Society of
PSYCHOS

SOCIETY OF PSYCHOS

CAROLINE PECKHAM
SUSANNE VALENTI

Society of Psychos
Dead Men Walking #2
Copyright © 2022 Caroline Peckham & Susanne Valenti

Interior Illustration & Formatting by Sloane Murphy

.
The Death Club/Caroline Peckham & Susanne Valenti – 1st ed.
ISBN-13 - 978-1-914425-31-8

This book is dedicated to unleashing your inner crazy…

The world demands you to be sane, but let's all board the crazy train.
Be wild! Be free! Shake your ass at a tree.
Hoot to an owl, hit a melon with a trowl.
Hug a goat, milk a cat, wave a coconut at a bat.
Dig a hole and meet a mole, have a real ol' fancy rigamarole.
Throw a party and invite a bunch of moths, make them tiny invitations out of tablecloths.
Go wherever the wind blows, and feel the sand between your toes.
You get one life, so don't waste it playing small.
Be the biggest badass of them all

NIALL

CHAPTER ONE

"**F**or the love of fuck!" I bellowed, my eyes tracking the prison transport vehicle as it tore away down the road, leaving me and Mateo behind as my little psycho was carted off fuck knew where in the back of it.

"We can catch them," Mateo growled, the distant howl of police sirens seeming to concern him as little as it did me. Men like us knew better than to fear the law. We were the real darkness in this world, the real price which evil had to face eventually, so no officer with a badge or the promise of a warm cell were ever going to scare us away from our goals.

My eyes tracked the winding route the transport bus was taking, my knowledge of this area and the surrounding roads spinning through my mind on fast forward. I was nodding in agreement to his assessment of it before I'd even fully formed a plan.

"Let's fuckin' catch them then," I demanded, turning and taking off across the perfectly manicured lawn outside the burning facility, sprinting as fast as I could run with one destination in mind.

Mateo kept pace with me wordlessly, Evangeline dripping blood in his fist as he kept hold of the heavy axe, no doubt still thinking about planting her sharp end in my skull. But I wasn't worrying over that right now. I'd seen his truth just as he'd seen mine and black hearted heathens that we were, we shared a single common goal. A single desire which we wouldn't be denied no matter our other needs or wants.

Her.

That crazy, stubborn, beautiful creature of chaos who had come crashing into our empty, bloodthirsty lives and had forced us to experience so much fucking more.

Who knew how we'd ended up in her web, but my little Spider had us trapped alright. Trapped and begging for the taste of her bite. And if we weren't able to bring her back to us then I had no doubt that we'd both starve in her web, the absence of her wasting us away until we were far less than the devils we'd been before her.

She was the bright point in our dark existence and we weren't going to let some fucking prison transport vehicle steal her away from us.

There were more than a couple of shouts of alarm as we passed through the sweeping gardens, the few guards who remained on site spotting us, though none of them took any shots, not seeming to realise that we were the architects of their ruin this very night.

I ignored them all. My desire to see them bleed tempered by my need to catch up to that bus and retrieve my girl from its bowels.

I spotted the wall up ahead, the razor wire topping it gleaming silver in the moonlight and making me curse. I'd tangled with that particular nightmare enough times to know it could be a cruel mistress indeed, and we had no time to waste getting knotted up in it and bleeding evidence all over the fuckin' ground.

I yanked my jacket off, shaking the thick material out and snatching Eric from my pocket before the little dagger could end up lost out here and all alone in the dark, shoving him into my pants' pocket instead. This was no place for a little stabber to end up abandoned and alone. I might have been a monster, but I had more heart than that.

There was a fucking inferno burning in my cock with every bounce of my damn balls as I ran, and I cursed my marginally more sober self once again for piercing the fucking thing in the first place. It felt like I was going to pass out here and now from cock agony alone, but I had to force my attention away from it, focus on what mattered and not my own drunken insanity, so I kept running despite the pain.

I threw my jacket up onto the top of the white wall as we reached it, covering the razor wire and giving us a route to escape.

Mateo leapt up and heaved himself over it without so much as a thank you for my kindness, jumping from the top and tumbling away out of sight just as gunfire rang out behind me. Rude. That was his problem. He was rude and ungrateful. I'd spent months and months feeding him and changing his bucket and he hadn't once thanked me, so I didn't know why I was surprised he was still lacking in manners while in the thick of the fight too.

I looked over my shoulder to the guard who thought he could try his luck with a pot shot from six hundred yards away and barked a laugh, flipping him off for good measure.

"Good luck with that, fella," I mocked, ignoring him as he yelled a command for me to stay where I was and leaping up to grasp the top of the wall a few feet above my head.

I heaved myself skyward, ignoring the protests of my freshly inked and pierced cock as I swung a leg up onto the wall and heaved myself onto the top of it, using my jacket to protect myself from the cutting wire which lined it. It was a damn shame because that had been a nice jacket too. A robust little fella who didn't show much bloodstain and kept the chills away from my nips. But now he was doomed, done for and dead. At least I'd given him a good life while it lasted.

I didn't waste time making my descent pretty on the other side, hurling myself into the undergrowth which marked the edge of the dark woodland

and rolling a couple of times before springing to my feet and taking off once more.

Mateo remained silent as we ran for the car together, the combination of our heavy footfalls thumping through the undergrowth and our harsh breaths exploding from our lungs the only theme tune to our desperate bid for our girl's freedom.

I cursed myself for the effort I'd taken to conceal the car as the seconds ticked into minutes, every one of them carrying Brooklyn further from us while we raced towards our only hope of catching her now.

Finally, I spotted the dark paintwork of the Jeep between the trees and I let out a triumphant whoop as I pulled the keys from my pocket, unlocking the beasty. She was a gallant steed who had done me good on countless getaways and I trusted her implicitly for this rescue mission.

Mateo ran towards the driver's side but I barked a denial at him, locking the car again before he could tug the door wide and making him turn to scowl at me.

"I thought you were too drunk to drive, hijo de puta?" he sneered, judgement dripping all over his tone as he looked me up and down like I was little more than a stray mutt come begging at his heels.

It looked like my cartel prisoner was starting to remember the man he'd been before my basement. That feral look in his eyes spelled trouble and I couldn't help but want to beat it out of him again. Or encourage it. Undecided. Not now though. Right now, we had bigger fish to fry.

"I find myself feeling remarkably sober now," I replied. "So move your arse over to the bitch seat or stay behind. I don't much care either way in this moment."

His eyes flashed with the offer of freedom, but he didn't even take a second to consider it before cursing me and vaulting over the hood of the car, dropping into the passenger seat as I unlocked the Jeep again, leaving me clear to get in behind the wheel.

I aimed my gun at his head as I shut my door behind me.

"Toss Evangeline in the back," I commanded in a low growl. "She'll never get over the trauma if you make her cut her daddy."

"You think you're its daddy now, do you?" he muttered, not bothering to protest as he tossed the axe into the back and I flashed him a crocodile grin.

"Oh yeah, I'm her daddy alright," I agreed, dropping my gun into the pocket in my door and starting the engine up without any further time wasted on bullshit. Mateo was still well able to attack me while I was driving, but the desperate need in his eyes told me he wouldn't risk Brooklyn for a taste of my blood, meaning I was safe enough from his hatred at least until we had her back.

I slammed the Jeep into reverse and swung her around before hitting the gas and tearing out of the trees in the direction of the main road.

"They went east," Mateo said in a low, dark tone, all full of malice and violent thoughts.

"East? What are you, Captain Compass? They went right," I replied, scoffing at him and he scowled at me while I kept my gaze fixed firmly on the road which was whipping past us at an incredible speed, the trees lining either side of it nothing but a blur in the darkness.

"I still can't figure out how you earned your reputation," he muttered in distaste, clearly not appreciating my lack of knowledge on the position of the North Pole right now, but if he was all about sticking a magnet up his arse so that he could ingrain a compass into his flesh then more power to him. I, on the other hand, relied on something far more infallible than the polarity of this globe we were all sitting upon. Pure, brutal, instincts.

"North, east, left, right. End of the day, there's only one direction that matters to either of us, el burro," I pointed out. "So I'll be heading due Brooklyn and not fucking about with nonsense along the way."

"Disfrutaré destripándote cuando esto termine," he muttered and that sounded like one hell of an agreement to me, so I just grinned as I pushed the car as fast as it would go and tore up the road in pursuit of the transport vehicle ahead of us.

Every second that slipped by had my heart thumping to an ever more frantic rhythm as we passed along the empty road, my eyes hunting the darkness for any sign of the fucking bus up ahead, doubts beginning to slip in alongside fear for the ramifications of us having made a mistake. She couldn't be lost. I refused it. So help the god of a world which let me lose her, for I would wreak hell and havoc on everyone and everything in my path until I held her in my arms once more.

"They went this way," Mateo insisted, either convincing himself of the fact or me, his hand fisted on his lap, his knuckles blanching as he stared out into the dark with the same intensity I was feeling, hunting for her, praying for her.

"I know," I spat, my anger not really aimed at him, more insisting it was true to the universe despite me knowing that bitch didn't give one fuck about me insisting on anything.

The universe hadn't given a fuck when I'd been hunting for Ava all those years ago. It hadn't listened to me then. Hadn't given me the chance to get her back and make everything I'd ruined right again. I knew what a cruel mistress fate could be and as the seconds dragged, the memories of my dead wife's screams began to pulse throughout my skull, their volume only intensifying with every thump of my erratic pulse.

Not again.

Not this time.

"Watch out!" Mateo barked and my eyes snapped into focus as a suicidal deer leapt into the road, a curse spilling from my lips as I was forced to swerve.

I turned my head as the car lurched to the right, my eyes meeting the startled big browns of the beautiful creature in a moment which seemed to stretch between us, its life flashing between both of our eyes.

For a moment there I was a little fawn munching in the long grass while mammy deer stayed close, all warm and furry and loving. Then I was gambolling about, making deer buddies and having the time of my life as I munched on the flowers in some big fancy garden, escaping the crack of gunfire as the owners spotted me and I bounded away. I was loving herd life, in my damn prime and then I was hopping out into the road as some Irish fucker in a Jeep sped towards me and threatened to steal it all away.

The deer skidded to a halt and my wing mirror damn near clipped the big fella as I yanked the wheel hard to the right, the wheels locking up in the dead leaves which were clogging the tarmac as his death hung in the balance.

Then we were past him.

My heart tried damn hard to leap outa my chest as I glanced in the rear-view mirror and saw him looking back at me, a note of thanks in his big browns as he was left to go on living his best deer life in the wake of my close call.

"Go get all that deer pussy, big fella," I said as I gave my full attention to the road once more. "Live your dreams."

Mateo was staring at me again and I was pretty sure that was a reverent kind of awe I felt coming from him. Or at least I did until he spoke again.

"I knew you were still too drunk to drive, you fucking idiota," he hissed.

I opened my mouth to tell him about the connection me and that deer had just formed, but before I could waste my breath on his close-minded ignorance, I spotted brake lights through the trees ahead.

"Bingo," I said, grinning darkly as I felt my little psycho drawing all the nearer and Mateo murmured more nonsense in his language as he spotted it too. Though I had to admit, it sounded like he shared my thoughts in that moment, and they were all entirely focused on one stunning, crazy girl.

Mateo brought the satnav up on the screen on my dash as I raced up a long hill, chasing after the distant taillights with a ferocious need building in me which had my blood pumping all hot and hungry.

"There's a curve coming up," Mateo said. "The road narrows, if you can get ahead of him, you should be able to drive him off the road there."

"I don't need instructions on how to force a fella offa the road," I replied angrily. "And I don't need no planner coming along trying to plan out my life like we have a wedding to arrange or some shit like that. You ain't my type, el burro. I'm not walking you up the aisle and I'm not making plans like some fucking Nancy ball rider. Today isn't a plan kind of day. I'll play this loose and free or not at all."

"It's the best chance we have at forcing them off of the road," he snapped, clearly unimpressed with my way of doing things but I was more than happy to prove to him just how impressive my brand of improvised chaos could be.

I ignored his suggestion as I sped up the hill and my eyes lit up like the first lights of Christmas as I spotted the bus ahead of us, just like I'd known she would be.

"Thar she blows!" I called excitedly and Mateo clipped his seatbelt into place as the engine roared and we closed in on our prey.

The transport vehicle was easily six times the size of my trusty Jeep, but she didn't pack the horse power I had at my control, nor did her driver pack the driving ability of a bloodthirsty O'Brien to be able to contend with me.

I shut my headlights off, using the dark as my mistress and she shrouded me obligingly as I closed in on the big bastard of a bus.

"What are you doing?" Mateo demanded as I remained in the shadow of the transport vehicle, aiming squarely for the back of it and grinning as I dropped a gear to give the Jeep a whole lot more growl.

"I'm just gonna give her a little kiss," I said.

"You're going to ram it?" he asked incredulously like I was insane.

"Yes, el burro, I'm going to ram it," I said with a huff as he took the thrill of the surprise from me. "Then the back doors will pop open and my little psycho will be able to hop right out."

"That won't work," he insisted, eyeing the back of the transport vehicle as I raced towards it.

"I've done this a thousand times," I replied dismissively. Okay, so maybe it wasn't a thousand. And maybe the one time I'd done it, it had been a DHL truck and not a prison transport vehicle with reinforced everything. And maybe that time things had gone more than a little wrong. But I still held firm to this plan. Not that it was a plan – it was more of an impulsive decision which I was sticking to until death.

"You need to cut it off," Mateo demanded, grabbing the wheel and trying to force it to the right, making the car swerve violently.

I punched him in the jaw and righted it again. "I'm ramming it," I snapped.

"I should have known you would fuck this up, you bastardo loco."

I ignored that shit in favour of pressing my foot to the floor and with a snarl from the engine, we flew forward and slammed into the back of the transport vehicle, the crash of metal and jolt of the impact sending adrenaline rushing through my veins.

We fell back and I cursed as the door remained shut, one great big bastard turning his head to look at us with his brow furrowing from the back of the thing where he'd been locked up in some sort of cage, long, white hair spilling all around his face as he watched us.

He didn't so much as flinch as I slammed into the back of the bus once again, and I whooped as they veered left and right, the driver clearly getting all kinds of spooked by my attack.

"You need to cut it off," Mateo hissed again as we were forced back again, the bus's rear doors remaining closed and the front of my car looking seriously worse for wear. Luckily, I had long since figured out exactly how hard you had to crash a car to set off the air bags. It wasn't an exact art, but

I pretty much had it down – I didn't need those fuckers going bang in my face in a situation like this and I didn't need anything tryna save my cursed life while I was working either. I already knew the Devil didn't want me and I wasn't inclined to rely on any judgement aside from his on the situation.

"This will work," I said, ignoring Mateo as the road took several sharp turns, the hills rising up around us as we closed in on the river ahead.

"No, it won't!"

"It will." I drove the car into the back of the bus again and I was thrown forward in my seat by the impact as I hit it harder that time.

Mateo cursed and smacked me, trying to grab the wheel and force me to go around yet again but I jerked it back, taking a hand from it to slap his fancy, freshly shaved face. Who did he think he was anyway? Don Fancy Face? Some kinda cartel somebody? That was bullshit and we both knew it – he was my little bitch and nothing more, and he never would be again unless I deigned it so.

The car hit the bus once more, but the fucking doors remained resolutely closed and the front of the Jeep began to release a little stream of smoke. Or steam. I wasn't sure which, but I was fairly certain that wasn't a good sign.

"You're making me fuck this up," I growled, knowing that it was Mateo who was cursing me in the endeavour with his sour attitude ruining the ambiance.

"You're the one who is going to destroy the car trying to batter down the fucking doors like an idiota. You need to drive it off the road!" Mateo shoved the wheel hard to the right as I put my foot down again and I cursed him as we sped out onto the bridge which crossed the river, jerking the wheel to the left once more as I slammed my knuckles into his jaw before grabbing a fistful of his ebony hair and cracking his face against the dashboard.

Mateo snarled at me like the beast he was, slamming an elbow down into my cock and I swear my balls leapt all the way up into my lungs as the burning in my new piercing blazed a path of pure fire from tip to base. I damn near blacked out from it. I tasted brimstone as I closed in on hell and wheezed like a football with a hole stabbed in the side of it.

I released Mateo who shoved the wheel to the right once more, his big fucking foot stamping down on mine as he forced me to accelerate, and I hissed out a breath laced with curses as I tried to blink away the pain.

The wail of the police sirens suddenly blasted through my skull, the flash of red and blue from the open road on the far side of the bridge calling me back from the abyss, and I roared a furious challenge at Mateo as I saw the end approaching. We were almost out of time and I refused to let this be it for my little psycho no matter what it cost me.

I gripped the wheel in both hands and ripped it to the left just as the nose of the Jeep began to pass the transport vehicle.

The crunch of metal and squeal of tyres against tarmac filled the air as the fucking thing was forced into a tailspin and my lips parted as I slammed my foot down on the brakes, the back end of the Jeep skidding out and the world rotating around us. The airbags exploded in our faces, keeping me in the car despite my lack of seatbelt.

Glass shattered, screams filled the air and an angry Mexican yelled 'I told you so!' as I grabbed the fucking door and held on for dear life while we spun in wild circles, and there was nothing left which made a whole lot of sense anymore.

But Ava's screams were gone, so there was that. No, I couldn't hear the hopeless pleas from the past anymore. Because I was fully engaged in the present and I swear I heard a scream which drowned out all other sounds of carnage as Brooklyn screamed in panic from somewhere all too close and all too far away at once.

"Hellfire!"

She needed me. She fucking needed me, and I refused to fail her the way I had Ava ten long years ago.

The car smacked into the barrier at the edge of the bridge and I hit my head on the window as it bounced down onto its wheels, blood trickling from my temple to the corner of my mouth as the airbag slowly deflated and the world beyond the shattered windscreen came into focus once more.

"Shit," I muttered as I spotted the destroyed railing on the far side of the bridge, the enormous splash confirming the location of the transport vehicle as the screams from the people inside it filled the air and it began to sink.

"Are you happy now?" Mateo snarled, shoving the airbag away from him as he glared at me with this indignant kind of rage which made me want to slap him.

"Ecstatic," I replied, hunting for my gun in the door pocket and grinning as I found it still lodged there. "That was my plan all along."

"Liar," he hissed, but we didn't have time to get into that as the howl of the police sirens and the blinding glare of the red and blue lights assaulted our eyes, announcing the arrival of the local sheriff and his band of helpful Harrys.

There was some yelling for us to get outa the car with our hands raised but the two of us ignored that shit, scrambling through the wreckage and dropping down among the shattered glass which lined the road as we took cover behind it, hiding from the police.

The screams from the sinking transport vehicle set my heart pounding to a frantic beat, but as I tried to make a run for the edge of the bridge to dive in after my Spider, a shot whizzed past me and forced me back into cover.

"Drop you weapons and come out with your hands raised!" a woman called and I fired a warning shot back in their direction as I swore beneath my breath, needing them to stay the fuck away from us while we found a way out of here.

"Shit," I hissed, my back pressed to the wreckage of my car as I turned to look at Mateo. "Any bright ideas coming to ya now?"

He narrowed his eyes on me and looked around as the police returned fire and we were forced to stay where we were, the prisoners' screams filling me with dread as time worked against us once more.

"I have one," he said, looking at the gas tank with the Devil in his eyes. "But it's as estúpido as it is brilliant."

"Well, I'm all for estúpido," I said vehemently. "So let's give it a shot."

JACK

CHAPTER TWO

The front of the prison transport vehicle sank beneath the water almost instantly on impact with it, the cab filling with the dark and murky contents of the river as I cursed within the confines of my own head and stood up in my cage at the back of the bus.

I watched as the rest of the passengers all groaned, touching their fingers to injuries if their hands were free or crying out for help if they weren't.

I was bleeding where I'd slammed into the cage door but the wound on my shoulder meant little to me in the face of the many things I'd suffered in the past. Besides, ever since my dark Rook had reappeared in my life, my focus had been entirely fixed on her.

Not that the time I'd spent mourning her escape from Eden Heights had been spent focused on a lot else, but now that the object of my obsession was within reach once more, I wasn't keen to let her out of my sight.

The two guards in the front of the vehicle made no attempt to save any of us, dropping a window and swimming away to the surface without so much as a backwards glance. Not that that was much of a surprise. I guessed they weren't inclined to risk their lives for the criminally insane psychopaths they'd been in charge of transporting. The problem was, with us all locked up and slowly sinking beneath the surface of the river, we were going to need help from someone or we'd all be drowning where we sat before long.

I gritted my teeth and rolled my shoulders back as I began to exert pressure on the cuffs which secured my hands behind my back, the metal cutting into my flesh as a growl of effort escaped me before they snapped suddenly, leaving the two cuffs dangling from my wrists and my hands free.

My eyes moved between the rest of the prisoners who were still chained to their seats, my position in my cage only offering me the small advantage being able to move freely, though it did me little good considering I was locked up.

There was one guard still here. Just one. He was fairly new to his role and mostly unknown to me, but I watched him all the same, taking stock of him as he blinked around in a daze, seeming to be unsure of what had even happened, let alone considering saving our lives. But I watched him all the same. He was our only hope after all.

He was bleeding. A cut on his head looking to have stunned him as he touched his fingers to the wound and unclipped his seatbelt, pushing to his feet while the water began to rise and the front of the bus sank further into the water. He staggered a little, not even seeming to notice the water rising up over his knees and I bit my tongue as I watched him, wondering if he might just drop down dead from that injury and curse us all to die with him.

"Mr Guard Man," Brooklyn called from her position still chained to her seat, her bright blue eyes wild with fear as she stared at him. Her voice had that same, husky, alluring tenor which I'd once lived for the sound of. I used to sit with her a lot, listening to her stories and drinking in all I could get of her. "I've given this a lot of thought in the past, and I came to the conclusion a long time ago that drowning isn't the one for me. I'm not about it. No siree. It's not glamorous enough, no flamboyance to it, no flare. If I'm going out, I need it to be bloody and brutal and all kinds of villainous. Please don't make this be my end all. Tied up like a burrito and trying to hold my breath before choking on dirty river water. I heard there's people poop in the rivers. I don't want the people poop to get in my mouth and give me the nasties."

I looked between the object of my obsession and the guard as more of the prisoners began to yell demands at him for freedom too, but he only had eyes for her. This wild, beautiful girl who seemed so out of place amongst the hellions who dwelled among us. I'd always thought that. How she didn't belong locked up with the rest of us, how she needed to be free like a bird being tossed to and fro in a storm. It was how I'd tried to force myself to come to terms with the loss of her after she'd escaped. But now that she was right before me once more, I was determined not to let her escape me again.

"I can't," the guard began, his gaze skipping around as he finally seemed to realise that time was of the essence here, his fingers trembling as he pressed them to the loop of keys on his belt. "I'm not supposed to unlock you until we reach the next facility."

"You're going to kill us?" Brooklyn gasped and he paled, his eyes widening as he shook his head and took a step towards her through the water which was now lapping over his knees.

"No. No, of course I'm not."

My muscles coiled with the need to strike at something, to fight for my freedom from this cage. But I stayed there all the same. Waiting to see what magic she could conjure. To see if she could use whatever power she had used to ensnare me on this man too, to bend him to her will. Waiting to see if she could lure us free of this death. Or perhaps she was only looking to buy her own life. Either way I found myself watching, wanting to find out, willing to accept my end if the cost of it had been these few stolen minutes in her company again.

The guard scrambled for the ring of keys at his belt, tugging them loose and quickly slotting one into the chain which was securing her to the floor.

The transport vehicle groaned as it pitched further forwards, the rear of it where I was contained tipping up into the air as the whole thing began to sink and I was thrown forward so that my weight was pressed against the cage bars. Screams and laughter carried around the bus, desperation and mania thick in the air as the prisoners all saw their deaths coming for them and either feared or welcomed such, depending on their particular brand of insanity.

Brooklyn pushed herself to her feet, balancing on the chair in front of hers in the slowly sinking bus, breathing a thank you to the guard as he turned and started unlocking more of the prisoners from their restraints, though he left plenty of them in their straitjackets, making me wonder how he expected them to swim for safety.

Brooklyn looked around as she stumbled into the aisle between the seats, her electric blue eyes sparking with cunning thoughts as she hunted for a means of escape.

"Rook," I growled, demanding her attention and earning it for myself as her head snapped around and her gaze fixed on me. My free flying bird who had already escaped without me once. But this time I had the hope that she might have wanted me to go with her.

She hurried towards me, scrambling over the backs of the chairs and using the heads of a couple of the restrained passengers to kick off of before pressing her cheek to the bars of my cage and looking in at me with something akin to fear in her eyes. But it was more vibrant than just that. A thrill along with her terror at the thought of us all drowning here in this place. I could tell she didn't want to die here but the thought of it was exciting her more than terrifying her.

"I'll get you out, Angry," she said, giving me a serious look. "Birds of a feather gotta snack together, right? And I'm betting you're real hungry, aren't you, big man?"

"Rook," I repeated, the simple word all I offered her, yet her brow pinched and she looked back to the guard like she understood fully. It had always been like that between us. No matter how little I gave her vocally, she still seemed to be on a level with me, understanding what I was struggling to communicate and making me feel seen in the anonymity of the facility where we'd been locked away to be forgotten by the rest of the world.

"You're right," she agreed as the bus tilted again, the rear levelling out with the first a little and allowing us to brace our feet against the floor once again. "I'll get it."

Brooklyn turned towards the guard just as he leaned down to unlock the chain securing Cannibal Carol, who had managed to get an arm free of her restraints and was grasping at the back of her head, struggling against the straps which secured the muzzle covering her mouth.

A cry of warning escaped Brooklyn's lips a beat too late as the insane woman lunged at the man who had just freed her from the muzzle and she sank her teeth into his throat, knocking the two of them to the floor where they tumbled back towards the front of the bus and fell into the rapidly rising water.

I caught sight of the guard's keys as they flew from his hand, my freedom spinning away in a flash of silver which was barely illuminated by the light outside the windows from the streetlamps on the bridge far above us.

Brooklyn cried out in dismay and dove headfirst into the water in pursuit of the keys, but with her arms secured by the straitjacket, I knew she had no chance of recovering them from the murky water now, that slim chance of escape eluding me and the reality of my fate closing in as I looked at the small cage I was locked in and found my death staring icily back.

I hadn't lived a good life. Certainly not since I'd been locked up in that forsaken place. And now it seemed I wasn't going to get a good death either. Honestly, I would have preferred to have met with the wrath of the Alonso brothers despite all of my work to evade them than this.

Almost all of the prisoners had been freed from their chains before

Carol had attacked the guard and they were fighting to get past each other, a couple of them loosening straitjackets for the others but most of them just clamouring to get the doors open so that they could escape, though I had no idea how they expected to swim to freedom with their arms bound.

They slammed into the double doors at the far end of the bus where the water was deepest, lapping up to their chests and I gritted my jaw as I saw my death coming for me in their attempts.

With a bellow of effort, I braced my back against the wall of my cage and threw my booted foot against the door in front of me. I kicked it again and again, driving all of my energy into the blows and making my cage rattle with the force of my strength.

The nurses and doctors in that place had had a lot to say about me and my mental wellbeing. A whole lot of nothing and a whole lot of everything. I'd confused them in more ways than they ever would have admitted, but this one had always been my favourite. They never had been able to figure out why I worked so hard to train my body. They claimed I didn't have the mental capacity to be doing it with any real intention. They assumed it was some kind of leftover routine from the life I'd had before my mental collapse. Of course, they didn't know the truth. That I had been working my body so hard not only to give myself something to focus on in that hell, but also so that I could be ready when my fate finally came for me. And now that destiny had come knocking, that joke was very much on them. I was stronger now than I ever had been when I was free, and I fully intended to break out of this fucking cage before I drowned here like a rat.

A muffled voice made me pause in my assault on the door, my muscles burning with the energy it had taken me to attack it that way and my chest heaving despite the metal which remained as solid as ever before me.

"I-ga-eet," Brooklyn said again and I hunted for her in the darkness of the sinking bus, leaning my head against the bars and looking down to find her on her knees amid the steadily rising water while she tried to get the key into the lock using her mouth alone.

I stared at her, unable to believe that she could manage such a task and yet unable to look away either. Over and over again she tried to fit the key in the lock while the other passengers kept trying to force the doors at the far end of the vehicle open.

That fucking snitch Norman was trying to kick one of the windows out like an idiot, the bars on the other side of the glass meaning he would only drown us faster if he succeeded in breaking it. I roared at him, pointing a finger his way and making him curse in fright as he whipped around to look at me from his position perched on one of the benches.

The light faded further as with a sudden dip, the rear of the vehicle sank beneath the surface of the river and the prisoners screamed as they realised death was inching closer to them. But as I looked down at the object of my obsession, I had a feeling salvation was coming for me.

With a jerk of her chin and a twist of her head, the lock to my cage snapped open and I sucked in a surprised breath as Brooklyn stood with a whoop of triumph, the keys still clasped between her teeth as she let the cage door swing wide. Her long hair was dripping wet and more droplets raced down her face but even in the darkness beneath the river's surface, her blue eyes blazed so bright they seemed to pierce right through me and take stock of all I was. And the way she was looking at me now said she liked what she saw.

I pushed out of the door with a dark and wicked smile trying to creep across my face, only supressing it through sheer force of will after many years of practice at maintaining a blank mask across my features, and I moved into her breathing space.

"Nithe boy," she breathed around the keys. "Ooo wouddun't hurt me. I'm your fwend."

Her words seemed out of place for this moment so close to oblivion and yet I heard them still, understanding what she wanted and eyeing her for a moment as I considered it. Yes. She had been my friend once. So far as people like us had friends. So far as I could trust her to be one without giving myself away. And unknown to her, she had been more than that to me. My secret obsession in the dark which I could never allow into the light. But here she was, offering me freedom and simply asking for the same in return. How could I deny her that? In fact, I fully intended to deliver her that wish plus however many more she asked of me from this moment on.

I gripped her arm and turned her around, my foot slipping on the uneven surface as gravity tried to make me fall into the water which was rising at the front of the bus and began to tilt further that way once more.

I pushed her against the bench closest to us, half bending her over it as my weight crushed her to it and I unhooked the buckles which secured her straitjacket in place while relishing the feeling of her body pressing to mine.

I ripped the straps open with a grunt of anger and tore the material almost in half as I ripped the fucking thing the rest of the way off of her body, leaving her in a simple white shirt and soft sweatpants beneath it, not unlike the outfit I was dressed in.

Brooklyn gasped as I released her, turning to look at me in the dark, the weight of her stare making my skin prickle with awareness as I gripped the handrail above my head and heaved myself back enough to let her move. She tugged the loop of keys from her mouth and beamed at me.

"Wanna join The Clit Clan?" she offered, making me frown just as the front of the transport vehicle hit the riverbed with a thud which almost knocked her away from the benches at the back of the bus and into the rising water below us.

I caught hold of her, my arm easily banding around her slim waist as I helped her stay balanced and she leaned into my embrace like she didn't fear me at all. Like my size and strength wasn't something to recoil from but something to embrace, and I liked the way that felt.

"Rook," I growled, my eyes on the doors which were now submerged.

Our only way out already looking less and less likely to work, though I refused to just give in and die down here like a bunch of worms caught in a can.

"I know. But Small Willy Norman has to die. He's on my list." She pointed at the snitch who whirled towards us at her words, his eyes wild and full of fear, his lank brown hair falling forward to shroud his features and I reluctantly released her as she pushed out of my hold.

"Stay away from me," he hissed, watching her as she stalked closer like we weren't just moments away from our doom and this vendetta meant a whole lot more to her than her impending death.

"I'll stay away from your gross little corpse," she replied, climbing up onto one of the benches and moving towards him where he still perched on the back of his as if we weren't all about to drown and the rest of the people onboard this thing weren't either trying to break out of here or sobbing uncontrollably. "I'll stay away from your little wet willy."

"I'm warning you," Norman growled, pointing a finger at her as she hopped from the back of her bench to the next and I remained where I was, my gaze roaming over everything that surrounded us as I worked to figure out what I needed to do to get out of this.

The guard's blood coloured the already mud brown water while Cannibal Carol still crouched over him up on a bench like a vampire Gollum guarding her precious, making it clear enough to me that he was dead and no longer able to offer his help.

I turned my attention from that particular form of carnage, eyeing the convicts who were still trying to force the submerged doors open instead. They hadn't gotten anywhere yet, but they were all smaller than me, weaker, likely unable to do anything close to what I could manage and so far as I could tell, that was the only viable exit.

"I'm gonna cut you up with these keys," Brooklyn hissed as she hopped onto another bench, threading the keys between her fingers and curling her hand into a fist while Norman scrambled along his bench to maintain his distance from her. "I'm gonna stab you with the blunt end and the sharp end, and I don't care if it takes all night for you to die because I'll enjoy every last second of your-"

Norman tried to leap across the aisle before me and my hand snapped out, catching him around the throat and making him scream in alarm as I moved my other hand to the side of his head.

"I never snitched on you, Jack," he pleaded as he met my eyes and began to quiver. "Never you."

"You ratted me out and got me sent to Lucille more times than I can count, you small willied, tiny penis man," Brooklyn growled and I cocked my head to one side, letting him see the utter emptiness in me as I held his life in my hands. Perhaps he had been too afraid to turn snitch on me, but he should have been paying more attention while he was running in fright from my shadow. Maybe then he would have seen the way I watched the girl beside us. Maybe then he could have anticipated what I might wish to do to anyone who caused her harm. Maybe then he would have seen this fate coming for him and made a different choice.

"Rook," I said simply, watching that terror spark in his gaze and drinking it in a moment before I snapped his neck and dropped him to the floor like the garbage he was.

"Wow," Brooklyn breathed, moving to perch on the edge of the bench right beside me, her hand reaching out to brush against my arm as she admired my work and my gaze roamed over her hungrily as the feeling of her fingers against my skin awakened something in me which I'd been forced to repress for far too long. "You just killed him with your bare hands, AJ. You're like a whole mood, aren't you? All dark and destroying and shit."

She bit her lip and I looked at her mouth, taking in her words as the water rose all around us and death whispered our names as it promised to come for us.

But I could hear the call of freedom all the louder after my kill and that was the mistress I was seeking tonight, my pulse thumping to a rhythm that demanded it.

The prisoners who were still locked in their seats were screaming and begging for help and I turned to them, grabbing the set of keys which Brooklyn still held and unlocking the closest prisoner without caring who they were.

"You want to help them all?" Brooklyn asked, giving me the doe eyes like I was some kind of hero, but I just grunted.

No. I didn't want to help them all. I wanted the distraction to help us escape. Most of these men and women were even more thoroughly cracked in the head than I was. They wouldn't be able to run with any real success. But they sure would keep the cops busy rounding them up while I played the smart game and got the fuck outa Dodge with my free flying bird.

The rear of the bus was slowly sinking towards the riverbed now, the water rushing up around my waist as it levelled out, the passengers in their seats forced to crane their necks to still draw in breath while I worked my way between them, releasing them all and ripping their straitjackets open too so that they could swim. I wanted the entire area surrounding this place swarming with psychopaths and hellions, their screams of excitement filling the air as they ran for freedom and buying us the time we needed to get the fuck away from here.

I made quick work of releasing them, baring my teeth at anyone who got too close to me or Brooklyn once they were free before turning toward the doors at the far end of the bus.

"Angry?" Brooklyn called out as I stalked away from her and I paused, turning my head to look back as the water rose up to my chest, the benches all submerged now and chaos unfolding all around us as the panicked prisoners realised that they really were about to die. "I can't really do the whole swimming thing," she breathed, still standing up on the bench and looking at the water like it had personally offended her sweet old grandma.

I grunted, turning my back on her once more but pausing, the offer there if she wanted it and barely a second later, she hopped onto my back, her arms and legs winding around me as she clung on tight and that smile tugging at the corner of my lips once more.

"I'll pay you back in cheesecake," she whispered into my ear. "You look like a cheesecake kind of guy."

I grunted again, stalking forward and shoving my way between the rest of the passengers who were still trying to break the doors open. I didn't want cheesecake. I had all I needed right here.

I grabbed hold of the railings either side of the door and braced myself using them, pivoting so that I could use all of my strength in the blow before slamming my foot into the double doors.

They rattled wildly, parting an inch and letting water rush in for a moment before slamming closed once more and I snarled as I braced myself to kick them again.

"Oh, there's a thingy up here which says 'door release' should I try that?" Brooklyn asked and I tipped my head back, squinting in the dim light as she wrapped her fingers around the red handle and yanked hard.

The doors burst open and water rushed in so fast that I was almost knocked on my ass, my grip on the railings firming as I fought the current and Brooklyn tightened her hold on me as she fought to cling on.

I sucked in a breath just before the last of the air was snatched away and the moment the onslaught of water eased, I kicked off of the steps I'd been standing on and propelled us out into the river with a whole host of criminally unhinged deviants scrambling to follow.

I began to swim, more prisoners forcing their way out all around us and crashing into me as they fought to claim their freedom in the icy embrace of the river too and I ground my teeth in determination as I began to swim for the surface.

Brooklyn clung to me as the light of the moon became clearer above us, her fingers digging into my skin as she held on tight but then suddenly she was gone, the rush of the current ripping her away from me and spinning her aside in the dark.

My gut lurched in panic as I felt her grip fail, my own escape becoming irrelevant as the thought of losing her again consumed me and cast my soul to cinders.

I twisted after her, her fingers brushing mine as I fought to see her in the murky water, my lungs burning with the need to take a breath as I hunted all around. But as my hand closed on nothing and my heart thundered with frantic energy, I found myself alone in the dark. Just like I had been when she'd left me once before and that empty, hollow place in my chest began to roar with a denial so potent it consumed me.

I kicked after her, my eyes wide in the dirty water and my hands grasping as I hunted for Brooklyn.

I wouldn't give up on her. Not now. Not when we were so damn close to the escape we both craved and a life beyond those fucking walls at Eden Heights.

BROOKLYN

CHAPTER THREE

The best thing about being free was the smile on my face which nearly burst my cheeks open. The worst thing though? I was sailing down a river, tossed in the current like a feather in a thunderstorm, and I couldn't swim.

I kicked and flailed, trying to make my arms and legs do the right thing and get me moving towards the surface, but every time my head made it above the waterline, I was bitch slapped back under it by the force of the current.

A stream of bubbles poured from my lips as I was tossed around in the water, losing knowledge of my up-ways and down-ways. I was being thrown around like a half dead duck, my kickers kicking and my flappers flapping, but it didn't do me any good.

Damn this was a shit way to die. I was in a cold wet washing machine left on the spin cycle and there was no way out. No one was gonna talk about that, it wasn't gonna hit headlines and be splashed all over the news like my death should have been. This was humiliation at its finest. I was going to sink all the way to the bottom of the river where the fishes were going to giggle and point at me. Then they'd eat me away, and I'd be swallowed into fish bellies until I was nothing but a pile of pointless bones on a riverbed. And no one would care, not one single person up there in this big wide world would miss me. Would anyone even wonder what had happened to Brooklyn with a B?

A muscular arm suddenly locked around my waist and in the next second my head breached the surface.

I sucked down air like it was Big Red's dick and I was his favourite slut. It tasted so fucking good and I couldn't get enough as I drank in more of that sweet, sweet wind whistling through my lungs.

I leaned back against the huge body that had hold of me, wondering if it was the Devil himself, come to haul my ass off to hell and spank it raw. Though, as I thought about that, I couldn't help but pout a little. Niall and Mateo had come for me – unless my drugged-up brain had conjured them into existence – but it made me wish they were the ones holding me now, ready to spank me, bend me over, and skewer me like a pinata. They got skewered, right? Lucky bastards.

I looked down at the arm gripping my body like I was nothing more than a half-drowned cat to them. But I didn't find any tattoos there, or even the deep bronze of Mateo's flesh. This wasn't an arm I knew. But it was a nice arm, hairy in a manly way not a gross way. There was a lot of muscle going on and a little vein or two was on display as I tried to peek at the underside of it.

"Still," a deep voice growled in my ear as my saviour powered through the river with his free arm, cutting through water like it was nothing but a slight inconvenience to him.

I knew that voice. It was the deep rumble of a man I'd liked to look at a lot a long time ago. A man who'd played steed for me in our attempt to escape the asylum we'd been enslaved to. The man who'd gotten me off of that bus.

"Angry Jack," I cried, clinging to him more tightly and grinning as he grunted at me in what was definitely an affectionate way.

He said nothing more but shifted me so that I could cling to his back and I twisted my head around to look upriver, spotting the bridge we'd crashed off of in the distance, the flash of police lights lining the bank on the left-hand side while the crack of gunfire echoed through the air.

There were prisoners swimming in the water behind us, their heads bobbing up like corks in a barrel and I watched as they turned for the shore, heading towards dry land and safety.

"We should climb out too," I urged, my grip so tight around Angry Jack's neck that it was a wonder I wasn't strangling him, but I didn't like the deep dark beneath me. Not one bit. And if I let go again, I knew nothing but a watery grave and a smug little arsehole of a fish would be waiting for me down there, ready to chomp on my soft flesh.

"Swim," he replied in what was a clear refusal as he continued to power his way through the water, ignoring the shore and heading who knew where while I just clung on to my boat man and waited to find out where he would dock.

An enormous explosion made a gasp of exhilaration speed through my veins and I twisted to look at the bridge just in time to see the blazing debris from the centre of it go sailing up into the air before it came crashing down in the water, leaving the centre of the bridge to bow and buckle as fireworks exploded above it in celebration.

"Oooh," I cooed as I craned my neck to watch the carnage, the gunfire falling silent while the police all took cover from the mayhem. Mayhem really was the most beautiful thing in this world.

The river turned around the sharp curve of a hill and I sighed as my view of the burning bridge was stolen from me, concentrating on holding on tight once more as Jack continued to haul himself through the water like a merman on a mission.

Minutes ticked by while he swam endlessly on, and I began to shiver in the icy cold of the water.

It was as freezy as a snowman's cock out here and I was dreaming all the good dreams of snuggly slippers and hot cheese grills and sunshiney days, when the distant whir of a helicopter engine made me look up.

"Do you hear that, AJ?" I asked. "I think it's a helicopter. Do you think Hellfire is flying a helicopter now?"

Jack tipped his head skyward, a shriek escaping me as the move dipped me further into the water before he growled like a beastie and turned for the riverbank without another word, little old limpet me still clinging on all the way.

He made it to shore, but didn't place me on my feet, shifting me into his hold and keeping me tucked under his arm as he strode up the rocky bank and ran straight into a dense group of trees. I couldn't say for sure how far we'd travelled from the bus, but I did know that we wouldn't be far enough until we were unfindable.

I shivered as the cold air gusted around us and I started to sing Cake by Melanie Martinez to stop my lips from chattering – or was it teeth that chattered?

Jack placed me down suddenly, shoving me up against an oak and clapping a huge palm to my mouth. He was as big as a tree and almost as conversational.

"Hush," he commanded and I blinked the water from my lashes, a smile pulling at my mouth. His long, white hair was damp around his shoulders, his features hard and the scar on the right side of his head drew my attention. I liked that scar. I'd always wanted to tiptoe my fingers across it and find out how big it was. I'd bet thirteen ladybirds could line up in a row along it.

He slowly lowered his hand while I raised mine, my fingertips brushing his scar and starting their walk to remember and for a few blissful moments, he let me until the whir of that helicopter engine called to us once again and we both tipped our heads back to look up at the canopy of trees which shrouded us from view. A light wheeled overhead, and the helicopter roared away across the river, leaving us in the dark and the quiet, never to be found. Or so I hoped.

Jack knocked my arm away, scowling down at me with a flicker of concern in his grey eyes.

The cold water had helped shift the fog of the drugs from my system and I was starting to feel less fuzzy now, my mind clicking into top gear. *Vroom vroom, little brain.*

It felt like we were the only two people left on earth as I stared at him, finding countless dark deeds in his eyes. Angry Jack was bad to the bone, that was as clear as day to me. I always could sense my own. He was a wicked man with a soul drenched in secrets, and I wanted to know each and every one of them. Starting now.

"Did they really cut out a slice of your brain?" I whispered curiously as the helicopter drifted further away until we couldn't hear it anymore. "Did they put it in a jar? Did they let you keep the jar?"

"No," he grunted.

"No, they didn't let you keep the jar, or no they didn't cut out a slice of your brain?" I asked, but he looked away as a dog barked in the distance, his gaze fixed on the trees.

"Move," he growled, gripping my arm and dragging me after him across the frozen ground. He had a good grip, all strong and manly and pin-me-down-demon-man-ish.

"I'd like to see the jar if you still have it," I breathed as I jogged to keep up with the pace of his stride. Every three steps of mine equalled one of his. He was so big that it made my heart race just to tilt my head back and look all the way up, up, up at him.

Leaves cracked beneath our feet as we moved, little night time animals darting through the canopy overhead, though they were so quiet it made me feel like they knew something I didn't. Was danger here, lurking within the shadows? Was there a beast in that bush? Was there a danger man hiding in the moss?

My heart did a pole-vault as we moved past a huge tree and a dog started barking ferociously at us. Jack drew me to a halt as I took in the ramshackle cabin we'd stumbled across. Smoke was coiling up from a little metal chimney on top of it and the dog was chained up out the front, snarling and snapping its teeth. It was a big grey beasty and scars covered its head and body like it knew the taste of violence all too well and liked it a whole hell of a lot. I'd guess it was some sort of cross between a pitbull and a bear, but I couldn't be sure.

"Well hello there, little cutie pie," I cooed, stepping toward the dog as it snarled viciously at me.

"Shut the fuck up, Hammer!" a man boomed from within the cabin, and Jack dragged me backwards behind the wide trunk of a tree, shoving me against it and crushing me there with his body. My face was smooshed to his chest and I lost all ability to breathe as he held me there without any mercy on my lungs. His shirt was all wet and clingy to his muscles and I was pretty sure a girl could find a worse place to be than pinned against that. His pecs could probably crack my head open like a nut. That wouldn't be a terrible way to go actually, I just hoped I got a lick of them before my brain spilled out.

The dog yelped horribly and my gut tied into a million knots as I realised what was happening, my head shaking in horror as another yelp sounded. I shoved at Jack's chest and he gave me an inch as I shifted sideways, peering out past the tree. A man with a big gut stood over the dog, his belt in hand as he whipped it and my ears started to ring, the moon drew closer in the sky and a bloodthirsty animal within me bayed for blood.

I went to the bad place, the one where bloody lullabies were whispered in my ears by my favourite demons. I let them all in, opened the door as wide as it could go and they filled me up until there was nothing but a song of wrath and evil playing in my head.

I wriggled past Jack, picking up a hefty rock from the ground and stalking towards the man as he laid into the dog. Jack came after me, but I was fast, and I didn't waste a second as I lunged at the monster hurting my new friend.

The man saw me a second before I struck his head with a blow which sent blood flying. He hit the ground with a garbled cry and I fell on him, beating his head in with the rock as the dog scrambled away.

The man was big and he rolled, fighting back and punching me hard enough to knock all the breath from my lungs, but I was in the swing of things now, all rabid and hungry for his death. I hit him again with a shriek of anger and Jack's hand slapped over my mouth as he came to stand behind me, though he didn't stop me from continuing to hit and hit and hit until the ugly monster fell still beneath me. I inhaled the scent of blood and admired the sheen of it on my hands, a muffled giggle falling against Jack's palm.

I breathed heavily between Jack's fingers as I let the rock fall from my grip and stared down at the bloody mess I'd made, my skin lit up with adrenaline. I tilted my head all the way back as Jack's hand remained plastered to my mouth and our eyes met. It was like a divine meeting as our gazes locked, something real and tangible bouncing through the air between us. He was devouring me with that look and I devoured him back as my chest heaved and I let my tongue slip out to lick his calloused palm. He tasted like a sea of sin and a shudder danced down my spine in delight.

His eyes widened as he peeled his hand away, looking down at it as if I'd left a mark on his flesh and I kinda hoped I had. A little B for Brooklyn so that he would never get muddled and spell it with a silent H.

The dog was snarling again as it shifted back against the wall of the cabin and Jack dragged me upright, towing me away from it and ushering me through the front door of the cabin. Heat washed over me from a fire behind a grate and I looked around at the cosy little space in surprise, Jack headed back out to the corpse and grabbed it by the ankles, heaving it out of sight and shoving it beneath the cabin which stood on little stilts before kicking some dead leaves over the blood staining the ground.

He glanced up towards the sky and I nodded, realising he was hiding what I'd done from the owls. And maybe those helicopter men too. We didn't want any of them knowing, that was for sure.

Jack strode towards me where I lingered in the doorway, crowding me back against the wall as I failed to move aside and tugging the door closed behind me before shutting off the lights which illuminated the space outside the cabin. We lingered there by that light switch, tiny me and massive him, looking at each other in a way that spoke a thousand words. AJ had never been very talky, but I'd always been super intuitive. He didn't need to speak when his eyes could talk for him, and my brain did the translatey thing and hey presto, here we were speaking a million, zillion words without a single peep passing between us.

"Peep," I breathed. Okay, maybe one peep.

"Peep," he replied, the echo of a smile ticking up the corner of his lips before it vanished like Casper the friendly ghost.

Jack headed off into what I guessed was a bedroom and I settled myself down on the couch, putting my feet up on the coffee table and picking up a glass of whiskey which the creepo must have been working on alongside a porno magazine. I knocked the whiskey back and thumbed through the pages, arching a brow at the nice tits of a girl in a cowboy hat, riding a motorised bull.

Yeah, I could get used to this place. Whiskey, porn, and a nice fire going. This was the life for me. I had it made. Me and Jack could really make something of ourselves here. Maybe we'd fall in love and make a few mini-Jacks and Brooklyns. Though as I thought of that, I wrinkled my nose. I didn't wanna push a giant Jack baby out of my tiny vagina. No, that wasn't the life for me at all. Maybe I could be like the girl in this magazine. I could set up a camera and have Jack go to town on me, then we could post it online and watch the money roll in. Mm, I didn't hate the sound of that idea. We could call it Jack and the Beanwhore. Or Jack Licks Her Magic Bean. Or Jack Stalks the Bean. Or, The Giant Comes Down from the Beanstalk and Fucks the Living Daylights out of Jack's Sister and-

"Change." Jack reappeared, tossing me a big old plaid man shirt and some black long johns. He had more clothes in his hands and as he pulled his soaking wet shirt off, my gaze zeroed in on his muscular chest, the abs that were cinching tight across his stomach, the hugeness of him that bulged everywhere. Eve-ry-where.

My pussy throbbed and I just stared as he dropped his pants and boxers too, showing me a cock that I swear was close to tickling his knee as it just dangled there like a fucking sea monster wrestled into submission. But something told me if I woke that sea monster, it would need a warrior to take it down again. Was I trained for that? No. But I'd don the armour and give it one hell of a battle.

"Hi," I breathed, my hand raising in a wave, the need to introduce myself to the monstrous cock in the room overwhelming me. It had so much presence it simply demanded it. "I'm Brooklyn with a B."

"Rook," Jack corrected, and my eyes snapped up to his again.

"Ca-caw," I said like a rook. I liked that nickname. I wondered what it would sound like being moaned in my ear. But then again, Jack didn't look like he would moan for anything. He'd grunt and roar and growl like a beast, but moan? Nah, nothing that soft could come out of those manly lips. Those lips were made for sucking on rocks and spitting tobacco. "Has anyone ever told you that you look like The Witcher?"

"Dress," he commanded, ignoring my words though his eyes were riveted to my face and drinking me in in a way that made me feel like he'd been thirsty for a long damn time.

I hadn't actually seen The Witcher, but I'd seen pictures of him and I was pretty sure I knew the gist of the show. Man says fuck, man makes witches' panties melt. Sounded like my kind of show.

Jack tugged on the large jeans, cinching them around his waist with a belt and leaving half his calves exposed. He pulled on a white shirt next and his muscles filled it out almost as nicely as the big guy's gut probably had.

I stood, stripping out of my wet clothes and Jack's eyes never moved from my flesh, though not a flicker of emotion passed through his gaze. Except maybe anger. But then when your name was Angry Jack, I guessed you were always a little angry. His fist balled at his side though, and his throat bobbed as my hard nipples turned his way, making it clear how cold I was, though they were also enjoying the feeling of his eyes on them while they put on a show.

I wiped the blood from my hands onto my sodden clothes then pulled on my new long johns with the large shirt, pouting down at the ugly outfit. So this was my life. I was a trollop in the woods, living off the land. I'd really thought I'd suit that lifestyle for a second, but now that I was faced with the reality of it, I wasn't sure I wanted to stay here. There were far better things out there for me and Jack. We could become pirates sailing the seven seas, or wandering nomads who travelled from state to state, slaying bad guys and staying in dodgy motels. Or maybe our destiny was even bigger than that. Maybe fate was calling our names, and this was just our villain origin story, waiting for us to step into our true roles as evil masterminds set to take over the world. Hell, we already had our villain names picked out. Angry Jack and the Pink Pussy unite. We needed signature weapons though. I'd have a serrated boomerang and Jack could wield a double headed hammer with a head in the shape of a roaring bear. It would have to be a big one, really, really big.

"How big of a hammer do you think you could hold?" I asked him just as the drone of a helicopter soared overhead. My heart did a flip and I wondered if maybe I still had an incy wincy bit of drugs still left in my system because something tugging in the back of my head said I should be shitting my panties right now. If I had any panties on, that was. So maybe I should have been shitting that dead guy's long johns. Instead, I was kind of enjoying this field trip and I was very curious about what time we were going to be having dinner. What did woodland people eat? Would I have to battle a peeping squirrel for his hoard of nuts? Could I win in a fight like that? Hard to say for sure, squirrels were nifty and all kinds of crafty too. Especially if they got their friends involved. I couldn't take down an army of squirrels, maybe Jack could, but not if there were a thousand of them. *Oh no, I don't want to die hungry being choked out by hundreds of tiny squirrel feet.*

Jack moved to the window, twitching the curtain aside as the wail of a siren sounded off in the distance. He scrubbed his hand over his jaw, a lot of thoughts and calculations going on behind those intense grey eyes. I could hear his brain working, or maybe that was just the sound him cracking his knuckles one by one.

"What do we do?" I whispered.

"Stay," he decided. "Think."

"Okay, big man," I agreed, heading off into the tiny kitchenette to rummage in the fridge for some food. I'd have to consider how to take on the squirrels later if there weren't enough snacks here. "You do that. I'm gonna refuel my jets."

MATEO

CHAPTER FOUR

The cops had kept us pinned down well after the prisoner transport vehicle had sunk beneath the surface of the river, and I'd experienced the most terrifying moments of my life as I'd been left helpless against the fate which was coming for mi sol. The light in my small and hopeless world had faded in those moments, each of them dragging into the next as I made an attempt to run for the edge of the bridge and dive in after her only to feel the keen sting of a bullet as it tore across my arm.

Niall had grabbed me and thrown me back into the cover provided by his destroyed car just in time to save my sorry life, and even now as we ran through the forest in hunt of the girl who had us both so irrevocably enamoured, I couldn't figure out what his motive for that act had been.

He'd been the one to see her surfacing. He'd spotted her as she scrambled to keep her head above the surface while the current of the river swept her away from us and the rest of the prisoners all started swimming for freedom too.

We'd watched as one of them had helped her, the two of them swimming towards the bend in the river and out of sight before we could free ourselves from our fucking predicament of being pinned down by the police.

I had come up with an insane plan to rescue us, taking the axe he'd named Evangeline from the back of the car and splitting the gas tank open with one mighty swing. Niall had lit a cigarette and started running, leaving me scrambling to race after him a moment before he flicked the burning smoke into the gas tank and the entire car had gone up in a fire bomb. Of course I hadn't known he had a trunk full of grenades and fireworks so the fucking thing had taken half the bridge out with it too.

We'd been hurled off of our feet, thrown almost the entire way to the far side of the bridge from the police as they all yelled and ducked for cover while chunks of concrete, metal railings and the remains of the Jeep were launched into the air and sent crashing down into the river.

Then we'd taken off into the woods without a backwards glance and had begun the task of hunting for my chica loca in the dark forest which surrounded this place.

We'd run and run, never slowing despite the sounds of more squad cars arriving, the baying of the hounds set to hunt the escaped prisoners or even the addition of the helicopter which swung back and forth overhead, the wide beam of its searchlights making us duck for cover whenever it got too close. If they were using heat detection cameras then our attempts to hide would likely be for nothing, but lucky for us there were countless insane criminals trying to escape these woods and the attention of the police was very much divided as they searched for them.

Any other man likely would have been terrified. But this was where I thrived. I'd been a hunted man for almost as long as I'd been a dead one and I'd escaped far more perilous foes than the police who currently stalked us through the dark.

"This way," I hissed, jerking my chin towards the riverbank once more.

We were more than a mile downriver from the crash site now, but I'd been making sure we checked the riverbank as often as we could, certain I'd find evidence of my chica loca's passage sooner or later.

In another life, I'd hunted people like this. I'd been the one sent to deliver the message of failure to those who incurred the wrath of the Castillo Cartel. Sometimes they knew I was coming, and they ran. In fact, sometimes I let them find out on purpose so that I could experience this thrill, push myself with the challenge of the hunt. It was a high like no other. I could track a man across country for days in all terrains and weather patterns. I'd made a hobby of it.

On occasion I'd even captured them and taken them out to some remote location and allowed them the chance to run, giving them a head start before my hunt began. My terms had always been the same. 'Escape me and live, but if I catch you, your death will be all the bloodier.' Still, most preferred the chance of survival no matter how slim. They took the risk and played my games, and I had never once lost. So I wouldn't lose her either.

"You can't even be certain she'll have gotten out on this side of the water," Niall hissed, not for the first time. He had a habit of doing that. Repeating himself as if his words held more meaning the second or third time I heard them. Or perhaps because he was so fucked in the head that he couldn't even remember saying them already.

"The river curves here," I growled. "The current pushed them to this side. She would have to be a strong swimmer to go against it which she isn't and even if that bastardo we saw helping her is still with her, it would be much easier for him to exit along here somewhere too."

Niall grunted, the noise an agreement or at least not a disagreement and I carefully made my way closer to the riverbank.

I eyed the water, hunting for the police boats which kept speeding up and down it, their searchlights scouring every inch of the riverside in pursuit of their quarry. But we had left the majority of their hunting grounds behind already as we raced away from the crash site, and they were focused closer to the bridge for the most part.

I licked my lips, my gaze dropping to the bank and a smile lifting the corner of my mouth.

"Two people exited the water there," I said, pointing out the disturbed mud at the water's edge and following it until I found a large male shoe print right beside the bare footed print of a little ray of sunshine.

"Looks like hers," Niall agreed before swinging his axe at a small tree beside us, felling the thing so that it covered the tracks and making me hiss a curse as I looked skyward, wondering if that helicopter had seen it fall.

But all was quiet in the sky, the whir of the helicopter's engine distant as it hunted elsewhere and we got away with that insanity.

"Giddiup then, el burro," Niall said, hefting the axe back over his shoulder once more and heading into the trees in the direction the footprints indicated. "We have ourselves a little psycho to round up."

BROOKLYN

CHAPTER FIVE

Sirens wailed closer and Jack finally looked to me as I snarfed down another chocolate bar. Mm, I'd missed chocolate. Three days in an asylum sure did give me the hungries.

"Follow," Jack growled, striding to the exit and I fell into step behind him as he put on some large boots beside the door. I frowned at the sneakers beside them which I could have sailed down a river in and figured I was gonna have to stay barefooted. I guessed Jack's brain had come up with an idea and I reckoned it was a good one judging by the twinkle in his eye. And eye twinkles were the best mark of a great idea.

Jack seemed to agree as he opened the door, taking hold of my arm and pulling me after him. The dog immediately barked at us and I looked to it with a frown and a whine in my throat. I twisted my arm out of Jack's grip, moving toward the enormous dog with my arms wide open. The poor little pooch just needed a big hug.

"Rook," Jack hissed in warning as the dog bared its huge teeth at me, drool sliding between them and hunger in its eyes.

I sank to my knees before it, wrapping my arms around its neck and petting its head.

"It's okay. The big, bad man is dead now. I killed him good for you. Here you go, little guy." I unclipped the chain from around the dog's neck, his body vibrating as a growl peeled back his lips.

I got to my feet, smiling down at him and Jack grabbed me, yanking me away from my new friend. The dog suddenly realised it was free, moving to take a piss on its dead owner where his feet poked out from beneath the cabin and I laughed as Jack dragged me deeper into the woods.

"Come on, boy!" I called and Jack's nails dug into my arm at the sound of the dog padding after us.

"Hush," Jack commanded and I found an inch of sanity to hold onto, realising he was right.

The whir of helicopters carried through the air and sirens filled the night from a road not that far away. Of course we couldn't have stayed there. That was stupid. Stupid, stupid, stupid. And I was kinda glad because I'd been seriously doubting my squirrel battling skills, and it had felt like the time for a nut battle had been drawing close if we'd stayed on.

We walked on through the trees, neither of us speaking as we listened out for sounds of approach and I worked to ignore the prickles and stones which poked into my bare feet and gave me little owchies.

The crack of twigs sounded somewhere off to our right and Jack pulled me behind the cover of some bushes, the two of us crouching low. I noticed he had a knife in his hand which he must have taken from the cabin and my fingers got twitchy for one too. It looked like a boring Brenda of a knife. She was organised, got the job done. Someone you could rely on, but would write you a snooty email or two when she didn't get her way. She'd do, I guessed. Though I kinda lamented my need for a Kevin – the kind of knife who stayed home without his family and killed for shits and giggles, not needing anyone to boss him about.

The dog was off sniffing in the tress, lingering close, but not moving to hide with us as he took his time peeing on stuff and things.

Another crack sounded somewhere ahead of us in the woods and I held my breath, picking up a rock from the ground. You could say I was a bit of a rock star today. Damn, the press would have lapped that up. *I should write them a letter, so they make sure I sound really cool in the news report tomorrow.*

I felt eyes on the back of my head and whipped around, hurling my rock with a growl leaving my throat and Niall appeared, lurching out of the way of it before he leapt on me. In the same moment, a huge figure collided with Jack and they fell into a furious tussle.

My eyes widened as Niall's hand stamped down on my mouth and I realised it was Mateo fighting Jack, as free as a bird with his luscious, long hair and beard now cut short and his face peeping out for all the world to see. Jack punched him so hard in the chest, he was forced onto his ass, but Mateo had gotten the knife and he held it to Jack's throat in the next heartbeat. *Oh Brenda, you two-timing whore.*

I couldn't figure out why Mateo had come here, wasn't I just his BFF BJ buddy? Hadn't he just been using my mouth for pleasure like Niall had said, and really, I meant nothing to him at all?

Niall was straddling me, keeping me down and I gave him a venomous look as he peeled his hand off of my mouth. My big bastard of a psycho was here, but the whys and the hows and the whats weren't clear to me. He'd come all this way and he'd actually found me in the deep, dark wood like the wolf who'd come to huff and puff down my little piggy house.

"The cops are close," he warned in that gruff Irish accent of his, and I could see the wildness of his ancestors in his eyes and smell the heather on him from the hillside of a craggy village called Killooney where they'd resided. But I wasn't going to be tempted in by his Celtic soul, not again, not after he'd flushed me away like an all-American turd. "We need to go, Spider."

"I have two words for you, Hellfire," I hissed. "*Fuck* and *you*."

"That's three words," he said.

"It's two. The 'and' didn't count."

"It does too," he insisted.

"Does not."

"Does too."

"Does not."

"Does too."

"Stop," Mateo snapped in a whisper shout. "I'll cut up this one's legs so the cops find him and give us a head start."

"No," I gasped in horror as Jack gave Mateo a murderous look and I got the feeling he was about to take a stab wound just so that he could aim his own demons at Mateo and fight back.

I tried to get to Jack, shoving at Niall's chest while he forced me harder down beneath him.

"Stop wriggling, Spider," he growled. "Yer not getting away again."

"If you hurt him, I'll scream. I'll scream until the cops come to take us all away," I said passionately.

"What do you care about the giant fella?" Niall demanded, his fingers winding around my throat and making me look at him. His green, green eyes swallowed me up like two beasties come to eat my flesh from my bones.

"He was the only one I ever had when I was locked up in that place for all those years," I hissed. "And when I was sent back there, he was waiting for me like he'd never once doubted I'd return. Plus, he killed Small Willy Norman and he saved me," I said simply. "So now I'm returning the favour."

"So, what do ya want me to do with him?" Niall pushed. "Because you're coming home with me, whether you like it or not."

I glared at him, fury bubbling in my chest. "You're the one who told me to leave in the first place. You don't get to just show up like a friendly axe murderer and whisk me away to your murder lair - *again*."

"And why not?" Niall asked with a manic gleam in his gaze. "That sounds exactly like the sorta thing I'd do."

I slapped him across the face and he instantly slapped me back. I gasped, slapping him again and he slapped me in return, the two of us falling into a furious slapping frenzy until Mateo kicked Niall in the thigh and we were left panting, nose to nose and wide awake from the slap war.

My cheeks were burning from his touch and a high was buzzing through my veins from that little fight, my hair fluttering before my eyes and my heart on overdrive. Holy tits, I forgot how much I liked playing psycho with Niall.

"We need to move," Mateo snarled.

"We came to save ya. This is a rescue mission," Niall told me. "Don't that count for somethin'?

I considered that with my lips pursed, but he was clearly too impatient to wait for my answer, rising to his feet and dragging me after him. He locked me to his side with one large arm and I leaned down to bite it, digging my teeth in deep but it only made him laugh in return like he liked it. And dammit, I liked him liking it. And double dammit, I liked liking him like it.

Mateo rose to his feet, gesturing for Jack to get up with the knife and Jack did as he was commanded, glancing from Mateo to Niall with raw death in his gaze. Ooh, I liked that. It gave me the shivers. He was all hell beast right now and that was my favourite flavour.

"It's okay, Jack. I know them. They're my…" I didn't have an end to that sentence. Friends? No, friends were squishy and these two didn't fit that description. Mateo had made me come a lot and Niall had made me want to come a lot. So I guessed we were…

"Hers," Niall decided for me. "We're hers. And we're here to collect her. So you can skedaddle off into those trees if it suits ya, lad. Or you can follow her and see where it leads ya. But I can't promise it won't be to yer death in the end."

Niall pulled me away from Jack and I glanced back at him, my heart a stampeding wildebeest about to kill Simba the lion cub as I saw the hesitation in his eyes. Mateo was huge, but Jack somehow had almost another half foot on him. He was a titan forced to sleep beneath the earth, but I'd woken him now and I wanted him to stay.

"Jack," I breathed in desperation and I saw all hesitation fall from his gaze. He wasn't going to be leaving me, I could tell. We were bonded him and me through death and destruction – my favourite kinds of bonds.

"Rook," he answered, taking a step after me and Mateo walked at his back, angling the knife at his ribs.

I looked around for my new dog as Niall picked up the pace, pursing my lips and trying to whistle for him. A faint noise came from my lips and I tried to make it again, but failed.

"What the fuck are you doing?" Niall hissed.

"Whistling for my dog," I said simply, continuing to blow air between my lips. The sound wasn't much, but it was as good as any whistle I'd ever heard.

"You can't even whistle," Niall tutted. "And what fuckin' dog? Are those drugs making you see things?" He seemed concerned, pulling on my hair as he made me look up at him and examined my eyes. His fingers carved along the side of my face like he was checking all the bits and pieces that made it up were still there, and I couldn't help but enjoy the attention as his concern fell over me. No one had ever been all that concerned about me. Not any time recently.

"I can whistle perfectly. Look." I blew air between my lips once more.

"If you could whistle, do ya think I'd let ya keep whistling while the cops are on our tails, love?" He shook his head at me.

The sound of paws padded through the trees to my left and I whipped my head around, spotting the dog as he arrived, baring his teeth at the band of men around me.

"Told you," I muttered to Niall. "That's my dog."

"Well shit," he exhaled. "That ain't your dog. That's *my* fuckin' dog."

"What?" I balked.

"That's Brutus." He pointed at him and I looked to Niall in confusion. He'd mentioned that he had a dog called Brutus before, but what were the chances I'd bump into him out here in the woods chained up outside some dodgy dude's house?

"Really?" I breathed, realising that fate must have truly been on our sides to have brought that together so perfectly. The stars had aligned, called our names and we'd said yes please Mrs Fate – because only a crazy person would ever deny the stars and risk their wrath. They were vengeful, spiteful creatures who would always get their revenge for such a snub after all. No one could win against them, anyone who tried would perish and rot and say bye-bye to all the good things they'd ever held dear.

"Liar," Jack growled and Niall bristled.

"Let's just get the fuck out of here," Mateo pressed and my gaze lingered on him, his new look every shade of hot. I wanted to see him in the light, drink in the lines of his newly emerged jaw and cheekbones, run my fingers up the shaved sides of his hair and bury them in the longer, messily perfect dark strands on top.

I'd missed him, really, truly, deep down to the bottom of my empty little heart missed him. And I hated to admit it – so I wouldn't ever – but I'd missed Niall too. I'd pined for them both in that horrible cell where the drugs had made my mind sleep and my nightmares sharpen. And they'd actually come for me, Hellfire and my Dead Man. They'd shown up to pull me out of that place, Niall had said so himself. This was a rescue mission. But I still couldn't forget the look of anger in Niall's eyes when he'd kicked me out of his house, the rejection I'd felt carving out my heart and throwing it against the wall so it splattered everywhere. Why had he come for me if he wanted me gone? I could have been permanently gone if he'd wanted me to be. But he was here, ensuring I was the opposite of gone to him. I was non-gone.

We picked up our pace through the trees, Niall seeming to know some route towards wherever we were going, or maybe just following his instincts. Brutus ran along behind us, occasionally snapping at Mateo and Jack's heels in a fun little game I quietly nicknamed snappy snaps.

Mateo cursed the dog, looking more than a little unsure of the game but I'd teach him the rules later – you could lose a finger if you didn't play it right after all.

Eventually, we reached a dirt track where a rusted old truck was parked up and my heart swelled as Niall kicked the door handle off to break into it. He quickly hotwired it and we all piled inside while Brutus leapt into the truck bed with such confidence that I had to wonder if this truck had belonged to the dickmunch who'd beaten him.

Niall found some rope in the glove compartment and dove onto Jack like a ninja from the shadows, tying his wrists and ankles together while I pouted the whole time. Angry Jack didn't fight him, but he had a scheming look on his face which said his fight wasn't done here. But I guessed he was happy to take the free ride away from the cops.

"He's not your prisoner, Niall," I growled, jabbing him hard in the ribs as Mateo drew me into his lap.

"Yer all my fucking prisoners," Niall insisted.

I opened my mouth to refute that but Mateo captured my cheek, forcing me to look at him and I fell into the depths of my Dead Man's gaze. There was so much evil in him, I could feel it painting my soul a deeper shade of black and my pulse picked up to a thunder.

"Hello, chica loca," he said in a rumbling tone that made my bones quake.

"Hello, Dead Man. You look pretty," I said with a shy smile and he frowned like he didn't know what to do with those words. So I carved my fingers over my lips, capturing the essence of them and slipped them into his pocket for Ron (first name Later).

Mateo's gaze intensified, sliding to Niall as a sneer twisted his features. I didn't see his next move coming as his hand shot out, snapping the windscreen wiper lever off and wheeling the jagged end of it towards Niall's throat. I screamed, shoving Niall aside before it could impale him and the lever sliced into the headrest instead. Niall roared in anger, shoving a hand in his pocket as Mateo yanked the lever free and I tried to keep myself between them as he swung for Niall again.

Niall ripped me off of Mateo's lap into his own and his thumb came down on a remote in his grip. Mateo dropped the lever before his strike could land and he growled in rage, slumping back in his seat as he spasmed under the power of a shock from the collar he was wearing. His eyes rolled back into his head as Niall bared his teeth and kept his thumb on the button far longer than I liked. The zappies were great for fun times, but they could set Mateo's heart on fire if Niall wasn't careful. And it didn't look like he was being careful at all.

"That's enough!" I demanded, turning in Niall's lap and cracking his head back against the window.

He grinned at me like he enjoyed that, and I did it again harder and harder until his thumb slid off that button.

"Have ya learned your lesson yet, el burro?" Niall asked as I clambered off his lap onto my Dead Man's once more, cupping his cheeks as he fought to keep consciousness. "I'm the governor of yer fate, so sit back, relax and enjoy the ride."

Niall settled himself in the driver's seat and I nuzzled Mateo's stubble to see how it felt against my cheek. He turned into the touch as if he'd expected something else and my lips caught on the corner of his, making my heart hitchhike right on up into my throat. My fingers explored his chest and I glanced at Niall as I bit down on my lip, heat pooling through my chest as he gave me a dark and hungry look which said he wasn't quite decided on what to make of my little crush on Mateo.

"Let's get the fuck outa here," Niall said, taking off down the dirt road.

It was a bad idea to go back to his den, but I was down to my last option. Besides, Niall may have thrown me out before and told me I was useless, but now he'd shown up, freed Mateo and come rodeoing in to rescue me. That had to count for something, even if I was just fooling myself into hoping he'd missed me like I'd missed him.

I wasn't going to forgive him like a friendly dolphin looking for its blowhole to be tickled though. I wanted a big fat sorry alongside a big fat French kiss, and maybe a little finger up the butt if I was getting all my wishes fulfilled.

I was fooling myself for the second and third part of my wants though, because Niall was engaged to a well-titted Russian. So I'd settle for the sorry, and if I didn't get it, I'd be leaving pronto, riding Angry Jack off into the sunset with Brutus chasing a squirrel at our side.

NIALL

CHAPTER SIX

We pulled up at my house at last, the shitty old truck I'd stolen wheezing and creaking as it rolled to a halt and I cut the engine. I was going to need to get the thing taken care of sharpish as it was likely registered in the name of that fella whose head I'd found smashed in back at that shack, and I didn't much need the headache of having a big lump of evidence sitting right outside my house.

That said, I wasn't in a whole lot of a rush yet. This place was untraceable, hidden from eyes all around and damn near off the map altogether. That was what had made it such a perfect hiding place for a man on the run from the most bloodthirsty cartel in all the world. And it was why I'd decided to stay after claiming it from him and locking him in my basement.

I snatched Brooklyn offa Mateo's lap, not liking the way he'd been pawing at my little Spider on the drive back here. I was liking the way she'd been appreciating his fancy new haircut even less. It wasn't even that fancy. I'd seen a baboon with fancier hair at the zoo once and that was far more impressive than Mateo and his stubble.

"I'm still mad at you," she hissed at me, yanking her arm outa my grasp as I directed her towards the door.

"Well, be mad inside. It's fucking freezing out here and you're dressed like a crazy person," I said.

"I am a crazy person," she said. "And I'd never choose to wear this."

She yanked the oversized plaid shirt off to prove her point, hurling it into my face and I didn't even catch it as my gaze fell to her bare tits and my throat bobbed with that hunger I'd been fighting against so hard ever since she'd run out on me.

Fuck, she was a stunning creature.

My tongue ran along the seam of my lips without me giving it permission to and I found myself indulging in fantasies of tasting her skin and sinking my teeth into the pert flesh of her hardened nipples before I could fight to keep the thoughts out.

I lingered there for a moment, ignoring Mateo's curses as he climbed from the truck too and just stared at her. My little psycho, all outraged and river-swept and *here*. Right fucking here where I could keep her safe. Not to mention the half-naked part which I was having a whole lot of trouble ignoring.

"Holy mother of a fucking goose," I cursed, doubling over and clutching at my cock as it enjoyed the show a bit too much, swelling at the sight of her and damn near making me pass out from the combined pain of the healing tattoo and the new piercing once again.

"I'm not your mother goose," Brooklyn growled from somewhere above me, but she was gone before I managed to catch my breath and look up at her again.

"Hijo de puta," Mateo muttered, spitting at my feet and stalking after her, clearly giving in to the fact that I would just shock him and haul his arse inside if he didn't do as I wanted. They left me with the beast man still tied up in the front seat and Brutus who looked seven shades of confused as he cocked his head at me from the truck bed.

"Out, boy," I snapped at the dog through the window behind me, wondering what the fuck he was playin' at, making me wait for him and pointing to the front door of the house which Brooklyn and Mateo had left wide.

The dog bared vicious looking fangs at me then leapt out, charging into the house like he was on the hunt for a kill and I smiled.

"Good boy. At least someone around here listens to me."

I turned my attention to the giant in the front seat next, his cold, soulless eyes staring right back at me with a deep kind of intelligence that made me scowl. I didn't need no clever men making themselves at home in my house. I didn't need no men at all. Just my little Spider. But now she'd brought another stray home, and with the tenuous peace I'd formed with her following my arsehole display of mass proportions, I was afraid to rock the boat by turfing him out right away.

She said he'd saved her? Fine. That bought him one night of leniency with me. One night of mercy, fresh sheets and food in my home. But that was it.

I tugged the door open and jerked my chin at him in command. "Out."

He surveyed me a little longer, his grey eyes dropping to my feet, taking in the gun holsters still strapped over my body and the desert eagles contained within them before shifting all the way up to meet my eye.

He held my gaze.

Not a flinch, not a blink, not a single emotion flittering through his pupils. Nothing. Man was as stone cold as me. Maybe even stonier.

Before I could lose my rag and clock him in the jaw, the big fella stepped outa the truck, unfolding himself from it like he was an origami figure or some shit and standing there before me all smug in the few inches of height he had over me. I couldn't say I'd been forced to raise my gaze to meet another man's at any point which I could remember, and I'd have been lying if I tried to pretend it didn't irk me some.

"That way." I pointed towards the open door and he strode away without a word, his gaze only breaking with mine once he'd passed me and I tutted loudly.

"If it's a brawl you're looking for, I could do with a workout," I warned him as I followed him inside. "You won't emerge looking so pretty after it though."

Nothing. Stone, cold nothing. Not even a denial about the pretty comment. And he wasn't pretty. He was rough and tainted in sin and full of dark promises, none of which would ever cause anything good to come of them.

I scowled at his back as I followed him inside. This wouldn't do. Not at all. I needed to reassert my authority here and get the prisoners back to where they belonged.

I followed him into the kitchen as he tracked down the sound of Brooklyn's voice while she jabbered on about all the things she'd been up to since she'd been gone, giving quite a lot of detail to the way she had choked her past tormentor with a twelve-inch rubber cock while not looking at Mateo at all.

There was tension hanging in the air between them. Tension I'd no doubt put there after finding her with his fucking cock in her mouth and accusing her of being a naïve little arsehole who had fallen for his tricks and let him use her.

He was probably salty about the way she'd run off and left him behind too. But hey ho, their drama wasn't my issue.

I moved to the drawer on the far side of the room, grabbing the taser from it and ramping up the power to 'might just kill a T-Rex' as I eyed the big fucker my little psycho had brought home with her.

As a backup plan I grabbed a knife too then hid them in my pockets and slipped towards him like a thief in the night. Or a psycho in plain sight, but who cared?

He twisted towards me just before I made it to him, his reflexes almost sharp enough to beat me, but I'd been ready for it, getting a sense of him from the moment I'd first laid eyes on him. This was a tricksy one, that was for sure.

His meaty hand wrapped around my wrist half a breath before I slammed the taser into his side and I cursed as I was gifted a secondhand dose of the blast myself through the contact.

He toppled backwards, colliding with the door to the cellar, his death grip on my wrist bringing me with him as the two of us took a tumble down the fucking stairs.

I swore as I hit every damn step on the way down, the arsehole's big body as fucking painful to collide with as the steps every time I crashed into it.

We landed in a heap and I groaned as I rolled off of him, leaving him twitching on the ground from the shock of the taser as I cupped my junk in my hand and tried not to black out from the pain of that big bastard slamming his knee into my freshly pierced cock.

"Fuck me," I wheezed as I gripped the railing and heaved myself to my feet.

I moved across the room, unlocking my killing parlour, and taking a pair of bolt cutters by the name of Jim-Bob from the wall and returned to the behemoth who was still resting in a pool of agony at the foot of the stairs. I made quick work of removing the broken metal cuffs from each of his wrists, making sure he couldn't turn them into a weapon somehow before tossing them and Jim-Bob back into my killing room and locking the door up tight again.

I hauled my sorry self up the steps one at a time before coming face to face with Brooklyn who stood at the top of them, her eyes narrowed and her hand on the doorknob as I fell still before her.

"Give me one reason why I shouldn't just lock you down there, Hellfire," she demanded, her voice all threat and no mercy in her electric blue eyes.

I wetted my lips, forcing my hand away from my dick as I took her in in the lilac jumpsuit she was now wearing, the thing covering her from neck to ankle yet clinging to every curve so perfectly that she practically looked naked before me.

"Pops," I said, the sound of the big fella groaning behind me making me shift uncomfortably. I'd hit him with the taser again if I had to, but I would rather just get that locked door between me and him then give him a night of reflection in the dark instead.

"Truly?" she breathed, her eyes going all wide and her lips parting.

"I saw your kills," I replied in a low tone. "Saw the way you'd pulled it off, how you made your demons suffer at your hand. It was a fucking masterpiece, love," I admitted. "I told you I'd reward you once you impressed me. And I'm impressed."

Brooklyn squealed with excitement, leaping on me and wrapping her arms and legs fully around my body so that I had no choice but to grab a handful of her arse to help hold her in place.

I stepped through the door while she hugged me tightly, sobbing something against my neck about how she still hated me, but she'd also really needed to hear those words after the day she'd had and I nodded.

I locked the door with my free hand before drawing one of my guns as I stepped further into the kitchen, unsurprisingly finding Mateo ready with a carving knife and a promise of my demise written all over his surly features.

"I thought we were in a truce, lad?" I questioned, the corner of my lips lifting as Brooklyn remained in my arms, squeezing me tight between her thighs and letting tears fall on my neck.

"That ended when Brooklyn got back to safety," he replied in that thick accent of his.

I nodded slowly, letting Brooklyn drop from my arms as she turned her attention to the violence simmering in the room.

"Fair enough," I agreed.

I kept my gun aimed at him and pulled my cell phone out of my back pocket with my other hand and casually opened up the app which controlled the perimeter sensor on that fancy collar he was wearing.

"You might wanna move into the lounge there, lad," I warned him, my thumb hovering over the accept button for the new boundary I'd just set.

"Why?" he barked.

"Because I am officially rescinding your invitation to the kitchen and the upstairs portion of the house too. I don't need you getting easy access to any weapons, and I don't wanna have to sleep with one eye open neither. You'll also find you can't get into my tool shed or the garage, just in case you were inclined to look there for something murderous. We can't have too much bloodshed in the house after all – it's murder on the carpet cleaning bills."

"What the fuck are you-"

I cut him off by hitting accept on my phone, a bark of laughter escaping me as he went rigid right away, his body twitching and jerking from the shock of the collar before he collapsed to the kitchen floor and the knife fell from his hand, skittering away across the tiles.

"Oooh, zappy," Brooklyn purred before turning and pulling the closest cupboard open as she searched for Coco Pops.

I left her to that as I crossed the room, taking hold of Mateo's ankle and dragging him away from the kitchen before that collar got too excited and fried his brains or some shit, hauling him along into the front room and past the grey couch which marked the line of his new boundary.

He kicked out at me before I could release him, his foot clipping me in the jaw and making me stumble back as pain blossomed through my face. I roared a laugh as I backed up, rubbing at it and admitting to myself that the man had a damn good kick on him. Like a donkey some might say.

I left him there to jerk and twitch himself back to normal while I made a quick sweep of the room, grabbing a couple of hidden knives and a gun from their hidey holes before striding down the hall towards the front of the house and gathering up a few more.

There were a couple of guest rooms on the ground floor beyond the front door, and I was feeling generous enough to let him have his pick between them for his new prison.

"You earned yourself a comfy bed with your help out there, el burro," I called to him as I made my way back to the kitchen and dumped the weapons well away from him.

Mateo hurled a bunch of Mexican cursing my way and I chuckled as I leaned my shoulder against the door jamb and watched Brooklyn continue her hunt.

She ignored me as she pulled cupboard after cupboard open, hunting ravenously and putting on a show for me while I let my heart settle back into a normal rhythm at last.

She was here. Safe.

The screaming which had been taking place in my head ever since she'd left me had fallen quiet at last and I just soaked in her company while she focused on her task.

"You liar," she hissed suddenly, whirling on me and pointing a spoon my way like she fully intended to do me bodily harm with the thing. "There's not a Pop in this place!"

"Calm down, little psycho," I replied, moving towards her and letting her press the spoon to my heart as I reached beyond her to one of the open cupboards and retrieved a bowl from it before grabbing the milk from the fridge. "I'm a man of my word. Come, you'll have your Pops."

I turned away from her narrow-eyed stare and strode out into the living room again, my gaze sweeping over the fire damage to the wall on the other side of the fireplace before I led the way up the stairs to the walkway above us, guiding her into the master suite.

Mateo had recovered enough to call after her, demanding she return to him, but she just looked down at him from the walkway and shook her head.

"Go have a rest, Dead Man. I have a prize to claim."

"You shouldn't be alone with him, chica loca," he insisted, shooting me a venomous glare as I looked back at him from my doorway.

"And you shouldn't be such a wet Wanda, Mateo. Now stop trying to Pop block me and go get some sleep." Brooklyn flicked her long, black hair and strode towards me without another word.

I met Mateo's gaze and gave him a taunting smile as I tugged the door closed behind her, enjoying his yell of rage as he was left all alone downstairs with no one but his own hand to keep him warm tonight. Or this morning. I had no fucking idea what time it was actually, but I knew I was feeling dog tired after all that running about.

"I like what you've done with the place," Brooklyn said and I turned to look at the room, remembering the way I'd hurled my bed over in a rage after finding out that she'd been arrested.

"I mighta gotten a bit upset when I saw the news report about them capturing you," I admitted, crossing the space and shoving the bed back down onto its legs again before realising she deserved better than to sit in my self-pity sheets which hadn't been changed since before the start of my dark spell. I quickly stripped the bedding from it, walking back out of my room and tossing the dirty stuff onto the walkway and flipping Mateo off as I found him still down there, glaring up at me like some kind of grumpy little ghost. Would he just stand there until the two of us came back downstairs? What if we slept for hours? What if we killed one another and never came down? Would he stand there until he died, his eyeballs drying out in his face in an eternal glare because his little feelings were all messed up by our girl picking my company over his? It was damn tempting to kill the two of us to find out. Then again, if I was dead and there was no afterlife, I'd never get my answer. And I didn't much like the idea of killing my little psycho even if I was planning to follow her into oblivion moments after the act was complete. Nah. Not today.

Brooklyn had spotted the bags of her new clothes which I'd tossed into the open closet and was thumbing through them, so I headed into my bathroom and quickly filled the bowl I'd brought with me using the stash of Coco Pops I kept hidden in the secret panel behind the towel warmer. Mateo had kept weapons and cash in there when he'd owned this place, but I'd quickly thrown those out in favour of the Pops. There were far more valuable things in this world than money after all.

I returned to the room, finding Brooklyn pouting as she held some pink and blue fabric in her fist, and I cocked my head at her in question.

"I'm still all river stinky," she complained, plucking at the jumpsuit she'd changed into like she was annoyed she'd dirtied it.

"Have a wash then," I replied, bobbing my chin towards the bathroom. "I'll get everything set up in here for when you're done."

I set the bowl of cereal down on the nightstand and she eyed it like a ravenous beast, seeming to decide she wanted to be clean before claiming her prize and scurrying towards the bathroom door.

I placed my arm across the doorway just before she could cross the threshold and leaned down to speak into her ear.

"You and I have things to say to one another, Spider," I said seriously, and I couldn't help but notice the little shiver which tracked down her body in reply to my words.

She turned her head to look up at me, devouring the space between our mouths until I could almost taste her. "I know, Hellfire. I haven't forgotten the way you hurt me. And Glenda."

"Who's Glenda?" I frowned.

"The tiny duck who lives in my heart," she whispered.

"I see." I swallowed thickly, dropping my arm and letting her pass before I did anything insane like lean in. So that was two casualties to my dickish behaviour.

While Brooklyn showered, I made the bed up fresh and closed the blinds against the assault of dawning sunlight which was trying to blind me, then gave the rest of the room a quick tidy around. I grabbed the liquor bottles which had been sitting beside my bed and deposited them back in the kitchen, ignoring Mateo's unending glare the entire way there and back.

When I returned to the room, I spotted a candle on the dressing table and lit it, wondering what the fuck I was trying to achieve with candlelight and deciding to blow it out again almost instantly.

But before I could manage that, Brooklyn stepped back into the room and I straightened quickly, trying to act like I wasn't some kind of candle lighting fancy man and folding my arms in a way that made my biceps flex.

She'd changed once more, this time wearing a little sleep set made up of a silky cami and shorts combo which was baby pink on one side and baby blue on the other. Her ebony hair was wet and she'd braided it over her left shoulder, leaving her face open for me to inspect, not a scrap of makeup in sight and making sure I couldn't for a single second forget how much younger than me she was. In mind, body, and soul. Yet there was still this connection there, this tug between us which wouldn't ever let me ignore the fact that I'd found something in her which I hadn't ever thought to find. A match. A soul akin to my own.

"No one's ever lit a candle for me before," she said, biting on her full bottom lip as she looked at it like it was something special and I cleared my throat, not sure what to do with the mixture of embarrassment and pride her words were shaking up inside of me. "Two-Toe Jill lit her hair on fire once while I was close by. But it's not the same."

"I was lighting my cigarette and it fell in there and did that," I said, wondering why I was even lying about it. There was no cigarette and we both knew it. But some part of me must have still been clinging to my sanity, and it was clear to that part that I shouldn't be doing anything to make her give me the big eyes the way she was. I shouldn't have been encouraging it. It was wrong because I was wrong. A bad decision darkened by worse consequences. And I didn't want any of my bad to come down on her.

Brooklyn frowned and I quickly changed the subject, crossing the room to her bowl of Pops and pouring the milk onto them before offering them up with only a little reluctance in my soul.

"I meant what I said," I told her as she reached out to accept them with a look of reverence on her face. "You did real good with those fuckers who hurt you. Real fuckin' good, Brooklyn."

Her eyes lit up with pride and I bit my tongue against the words which wanted to follow them, the shield I was so tempted to place between us by pointing out how spectacularly she'd failed at evading the cops, but I didn't do it. She didn't need me to remind her of that and despite me knowing full well that I couldn't be what she needed, couldn't give her what she deserved, I simply had to steal that look in her eyes.

"We still need to talk," she whispered and I nodded.

"Enjoy your Pops first. I'll get myself cleaned up before we get into it."

I turned from her and headed to get myself a shower, cursing and spitting and biting my tongue against the pain in my fucking cock as I washed and fought back the thoughts of her which kept pushing into my brain. Because every time my dick got excited, liquid magma seemed to boil its way through it from the new piercing and it was a hell unlike any I'd ever known before.

I grabbed a loose-fitting pair of navy sweats and pulled them on once I was dry, leaving my chest bare. She deserved to see the ink I'd gotten for her, even if it was going to raise some questions I might not have been comfortable answering.

I returned to the bedroom just as Brooklyn placed her empty bowl down on the nightstand, a contented sigh escaping her as she smiled to herself and leaned back into the pillows on my bed. But as she turned those big, electric blue eyes on me, her smile fell away and the silence in the room deepened until it felt like it was pressing in on us from all around and I would suffocate on it if something wasn't done to end it.

"I was an arsehole," I admitted, leaning my shoulder against the wall as I watched her, my inked fingers curling and unlocking again like I didn't know what to be doing with them. "The things I said to you before you left-"

"Before you kicked me out like an owl in a storm," she interrupted and I heaved out a deep breath.

"I'm bad, Brooklyn. All the worst kinds of it. Toxic. Poison. Whatever you wanna call me, I'm it. Ava…" The screams of the past rose up inside me until all of my muscles were locked in place and I wanted nothing more than to just turn and leave, to never speak of this again, but I couldn't. She deserved to hear this, even if I had to cut myself open to say it. "Ava was sweet, innocent, blind to this world of mine through ignorance or a stubborn refusal to see the truth of it. When I was with her, I was a different man to the bloodstained one you see before you. Not because my grief and guilt didn't hang on me then but because I was just Niall. Just this fella with a normal job who earned an abnormal amount of money for it. I could be different when I was with her. It was like…living this whole other life."

"But wasn't that life a lie?" Brooklyn asked, a frown pinching her brow which made me still.

I wanted to bite back at that accusation, but I couldn't really. She'd gotten to the truth of it.

"Yeah. A pretty lie that I let myself believe in whenever I walked through our front door. That I left behind whenever I went to work for my pa and listened to my victims scream their last screams. I was two men but both of them wanted that lie to be true at least some of the time." Her screams echoed on inside me and I swallowed thickly. "And that selfish desire was the lie that cost her her life."

"Hellfire, I don't understand what this has to do with me," Brooklyn said slowly.

I swiped a hand down my face and looked away from her. "I'm just trying to explain what happens to people who get close to me." I needed to warn her away, but I wasn't sure I could keep hiding how I felt about her, so maybe if she understood the cost of loving me, she'd keep herself from me all on her own.

"But…she wasn't close to you, was she? Not like I am? She didn't see you like I get to. All bloody and broken and beautiful in your destruction. So I'm not like her in that way. I can fight, I can kill, I can-"

I stepped forward and cupped her cheek in my palm, looking down at her where she still sat on the bed and shaking my head.

"You're still too close," I said. "That's why I wanted you to run. You have no idea how many people want me dead, little psycho. How many of them want to strike at me and hurt me in any way they can. Even most members of my own family want to see my head roll. I can't always be there to protect you from that. I couldn't protect her."

Brooklyn's lips parted and I forced myself to withdraw my hand, making a move to step back, but she caught my forearm, her fingers seeming to burn where they pressed against the tattoo of my dead wife's name.

"Sit with me," she said, her voice firm but not demanding, more of a plea which I couldn't refuse.

I moved onto the bed beside her, my entire body aware of her as I made myself comfortable leaning against the pillows to her right, her bright eyes keeping me captive the entire time.

"You lied to me," she said just as I thought the worst of this conversation had passed and I winced as I remembered there were other issues to discuss. "About your big tits fiancée. If you can't have people close to you then why are you marrying some big titted, big boob woman?"

I cleared my throat, looking away from her at the stark reminder of my own bleak reality and shrugging.

"My pa arranged it. I don't want it. I even told her I don't want it. But this world I live in doesn't make way for wants and dreams. It's all about power and transactions."

"You've been sold?" she gasped. "Just like me?"

I looked at her again, my eyes moving to the thin straps of her cami and the way the silky material barely kept the swell of her breasts hidden from me. My mouth dried out. I wanted things from her which I hadn't wanted from any woman in ten long years. She was tempting me in ways I didn't even think I was capable of being tempted in anymore, and I was finding it damn hard to fight those wants away. More and more often they came to me while I slept or whenever my mind wandered and now, with her sitting right here before me, I found I could hardly think of anything aside from how soft her skin had felt when I'd touched her before or how sweet her kisses had tasted against my lips.

"Do you wish I'd never bought ya?" I asked her, unsure what I even wanted to hear to that.

"No," she replied instantly. "Anyone else could have just used me any way they liked. But you…"

"I used you too," I grunted, not wanting to accept that grateful look in her eyes because I didn't deserve it. "Don't go thinking I rescued you outa the kindness of my black heart, Spider. I don't have any of that left in me. I was just a lonely man sick of living in a lonely world and you…"

"Yes?" she breathed, drinking in my words and forcing me to finish them.

"You helped me to focus," I admitted. "I get lost in the dark sometimes. A lot of times, actually. There are probably some pills I could take for that or some shit, but I figure I'm owed my misery for what I cost that woman I married. But since you, I haven't gone into the dark nearly as often as I used to, and I find…I find that I have more reason to return from it when I do."

79

"So you…like me?"

"No," I barked and she flinched, making me feel like a royal arsehole, so I huffed out a breath. *"Like* isn't what it is," I went on, taking her hand and moving it to my side, placing her fingers on the fresh ink I had there and embracing the slight tingle of pain which came from her touch.

Her lips parted as she moved her fingers over my skin, the spider on her thumb brushing against the one I'd gotten for her as she licked her lips and my breathing grew shallower. She had to see it for what it was, had to know my reason for getting this particular tattoo. There was no other motivation for it beyond wanting this reminder of her permanently branded onto my flesh.

I cursed as my cock stiffened, the blinding pain reminding me of myself and making me draw back before I could do anything stupid like try to kiss her again.

"What is it?" Brooklyn asked in alarm.

"Nothin'," I ground out, cupping my dick and trying not to buckle in on myself as I gritted my teeth against the pain.

"It's not nothing. It's clearly a something," she insisted. "Let me see the something."

Brooklyn grabbed my wrist, trying to pull my hand away from my cock and I growled at her.

"Honestly, love, it's just my own stupidity reminding me what happens when I act before I think," I grunted.

"Let me see," she hissed, trying to yank my pants down and making me curse again as my dick got even harder.

"Fuck, Jesus, stop pawing at me or it's going to fuckin' fall off," I groaned.

"Have you hurt your cock?" she breathed. "Because of me? Did someone do this to you? Did they cut it off? Is it nothing but a nub now? Just a bloody, bleeding nub of doom? Did they leave your balls behind or are they gone too? Will I have to call you Nubby Niall now?"

"No one cut anything off of me," I snarled.

"Then why won't you let me see?" she insisted, yanking on my sweatpants again and knocking my hand hard enough to make a fresh wave of agony explode through my manhood.

One moment I was calling her a she-witch and the next she'd managed to pull my fucking pants down to reveal my freshly decorated dick.

"Oooh," she gasped, leaning down to get a better look and I gripped her by the throat, forcing her back, mostly because the thought of her touching it was at least as terrifying as it was tempting in that moment, and I was pretty certain I'd pass out from the pain if it got any worse. "I've never seen one this fancy before."

"I was drunk off my tits and thinking fuck knows what," I snapped, not bothering to fight to get my pants back in place now that she was already getting her eyeful.

"It looks ouchie," she said. "And it's really swollen up – it shouldn't be that big, should it?"

"That is your contribution to my problem, Spider," I said roughly. "It hurts like a bitch when I get hard, so I'd appreciate you backing up a touch."

I bit my tongue on the alternative offer which was burning through me because for one, I was pretty certain that I really would black out from the pain of her touch if she got any closer to my cock. And for two, this was a terrible idea. A terrible, irresistible, all-consuming idea.

Brooklyn backed away and I tugged my sweatpants up again.

The intensity of the look which burned between us had me questioning all of the decisions I kept trying to stick to about keeping a distance from this creature.

I had a list of reasons not to give in to this. A whole fucking list. But they were gone now, swept away on a wind I could no longer feel, leaving me staring at her with a pain in my soul which said that if I didn't kiss her, I might just shatter into a thousand pieces which would never fit back together right.

"I'm marrying her," I blurted before I could lean in and do it. Because I would. I was weak. Which meant I was going to take the coward's way out and make her stop this. "Anastasia."

"She has a princess name?" Brooklyn breathed, the flash of hurt in her eyes making me feel like a royal cunt as I swallowed thickly. "As well as big tits?"

I nodded, hating the coldness which was slipping in to take the place of all the heat which had been building between us.

"And is she too young for you?" she asked and I shook my head.

"She's my age," I admitted.

"What does she look like?" she asked, shifting back inch by inch, retreating against her pillows while I felt that wall building up between us and hated myself for every brick she laid.

"Blonde." I shrugged. "Tall. Russian."

"Beautiful?" Brooklyn whispered and I shrugged again, my eyes clinging to every piece of her and knowing in my soul that I'd never once seen beauty that came even close to hers. It was there in every line of her features but more importantly than that, it was painted through every stroke of her dark and twisted soul. There was no beauty beyond this woman before me, but admitting that would have been admitting to so many more things which would only end in her death, just like it had for Ava.

"I suppose so," I agreed, but I had no interest in any part of Anastasia and I couldn't say I'd felt even the slightest stirring of attraction towards her. I just couldn't let myself voice those words.

"When?" she asked quietly.

"Soon. The whole thing is going to be some big showy event. I haven't paid much attention to the details, but our families want this union."

Brooklyn nodded again, her gaze moving to her hands where they twisted in her lap and I felt like the biggest piece of shit to ever draw breath, but I wasn't going to back down. I couldn't risk her for my own selfish desires. I wouldn't.

"I took the tape of you killing Andrew Fig and his bitch of a wife from the scene of the crime," I said suddenly, wanting to put a smile back on her face even if it had to be for reasons aside from me.

"You did?" she asked, her big blues brightening at the thought and I nodded, hooking it up to the TV so that she could get an eyeful of her victorious moment on the big screen.

I started it playing from the point where Brooklyn got the upper hand, knowing I couldn't bear looking at that motherfucker hurting her again without losing my shit and watching her face light up like a kid in a candy store as she re-lived their deaths with a moan of satisfaction escaping her that made my fucking cock pulse with pain once more.

She kept making those noises while their screams filled the air and I couldn't tear my attention from her, my heart thumping, blood heating and so many unspoken words tying my tongue in knots. But there was only one thing left to say that really mattered anyway.

"Will you stay?" I asked her softly, drawing her attention back to me once more and she nodded slowly, making the tightness in my chest ease at last as I took in her answer and tried not to grin like a kid smashing pumpkins on Halloween.

"Yes, Hellfire. I'll stay."

BROOKLYN

CHAPTER SEVEN

"Right, Spider, where can I find this armadillo that wronged you?" Niall asked over the breakfast island.

After last night's gift, he was back to hoarding the Coco Pops, serving me pancakes instead. I liked pancakes, but if he thought I'd forget about those delicious Pops anytime soon, he was kidding himself. I was a Pops expert and I'd sniff them out eventually, then I'd hide them somewhere he'd never ever think of and hoard the Pops all for myself. Then he'd see who the real Coco Pops master was. He'd come begging me for them and I'd make him kiss my feet in payment for them. One kiss would equal one Pop. I'd get him to kiss his way up my legs, spread them wide and call me the Pop queen as he rolled his tongue all the way over my- *wait a second, what did he just say??*

"What armadillo?" I asked through a mouthful of pancake and syrupy goodness.

Mateo sat beside me with a bowl of oatmeal in front of him that Niall hadn't even put extra milk or sugar on. It looked overbaked too, like a gloop made of poop.

I made a point of feeding Mateo pieces of my pancake and he sucked the syrup off my fingers too. His teeth dug into the pads of my fingers every time he accepted a bite, and the small pain made my skin all tingly while the warning look in his eyes reminded me that I was toying with a monster. But that was my favourite kind of playtime.

Niall watched with the fury of a madman on his features. But I didn't know why he cared what I did with Mateo, he was getting married to his flouncy titted bride. Not that I cared about her or her giant beluga tits either. He could marry them too if he liked and shove them up his butt on their honeymoon. Whatever Trevor.

I looked down at my perky boobs, pushing my arms together a little to try and get some cleavage going within my hot pink strappy bodysuit. I'd paired it with a ripped denim skirt that had two skeleton hands stitched over my ass cheeks. It looked cute. Or at least I had thought it did until I let thoughts of tall, blonde, Russian, big-titted women push into my mind and couldn't help but think about the way I was just a tiny, ebony-haired, plain old American, perky tits girl who was 'too young', though I hadn't quite figured out what the numbers had to do with anything. I was as mature as an old cheese and as worldly as a goat on a hill. I'd seen things. Done things. Just like that goat. So who cared if I didn't have any butt wrinkles yet – were butt wrinkles even all that desirable anyway?

"The one on yer kill list." Niall took my kill rock from his pocket, sliding it across the table and I gasped, grabbing it and hugging it to my chest. *Rocksie.*

"You kept it?" I breathed and Niall shrugged one shoulder.

"Sure I did. Why would I throw away a perfectly good rock?"

Mateo gave him a dry look then turned his attention back to me, every crime he'd ever committed written into his features. He was danger lurking in the forest, death riding a black tide, and hell did it give me the flutters.

"You got some of them?" I breathed as I stared at my murder rock, my eyes going all wide and adoring as I looked at the names which had now been struck out. I looked up and found Niall smirking back at me like the cat who'd gotten the bean.

"He helped," Mateo said, his hand moving to grasp my chin and drawing me around to look at him as his fingertips dug in. "Do you want me to tell you about the way their blood felt as it speckled my skin?"

A moan escaped me, all filthy and sexual and full of desire, and I nodded as I stared up at this dark creature of mine who had wetted himself in the blood of my enemies.

"Tell me about the crunchy bones and the stabby stabs, Dead Man," I begged breathlessly, heat burning between my thighs. "Tell me about when the screams were hushed and the blood turned cool against your skin."

Niall took the remote for the shock collar from his pocket and zapped my Dead Man good, making his hand fall from my face as he fell from his stool, and I pouted as I turned my glare on him.

"I want a turn with the zappy," I demanded and Niall gave me a heated look which made my toes curl.

"Later," he promised and I swallowed as I considered that, nodding my agreement and hoping he gave me a good one when the time came. The kind that sent the zips and zaps right to my clit and had me writhing like a snake in the sun on the ground. "I think you said something about killing the Lucille bitch earlier?" he added, offering me a Sharpie, and I smirked like a hell cat as I took it.

"I did," I agreed, striking her name from the rock with a flourish before twisting it and marking off Small Willy Norman too. "And Jack snapped Small Willy's neck for me with his bare hands. It was so hot, Hellfire, you should have seen it."

"I've snapped plenty of necks with my bare hands," he replied with a scoff as Mateo managed to get to his hands and knees on the floor beside me. "Ain't nothing fancy about that."

"Yeah, but AJ did it with pizazz," I protested. "It was something special."

"I have pizazz," Niall growled. "And dramatic flair. And I can speak in full sentences."

"Yeah, but Jack can convey full speeches with a single word," I pointed out. "It's beautiful in its simplicity. He's a deep soul."

"About as deep as a puddle," Niall grumbled.

"Yeah, the ocean puddle," I shot back. "Besides, he killed someone on my list and he did it for me, so you can't be mean to him. It's the rules."

"What rules?"

"The club rules," I growled, knowing he knew that and was just trying to spite me by pretending he didn't.

"We ain't no club."

"We are, and Jack is in it now too."

"He absolutely isn't," Niall snarled just as the sound of Jack breaking something in the basement reached our ears.

Mateo cursed as he hauled himself back up onto his stool, saying something in his language which most definitely threatened violence and made my muscles clench in a yummy kind of way. But he must have liked it a little because he said the word 'coño' and that definitely meant thank you.

"Enough about non-existent clubs," Niall barked. "Tell me more about this armadillo."

I frowned, shaking my head fiercely. "There's no armadillo, Hellfire. And even if one chewed my legs off and called me a flat tit bitch, I wouldn't want to hurt it."

"So why'd ya put one on your list, woman?" Niall demanded, pointing at Rocksie which was now down to only two names, and I had to admit the knowledge of all that bloodshed happening on my behalf and by my hands was making me flustered.

"I didn't," I growled, having no idea what he was talking about. Sometimes he really was a riddler on a hot tin roof. "Would you contradict the armadillo if it said that, Niall?"

"Said what?" he asked, stuffing more pancake into his mouth and speaking through it.

"That I'm a flat tit bitch?" I glanced at him then to Mateo, wondering if either of them would fight an armadillo for the honour of my tits. Or if my tits just weren't worth invoking the wrath of an armadillo for.

"Why the fuck would I waste my time contradicting an armadillo when I could be off killin'?" Niall scoffed and hurt flashed through me as I pouted.

"So you agree with the armadillo now?" I asked, trying to hide my hurt, but Mateo was watching me closely like he could see through every crack in my perfectly polished armour.

Niall shrugged like he wasn't listening anymore and I grabbed a knife from the table, slamming it down into the wood.

"Well maybe I *would* kill an armadillo."

"Mi sol," Mateo growled, leaning in close so his hot breath fanned against my neck. Ooh I loved when he did that. His breath was a heated breeze sent straight from the depths of hell to stir the sin in me. "Tell us who else is on that list."

My gaze moved from his intense eyes to his tempting mouth then I let my eyes fall all the way down to my murder rock.

"Ooh, can we kill the judge next?" I asked as I spotted the name of the man who'd shown me no mercy after I'd been terrorised at school by those monstrous bullies and gotten stabby with a couple of them. Cedric Rawlings.

"Killing a man of that position will need some careful consideration," Mateo said slowly.

"And who says you're a part of this discussion, el burro?" Niall sniped at him.

"I do," I said firmly. "He's part of our gang. We're The Clit Clan, The Club of Death, The Axe Swinging Bandits, The Pink Pussy and the Muscle Men."

"There's no gang," Niall said. "There's just me, my apprentice and a couple of prisoners I'll take pleasure in carving up once I get bored of torturing 'em."

"And what about Brutus?" I huffed, pointing to the dog who was chewing on a cushion, ripping the stuffing right out the middle of it. It was a beautiful murder, chaotic, savage, perfect.

"What about him? He's always been here. I ain't gonna do no harm to my own dog," Niall said, waving a hand at me.

"You're getting off topic," Mateo stepped in and Niall's head whipped towards him.

"You ain't a part of this discussion so whatever topic we're on is the right topic," he bit at him then shoved to his feet. "Let's look at the info I've had gathered on this fella's house and see what we're dealin' with security wise." He headed off to fetch his laptop and Mateo immediately grabbed my stool, dragging me to his side so our legs pressed together. My breaths came quicker like a little windmill was whirring in my lungs.

His large fingers curled around my bare thigh and I bit my lip as he leaned down, so close there was only him, a demon summoned to me from the dark.

"Did he touch you last night?" he asked, unblinking and I swear I could feel the rage in him winding all around me as it hunted for an outlet.

I thought back on my night with Niall, a rush tumbling through my skin at the way our legs had brushed, our arms, fingers finding each other's one too many times. But nothing more. Sleep accidents, that was all it was. I'd barely caught three winks because of the electrical current that zapped between us every time he touched me. It was like he'd left my shock collar on and he was the source of its power now.

"Not on purpose," I said and he frowned at that answer.

"Did you want him to?" he asked dangerously and my little heart grew stubby wings and tried to take off in my chest, but it couldn't get its feet off the ground.

"He's engaged," I blurted. "He's going to marry a busty bitch who probably has two large mice employed full time to sit under her perfect tits and prop them up. I bet they're not even paid well. Poor little tit mice, forced to work for that heartless, big breasted bi-"

"Brooklyn," Mateo growled, my name rumbling through his chest and capturing all of my attention. "Who gives a fuck what Niall is going to do? You are the only thing that matters to me."

I slowly ran my tongue over my lower lip, tingles starting up in my clit and a few danced around my butt too. "Me?"

He nodded, his eyes hooding as he leaned in almost close enough to bite my nose off. "Every time I've licked your fingers this morning, I've been tasting you, mi sol. You're sweeter than any syrup. Your skin is a drug to me. And I want more of it."

"I wasn't just your BJ buddy?" I breathed.

"No, mi sol. You are everything to me."

Shivers tracked along my flesh as he hovered on the line of kissing me and not kissing me. I could taste him in the air, sense him in my bones. Mateo was a lightning strike and I was the tree he had been drawn to, so much power and energy pouring from him that it made my blood spark like fireworks.

"I'm sorry I left you behind," I whispered, reaching up to carve my fingers over the stubble on his jaw. I'd always known he had a nice face, but now his beard was sheared away, I could see just how beautiful he really was. If I'd been more skilled with a blade, I'd have been tempted to cut his face off and see how perfect his bones were beneath it. But I didn't want to hurt my Dead Man. He was perfect just as he was with his face perched right there on his skull.

"You won't fuckin' believe this, Spider." Niall strode back into the room then a growl sounded from him half a second before he yanked me away from Mateo by my hair. "Watch yerself, lad." He swung a finger in

Mateo's face then scooted my stool away from him, the feet squealing as they scraped over the kitchen tiles. Then he grabbed his own stool and planted it between Mateo and I, dropping onto it and placing a laptop down, showing me the satellite photo on the screen of someone's house.

"There'll be too much security on a fancy pants house like that," Niall said thoughtfully then tapped onto another tab, opening a file headed with the judge's name Cedric Rawlings.

A stream of information came up and the top hit was a news report stating that the judge had been involved in a scandal after his wife had walked in on him mid-orgy with four men in the Terrance Hill Hotel. From the photos that accompanied it, he was clearly a party animal and the article stated he was there every other weekend partying. There were other stories about him having been caught with women too so all in all it seemed like he was of the wandering cock variety.

"Seems like he's into young men, expensive wine and being an insufferable cunt," Niall deduced and I nodded at that assessment.

"I could dress up as a teenage boy who's a wine salesman and go knock on his door?" I suggested.

"That's not a half bad idea," Niall said.

"It's a ridiculous idea," Mateo muttered.

"Oh, like you have a better one?" Niall scoffed, rounding on him.

"I do actually," Mateo said lightly and I bounced in my seat.

"What is it, Dead Man?" I asked.

"Yeah, come on, *Dead Man*," Niall mocked. "Let's hear your clever clogs idea then, shall we?"

"We sneak into his house in the dead of night," Mateo announced.

"I see a lotta security on his house, Mr Genius." Niall arched a brow. "How do you suggest we get in? Not every arsehole is stupid enough to leave their windows open all night for psychopaths to hop in through."

Mateo muttered a few curses at him and seized the laptop, panning through photos of the house interior which seemed to have been gathered from various social media accounts to piece the place together and I looked over his shoulder as I drank it all in, admitting that I was impressed by how much information Niall had gathered for this. I knew he enjoyed the freedom of a wild kill but when he put the effort into planning one out, he really made my jaw hit my knees.

It was a massive modern structure, all white and blocky with glass balconies everywhere and a huge L-shaped swimming pool that hugged the edge of it. Mateo leaned forward and tapped one of the photos, showing how the pool connected to a big indoor conservatory.

"That's a shitty design there," Mateo said and I frowned as I leaned forward to see the picture better. "The indoor pool is connected to the outdoor pool. There's a sliding door here that can open."

Mateo tapped back onto a photo of the pool. The long conservatory met with a metal door that was shut in this picture, but as Mateo scrolled onto another one, it showed it wide open. "That's gotta be an inch of metal at best. We get through that, we're into the house. We'll bypass the security he's got in place surrounding his doors and can get in and out here without anyone ever knowing we were there."

"There's no we," Niall hissed.

"There is too," I insisted. "Mateo is coming or I'm not going."

"Fine, I'll go by myself," Niall said lightly.

"It's *my* kill list," I growled, picking up my rock and pointing it at him. "You don't get a say in how the kills go down. This is my revenge, and I want Mateo there when I cut Cedric's tongue out and shove it up his ass, just like I want you there too, Hellfire."

"Fine," Niall spat, drumming his fingers on the surface. "But we gotta wait until the heat dies down around yer escape. Have ya seen this shit?" He tapped onto another tab, bringing up a news report with mugshots of me and Angry Jack alongside a bunch of the other inmates from Eden Heights.

"Ooh!" I cooed, leaning in closer to read the article entitled Dangerous Criminals at Large. "Oh my god, Niall, look -look! They have a bounty on my head. Fifty thousand dollars, that's a lot, isn't it? Holy tits, there's a hundred thousand on AJ's head – oh but they've got his name wrong. Jackson Door." I giggled, shaking my head. "They're not going to find him if they can't even remember his first name."

"This is bad," Mateo said in a low tone, leaning in to read the article. "Mi sol can't leave this place until this news dies down."

"That's precisely what I just said, ya big donkey," Niall said, coming off of the page and going back to the photo of the judge's swimming pool. "Anywho, that's deep there. I can cut through it underwater no problem. It'll keep the sound quiet."

"But I can't swim," I whispered, staring at the water longingly.

"Well now I've got time to teach ya," Niall announced, getting to his feet. "Go get yer swimsuit on."

"Ooh, should I wear a bikini? Or a tankini? Or a mankini?" I ran out of the room towards the basement, snatching the keys off a hook by the door and letting myself in to get my stuff. A roar preceded a battering ram colliding with me just as Niall shouted, "No!" and I was knocked to the ground beneath the weight of a mammoth.

"Oh hey, AJ!" I squealed with glee as I hit the floor like a sack of potatoes and wrapped my arms and legs around him in a hug. His big body squashed me real good, and I couldn't say I hated that. I was an ant in love with a boot, the big shoe coming down on my head while I smiled my way through my death.

Angry Jack paused, staring down at me in shock at what he'd done. "Rook."

That was all it took for Niall to appear, slamming into Jack and smacking him over the head with a frying pan. Jack tumbled off of me, shoving to his feet and throwing a powerful swing at Niall's head. He jerked back a second before it could impact with his skull and Niall lurched forward and hit him over the head with the frying pan again. Jack stumbled backwards, clearly dazed by the blow and Niall kicked him squarely in the chest, sending him crashing down the basement stairs.

Niall slammed the door behind him, locking it tight with a triumphant laugh before his eyes fell on me and he hauled me to my feet, twirling me around to inspect the back of my head which had bumped against the floor.

Mateo appeared beside me, but before he could reach me, Niall took the remote control for his shock collar from his pocket and pressed the button on it again.

Mateo hit the floor under the assault of electricity and I gasped as Niall whistled lightly and went back to inspecting my head for injury.

Brutus was barking and snarling, but as Niall snapped his fingers, he fell surprisingly quiet at his command.

"Is it cracked open like a nut?" I asked in concern. "Is a squirrel going to come and feast on my brains?"

"I can't see any brains," Niall said, rubbing his thumb over the ouchy part of my head. "But that might be because you don't have any."

I whipped around, punching him in the gut and he wheezed a laugh. "That's for Jack and Mateo." I folded my arms. "How am I supposed to get changed into a swimsuit when all of my swim thingies are down there?"

"Just stay like that for yer swim," Niall decided.

"But my swim thingies won't fulfil their destinies," I whispered in horror.

"They can fulfil their destinies when ya can actually swim. You wouldn't want them to see the shame of you flailing about and unswimmable, would ya? Now come on, love. You want to be the best swimmer in swimsville, don't ya?" He strode away from me, kicking Mateo in the gut as he stepped over him and my Dead Man growled in rage as he managed to get up.

"The best swimmer in the whole of swimsville?" I breathed in awe, moving to Mateo and gripping his shirt in my fists as I looked up at him. "Did you hear that? The *whole* of swimsville, Dead Man. Do you really think I could be that good?"

"Maybe one day, if you practise." He skimmed his thumb along my cheek.

I released a squeak of excitement, grabbing his hand and towing him after Niall, spotting him outside by the pool. I shoved the back door open, jogging out there as rain dotted my cheeks and Niall worked to wind the cover off the pool. Steam coiled up from it into the cool air and I hurried towards Niall in anticipation, leaving Dead Man to sit on one of the loungers at the edge of the water.

Niall had a coil of rope with him and he moved forward to tie it around my waist, securing a knot in place. Then he took hold of my skirt, unbuttoning it and making a breath get stuck in my throat, never to come out. It was going to live there like a bee in a jar, throwing its buzzy little body at the walls.

Niall shimmied the skirt over my ass then let it fall to my bare feet. I stepped out of it and his green eyes fell down my body for half a second before he picked me up and threw me into the pool.

My scream was lost as I hit the surface and went under, sinking deep, deep, deep, sending my arms and legs out in every direction as I tried to get back to a source of air. But every time my leg kicked, my arm flailed in the opposite direction and I sent myself spinning instead of swimming.

The water burned my nose as I accidently inhaled it and I gave up thrashing and tried playing dead instead.

I released a stream of bubbles from my lips and sank deeper, my back hitting the tiles at the bottom of the pool. Light danced far above me at the surface and the droplets of rain sent a hundred thousand ripples across it. It was such a pretty way to die, but I didn't like the ouchies in my lungs. Maybe if I laid here a while longer, I'd float on up to that lovely light and break out into the rain where it could tickle me all over.

But the longer I lay there, the more my lungs felt like they were going to pop instead.

Two shadows appeared above the water and they seemed to be struggling with one another, shoving, fighting maybe. A final bubble left my lips and that was it, the last piece of air I had to give. It danced its way to the surface, doing a little rumba as it wiggled its bubble butt left and right then popped at the top.

The rope suddenly went tight on my waist and I was hauled skyward a second before a huge body dove into the water.

Mateo appeared, swimming forward and grabbing hold of me with wild eyes and a bruise swelling on his jaw. He swam faster and my head broke free of the surface, beautiful air tumbling into my lungs as I took a massive breath. Niall kept reeling me in with the rope, forcing me out of Mateo's arms to the edge of the water and yanking me up out of it.

"What the fuck was that?" he snapped as I continued to pant.

"You could have killed her, you hijo de puta," Mateo spat from behind me.

"I'm teaching her the way my father taught me, el burro. It's a perfectly good method," Niall growled then grabbed my waist and launched me back into the pool. "Kick this time, love!" he cried just before I went under and started sinking like a stone.

I kicked my legs, placing my hands against my sides in case they were hindering me and trying to use a dolphin technique to get back to the surface. I could do this. I had flippers and fins and a blowhole. I just had to be one with the blowhole. *Ohm.*

My toes hit the bottom of the pool and I continued to thrust my hips and kick my feet, my chin doing a jerky thing as it tried to lead the way back up, but I didn't seem to be going anywhere at all.

Mateo appeared again, shirtless and diving down towards me like a Greek god in one of those yummy yoghurt adverts on TV. He scooped me up under one arm whilst powering back towards the surface like his toes had built in rockets. We breached the surface and the rope went taut as Niall tried to haul me from Mateo's arms, but my Dead Man wouldn't let go this time.

"Enough," Mateo barked, grabbing the rope at my waist and untying the knot.

The rope went slack in the water and Niall's eyes flashed with fury. He picked up a sun lounger, launching it over his head and sending it crashing into the side of the house.

"You're going to fucking kill her," Mateo snapped. "Stop acting like a two-year-old in a tantrum."

Niall's face soured as he watched us. "Fine," he said lightly like he didn't care anymore. "Let's see what the great donkey can do with her." He moved to another sun lounger, throwing himself down on it and staring up at the rain, focusing on the sky instead of me.

"Place your hands on my shoulders, mi sol," Mateo encouraged.

I did as he said, looking to him for more instruction as he wrapped his big hands around my waist to keep me above water. He looked good wet. Like an oiled-up G. I. Joe, ready to slide into a tight hole.

"Legs out behind you and start kicking," Mateo instructed and I did as he said, holding onto him tight.

I adjusted my kicks at his prompts until I felt like I could really move forward if Mateo wasn't blocking me. He started swimming backwards until his feet hit the shallow end of the pool then he walked wherever I pushed him with my kickers. I was on the move, my inner fish freed. Laughter kept bubbling from my throat and Mateo smiled at me darkly like he enjoyed that sound.

"Niall – look! Look at me!" I called, glancing over my shoulder, but he was still stubbornly staring at the sky.

"Don't worry about him, chica loca." Mateo drew me to my feet in front of him, pushing a lock of wet hair behind my ear. "Focus on me. If you do good, I'll give you a reward."

My heart raced as I nodded hopefully. "What's my reward? Is it candy? A pony? Oh my god, is it a little paper man called Clyde?"

"No, mi sol." He shifted forward, his fingers sliding between my legs and rubbing against my clit, making a moan roll up into my throat.

He pressed a finger to his lips in warning and I nodded, swallowing the noise back down like a sugar lump, my heart beating rampantly. His fingers moved in a teasing motion and I kept my hands against his shoulders for support as he played with me.

"Good girl," he said gruffly then flipped me around by my hips and nudged me forward. "Now you need to learn the arm motions. Stay in the shallow water and copy me." He dropped into the water while my head still spun in circles from his touch and my clit throbbed with the need for more attention.

His powerful arms cut easily through the pool in large circles and I watched him carefully as I prepared to copy him. I'd once mimicked a mailman for a whole hour, going house to house behind him, planting my hands on my hips when he did and echoing back to him the insults he hurled at me. I'd have been a pro at if he hadn't called the cops on me, so I could definitely copy Mateo with perfect accuracy.

I let myself sink down into the pool and did what my Dead Man was doing, my arms wheeling around and sending water splashing everywhere. Mateo kept calling out orders until I made improvements and when he taught me how to combine the arm wheelies with the leg kickies, I really started going places. Not faraway places, but still. I was really moving through the water instead of sinking like a goat with its hooves bound.

"Look, Niall!" I shouted, desperate to get him to see as I swam back and forth between Mateo's chest and the edge of the pool.

Mateo increased the distance each time, stepping backwards so I had to work harder to get to him.

"Niall!" I glanced over at him where he lay still on the lounger, not looking my way and in my moment of distraction, I forgot how to put all the movements together and sank underwater.

Mateo scooped me up in the next second, moving me against the wall and standing in front of me so his back was to Niall. His fingers slipped easily between my thighs, pushing the material of my bodysuit aside and driving inside me with a firm thrust. I lurched forward, biting into his pec to stop myself from crying out as his fingers worked to a heady rhythm, making my hips buck and grind as I ached for more. He raked his thumb over my clit through the material still covering it and I licked his skin, hungry for more as I let his body devour away the sound of my moans.

"You don't understand what you do to me, chica loca," Mateo growled in my ear, his words for me alone as I gasped at the feeling of his fingers working me over and playing me like a fiddle destined to jump right over the moon. "The hunger you raise within me."

"I make you hungry, Dead Man?" I whispered, biting down on a moan which tried to follow my words and his gaze dropped to my mouth, making me wonder if he might finally kiss me and I'd get to feel the pressure of his tongue against mine and taste the sin on his lips at last.

"You make the demon in me hungry too," he replied, his muscles tensing like he was trying to fight that demon even while he drove his fingers in and out of me, and I wondered if I should have been hoping he could beat it or encouraging to let the little beastie inside him come out to play. It had to be sad all locked up and denied inside him after all.

"And that's...bad?" I breathed, a whimper in my tone as my pussy gripped his fingers tight and I felt that impending bliss approaching.

"Endlessly bad, mi sol. I fight it with all I have every time I'm close to you," he said in a low warning and the darkness in his eyes made a delicious tremor of fear tingle down my spine, forcing me even closer to the release I could feel building as my fingernails bit into his flesh and I fought the needy moans which were rattling around inside my lungs, desperate to break free.

Mateo edged me towards a high I was aching for, but before he let me have it, he pulled his fingers free of my pussy and smirked down at me instead as he adjusted the bodysuit back into place.

He shifted forward so the hard ridge of his cock ground into my stomach and my eyes dipped to the crucifix burned into his chest, a complete paradox to this man who was so full of sin, no divine being in the world could save him.

But I couldn't be saved either. I wanted to stay down here in the dirt where the world was for the taking. We were different, we made our own laws while reaping blood and making deals in death. When the men in this place looked at me, I saw myself reflected back, and it made me feel like I belonged somewhere at long last.

His grip on me tightened as he boxed me in against the wall of the pool and that dark in his eyes grew all kinds of restless as he tensed like a man standing on the edge of an abyss. His jaw ticked and his cock ground against me again, giving me wicked ideas and things to wonder about before he snapped his eyes shut and moved his hand to grip the edge of the pool instead of my body, inching himself back just enough to break the connection between us while I practically panted for him.

"If you can swim one length of the pool alone, I will make you come all over my fingers," he said in a low voice and excitement rippled through my chest even while he stood there fighting his demon.

I launched myself past him, swimming for the other end of the pool with determination dragging through my being. Water flew everywhere, huge splashes spraying up around me as I kicked and swam like a mad thing. I moved faster than I had so far, and a grin split my cheeks apart as the end of the pool loomed ahead of me.

"Niall," I spluttered, catching glimpses of him lying on his sun lounger, his eyes still firmly fixed on the sky without a care in the world between the giant splashes of water flying up around me. "Niall!"

"Go on, chica loca!" Mateo called to me, igniting pure sunshine in my chest.

I can do this. I'm Flipper the dolphin. Derrick the dogfish. Spongebob Squarepants.

I lost sight of everything as water exploded around me, but I kept moving, my hands reaching for the wall and suddenly I had hold of it, whooping loudly and finding Niall sitting up on his lounger watching me.

He had a smile dancing around his lips, but he scowled the second he caught me looking.

"Next time, keep some of the water in the pool, yeah love?" He shoved to his feet, striding inside without a backwards glance and failure fell over me like a weighted blanket.

Mateo came up behind me, capturing my waist and pressing a kiss to my throat, making me instantly forget about the grumpy Irishman who was rarely pleased with me.

"Now he's gone and done it," he growled as he drove me back against the wall and made me moan softly in anticipation. "Left you alone with the Devil."

Mateo kissed his way up to my ear, the feeling of his mouth on my flesh making my lips ache for the same attention before he stole a gasp from me as he knocked my thighs open with his knee, gripping the edge of the pool to hold me in place as he unbuttoned the bodysuit to give himself full access and drove his fingers into me.

"We have to hurry," he said, a dark warning in his voice. "While I still have control of the demon in me and before the bastardo comes back."

"Aye aye, captain," I said breathlessly, his fingers pulsing in and out of me as his thumb tormented my clit.

I bit into his shoulder as he crushed me there against the wall with his huge body, his mouth nipping and torturing me but never meeting my lips as I tried to kiss him. Oh how I wanted to kiss him. The denial of that sweet pleasure was enough to make my chest ache even while his hand worked to destroy me so beautifully.

I was so close to bliss already, teetering on the edge of fun town as my hips bounced in time with his hand. He pushed another finger inside me, making it a hattrick and I moaned as he stretched me, leaving me hovering on the edge of pain. But I liked the edge of pain, it was a place where I danced barefoot howling to the moon.

His thumb moved to an endless, delicious rhythm against my clit and as I started to come, Niall's voice bellowed in my ears.

"What the fuck are you doing?!" he roared and suddenly electricity was pouring from Mateo's body into mine, his fingers zapping my pussy in all the right ways and making me come even harder.

I couldn't keep quiet even if the Devil had commanded it. I cried out, my head tipping back against the wall and Mateo continued to pump his fingers like a man possessed to fulfil this one deed even as he growled through the pain of the shock collar.

The water carried the charge all over my flesh, my nipples hard and aching as the electricity crackled across my body.

"Holy tits, Batman," I said breathlessly as I came down from the high and the electricity finally subsided.

Mateo was gripping the wall tightly, pain written into his face as he sneered up at Niall.

Niall's hands suddenly knotted in my hair and he hauled me out of the pool by it, dragging me away from Mateo and wrapping me in a huge towel which he must have brought out for me.

"Bad little psycho," he growled and I swear for a second, I felt the huge length of his cock driving into my ass before he shifted back enough that I couldn't be certain.

He led me inside and I glanced back at Mateo as he climbed out of the pool, dripping water and looking like a model as the water streamed down his bare chest and he offered Niall a murderous glare.

"Get inside, ya fuckin' donkey," Niall barked back at him. "Or I'll leave yer shock collar on full blast for an hour and see if your heart can take it."

Mateo trailed after us, smirking at me like a heathen and I swear the demon inside of him winked at me like it had barely even begun with me yet. Niall yanked my head around to face the way I was going as he marched me along like a prisoner of war.

"No more games with my captives," Niall warned in my ear. "You're my apprentice, under *my* command. If you wanna be a fully-fledged killer, then you'd better keep your legs closed and stop bewitching Mateo with yer pussy. Got it?"

I didn't answer, not agreeing to any such thing. My pussy was a free entity, a bird on an updraft riding the wind. I couldn't contain her wants and needs any easier than I could contain a fox in a box. And after I'd just fallen at the mercy of Mateo's fingers and Niall's zappy, I was only thinking about one thing. How and when I might get to do that all over again.

"I'm gonna have to cut down on your distractions," Niall muttered to himself, pushing me towards the stairs. "Go up there, shower and think about what you've done."

"With pleasure," I said excitedly, running away upstairs with a giggle.

"I didn't mean it like that!" Niall shouted after me, but I just laughed harder as I slipped into the bathroom, peeling off my clothes and diving into the shower.

By the time I returned downstairs dressed in neon blue leggings and a matching crop top, I'd gotten myself off twice with Niall's soap and had a smug grin on my face.

My grin fell away as I found Niall tying Angry Jack to an armchair, his head slumped forward like he'd just fallen prey to a zappy.

"What are you doing?" I hurried forward, but Niall stood upright, snatching a machete from the table beside the chair. Mateo dragged me away from him as if he really believed Niall would get slicey and dicey with me, but I knew he would never do that.

"Well I can't kill, el burro, because I need the information in his head, but this one's got nothing but a bunch of bluebottles buzzing around in his brain." Niall smiled like a clown, turning to Jack and I screamed, lurching out of Mateo's grip and running to my AJ.

"You can't kill him!" I grabbed Niall's arm, hanging all of my weight from it as I leaned backwards and he tried to shake me off.

"And why not?" he demanded.

"Because I said so," I growled.

"I'll just chop a few inches off him then, he's got plenty to spare. Though if I take those inches from the top, I can't promise he'll be all that pretty when I'm done."

Niall shook me off, leaning down and holding his machete against Jack's cheek before lowering it to his chin, then his neck like he was deciding where to strike.

Jack glared up at him with his teeth bared and I ducked under Niall's arm, throwing myself onto AJ's lap.

I hissed at Niall, spreading myself over Jack like a starfish and Jack's rough stubble grazed my cheek, starting a fire in my blood that quickly got out of control.

"Ah for the love of Christ, not this again. Move outa the way, Spider," Niall demanded, pointing the machete at Jack's head, but I shifted so my face was in the way and the machete grazed my lips.

Niall yanked the blade back just as a shadow came up behind him and locked a muscular arm around his throat, dragging him backwards. Niall cursed, falling into a kerfuffle with Mateo and I twisted around in Jack's lap, sitting up and working to untie him, but the knots were too knotty.

"Rook," he said gruffly and I looked into his deep grey eyes which were like two whirlpools, dragging me in and pulling me all the way to the bottom of the ocean.

His arms bulged against his restraints and the rope creaked from the power of him, but it didn't give. I could read a hundred stories in his gaze and I got lost as I brushed my fingers along the perfect line of his jaw.

"I know, AJ, you want to smash things. I'll get you some things to smash, kay? I'll bring you porcelain plates and vases and all the best things to smash," I promised then leaned in close as his eyes travelled over my face, roaming like a wandering man lost in the desert hunting for water. "Do you want to smash me?" I whispered and his eyebrows arched. "You can smash me if you want. Throw me around and make me bounce off of things. I think I'd like that, AJ. I might even like it when my bones go crunch." My pulse skipped around like a girl in a school uniform and Jack's throat rose and fell, my fingers gliding down to feel it move like that.

The sound of Niall roaring made me whip around and I pouted as Mateo hit the ground beneath him under the onslaught of his shock collar. He was always playing with Shocky McZaps without me, and I was getting sick of it.

Niall left Mateo there to twitch through the aftermath of the electricity, swiping up the machete which had been lost beneath the coffee table and striding back towards me, his inked neck reddened from Mateo's attack.

I snuggled closer to Jack, nuzzling him like a cat and Niall's eyes flashed with rage.

"Enough of this. You're my psycho. I ain't sharin' ya. I bought ya fair and square." Niall grabbed me, yanking me off of Jack and tossing me on the floor.

I rolled like a ninja, bumping into Mateo and leaping back to my feet in a panic as Niall raised the machete above his head.

"Stop!" I screamed, running forward in desperation to save my AJ but the machete came cleaving down through the air and I swear it tore a hole in the fabric of the universe before it collided with Niall's target.

But somehow, impossibly, it wasn't Jack. It was the rope binding him to the chair and Niall hauled him out of it as the tatters came loose and he held his machete to Jack's throat as he dragged him along.

He yanked the front door open and shoved Jack out of it. "There, you're free, ya big bastard. Now get outa my sight," Niall barked, throwing the door shut in his face just as Jack looked to me, a furious expression on his face.

"Wait," I gasped, running across the room and trying to get the door open again, but Niall twisted the lock and stood in my way.

"He can't leave, he's part of the club," I insisted, panic rising in me as I tried to get past him again.

Niall knocked me away with a glint in his gaze. "Nah, he's a goner now, love. Bye bye, Jack." He waved out the window then yanked the blind down just before Jack's fist slammed into it.

"Rook," he growled.

"Off you go!" Niall called to him. "Go back to your mountain, Bigfoot."

I turned around, looking to Mateo for support but he was still on the floor, no desire to help in his eyes.

"I need him. He's my Angry J. He was there when no one else was there. He was there when Madam Lucille did her taunting and taking and hurting." I launched myself at Niall again with a snarl, but he knocked me off with a dark laugh.

"He ain't even got thoughts rattling around in that big head of his, Spider. He'll be happier off in the wild, living off the land like some kinda giant horse. It's what's best for him."

"No," I snarled through my teeth, but Niall leaned his chin down and shadows fell over his face.

"Yes," he growled. "I'm the boss here, and I say he's out."

Tears burned my eyes and my lower lip wobbled. I whipped around, my wet hair slapping him in the face as I ran to the couch, throwing myself on it and sobbing into a pillow. I threw some fists into it too, rage and hurt stomping through my chest like an elephant.

"It's not fair!" I screamed into the pillow.

"Life ain't fair, little psycho," Niall chuckled. "Get used to it."

JACK

CHAPTER EIGHT

I stood in the yard of the imposing house, staying utterly still and staring up at the windows while I waited. After realising I couldn't break back into the fortress of a house, I'd simply circled the building and come to stand before the huge windows which looked back into the lounge and begun my wait.

I'd had a lot of practice at this kind of patience while I was incarcerated within Eden Heights Psychiatric Facility, so it wasn't hard. I just let my mind wander, take me back to a place of sea and sunshine where I'd once spent my days, and concentrated on the feelings and sounds associated with that memory until I might as well have really been there. Or at least somewhere between here and there.

I didn't move, didn't shift or fidget. Not even when the rain poured down harder on me and my long hair was plastered to my cheeks and my shirt clung to my frame. Not even as the cold wind blew and the chill in the air bit into me.

I stayed where I was, staring up at the windows of the house and waiting.

One way or another they would have to do something about me

standing here like this. It was disconcerting even if it was harmless.

They wouldn't be able to leave me here. And I wasn't going anywhere. Niall may have decided he no longer wanted me in his house, but now I was free, I found myself still chained to the girl he kept within those walls.

She had been my secret obsession when we'd been locked up together and now that we'd stolen this freedom, I found that I was ready to let that secret out. I'd wanted her for too long, fantasised over her too often, and now she was within my reach I wouldn't be backing away.

I wasn't going to allow them to move me away from here, from her. So that would leave Niall with a choice. Let me in or end me now.

I found myself comfortable with that ultimatum.

I had seen enough of the set up here and the kinds of people they were to know that they weren't doing anything legal in this place. There was a torture chamber in the basement and the hollow, compassionless look in Niall's eyes let me know exactly what he was. The Mexican one, it seemed, was a prisoner too. Though he was offered some amount of freedom to move about the place. I didn't miss the way he watched my Rook either, my motionless gaze drinking in everything that had played out within that house in the hours that had passed since I'd taken up this position.

He watched her like I watched her. He saw her just as I did. But I was the one who saw her first.

If it hadn't been for her, I wouldn't have stacked my odds this way. But I'd seen enough of her to make me think that this might work. We had a connection, the two of us, bound in the months we'd spent locked up together and the death and carnage we wreaked during our escape. It was as though a chain bound us to one another and it wouldn't be severed now. Not if I had anything to do with it. And if the screaming and shouting and raging I'd watched her display through the window was anything to go by, then I knew she felt it too.

She'd stood at the window looking out at me for a long time, her hand pressed to the glass and the rain washing down it making it appear as if she were crying. I had almost moved then. Wanting to brush those false tears from her cheeks and see that wild smile of hers once more. But of course, I could do no such thing through a pane of glass. So I'd just maintained my vigil, setting my stance and holding it as I waited. I'd made my decision and it was her.

Even discounting the pull I felt to my Rook, I wasn't a man who could blend in anywhere easily. And more than just the authorities would be out for a piece of me once news of my escape spread. I had enemies upon enemies.

The skin in the centre of my chest itched just thinking about it. About the man I'd once been and the crimes I'd committed in the name of what I'd been then. It was so long ago that it almost seemed like someone else had lived that life. Followed those rules. Been that man.

The wind changed and the rain drove into my face, but still, I didn't move. I was long used to the cold. I'd even spent time suffering the discomfort of wet clothes for hours at a time before now thanks to the punishments Madam Lucille had liked to dole out to those who she deemed disappointing - which I often had been in her books. It had felt good to watch her die, to see Brooklyn drive that taser into her flesh until her pitiful heart gave out. I relived the memory over and over in my mind as I waited for this to end, for the doors of that house to open and for my fate to be decided once again. I'd faced far harsher trials than this before anyway.

I watched through the windows as the Irish one came and went, prancing around the place like he was high on life, sinking whiskey and chain smoking while dancing around the front room with his shirt off to reveal a muscular chest stained with brightly coloured ink and marked with countless scars. He had lived a life which ran damn close to death, that one. I could see it in everything from the marks on his flesh to the look in his eyes and the tension in his body. He wasn't just ready for the fight – he was the fight. A harbinger of the apocalypse fully invested in his duty to dance with death, and yet tempted by the joys of life which he chased through the dark.

Brooklyn scowled at him, starting to dance angrily to one side of the room to Twinkle Twinkle by Holy Molly and I could hear every word which escaped Niall's lips as he sang along even through the thick glass and pounding rain. He was manic that one. I'd seen plenty like him in the facility. Up and down like a yoyo yet far less predictable than that. Men like him were impulsive and that equalled dangerous of the most volatile kind. Something that made him laugh one day was likely to make him kill another. At least it was with most people. But if the way he watched my Rook was anything to go by, he wouldn't be turning on her.

She had him under her spell too. That made three heathens snapping at her heels and hoping for a taste of her. Question was, what would she do about that hold she had over us?

She was the real power here. And if the way she kept throwing furtive glances out at me and pouting petulantly was anything to judge by, then I might just have found my ticket to staying in this place. The chain which bound me to her was tightening with every moment that I spent out here, and I could feel her tugging on her end of it, wanting me closer and making my heart thump to a powerful beat as it ached to answer her call. And I would. It was all a matter of time.

So I let the rain crash over me and I lost myself in the sunshine within my own mind as I waited and watched her. Because if I had judged this little haven from the real world correctly, then it was my best bet at remaining as free as I was now, and I didn't want to let that opportunity pass me by. Not to mention the fact that my sweet obsession was waiting for me inside that house and I wasn't going anywhere without her, so death could come for me if it liked or that door could open and allow me back into the warmth of that house, because those were the only options I would allow. It was just a matter of waiting to find out which one of them it would be.

BROOKLYN

CHAPTER NINE

Mateo watched me as I shot cold looks at Niall, swaying my hips to the music as he tried to outdance me. I was a queen of dance, a dance master. And if Niall thought he could beat me with his shimmies and his slut drops, he was going to find out who he was up against. I wasn't just dancing for me today either, I was dancing for Angry Jack who was stuck out in that rainstorm like a stray cat kicked to the curb.

Brutus had taken one of Mateo's boots, chewing on it and growling any time one of us came close to him like we might want to steal it away from him. Mateo had made a few swipes for it, cursing under his breath in his sexy man language whenever Brutus took a chomp at his fingers. Mateo had looked to me for help, but I wasn't going to take Brutus's little bootie away from him. It was giving him the happies. Besides, Mateo still had a second boot which he could put his feet in all he liked.

Circus by Britney Spears came on and Niall leapt onto the coffee table, showing me up as he kicked a set of coasters into a wall. Mateo moved to pick them up, shaking his head in irritation as I leapt onto the couch arm to get higher than Niall.

"Ya think you can outdance me, Spider?" Niall scoffed.

"I once outdanced a fox in an alley," I said proudly, rolling my hips and running my palm up between my tits.

"I once outdanced a goose in a parking lot," he countered.

Dammit. How was I supposed to compete with that?

"If I win this round, you have to let Jack back in and he gets to stay here always and forever," I demanded.

Niall roared an obnoxious laugh. "No."

"Yes," I snapped, leaping across the couch and landing precariously on the other arm, knocking a lamp flying as my foot shot out to balance myself.

Mateo ran to catch it before it hit the floor, picking it up and placing it back down with a frown drawn on his brow. I guessed he didn't want more things to join smashy corner. There were lots of broken bits of things all swept over by the window and I realised Mateo must have cleaned up last night and put them all there because his collar wouldn't let him get to the trash bags in the kitchen. I quite liked the ambience smashy corner created, it was like modern art, giving us a real sophisticated flare to our club. That was probably what Mateo had been going for.

"You're too afraid to lose, Hellfire," I taunted, lowering into a squat and tumbling back onto the couch cushions when I lost my balance. But I styled it out, so no one noticed. "You can't handle the heat."

"Oh, you think so, do ya?" he growled, doing a pirouette which sent the coffee table flying backwards. Niall leapt off of it, hitting the floor and spinning with such technique it made me stare for a long second. Damn, he was good.

Mateo bent down to pick up a bunch of books which had tumbled from the coffee table and Niall squatted at that moment, his ass grazing Mateo's face on the way down and on the way back up. It happened so fast that Mateo hadn't even had a chance to move aside.

"Hijo de puta," Mateo snapped. "Watch where you're putting your ass cheeks, bastardo."

"I'll put 'em where the rhythm take' em, lad," Niall answered, shaking his butt and making Mateo back away with the books in his arms and a scowl on his face.

I grabbed a blanket from the back of the couch, tying it around my neck like a cape and leaping forward through the air so that it sailed out behind me. I was like a Pegasus gliding through the sky, my wings stretching either side of me, my horn glinting and sparkles tumbling from my flesh.

Niall looked to me with his eyebrows raising and a challenge flaring in his gaze as I landed perfectly and trotted past him, my cape whipping him in the face.

"Fine," Niall spat. "I'll dance ya into the dirt. And when you're down there as a failure, you can wave yer giant friend goodbye."

I spun towards him, planting my hands on my hips and smiling keenly. "Deal. And if I win, you have to kiss Angry Jack and tell him you're sorry."

"Deal, because I won't lose," Niall said with a smirk.

"We need a referee." I pointed to Mateo.

"No fuckin' chance. He'll side with you because he's all pussy dazzled by ya." Niall glared at me and I glared back.

"Then what do you suggest?"

"Brutus picks," Niall said and I looked to the dog who was still busy destroying Mateo's boot. "We'll both dance for him then see who he comes to when we call him once we're done. I'll even let you pick the song, little psycho." He gave me a taunting look and I moved to his phone which was connected to the Bluetooth speakers in the room, picking out Heads Will Roll by Yeah Yeah Yeahs. I'd wipe that smug as a Bakewell tart look off his face in no time.

Niall moved to my right, sneering at me and Mateo hovered close by like he expected us to break more stuff. But the only thing I planned on breaking was Niall's ego.

I rocked my hips to the beat then Niall dropped into a squat dance, his hands on his hips as he kicked out his legs. Holy tits, it was good. So I leapt over him, waving my arms and rolling my head dramatically. I threw in a little Macarena as Niall swung over onto his stomach and did some kind of sexy worm thing where he looked like he was fucking the floor. It drew my attention for way too long and I realised I was stuck in a repetitive hip swirl. I needed to short circuit it, but with style. *Come on, get out of the swirl, Brooklyn!*

I did some jumping jacks then dropped down and did a forward roll, only managing to go half way before I rolled back and tried it again. My legs went over my head this time and my feet hit Niall in the face.

"Yer throwing me off, woman." He grabbed my ankles, getting to his feet and starting to spin as he held onto them. I gasped as I was spun out around him as he swung me in fast circles and I whooped in excitement before he threw me onto the couch so hard that the whole thing toppled backwards and crashed to the floor.

I peered up over it as Niall did an Irish jig and Mateo moved to help me up, checking me over before I sprang back towards Niall and kicked my feet left and right to show him what a real jig looked like.

The song came to an end and both of us struck a pose, my arms out either side of me and my fingers wiggling with some perfect jazz hands. Niall had bent right over, sticking his head between his legs as he gripped the backs of his knees.

Mateo shut off the music and I beamed at him, my heart swelling as he started clapping for me. Just me. His mouth twitched into a smile and I swear a balloon expanded in my chest and my toes came off the ground as I started to float.

"Perfect, mi sol," he said and a blush lined my cheeks.

Niall snapped upright, knocking me sideways so I lost my balance with my pose. "It doesn't matter what you think, el burro, it matters what my dog thinks."

We both looked to Brutus as he pulled the insole out of the boot and Niall patted his knees. "Come here, boy. Come to Daddy."

I scowled, patting my own knees. "Here, Brutus. Come to Momma B."

"You're not his momma," Niall growled. "He's my dog."

"He's mine too," I insisted.

"He is not," Niall said.

"Is too."

"Is not."

"Is too."

"Here Brutus," Niall called, dropping to the floor and Brutus finally gave us his attention, glancing between us with a growl.

"Here baby," I cooed. "Come on little love puppy. Come to your best friend."

"I'll cut you out a nice liver to eat from the mailman, how about that, pal?" Niall offered.

Brutus got to his feet, his upper lip curling back as he bared his sharp teeth at us.

"Move away, mi sol," Mateo warned as I reached for him.

"Don't be silly, Dead Man," I laughed. "Brutus is a big softy wofty with a snuggly heart."

Brutus moved towards us with his hackles raised and Niall and I called him more excitedly, patting our legs.

Brutus snapped his teeth at Niall and I was sure I'd lost, my heart thrashing with panic at the thought of having to say goodbye to Angry Jack. But then the dog swerved towards me and sniffed my throat as a low growl rolled through his belly. I hugged him tight with a squeal and Mateo shifted closer like a looming shadow.

"Brooklyn," he said urgently as Brutus snarled ferociously. But he was just playing snappy snaps with me. It was his favourite game and I was winning.

I released Brutus, narrowly avoiding a snappy as I got up and I pointed at Niall, laughing in his face.

"I won! You lose!" I cried and Niall's face turned red with rage.

"Ya cheated!" he bellowed.

"I did not!" I cried back and Mateo stepped forward to get between us as Niall rose to his feet.

Brutus snarled at the shouting but got distracted by his boot and ran back to grab it without getting any more involved.

"She won fair and square, Niall," Mateo hissed. "Don't you dare go back on your word to her."

Niall's lips twitched with irritation as he mulled over Mateo's threat, looking at me over his shoulder. I was sure he was going to call me a cheat again, but then his shoulders dropped and he nodded to Mateo.

"Sure, whatever, like I give a fuck anyway." He strode over to the couch, flipping it back upright and dropping onto it like he had no cares in the world.

I leapt up, kissing the back of Mateo's neck then turning and sprinting away to the door. I unlocked it, throwing it open and racing out into the windy wetness, running to Angry Jack.

I sprang into the air, forcing him to catch me as I wrapped my whole body around him and I grinned from ear to ear. The cold, wetness of his hard body surrounded me as he crushed me against him and he looked deep, deep down into the depths of my eyes.

"You can come in now. I won the dance off, AJ. I won you back," I said proudly and his grip on me tightened as this delicious kind of victory danced in his gaze.

I bounced in his arms as his eyes widened in surprise. "In?"

"Yes!" I cried, hugging him tight. He smelled like rainy goodness and beneath it was something so masculine it made my toes turn into curly fries.

"Rook?" Jack asked and I looked up at him as I interlaced my fingers behind his neck.

"What's up?" I asked. "Oh, is it because you're wet and windyloo? I can dry you off with a towel when you come inside. I'll need a big towel though, a big, big one. As big as a horse, or a van, or ten herons stitched together-"

"Rook," he growled, peering down at me with water droplets rolling down the sharp lines of his cheeks.

"Yes, Jack?" I asked a little breathlessly. Despite how long he'd stood out here in the cold, his body was as warm as a burning beehive and I snuggled into it as rain dripped down the back of my neck.

"Stay," he said and I wasn't sure if it was a question or if he was commanding me to do so.

"I'll stay with you always if that's what you want, but I can be very annoying long term. People say I'm odd, do you think I'm odd Jack?"

His penetrating gaze roamed all over my face like he was drinking me up drop by drop and my skin tingled under the intensity of that look. He was staring at me like I was someone. Like I was worth something. Something so much more than anyone had ever thought I was worth before I came to this place which seemed to draw these wild men to live in it.

"No."

"What do you think I am?" I whispered, my fingers itching to explore more of him. There was so much of him to explore too. I was a shipwrecked pirate on his island, and I had a feeling there was buried treasure right where his heart lived.

"Here," he said, wrapping his arms tighter around me and I bit down on my lower lip as he tucked me tight against him, his lips brushing against the side of my neck and against the shell of my ear while I inhaled the rich scent of him drenched in the taste of the rain.

"Did you miss me when I left the asylum?" I asked, rubbing my face against the prickly stubble on his jaw as we inhaled each other. "We spent lots and lots of time together in there, didn't we? I forgot about that a bit. The drugs made my mind woozy and swooshy, but I remember it better now. You were always there, Angry Jack. With your angries. Watching me while I fought to hold onto the me parts. I always liked your angries. Let's go inside."

He nodded, carrying me back to the house and shoving the door open, ducking his head to make it through and making my heart fall into beat with the solid thump of his stride.

Niall stood there with his arms folded and he lunged toward me, ripping me from Jack's arms and pushing me behind him as I stumbled to regain my balance.

"She's *my* little psycho, you get that big man?" he demanded, violent energy crackling from every inch of him and making my breath catch as he rolled his broad shoulders and faced off against certain death like it was nothing but a cat in a tulip patch. "Now I owe ya somethin' for losing that dance off." He strode forward, leaning up with his lips puckered and I giggled as Jack's eyes slid over his head to look at me in confusion.

Niall didn't give him a moment to avoid the kiss and their mouths collided in this dominant, masculine kind of way that got my Glenda all of a flutter as my teeth sank into my lower lip and I took a mental snapshot for the forever bank. But the moment Niall kissed him, he also slid something from his pocket and rammed it into Jack's side, using his luscious lips as a distraction the way I'd always dreamed of doing as a honey trap.

The taser sparked and flashed and I gasped as Jack hit the floor under the assault of it and Niall jerked back to avoid shocking himself as well.

Niall left him kicking and twitching as the electricity poured into AJ and I beamed, hoping he was enjoying Niall's gift, though I was tempted to drop down and steal some of the crackles for myself.

When Jack fell still, Niall grabbed hold of him beneath the arms and dragged him down the hall and through the kitchen towards the basement, shoving him inside and throwing the door shut. He locked it tight just as I ran into him, scratching his arms as Niall laughed.

"Not in your boring murder lair," I begged.

"I said he could come back in, not that he's a free fuckin' man, Spider." Niall caught hold of me by the throat, squeezing just enough to hold me still as he smirked in my face and I pouted up at him. "And I'm gonna be out all day tomorrow, so do you think I'm gonna leave that big beastie loose in my house?"

"It's *my* house," Mateo snarled from behind him, making me look his way as he stood in the corridor, as close as he could get to us without setting off his collar.

"Not anymore, el burro," Niall said, drawing me closer and my pulse started to skip wildly.

"Where are you going tomorrow? Can I come?" I asked, my voice tight against the grip he still held on my throat while my body tingled from the tightness of his hold. I had to admit, Hellfire got me seriously worked up when he went monstrous on me like this, even if I was mad about Jack being locked in the basement.

"No," he said simply. "I'm going to see my fiancée."

A lump lodged in my throat that was full of pins and sharp pieces of glass. Something shuttered within his crocodile green eyes like he had seen the way his words cut me and wasn't going to let himself regret a single one of them. "Oh," I breathed.

"Yeah. Oh," he said, eyeing my face closely. "That a problem?"

"Problem?" I scoffed, laughing a little too loudly. "Problems are for squirrels in the middle of winter with no nuts and no one around to peep on while they poop. I don't have a problem. Why would I have a problem with you going to see your busty bride? You should bring her a big bra for her big tits."

"Maybe I will," he taunted, his fingers flexing against my throat like there were more words getting knotted up inside of him, but he didn't give them to me if there were.

"Good," I said lightly, but inside my heart was screaming. "I hope you have a wonderful time bagging up her milk monsters in her new bra, just be careful you don't gouge an eye out on one of her pokey nipples." I shoved him in the chest, forcing him to release his hold on me, his jaw gritting as his hand fell back to his side.

I ran away towards Mateo, shoving past him into the lounge and picking up Niall's coat on the way, hurling it ahead of me. It landed on the stairs and I trampled it, jumping up and down on it a few times with a huff then sprinting upstairs into his room and throwing the door shut so hard the house rattled.

I didn't care one bit about his uddery fiancée. Not one tit of a bit.

I pulled my crop top off, looking in the mirror on the wall and staring at my little boobs, gritting my teeth as I willed them to grow bigger. But they just remained there, staring back at me like two disappointing dandelions caught on a wayward breeze.

My lower lip pushed out and I moved to the window, pressing myself to the cold glass so my face and boobs were squashed against it.

I thought about Niall leaving here tomorrow to go stick his dick in his bride. I bet she'd ride him like she worked for the Pony Express and had an urgent message to deliver to the mayor of Important City. He'd come home all freshly fucked and satisfied with the woman he was going to marry.

Was she going to move in here after that happened? Was I going to have to watch her kiss my Niall and take him away every night to screw the senses back into him?

Oh god, what if he got more sane every time she fucked him? What if her vagina made him wear suits and get a nine to five job? What if he bought an Apple Watch and wore it like some city man with a big job and deadlines to meet?

I slid down the glass, a squeal sounding as my skin rubbed against it before I sank to my knees and screamed.

NIALL

CHAPTER TEN

And so the day of doom commenced. Dramatic. But also true.

I heaved a sigh as I leaned back in the seat of my BMW right outside my pa's house, taking a long drag from my cigarette and narrowing my eyes as I thought of Spider all alone back at the house with those two big, ugly bastards who were annoyingly not even ugly at all.

Mateo had been eyeing her like he was a dog desperate for a bone – even more so than Brutus was – and the thought of him having free access to her while I was gone made my skin all hot and prickly. I had considered just locking him back down in the basement so that I wouldn't have to worry about that. But then I'd considered the idea of someone finding their way to the house against all odds and trying to hurt her. I knew it was the least likely of scenarios, but I also couldn't bear the thought of one of my many enemies taking advantage of my pride and hurting her just because I'd believed she was out of harm's way in that place.

So, all in all, I'd had to accept the risk of Mateo getting his cock near her because that was marginally more bearable than the risk of her being left to protect herself in my absence, no matter how fine of a killer she had the potential to be. Though I was still hoping he kept his fucking dick to himself and I thought a whole lot about castrating him to alleviate the concerns I had over that.

It wasn't that I wanted her. Because of course I knew now that I did. It was more that I didn't want *him* to have her. Him or any other fucker who mighta lain his eyes on her and gotten the kinds of ideas that would cause me to carve said eyes from his face. For reasons. Reasons which I wouldn't allow myself to think on – at least while I was awake.

Dreaming Niall had a whole lot else to say on the subject, but I refused to listen to him beyond banishing those thoughts with the aid of my right hand as often as necessary. Or my left. Had to change it up sometimes. Couldn't let righty go thinking I'd been caged and made monogamous or anything. Not that I'd even been able to do that since insanity had struck and I'd gone and gotten a bolt pierced through my cock. Though it did feel better today, and I was thinking it might just be healed enough to allow me that form of relief. Healed and feeling all kinds of interesting I had to add. It had been a long damn time since I'd gotten laid, but since getting that fancy silver Prince Albert, I had to admit I was thinking about relieving those urges in my body more and more than I could ever remember doing so in my life.

Then again, that mighta pre-dated the piercing. And if I was being totally honest with myself, then it may have had a fair bit to do with the object of my desire and all the things I kept fantasising about doing with her. Not that there was a her. Because if there was a her then that meant I really was going to hell. Because I was breaking that one last, sacred promise I'd made to my wife all those years ago.

I knew that her death was supposed to release me from my vows of fidelity, but it hadn't. Not for me. It had only bound me tighter to her memory, made me want to be a better man and a worse one all at once. Even bathing myself in the blood of all those who had hurt her had never helped with that.

I sighed, exhaling a mouthful of smoke and closing my eyes as I begged for an oblivion which wasn't coming.

I had a real day of it headed my way. Pa was insisting I sit in on a bunch of meetings with him where the plans he was making with the Russians were going to be talked to death while I fought not to die of boredom and had to force myself to offer up opinions. Not only that, but he wanted updates from me on my hunt for information on the infamous missing man from the Castillo Cartel. The one who I had had to fake all kinds of information about without running the risk of any of it being proven as fabricated bullshit. I needed to lay a trail which had long since gone cold without anyone ever realising it should have led to my own door.

Mateo was *my* donkey. The money he'd stolen from the man he'd once worked for was destined to buy me a new life, a whole continent away from here or more. I wasn't going to let my pa and his grubby little Russian buddies get their paws on it *or* him. He was my One Ring, and I was booked on a one-way trip to the paradise of Mordor regardless of anything they had to say on the matter.

Aside from the tedium of those meetings today, I also had the anticipated hell of an evening in my dear fiancée's company.

Anastasia.

I sighed, taking another drag on my smoke as I tried to picture the kind of life I was being forced into with her. For all my big talk of running, I still hadn't managed to drag the location of Mateo's stolen treasure from him. And without his treasure – which I was firmly imagining to be a big fat chest filled with doubloons and diamonds instead of a hoard of stolen dollars – I was stuck here.

My heart crashed and thundered against my ribs in a riotous act of defiance as I considered the idea of waiting in a church for Anastasia to arrive in her white dress. Virginal certainly wasn't something she could pull off, but I knew she'd try. She was of the flashy, bullshit variety and she'd want a thousand photographs of her draped in something unbearably expensive while she hung all over me like a possum on a branch.

Worse than that, I pictured our wedding night. Her there in some skimpy scrap of nothing with her fake tits pushed up to her chin while she panted all over me like a rabid chipmunk tryna find its stash of winter nuts while my fancy penis tried to pull a turtle act and retreat all the way away from her.

The dark place was calling my name. It was calling and I was damn tempted to give in, follow the sound of its voice and wait to emerge bloody on the other end, hoping I might find myself absolved of my commitments by my half-cracked self accidentally butchering all of the fuckers who were trying to force this hell upon me.

I rested my head back against the headrest and enjoyed the breeze coming in through my car window as I fought against the temptation to wallow in my internal agony. I only realised I'd closed my eyes when I felt the prickle of a pair of beady little eyes on me, heard the scuff of poorly concealed footsteps on the drive as the fucker tried to sneak up on me.

I parked my cigarette in the corner of my mouth and opened my eyes just as my brother, Connor bent down and pressed a hunting knife to my neck, a smug smile on his face and a new haircut on the top of his head to fix the mess I'd made when I'd severed his ponytail.

"Looks like 'the greatest hitman in the state' isn't so hot after all," he sneered, looking like he really did want to kill me, and the corner of my lips hooked up as I turned my eyes to him.

"You made a mistake though, Connor," I pointed out, making his brow dip and scowl sharpen. "Six, actually."

"What's that then?" he scoffed.

I fired the gun which I'd pulled, not even bothering to lift it up and just shooting straight through the door of my car so that it hit him in the thigh. He fell back to the ground with a scream of pain, his knife not even managing to scratch me as he went.

"First off, you brought a knife to a gun fight," I pointed out as I opened

132

the car door and stepped out, holstering my Glock and grinning down at him as he tried to scramble backwards across the drive, blood staining the pale stones beneath him.

"You fucking animal," he hissed, clutching at his leg. "You shot me. Pa is going to fucking kill you. He-"

"Secondly, you breathe too loud, not to mention the way your fancy loafers sounded on the ground as you approached me," I went on, ignoring him as I moved to step on his wrist, grinding my heel down until he dropped the blade he'd tried to threaten me with. "Third, you stared at me too hard. Stared and stared until I could feel the unpleasant crawl of your slimy eyeballs rolling all the way down my spine."

"You can't feel people staring," he hissed, trying to take a swing at my leg to stop me from crushing his wrist.

I plucked the cigarette from my mouth and flicked it right into his eyes, making him yell again as he batted it away, sadly managing to put out the sparks before the rest of his hair went up in flames.

"Fourth, you wasted time on small talk – now, don't get me wrong, I love to have a natter with my marks before I end them. But I'm a pro. I don't have to worry about the extra time I'm offering them to come up with a plan to fight me off, because I actually enjoy the killin' all the more when they try and fight back. But you – you aren't made of the same stuff, Connor. You need to go for a quick kill because if you give someone else the chance to get the upper hand then they most certainly will. You're too dumb. Too easy to outsmart."

"I'm going to bleed out while you keep talking," he snarled, giving up on trying to remove my foot from his wrist for a moment and clutching at the gunshot wound on his leg once more.

"Suck it up, Betty, it's a fuckin' flesh wound," I scoffed.

"You could have hit an artery," he shrieked and yeah, I liked that look of fear in his eyes.

"You're right," I growled, leaning down to let him get a good look at the dark in me. "I coulda. So don't you want to thank me for having such impeccable aim and for taking pity on you outa nothing but the pure, sweet love I have for my brother in my heart?"

We both knew I loved him less than a sun-baked turd on the street, and his hissed curses quickly turned into a yell for help.

That was a mistake.

I could already tell we had an audience anyway and I knew no member of our rotten family would step in to save him just as well as he did.

"Fifth," I continued, wanting him to know his failure well because I was a good brother, and this was the kind of learning curve which could truly benefit him long term. "You need to wash more. Shower, bath, scrub your balls with a rag, I don't really give a fuck how, just get that stench offa ya skin. And stop spritzing yourself with all of that damn aftershave to try and cover up your stink. Even if you'd been as silent as a gnat's fart, I still woulda scented you coming like a warthog in a mud hole. It's fucking unseemly."

"I'm going to kill you!" Connor roared and I sighed as I lifted the foot that had been crushing his wrist before stamping it back down again so hard that I heard the bone snap like a crack of thunder. It truly was a beautiful sound.

His screaming was less euphoric unfortunately.

"And sixth," I called, making sure he could hear me over his screams as I picked up the hunting knife he'd thought to threaten me with and twirled it in my fingers.

Connor seemed less than inclined to hear me out though and he rolled over, scrambling away from me in a kind of strange caterpillar wriggle thing which made his arse strain against the confines of his fancy slacks as he dirtied them all over the ground.

I stalked him calmly, spinning the blade in my hand and sighing at the pathetic display he was putting on. Where was the O'Brien fight? Where was the backup weapon? The venomous words? Something, *anything*.

But no. Turned out that when we got right down to it, Connor O'Brien was no fiercer or more fearless than any other fucker I'd come knocking for, and that really was disappointing.

I let him crawl all the way up to the base of the steps which led into the house then dropped down over him, fisting his freshly barbered hair in my tattooed hand and forcing his head back so that he was looking right up into the disgusted face of our pa.

"Please," Connor sobbed, cradling his wrist and making some weak attempt to buck me off of him which did little more than make me tighten my grip as I moved his own blade to his throat.

I raised my eyes too, the thrill of the hunt on me and the bloodlust hot in my veins as I met our pa's gaze and gave him a choice. I had no qualms over killing the rotten sack of shit beneath me. Only the thought of breaking our ma's heart would have stayed my hand and she was long since dead and beyond the point of caring, so I had no need to worry on that point.

Connor sobbed again, no doubt begging our father with his eyes for mercy, and I watched the old man sneer as he looked down at his fourth son with disdain.

For a moment I thought he was going to give me the nod. For a brief little beat of time, my grip tensed and I prepared myself to do it.

But no. As always, the man who had sired this pit of vipers refused to let me cross that final line and he gave me a slight shake of his head.

It was a test of course. I hadn't bothered to turn my attention to Ronan or Dougal at his back, but I could feel the aim of their guns on me. If I disobeyed here and now then I'd buy myself a bullet to the head for my insubordination. Liam O'Brien's mercy was as much a test of his hold over me as it was an act of kindness to his other boy. Probably more so.

My muscles locked and I bared my teeth, knowing I must have seemed like little more than a rabid creature before them and not caring much either way. I fought back the need for death and carnage which warred so fiercely within me until I somehow managed to regain control of myself and pull back.

"And sixth," I snarled again, determined to finish my point at the very least as I shifted the blade to the top of Connor's scalp instead. "You were stupid enough to go up against an opponent you never had any chance of beating," I finished. "So now I want to hear you say it, nice and loud for me, dear brother. Tell me you fear me, or I'll work harder to make it so."

Connor trembled beneath me, the blade cutting into his scalp at the edge of his hairline as I made my final threat to him clear. I might not have been gifted permission to kill him, but I hadn't been told to stop with the torture and he knew it. So this was all down to him and me.

"Of course I fucking fear you," he hissed. "You're a mad man. A psychopath, a liability. We all fear you, and we all want you dead."

I grinned widely, enjoying that admission to no end and deciding to go easy on him in payment for it.

I shifted my blade just a little before sawing through the dirty blond hair I still held in my fist and giving him a monk's cut right down to the skin, showing my skill by not so much as giving him a scratch.

I shoved him away from me with a bark of laugher, dropping both the blade and the ruins of his hair onto the drive beside him and turning aside dismissively as I began to head up the steps to the house.

"Be thankful I didn't go the whole hog and scalp you, dear brother," I called back over my shoulder as I went. "Next time I won't be so merciful."

"Your brothers and I have a matter to finish up before we start with the real business of the day," Liam said as I stalked towards him and I said nothing, the two of us knowing I had no interest in his so-called businesses whatsoever. I was a man made for bloody work, not money laundering and racketeering. "Kyan and some of his friends are staying in the house if you feel like amusing yourself with their company. I won't be needing you until after lunch."

I bit my tongue on the angry retort I wanted to give, pointing out the fact that he had insisted upon me being here this early and that I wouldn't have shown up for hours if I hadn't been required - which he damn well knew.

"I guess I'll be seeing you at lunch then," I said, stepping between my two other brothers as if they weren't aiming their guns at me. "Oh, and Ronan? You left the safety on, so I'm about as terrified as a cat on a sun lounger right now."

Ronan turned his gun to check my claim and I snatched Dougal's revolver from his grip so fast that he didn't even get a chance to try and fight it away from me. Before Ronan could aim at me again, I'd already hurled the revolver into his sneering face and he yelled in horror as the thing slit his forehead open and sent blood pissing down his nose, his own gun falling from his hand with a clatter.

"Amateurs," I muttered, striding away into the house.

"That's my boy," Liam said proudly as I walked away from them, and the saddest part about that was the way my pathetic heart lifted at those words, like some sad, lonely little part of me still gave a fuck if his daddy was proud of him or not.

Jesus, I needed to get my head looked at.

I sighed, mentally chastising myself while replaying my brothers' humiliation over and over in my head until my amusement banished a few of my demons.

I wondered whether I should track down my favourite nephew or stuff my face first…

I decided to grab a couple of bagels from Martha in the kitchen and eat them on the go, uncertain where Kyan was at anyway and figuring I'd do a quick restock of a few of the things I'd lost when my dear Jeep had gone boom on that bridge.

I headed through the stupidly big house, chewing my buttery bagels thoughtfully as I tried to think of the tools I was in need of and saying a silent farewell to those I'd lost. Gerald had been a good knife. And poor Evangeline had only just been starting out – she'd been broken in by that savage, el burro, and now she lay shattered at the bottom of the river somewhere after he'd ridden her hard and discarded her easily.

My mind shifted to Brooklyn as I thought those words and a growl formed in my chest. A real growl. Like a dog or a bear or a beast from some fancy story about Dragons and lost princesses who fought for a throne made for one and coveted by all while falling in love and saving the world only to find themselves doomed in the end. One of those. I woulda done well in a fancy story. Instead, I was locked in an endless nightmare and that girl had become the treasure I was never destined to claim.

But I'd be damned if that fucking ex cartel prick would claim her either.

With my mood souring more with every step, I pushed out of the back door and started across the yard to the little maintenance shed I called the 'Bloodshed'. I'd taken it for my own when I was a teenager. I'd tortured my first few victims in there, my pa watching on with hungry, proud eyes as I cut them apart and I had to admit that it was one of the few places in this monstrosity of a mansion which I had truly fond memories of from my childhood.

I'd found my calling between those four walls. Found peace for the voices in my skull within the sanctity of carnage. When the teacher from my school had first suggested to my pa that there was something wrong with me and that my violent streak needed addressing, I doubted she'd ever expected him to nurture it. But he had. It was one of the few things he'd encouraged in me which I could ever be truly grateful for.

He'd elevated me from beating the shit out of pricks at my school to cutting up men who deserved the very worst of me and letting my demons feast to their hearts' content.

I strolled down the path to my den, pursing my lips in anticipation of a whistle before pausing as a throaty female moan coloured the air in what was undoubtably an expression of deepest sin-filled pleasure. The moans got louder and I realised I recognised the girl's voice as my nephew's wife, who had very clearly had an orgasm which blew her damn mind.

I chuckled to myself, pausing a moment as I waited for them to finish up, then falling endlessly still as the sound of two male groans answered her cries. Male groans I did not recognise.

Ice trickled through my veins in a deadly kind of way which set the hairs along the back of my neck rising to attention, my muscles prickling and coiling in anticipation of the kill yet again. And there was me thinking I was going to have a nice quiet visit home. Well, not nice. I hated this fucking place and every bastard in it, so there was no chance of that. But quiet.

I slipped towards the den on silent feet, the little stone structure making it all too easy with its drawn blinds and closed door. I doubted anyone inside that place had a clue that their death was stalking closer, but it was.

I loved precisely one member of my family, and that was Kyan. So if I found someone else fucking his woman, you could believe that I was going to be offering him their heads on spikes before tossing her at his feet and letting him decide if I was to sever hers too.

The door wasn't even locked and I swung it open, my gaze taking in the sight of two of Kyan's best friends, the men he'd referred to as brothers on more than one occasion, sandwiching his woman between them.

Lucky for them, they were still mostly dressed. Tatum was wearing a man's shirt which fell down to her bare thighs, while the la-dee-da one, Saint, kissed her and pushed her back against the football player, who I was pretty sure was called Snake or Jake or something equally forgettable.

The space was fairly big, one side of it dedicated to my work, a bench there alongside a whole array of tools which I supposed could be mistaken for a plain old work shed considering how meticulously all of the blood had been removed from the place. On the other side of the space was a couch, TV, mini fridge, all things I'd added to the place in my youth so that I could avoid the house as often as possible.

I didn't waste time on announcing myself, seeing more than clearly with my own eyes the state of infidelity my nephew's woman was in and having no further need for bullshit excuses or lies to reach my ears.

I darted forward, snatching a crowbar by the name of Herbert from the workbench beside me, then grabbed the back of Saint's shirt and ripped him away from Tatum and threw him to the floor. I whipped around with a snarl of anger, swinging the crowbar to finish the conniving bastard off.

"Stop!" Tatum screamed in fear for her sidepiece, jumping into my way, but I knocked her aside like an irksome fly, swinging for Saint with a blow that would shatter bone.

The fucker rolled aside, kicking my shin hard enough to make me stumble back a step, a stream of cursing breaking out inside my head alongside the blare of a whole lotta aggressive rap music. It was a pretty nice place to be actually, aside from the cuckolding little fuckers who were evading my kill strikes. Then again, I always had preferred a proper fight.

The footballing lad grabbed my nephew's girl, pushing her behind him and trying to shield her half-dressed body as the t-shirt she was wearing fell down to cover her bare arse, and she gave me those wide eyes people always got when they'd gone and let themselves forget what kind of creature I really was.

"Ya think you can come into my family's home and fuck my nephew's bride, then live to tell the tale, do ya?" I roared as I swung the crowbar at Saint again, focusing my efforts on him first and planning on ending the other one after.

But before I could give Herbert the blood he was craving, the footballing fella leapt onto my back, locking me in a chokehold as he fought to drag me away from his little partner in crime.

"Call Kyan!" Saint barked, throwing his phone to the girl as he got to his feet once more, clearly thinking my nephew might be more lenient than me in this matter. But that was where he was wrong. Kyan mighta been working to distance himself from our family, but O'Brien blood ran in his veins, hot and thick, and he was a beast just as bloodthirsty as the rest of us.

I swung around as I fought to dislodge the big, burly limpet on my back, my muscles straining to support his weight as he hung from my neck and cut off my oxygen. I always had enjoyed a bit of choking though. There was something about brushing that close to death which always made my heart flutter like a ladybird having the time of his life in a tornado.

Saint grabbed a plank of wood from a stack by the workbench and I grinned as the game suddenly took a turn that was a whole lot more interesting.

I threw myself backwards onto the floor, crushing the big fella beneath me and hearing a nice, meaty crunch as his head hit the hard floor, forcing him to let go of me then rolling over, tossing Herbert aside and wrapping my hands around the fucker's throat instead, squeezing until the tattoos coating my fingers bleached.

"When I'm done wringing yer scrawny neck, I'll cut your balls off and make a necklace of them for Kyan to wear," I promised, giving that idea some serious thought as the beautiful feeling of his windpipe crushing beneath my fingers sent me to nirvana. I guessed the blood could be an issue, but if I had them dried out all nicely then I could thread them on a chain. Something platinum, not gold. Kyan wasn't really the type for gold jewellery.

"Stop!" Tatum screamed behind me, her voice all kinds of distant as I just looked into the eyes of the man I was killing and grinned as he fought uselessly to pull my hands from his throat.

Saint yelled something, the plank of wood crashing down on my head and breaking in half like we were in some kind of kung fu movie, and I couldn't say I hated the idea of that visual, even while I bellowed in anger and the pain of the blow made my vision swim. It wasn't enough to break my grip though. Not now that I had death in my sights and my grip was locked tight around my victim's neck.

His name suddenly came to me as I drew closer to the point of his death, like a little dicky bird had whispered it in my ear. Blake. I remembered now. I'd watched him play ball with Kyan a whole bunch of times when they were kids. He'd even gotten me to show him my best killing knife once. He'd been a cute kid, sweet in a conniving little fucker way. What a shame I was going to be killing him after all that.

Blake punched my sides furiously, making pain sing through my flesh as Tatum leapt onto my back, yelling and clawing at me in a desperate attempt to save her lover. But she really shoulda thought of his mortality before letting him sink his sausage into her. She must have expected this after all. There was one thing an O'Brien could be counted to fight for, and that was the honour of our family. Even if we were the most dishonourable bunch of fuckers anyone was ever likely to meet. We weren't going to admit that shit, after all.

Saint snatched my crowbar and I snarled as he took Herbert for a swing he hadn't asked for, bracing for the blow I knew was coming and somewhat relishing the thought of it. I liked pain. Not in a sexually explicit kind of way. But more in a 'I deserve it' situation. Because I did. I deserved all the bad in life and I was only ever taking my punishment for my past crimes whenever a strike was made against me.

But before I could taste the power of Herbert's blow, Kyan came barrelling through the door, tackling Saint to the ground and sending my little iron friend clanging across the floor.

"Kyan!" Tatum screamed as Blake started turning blue beneath me, his punches growing weaker as my gaze locked on his and I held my breath in anticipation of his end, the rush of it building all around me like a rising storm. I could hear that storm inside me, billowing and calling out for this death, aching to sweep another soul into the abyss at my hands. I could taste blood on my tongue, feel the need for oblivion in every inch of my body and I tumbled into that feeling as I sensed the moment of his death approaching and prepared to steal it for myself.

Kyan pushed his girl away from me as she continued to try and fight me off, but before I could take the final beat of Blake's heart from him, a punch with the force of a sledgehammer behind it slammed into the side of my skull, waking me up and calling me away from the death march I'd been lost to.

My gaze snapped up to meet my nephew's, my teeth baring as he forced me out of my moment and the desperate, final beats of Blake's pulse thumped against my fingers.

"Let him go!" Kyan barked, punching me again and taking me by surprise, but I could see the demand in him, the need for something more from me than death in that moment, and some part of me was still able to listen.

I forced my grip to release, sitting back on my haunches as Blake began to cough and splutter beneath me, fighting to regain the air I'd been denying him.

"Get away from him!" Tatum screamed, shoving and pushing at me like a bee who'd lost her way into the hive.

Kyan gripped my arm and I let him haul me up, frowning at him as I stepped away and Tatum fell over her little side piece with a sob.

"They're fucking your wife, lad," I hissed, my gaze on Kyan's as I gave him the explanation he still seemed in need of and a new, much more appealing idea occurred to me. "We can kill 'em together, if you prefer? I'll tie 'em down and we can take turns to cut off limbs. We can even start with their coc-"

"Tell him," Tatum barked at Kyan, a furious fire in her eyes which made me frown because she should have been begging, right? Sobbing and

143

apologising and all that shit that cheaters did when they got caught in a killing shed with their fella's best buddies and no panties on.

Kyan's jaw ticked like he didn't much want to do as she'd commanded, but he gave it to me anyway.

"She's with them too," he bit out, giving me a hard stare as he rolled his shoulders back like he was anticipating a fight. From me! His sweet old uncle Niall who had never been anything but good to him in all my life. I didn't know where he was getting the impression that I mighta been the kind to hurt my own flesh and blood, but he was seriously mistaken on that. He could ask my brothers...well, no, maybe not them because I'd gladly kill each and every one of them. But my other nephews and nieces...then again, I hated almost all of them too. Or at least held contempt and disdain for them. Huh. Maybe he had a point then; I *was* inclined to hurt family members. Not him though. Never him. Unless he did something to piss me off of course.

"And Nash. All four of us. We're hers and she's ours," Kyan went on like people just casually dropped that kind of information into conversation all the time. Oh hey, have you met my wife and the three other fellas she fucks? I'm so glad to have brought them all to this birthday party for ya to meet. No. Didn't seem like a usual kind of opener, that was for sure.

"But she's your wife," I pointed out in case he'd forgotten. Maybe that was it. He'd forgotten and their cocks had all just slipped into her a few times while he'd been trying to remember.

"I know, but she's theirs too. Not by law. But by... agreement. I dunno what else to call it. They love her and she loves them. It's all of us, that's just the way it is," Kyan snarled, his anger clear as he seemed to be fighting against the desire to spill blood almost as hard as I was. Though on that note, the bloodlust was fading fast from me in light of this new puzzle because I was trying to figure this out and it was actually making a whole lot of sense.

Saint had positioned himself between me and their girl now, his fists curled and his intentions clear no matter who I was. He wasn't going to let me hurt her. And I had to admit, despite how close I'd just come to killing dear old Blake, there were two more of them here who would have fought tooth and claw to keep me from Tatum if I'd gone and turned my killing intentions her way. They'd have done all they could to keep her safe and I had to admit that even with my superior skills and thirst for blood, I likely wouldn't have beaten all of them before they'd ended me. Which meant that even if I had taken out Blakey, she'd have still been safe.

Interesting.

But then I thought of the other mechanics of that set up and I had to admit that that was the bit which boggled me the most.

"And you're okay with that arrangement. Multi-dicks and all, lad?" I asked, wondering how that worked. Did they have a ticket system? A day of the week each? But then they'd need seven of them if it was one a day or that wouldn't work. A four-day cycle? A ballot? A lottery? A goat with impeccable taste who independently selected which one of them got to-

"Yes," Kyan said firmly, cutting off that wild thought and I put it away for later.

"And you're okay with it too, lass?" I looked over to Tatum, who seemed to be out of sorts for some reason, her hair all crazy-like and her eyes blazing with unshed tears.

Blake pushed himself up to sit at last, rubbing his neck as he glared at me like he was considering another fight which I wasn't wholly opposed to, but I had questions right now and I was more interested in those. Saint placed a hand on his shoulder in warning and he didn't move again, which was handy because I was still waiting.

"Yes," Tatum said firmly, surprising me with the vehemence of her words. "I love them equally. And I know you were trying to protect Kyan, but fuck you, Niall."

"So it's like a pick and mix for you?" I asked curiously, ignoring the suggestion for me to get fucked because I hadn't done that in a long damn

time, so it wasn't likely now. "If one of your boys is pissing you off, you can just go find another?" I asked, needing more information, all the information. I was like that beast in his library with the annoying little French woman who crept into his house and kept stealing all his books. I needed the books. I needed to know.

"It's not like that, I lov-" she started, but I was getting it now, so I cut her off because fuck me, I think I was having an epiphany.

"That actually makes a lot of sense," I said. "I always did feel sorry for my wife having to weather my brand of insanity alone. If she'd had a boyfriend too, maybe he could have given her some reprieve from my company. Of course, I'm not certain I could stand another man sticking his cock in my woman..." I rubbed my chin in contemplation, considering the idea while forcing my thoughts firmly away from my little Spider because this wasn't about her, it was about a theoretical reality in which I might not have had to live through the brutality of my wife's murder. Then again, wasn't a lot of my objections to having a woman because of my fear of what might happen to one who got close to me again?

I bit my own tongue, needing the pain to force out the thoughts which I wasn't going to be having about any kind of future which didn't involve me dying alone.

"My Ava wasn't likely to have wanted that though. And my bed has been emptier than a nun's vagina since she was taken from me, so I'm not likely to ever find out if I'd be able to allow it without castrating the other fella-"

"It's a family," Kyan snapped, interrupting me. "I wouldn't just let any man fuck my woman. But I love the three of them too. It's the only way that it ever could have worked for us."

"So you fuck them as well?" I asked him, pointing between Saint and Blake and tilting my head as I pictured that. It made sense actually. A woman only had so many holes and the two of them looked like they could suck a dick as well as anyone. I hadn't had much experience of men sucking my cock but then again, I'd married my high school sweetheart and been celibate for the ten years following on from her death, so I hadn't done a whole lot of experimenting.

"No," Kyan grunted, his lips lifting with a hint of amusement. "They couldn't handle me."

I barked a laugh, believing that well enough. Kyan was his own kind of monster, and it took a strong woman like his to wrangle one of those. Or four. Fuck me, what a turn out. Two's company, three's a crowd, but four? That was a number right there. That was the makings of an army.

"Well, I can't say my horizons are broadened every day, but you've definitely given me food for thought," I said, chuckling as I looked to Blake, who still seemed a little salty about his near-death experience. Whoops. "Sorry about that then, lad. Look at it this way though, now you can say you survived the wrath of the best hitman in the state – which I don't think anyone else has ever done. Ever. Not once. I don't leave bodies kicking. Or twitching. So everybody wins." Blake didn't seem inclined to agree but I'd said sorry, and that made everything okay. It was the law. Everyone knew that.

I stepped closer to Kyan, lowering his voice as the questions in me just kept coming, an idea I wasn't allowed to indulge in spinning around inside my skull.

"So tell me more about this arrangement? Do you have a schedule? Or do you all just whip your dicks out and-" I waved my hand between the group of them. "Act like animals whenever the feelin' takes ya?"

"I'll tell you about it another time," Kyan muttered, stepping away from me like there were more important matters at hand and helping Tatum to her feet.

He checked her over closely then kissed the corner of her mouth when he was satisfied she was okay.

It was…well, fuck me, they were all looking at her like that and I had to say I could see the appeal. She was there in the middle of a wolf pack, kept safe from the monsters of the world with enough love surrounding her that even if one of her men died in the name of protecting her, she'd still have more to keep her heart beating on.

"Well," I said, moving to pick up Herbert then heading over to the tools hanging on the wall as I got back to my original reason for coming here, my brain officially full. "I just came here to grab a few new friends." I grabbed a couple of saws and a hammer by the name of James plus a pair of pliers called Tilly.

I did need to get on with some other shit today, but I was all ears for whatever my nephew had to say on this matter when he had the chance to talk through it with me further.

"I have places to be, skulls to batter, eyeballs to pluck out. I'll be wanting that chat though, Kyan. And I'll keep my mouth shut too – Pa won't like you letting yer friends touch your girl, no matter what way you wanna paint it to him. See ya around." I headed out the door, leaving them there to chat or have a gang bang or whatever, whistling a tune which wouldn't quite come to me and trying to keep that pep in my step while I headed back to the house and the boring arse afternoon ahead of me.

A day in the company of my father and brothers was not the most relaxing of days. In fact, by the time I'd been forced to attend countless meetings and offer up opinions on so many things I gave no fucks about that my head was spinning with it, I was damn inclined to go on a killing spree.

There was rumour I'd heard about a cult up in the mountains who lured young men and women into it to serve under the rule of the old bastards who had tricked them into believing in some greater power or mystical fountain of knowledge or transitional veil of fire or some shit. I wasn't entirely sure which, but I'd heard a bit about sacrifices of the flesh and bodies being burned in the dead of night, so I was pretty certain there was a whole organisation up there just ripe for the killin'.

I'd bet my little psycho would enjoy that particular road trip with me. We could take one of those great big RVs which were practically a house on wheels. There would be a bed in the back and plenty of room to pick up hitchhikers who we could assess for psychotic tendencies before dropping them off or taking them out. It would be grand. An adventure of death and carnage fit for a queen of chaos and the broken fool who travelled at her back.

I pursed my lips as I considered that though. If I was at her back, then who was covering her front? Or the sides? I wanted her to run free in all of her beautifully lethal glory, but I needed her protected too. She was innocent at least as much as she was guilty, and I wanted to shield that part of her from this brutal world with all I had.

"Cat got your tongue, Niall?" Ronan asked loudly, stacking his hands over his stomach as he gave me a taunting smirk across the table in our pa's office where we'd been summoned for this final meeting.

Or at least I hoped it was the last one. I honestly couldn't remember if I'd been told that or had just decided it for myself.

The entire family had been showing up as the day progressed into the evening, and Pa had been calling different members of his family in to discuss the various arms of all his businesses throughout the day. Between discussions, we moved to different rooms and each time he summoned or dismissed my brothers, sister, nieces and nephews, cousins, uncle and the like, gathering different groups for each subject. Everyone had been cut out of at least one of those meetings if not more. Everyone aside from me that was.

I knew what he was doing. The game he was playing by sitting me at his right hand throughout the day no matter the subject. I was in on talks I had no business or interest in while he cut out people who mighta had something more to add to them. He wanted them all to think he was leaning towards me as his successor. He wanted them riled up and aiming their jealousy at me. But I was yet to fully figure out why.

The simplest explanation could of course have been that he really was considering me the front runner at this point. When I compared myself to my siblings, I could hardly blame him on that front. But Liam O'Brien just wasn't a simple man. So I had to think he was up to something far more conniving than that.

I probably shoulda been trying to figure it out with a bit more determination, but the thing was, I just didn't give a fuck. So far as I was concerned, this moment in time was just a place holder pre-empting my escape from this life. I had my donkey ready and waiting at home, his head full of all the information I needed to make a clean escape and just as soon as I'd cracked his skull open and peeled all the secrets outa it, I'd be off. Gone with the wind and travelling on a breeze. They'd never catch up to me. And if by some miracle any of them did, I'd just kill them and keep on floating once their blood was wetting my flesh. It was simple. Easy. And yet entirely too difficult all at once.

"Hamster got your cock, Ronan?" I shot back at him.

"What?"

"Well, I assumed you musta done a trade with the little fella for yours. That would explain that tiny pecker you've got resting on your balls like a worm sunbathing on a beanbag."

Pa chuckled and Dermot joined in like some kind of echo, always ready to team up against one of his siblings no matter which of us that meant he had to side with. Connor just glared at me from the foot of the table, his hand all tucked up in a cast and his hair now fully shaved off after he'd spent the majority of the afternoon getting bandaged up following on from our play date this morning. I preferred his hard-boiled egg look to his ponytail days anyway. Mostly because it felt like I had a bongo ready to go at all times while he was near, just in case I wanted to drop a beat and break into song.

"You think you're so funny, don't ya Niall?" Ronan growled and I just smiled because, yeah, I was pretty funny when I wanted to be. Like right now, as I looked between Ronan and Dermot and I thought about the way I'd paid to get a hooker into their beds with our daddy's money and the way the two of them constantly professed their love to her, spilling all of their sordid little secrets and affairs into her listening ears while rutting their cocks between her thighs, and never once realising who paid for her moans or who was laughing at them behind their backs.

I considered telling them right now. Just so that I could see the looks on their faces when they realised they'd been played by me and their mistress for years now. Dermot had bought her a fucking house. It was hilarious. And Ronan had gifted her so many diamonds and rubies and the like that she was legitimately able to employ a guard for them and set herself up like the queen with her crown jewels. I mean, I was pretty certain she just pawned them all, but it was totally an option she could have gone for.

"It's been a long day," Pa interrupted, maybe sensing how thin of a line I was treading right now and thinking to save two more of his sons from a trip to the hospital or maybe just not in the mood for violence before dinner. Blood and gore tended to get my appetite up, but it had the opposite effect for some.

"That it has," I agreed, pushing to my feet and almost knocking my chair over in my haste to be gone from this place. I'd been asked some kind of question towards the end of this latest meeting, but I couldn't for the life of me remember it now. Nor did I care to. All I wanted was to get the fuck out of here and head home to my Spider and my house and my bed. I'd hardly even touched the liquor throughout this most tedious of days because I didn't want to be unable to drive home late and get stuck here over night.

"Don't forget you have dinner with your fiancée tonight," Pa said and I could feel his eyes pinning themselves to me as I fell still there, my jacket halfway onto one arm and my jaw ticking with fury because I absolutely had forgotten that.

"It's been a long day," I said in a low rumble, tossing his words back at him and seeing my brothers all bob up and down in their seats like a row of ducks hearing the rustle of a bread bag. "I'm sure she would understand if I rearranged."

"I'm sure she would," Pa replied, his tone unyielding. "But an O'Brien never breaks his word. And I made it clear that you would be in attendance. Her father owns a hotel downtown and he has gotten the staff in despite the pandemic so that they can be open exclusively for the two of you. You will be there Niall."

The threat in those last words were all too clear for everyone in the room and Connor practically preened, his bald head shining in the light from the chandelier above him.

I considered my options, taking a great deal of pleasure in the one that involved patricide, fratricide, sororicide, nepoticide – there were a hell of a lot of fancy names involved when you started killing your family members that was for sure – but once again, one look around the room made it clear that the fuckers had all come armed to this tea party.

"Fine," I barked with all the petulance of a three-year-old who had been told what for. "But one of these days, you cowardly bastards should try threatening me with fists instead of gunfire. I like my odds against the entire family if no one is cheating with a gun in hand. Hell, I'd even let you all have knives and I'd still put money on an unarmed me."

My brothers glowered at me while Pa chuckled in a way that said he not only agreed but liked the fact a whole hell of a lot.

"Your opinion of yourself is too high, little Niall," Dermot sneered, his jealousy making his pug face all scrunch up.

I finished pulling my jacket on and stepped towards him as I adjusted the deep blue fabric of it.

"Is that so?" I asked, nice and slow, prowling closer. "Would you like to put your money where your mouth is there, Dermot? We could play a little game of cat and mouse if you like? I'll be the cat who comes creeping into your home while you're sleeping, and I'll even let you run all about the place while I hunt ya. Fair warning though – this cat always finishes his meal once he's done playing with his food."

Dermot swallowed thickly, trying to scoff and sneer at that suggestion, but I could see the fear in his eyes. I could see it and taste it and I was licking my lips in hunger for a whole lot more of it.

"Don't forget," I breathed, placing my hands on the arms of his chair and leaning right down so that we were nose to nose. Dermot pressed his pistol to my chest in a clear threat, but we all knew he wouldn't pull the trigger without Pa's permission, whipped little bitch that he was. "I know where you live," I purred.

The tension snapped like an elastic band as our father barked a laugh behind us and I straightened, finding my other brothers and my sister also openly aiming their guns at me. Pathetic little arseholes.

I took a cigarette from my pocket and sparked it up, placing it between my lips as I opened my arms wide and laughed like a heathen, waiting for one of them to grow the balls to do it.

"Come on then," I urged. "I've been waiting a long time for death to stop edging me and let me have my release, so give it to me, lads. But don't be gentle. I want it to be rough and dirty, just like the way I've lived. If I'm not choking on my own blood for a good fifteen minutes, then I'll be sorely disappointed."

Pa gave them a good thirty seconds, watching, waiting, judging. No doubt he saw their hatred, hesitation, fear and envy plain enough but when he circled the room to stand before me, it was harder to tell what he was looking at.

I grinned at him, still awaiting my death while I dragged a lungful of smoke down between my teeth and held it there, relishing the nicotine almost as much as I hated it.

"Life's been rough on you, my boy," Liam O'Brien said softly, almost sounding like an honest to shit daddy who gave a fuck as he stepped closer to me and fool that I was, something twisted in my chest at those words. "Ava…" he sighed and for all his faults I could see there was real regret there. He'd liked her. Been amused by her, no doubt too, with her innocence and the way she'd always turned a blind eye to so much of the dark in me and the rest of our family. But I knew he'd liked her at least as much as a man such as him could. "It's a terrible pity what became of her. But you did her justice in the end." He reached out to place a hand against my cheek and my siblings all shifted in their seats, no doubt so jealous over this small display of affection that they were close to combustion. "You made the men who hurt her pay. That's what counts."

"Didn't bring her back," I grunted, smoke spilling from my lips as I plucked the cigarette from them and held it loose between my fingers, somehow unable to move from that spot while my father cupped my cheek and looked at me with the closest thing to love I think I'd ever seen in him.

"No," he agreed. "But the Holy Father will have her in a better place now. Away from this. Away from us. Away from *you*. You know that's the best thing for her, don't ya, lad?"

I hadn't been prepared for that blow so when it struck me dead in the centre of my chest, it was a miracle I didn't buckle. Pain and the ache of my own endless failure speared through me until my throat locked up and the screaming inside my own skull reached a pitch high enough to damage all the most vital pieces of me.

Fuck.

I knew it was my fault that Ava had been gifted a brutal end. I knew that I never should have gone anywhere near her in the first place. That I shouldn't have dragged her into this place of sin and violence with me or fooled myself into believing that she'd be safe just so long as she kept herself on the side lines of it all. But no one else had ever dared say that to me before.

The bluntness of my father's weapon was what shook me most, the way he wielded it so casually after luring me close with a promise of the love he'd always denied me.

"And now, you're being gifted a woman better suited at last. One who you don't have to try and protect from this world of ours. One who you don't have to lie to and corrupt and tarnish the way you did that sweet girl all those years ago."

My fingers ached for a weapon, something that I could use against the power of his words and the cold, hard look in his eyes which he used to hold me captive in that spot as his thumb scored a path up and down my cheek in this mocking pretence of affection.

"You're the only one of my offspring yet to produce their own children," he added. "And let's not forget that if you're to rule after I'm gone, you'll be needing your own successor."

Liam smiled then, slapping my cheek and stepping back like he couldn't feel the rot and poison he'd just slipped into me, and he couldn't hear the screams of the woman I'd married all those years ago bouncing offa the walls all around us.

My brothers were smart enough to remain silent even in the wake of my destruction right before them, no doubt knowing how likely I was to shatter if I was pushed even a little further in that moment. I wouldn't care if there were guns pointed at me from all angles. Wouldn't matter to me one single bit. I'd rip them all apart limb from limb and welcome any death they might be able to offer if they gave me even the slightest motivation to do so.

"You have twenty minutes to make the reservation on time. It's at the Grand Avalon. Don't keep your new bride waiting," Pa said firmly, like nothing else had just passed between us at all.

I turned my eyes from my father and the rest of my rotten family as I strode from the room, nothing in my head but screams which grew louder with every step I took as they worked to drag me down into the dark place.

I stalked down the long hallways neither noticing nor caring if I saw anyone on my journey to the exit before throwing the double doors at the front of the mansion open and heading down the stairs to the drive where I'd parked my BMW.

I opened the door which now held a little bullet hole and dropped into the driver's seat, taking a long drag from my cigarette before flicking it out the window and starting the engine.

The roar of the powerful car starting up gave the screaming a run for its money as I tore away from my father's house and raced down the drive towards the setting sun and Hemlock City which awaited me in the distance.

The roads sped past in a blur of motion and I wasn't even lucky enough to run across a patrolling cop car on the lookout for anyone breaking lockdown on my journey to the hotel, pulling up outside it three minutes early with Eminem trying his damn best to drown my pain in lyrical acrobatics which unfortunately didn't even seem to be scraping the surface in that moment.

My fingers curled tightly around the steering wheel and I started counting in my head, working against the screams and the need to save the woman who was causing them. But that ship had long since sailed.

I was shaking. My muscles trembling from the force of my grief and self-hatred and worst of all, I couldn't even remember Ava's face anymore. Not really. She was all soft edges and half memories now. I couldn't even be certain if the things I thought I remembered of her were true anymore. Had she loved strawberries or was it peaches? Was her hair to her shoulders or just below them? Had she been happy living the lie I'd let her paint for us? Had she really loved Niall the motor mechanic with the incredible bonus package, or had those lies eaten into her at night when I was late to come home once again? Had the times when she'd inadvertently seen me with blood staining my clothes or my hands really been forgotten as easily as they seemed to have been? Never to be mentioned after the moment when her eyes widened at the sight and she hurriedly turned away and took herself to bed. Did the lie of me make her happy? Had *I* even been happy? Or had I just been playing make believe like some kid who never quite figured out how to grow up?

I reached for my phone as I shut the engine off and the music cut out, my thumb moving to the familiar app as it hovered over the camera reel and I prepared to make myself watch Ava's last moments all over again.

But I fell still with my thumb not quite finding it, my gaze slipping to the call list instead and before I could second guess myself, I opened it up and dialled out a number I hadn't thought I'd need to dial in a situation anything like this one.

The phone began to ring and a stillness came over me like the surface of a pool where a crocodile lay in wait, eyeing the creatures fool enough to want a drink from it.

On and on it rang and the darkness seemed to push in deeper around me as the sun set somewhere in the sky and night began to take hold.

Finally, the call connected as I released a long breath at the sound of Brooklyn's voice on the other end of the call.

"Hello?"

I said nothing, too lost in my demons to offer her more than my silence, but something unfurled in my chest at that simple word, at the knowledge that she was still there in the house, up to fuck knew what but safe at least, answering the house phone like she thought she lived there or some shit.

"Is that you, Horny Barry?" she growled suddenly. "Because I told you, if I catch sight of your beady little masturbation eyes ever again, I'm going to pluck them out of your face and feed them to a honey badger."

"It's me," I murmured, a breath falling from my lungs as the tightness in them eased.

"Oh ho," she said, her voice all full of outrage. "Needed a break from the big-boobed sex woman, did you? Thought you'd just call up tiny tata Brooklyn and remind yourself what small boobs sound like?"

There was hurt in her voice that I'd put there and bastard that I was, I couldn't do anything to soothe it. This was better. She needed to hurt over me, hate me if she liked, anything other than want me. Because she couldn't want me and I couldn't want her, that was the one thing I was certain of. I couldn't do it again. Not to her. Not to a woman who actually knew me, saw me and didn't even shy away from the truth. She was...

"Well, here they are and I'm shaking them right now and nooo, you can't hear them slapping together because they can't do that. They just bounce, Niall. They bounce and I'm bouncing too and if I take my shirt off, they-"

"Mi sol, what are you doing?" Mateo rumbled in the background and I gritted my jaw.

"Just telling Niall some important things about myself," she replied haughtily and my lips lifted just a little.

I wasn't sure if she really had been topless with her tits bouncing up and down or not and I was trying pretty hard not to think about that, but my cock was seriously interested in the subject despite my protests to it.

"Give it here," Mateo said and Brooklyn huffed out a breath before he took the phone from her. "What is it?" he growled down the line a moment later. "Is she in danger? Do I need to do something?"

My mind went to the way Kyan's boys had circled around Tatum like a pack of wolves when she'd been under threat this morning, and my brows arched as I realised Brooklyn was forming her own pack of attack dogs too. I liked the idea of that.

"There's no new threat," I replied, unable to give any excuse for my call. "Just keep her safe from that giant in the basement," I added, unsure when I'd started trusting Mateo with my little psycho, but I was somehow unworried about him doing anything to harm her while I was gone.

"Of course I will," he replied scathingly then the line cut out and I was left in silence.

True silence.

Ava's screams had abandoned me and I was left there in the cool air inside my car, with nothing but my own thoughts in my head and my cock aching for release.

The fucking thing was healed at least now, but I was yet to give it a whirl with the addition of my piercing and with the mental image my little psycho had just gifted me, it was damn tempting to do so right now before I was forced to endure the agony of Anastasia's company.

But just as I moved my hand to my waistband, an obnoxious knock sounded on my window. I turned to look out at a very grumpy looking Russian arsehole who seemed to have been waiting a while.

"Well shit," I said, throwing my door open so suddenly that it hit him in the gut and made him double over with a wheeze of pain while I stepped outa the car. "Don't go sneaking up on a fella like that."

Another bodyguard type fella stepped forward, his gaze lowering to my hands like he was expecting me to pull a weapon.

"The lady is waiting inside," he growled, seeming offended by my lack of haste and I had to assume they'd been standing out here the whole time I'd been sitting in my car. Probably a good thing I hadn't started jerking off into my cup holder in that case, but my cock was still sad about it as it slowly began to give up on its quest for satisfaction and deflate.

"Well, we can't be having that, can we?" I asked brightly as I swerved him and headed for the entrance.

"We ask that you go in unarmed," the bodyguard man called after me and I shrugged, opening my arms wide to allow him to check me. I wasn't carrying a single thing because I knew it would have made it too tempting to kill my family members earlier on, so it didn't take him long to usher me inside.

The hotel was eerily quiet, the lockdown on the country preventing the usual hustle and bustle. I walked in silence into the restaurant set beyond the bar, finding all but one of the mahogany tables empty.

Anastasia sat there waiting for me, her long, blonde hair all coiled up on top of her head and a silver scrap of fabric which I guessed passed for a dress clinging to her body.

"Niall," she purred as I closed in on her and nodded.

"Glove." She still hadn't even noticed I addressed her as if she were winter handwear instead of using an endearment, and I was all giggly over the fact, so I even managed to give her a smile.

"It's good to see you," she said, giving me a heated look.

I didn't reply to that, placing my jaw against her cold cheek in an imitation of a kiss as she stood and damn near forced it against my lips by trying to turn her head into it. I dropped into my seat and man spread myself until I was comfortable.

"I took the initiative and ordered for us, I hope you don't mind?" Anastasia asked, crossing her legs and smiling at me with her deep red lips.

"So long as it comes with whiskey, I'm game," I agreed, looking towards the lone waiter in the room and arching a brow to let him know I wasn't in the mood to wait on that drink.

He hurried to comply, grabbing a fancy decanter and whiskey tumbler before heading over to me.

"Ice?" he inquired as he set the glass down and held the decanter ready to pour, but I just reached out and took it from him.

"No need," I said. "And you can leave this here – I'm feeling inclined to get shit-faced."

He glanced at Anastasia who nodded once, encouraging him to leave me with my decanter, and I poured myself a healthy measure before knocking the entire contents of my glass back and refilling it once more.

"My father tells me that you are close to securing the position as head of your organisation after your own father's death," she said, apparently in no mood for bullshit today which I was glad for.

"I wouldn't hold too much stock by anything my pa says on that subject," I replied. "He likes to use that possibility to keep his children in line and working hard for his approval."

"I know this," she agreed. "But I also know that he has plenty of reason to select you for the role and I intend to help you give him more."

"You want to help me take my father's place as head of the Irish mob?" I asked, sinking another whiskey because her company was sending me towards the dark place once more as I pictured us married and the reality that presented to me.

"Of course. I made it clear to you already that I am a woman who gets what she wants."

Food arrived, offering me a reprieve from replying to her and I looked to my plate, eyeing the fancy pasta stuff and trying to decide if I was going to eat or not. Avoiding the food would give the booze a faster journey to getting me wasted so I had good reason not to, but it did smell nice.

I glanced up at Anastasia just as she dropped a pill into my drink, her eyes flashing with fear as she realised I'd seen whatever the fuck that was and I arched a brow at her.

"Well, well," I said slowly, reaching out to take my over full glass of whiskey into my grip and looking into it as the little white pill bubbled and dissolved before my very eyes. "Look who's playing dirty tonight."

To her credit, Anastasia just lifted her chin. "It won't kill you," she said defiantly, not bothering to deny what she'd done, and I hummed thoughtfully.

"No. Even the Russians aren't fool enough to try and kill an O'Brien so obviously."

That left the question of what exactly it was that she had been trying to dose me with. I cocked my head at her, taking her in and trying to decide what she was capable of. Not rape – she was far too vain for that. So she wouldn't be looking to dose me with some form of date rape drug to get me senseless beneath her while she rode my cock. No…

I really was confident that she wouldn't be dumb enough to try and cause me harm. So that had to leave mood enhancers on the table. Valium maybe. Ecstasy. Something to put me in a better mood and make me more interested in her and her agenda I'd bet.

Anastasia watched me warily, clearly expecting me to lose my temper, but I wasn't that kind of predictable arsehole.

I gave her a wide smile, lifted the glass to my lips and drank down every drop.

Anastasia sucked in a sharp breath, her pupils dilating with unmistakable desire and I banged the glass down on the table with a bark of laughter.

"Let's see if your little pill gets what you're hoping for outa me then," I said in a dangerous tone. "But I warn ya, missy – I don't tend to have the expected reactions to recreational drugs. They can make me all kinds of unpredictable and violent and I'll be holding you responsible for anything I may or may not do while under the influence of whatever the fuck it is you thought would be such a clever thing to offer me. You wanted to play this game. So let's play."

"Let's play," she agreed, raising her glass and I refilled mine before clinking it to hers and sinking the lot again. No one ever said it was a bad idea to mix drugs and alcohol. Right?

I picked up my fork and speared some fancy little pasta pocket onto it, concentrating on my food while Anastasia took the opportunity to fill the silence. I had to say, this was the only kinda pasta that had the right to claim it was different to all the others. Penne, fettuccini, macaroni, tortellini, rigatoni, spaghetti. You could string as many fancy letters together as you liked Mr Italiano, but I wasn't fooled into thinking that made any of those pastas worthy of their flouncy titles. There was only one thing different about them and that was their shape, but they all tasted and looked the same once they were chewed up in my mouth, didn't they? It didn't matter if they were in a twirly whirly coil or posing as a piece of string, I wasn't falling for the con the rest of the world was falling for while Italy laughed at us all behind a piece of bruschetta.

Apparently, Anastasia had decided to make this soiree into a sales pitch, using it to tell me all manner of things about herself and her capabilities. She was smart. Had gone to law school and had studied accountancy too which let me know she was helpful for any time that I might find myself in need of a loophole in the law to get me out of a sticky situation or a solution to any tricky monetary paper trails my businesses had to deal with.

I pointed out that not only had I never once found myself under scrutiny by the law because I was as wily as a fox in a top hat - and a little because my pa had enough lawmen in his pocket to bail me outa trouble if ever I got into any - but that if ever I was arrested, I'd likely just go on a killing spree to free myself. So those la dee da credentials of hers weren't much help to me. I also told her that I didn't have my own money and that I lived on handouts from my pa, which was bullshit, but I didn't much care about that. I got wired plenty of cash from fellas who wanted to hire me for a hit, but that money was more secret than a dollar bill tucked up a snake's vagina.

Wait…did snakes have vaginas?

I whipped my phone out to check the whole vagina/egg snake situation and got some pretty confusing answers.

"Holy shit," I barked, making Anastasia drop her fork in surprise as my fist landed on the table and made everything sitting on it rattle. "Snakes have two penises!"

"What?" She scowled at me, no doubt because she'd been harping on about her years of gymnastics training and how flexible that had left her, but I had no interest in her bendy bullshit.

"Two penises," I repeated. "And so do sharks! Fuck me, I need more information on this because Spider is going to lose her shit when she finds out. Unless she doesn't believe me. And maybe she won't because it's only come from the man in the phone, and we all know you can't trust him." I shoved to my feet. "I'm going to need to find a shark. Or a snake. Or both. Ideally both. Do you have any idea where such a hunt could begin?"

Anastasia was staring at me like I'd fully lost the plot and I realised that I'd gone off script here. It was an unfortunate habit I had of running my mouth to follow every errant thought in my head, but I happened to think that an inquisitive mind was an interesting one. So fuck her gymnastics bullshit because this was real prime information I was gathering here.

My fiancée blinked and suddenly she was smiling, getting to her feet too and revealing all twelve inches of her skirt which looked in danger of flashing her lady parts to me at any moment. I had no interest in a meeting with her eager beaver, so my gaze didn't linger there.

"I happen to have a tank with a shark in my suite," she said, her voice dropping in a way I was guessing was meant to seduce me and I sighed.

"If the 'shark' turns out to be you naked, I think we've already had this conversation, glove," I reminded her.

Anastasia tittered a laugh like me rejecting her point blank hadn't enraged her one bit and shook her head.

"It's a real shark, I promise. I live here full time and his name is Finley." She took my arm and I reluctantly let her tug me along, snatching my glass and emptying it for the final time before tossing it to the closest Russian stooge.

He just about caught it and I grinned widely as I recognised the fella I'd pegged for Anastasia's side piece the last time I saw him, noting the furious look of jealous rage in his eyes as he watched her lead me away towards the elevators.

"Don't look so glum, buddy," I told him. "You're welcome to have a round with her once she gives up on trying to climb my pole."

Anastasia's fingernails bit into my arm through the fabric of my suit and I looked down at her mildly, wondering what she might want to say on the subject of me not wanting to fuck her.

"Regardless of what we do behind closed doors, I won't allow you to speak about me like that when we are in the company of others," she hissed, a warning in her eyes which said she really would do something about it if I pulled a stunt like that again.

"You know, you're an objectively attractive woman, glove," I told her as we reached the elevator and she pushed the button to call it. "So why waste your time trying to win over a worthless fucker like me when you could have your pick elsewhere?"

She didn't reply until the elevator opened and we were sealed away behind the golden doors, rising up towards her rooms where she no doubt planned to try and seduce me again.

"Tell me what it is," she hissed, pressing a hand to my chest and shoving me back against the wall. "Do you prefer men?"

I barked a humourless laugh. "My life would be a whole lot easier if I did," I shot back.

"It's okay if you do. I don't mind bringing others to the bedroom if you require them," she pressed and I just rolled my eyes.

"I appreciate the offer, but it isn't a sexual preference issue."

"So you prefer women?" she pushed and I clucked my tongue.

"Yes."

"Blondes?"

"Ebony is more my thing," I shot back, my mind instantly filling with a picture of my little psycho as she moaned beneath the shock of her collar for me.

I swallowed thickly, trying to force the image away but Anastasia was smiling as I focused on her once more, her hand shifting down my body and making me frown before she grasped my dick in her hand and moaned in appreciation. Mostly because for some unknown reason, the thing was rock fucking hard and ready for action.

It definitely wasn't about her. And I refused to believe that small memory of Spider woulda brought on the straining hard-on so fast, but I had little else to pin it to.

I snatched Anastasia's throat into my grip and shoved her back, knocking her against the wall of the elevator and snarling at her as her hand fell from my cock and her eyes widened in lustful surprise.

"You're gonna wanna keep your hands offa me, glove," I warned.

"I knew you'd be huge," she panted, not seeming to mind the manhandling so much and I shoved away from her, not liking the way she was looking at me one bit. "You're the kind of man a girl can feel between her thighs days after the event, aren't you?"

"I'm the kind of man who doesn't fuck anyone, so I'd have no idea how long they might feel the after effects for," I replied, turning my back on her just as the elevator arrived on her floor and stepping out.

"Is that what you like? Purity?" she asked, hurrying after me despite my long stride and running her hand down my arm.

"I've warned you not to keep touching me," I said.

"I can do pure if you like that," she went on like I hadn't spoken. "I can do afraid too if that's what you want? Is it normally your victims who get to enjoy your appetites-"

"No," I barked, jerking to a halt and rearranging my still rock-solid cock in my pants as the corridor spun a little. Fuck, I was drunk. And whatever high that pill she'd slipped me had been intended to provide was not making an appearance.

Anastasia cocked her head at me like I was a puzzle she was in the midst of solving. She turned to a door before she figured it out though, opening it and ushering me inside.

I was about to tell her goodnight and leave before she asked me another question which could so easily end in her strangulation, but I spotted the enormous aquarium inside her suite before I could get the words out and forgot about them anyway.

"Is it a boy shark?" I asked, heading into the room and walking straight up to the tank.

"I have no idea," she replied, closing the door to keep me here and following too close behind me.

My damn cock was throbbing now and as I adjusted it again, my thumb rolled over the piercing and I nearly fucking groaned at how good that felt. Jesus. Thoughts of my little psycho dancing for me kept pushing into my mind and I had to fight tooth and claw to deny the memories of her mouth on mine, her legs around my waist, how deeply I'd been tempted to…

I cleared my throat as I tipped my head and watched the shark swim past, ignoring the rest of the lavish suite in favour of trying to spot its penises. I needed facts if I was going to tell Brooklyn about this.

Fuck, I shouldn't have let myself think about her again.

My cock throbbed and I groaned, fisting it to release some pressure and only making it ache more.

"I see it's kicking in," Anastasia purred. "I figured it could be performance anxiety. I know I am fairly intimidating, but I promise, I can be gentle if that's what you want."

She moved close and ran a hand down my spine which made my gut knot and twist with imaginable discomfort.

"Viagra?" I guessed on a growl as my dick throbbed again and she smiled like a predator who was inches from its prey.

"Just to help create the right mood." She shrugged innocently, licking her lips. "It's just physical, Niall. Why deny yourself? I can be whatever you need me to be. And once you've had a taste of me, I know you won't keep on denying yourself in the future."

I shook my head, finding the dizziness waiting for me there and cursing my dumb arse for giving in to the temptation of booze. I'd wanted to be able to drive home after this horror show, but I'd allowed the boring personality of my bride to drive me into a drunken stupor, and now look. I was hunting for shark penises in her suite with the hard-on from hell and half a bottle of whiskey swimming merrily in my gut.

"What reason is there to hold back? We'll be married soon. I'll be yours to use as you want and I want that too," she insisted, still stalking me even as I swiped a hand down my face and tried to fight off the effects of the booze so that I could think a little clearer.

She reached for me again, her hand landing on my chest as I cursed, my dick throbbing with urgent need and my mind so muddled that for a second, I let myself consider it.

Would it be so bad to use her when she so clearly wanted me to do so?

Ava's screams didn't even start up in my head as I thought about it and Anastasia noticed my hesitation, taking it as encouragement as her fingers rolled down to my belt, making a shudder pass through me which was in no way linked to desire.

No, it wasn't Ava's screams that filled my head as I looked at this woman who was supposed to become my next bride. It was thoughts of the girl I'd kept locked in my basement. The way she lit me up like a bonfire, the way she fought against me like a warring tomcat, the depths of her electric eyes and the darkness in her soul which was a match to her onyx hair.

She was the one who I thought of as Anastasia tried to unbuckle my belt and a growl of anger escaped me as I realised what that meant. It was already too fucking late for me when it came to Brooklyn. She was already in too damn deep. I couldn't cut her out. In fact, I wouldn't. And I didn't know what the fuck I was supposed to do about that, but I did know that this Russian bride who I in no way chose for myself was absolutely not the answer.

I shoved away from her, shaking my head as I turned and headed for the door, not even bothering to explain myself as I left her there, yelling my name like she expected me to give in to the power of her seduction.

But I'd already been seduced. And no tiny dresses or pouting lips, or fantasy fulfilling promises or fucking Viagra were going to be calling me away from the one who had me under her damn spell.

I ripped the door open but instead of finding myself in the corridor, I had somehow made my way into an enormous bathroom all decorated in black and gold like a Kardashian had puked all over it.

I turned to leave and found Anastasia racing after me, peeling her dress off as she came and raising her chin as she blocked my exit.

"You'll feel differently once you've had me," she hissed. "And my men won't let you out of here until sunrise. So between me and that little happy pill you took earlier, I know you'll give in eventually. Why not stop fighting it?"

I considered that. Considered fighting my way past a hoard of Russians to escape this place while sporting a massive hard-on. Considered how pissed my pa would be when he found out and the tedious reality of having to listen to him harp on about it for hours on end. Then quickly slammed the bathroom door in her face and locked it.

"What are you doing?" Anastasia yelled from beyond the door and I promptly turned away from it, flicking on the shower so that the sound of it would drown out her continued yells before leaning my back to the wall and unbuckling my pants.

I tugged my aching cock out and groaned as I just gave in to the inevitable, rolling my thumb over the piercing and letting all the thoughts of Brooklyn that I wasn't supposed to be having come charging into my brain.

Tonight, I'd let myself have her. In my mind and in this room with Viagra making my cock throb with desperation, and the time I'd spent healing from the fucking tattoo and piercing making that need all the more powerful,

I was giving in.

I pumped my dick as I thought of her, my thumb teasing the piercing and making me curse because it felt like heaven had just licked her tongue along the full length of me, and I was about thirteen seconds away from coming for her.

"Fuck me," I cursed, the words practically a plea to the woman I was picturing, though I knew I'd have to reign in that desire when I finally returned to her.

But right now, she could have me. Alone and in my fiancée's fucking bathroom. It was a hot mess but then again, so was I.

I pumped my cock a few more times, remembering the way Brooklyn had kissed me, and groaning her name as I came all over the floor, my chest rising and falling rapidly from the release.

My dick didn't so much as pretend to deflate as the Viagra kept it captive, and a laugh tumbled from my lips which I knew was the edge of the dark place creeping in on me again.

I was going to leave this place a broken thing come morning and I knew it. This reality my pa had mapped out for me wasn't going away even if I did spend the night locked in Anastasia's bathroom, jerking off over a woman I couldn't ever claim for myself.

In the morning I was going to go downstairs, pass by all of her merry men and let them think whatever the fuck they wanted to think about me as I went on my way. But right now, it looked like I was going to hell either way, so I was going to enjoy myself on the way down. And with that hopeless thought, I began pumping my dick in my fist once more, letting all of my attention fall onto my little psycho as I gave in to the dark and let myself pretend, just for a little while, that she was mine.

BROOKLYN

CHAPTER ELEVEN

The front door flew open with such force, I half expected a dinosaur attack before Niall appeared out of the shadows without a T-Rex in sight, the morning light filtering in behind him.

"Holy tits, Niall." I held a hand to my chest and glanced over at Mateo who was on his feet with a kitchen knife in his grip and a savage sneer on his face. I'd given him that little stabby last night when he'd told me he'd need it if anything bad happened. I guessed he was prepping himself for an attack, though I didn't know what he expected to come find us all the way out here in the middle of nowhere. An angry badger maybe, or a squirrel who was tired of living on nuts and wanted to steal our clothes, pretend to be human and rise up into high society. Yeah…that was just the sort of sneaky thing a squirrel would do.

Brutus was on his feet too, a snarl peeling back his lips and his hackles rising as he glared at Niall. I'd made a bandana for him out of a sparkly pink top and he'd almost taken my hand off when I'd tied it in place. He was such a good boy.

Niall ignored all of us, a cold detachment dripping from his dark eyes as he walked slowly towards me.

The television was still on and my snuggly blanket was still tucked around me. I'd been up all night long, except okay, maybe I'd drifted off for an hour or two or five, but mostly I'd been awake. And I'd been confused and worried too, because Hellfire had sounded seventy shades of off on the phone when he'd called last night, and thoughts of him had been whirring around in my brain like little flies trying to fix together a chopped-up piece of string.

When Niall hadn't come home, I'd realised he was staying the night with his fiancée and that was when the tears had started and I'd ripped the stuffing out of a pillow with my bare hands. It was all in smashy corner now, joining the rest of the broken things, and I was starting to think I belonged over there too.

Mateo had refused to sit anywhere near me while Niall had been gone, his fingers constantly flexing and his muscles bunching like he was a ticking bomb set to explode. I wasn't sure what was going on behind his eyes, but the fierce looks he kept giving me made me wonder if it was to do with little old me.

"Mateo and I are having a Lord of the Harry Potter-thon," I announced, hoping Niall might want to join us though equally not wanting him to because he was probably fresh from his fancy fiancée's bed after his dick danced the rumba with her giant chimichongas. Still, I couldn't fight the need in me to have him close, even though my heart felt like it was being stabbed repeatedly by a tiny man with a tiny pitchfork.

"A what now?" Niall mumbled, not seeming interested in anything much, but his eyes kept wandering to me as he drifted through the room like a sad pirate ghost caught on a sea breeze.

"We watch the first Harry Potter then the first Lord of the Rings, then half way through, we turn it off then watch the second Harry Potter, the rest of the first Lord of the Rings, then-" I babbled and Niall cut over me.

"Now why in the fuck would anyone do that?" he growled, irritation flashing over his features, but my intuition was buzzing around my ears like a wasp looking for some jelly and I was fairly sure that wasn't why he was angry.

Mateo took a step towards me as Niall got closer, his knife still raised and Niall ignored him like he wasn't even there as he came to a halt right in front of me and just stared down at me.

"*Because*, Hellfire, then you get the real story. The secret story," I said seriously. "Oh! And we found out Mateo's a Hufflepuff, isn't that great?"

Mateo grunted like he wasn't in agreement of his Huffly-puff ways, but that was such a Hufflepuff reaction. "I'm a Slytherin, obviously, and so are you. And Angry Jack's a Ravenclaw!"

"Ain't that the clever one?" Niall muttered, scowling deeply. "Jack ain't no fucking Ravenclaw. There isn't thoughts in his head. Not fuckin' one of them."

"Not true. I've seen the sparks in his eyes and the cogs whirring in his ears. You could carve all of our brains out, stack them up like a totem pole and it still wouldn't be as big as Jack's brain," I said firmly.

Niall stared at me for a long time, a dark cloud seeming to hang over him, threatening a rainstorm. He shrugged finally, turning away from me and finding himself face to face with Mateo's knife, Harold. Harold wasn't much to look at but he really had a glint about him that spoke of the pain he could cause, and I didn't much like him being so near to Hellfire's lovely face.

"Move," Niall growled, letting the tip of the knife press against his cheek.

"I could cut your eyes out in under thirty seconds, bastardo," Mateo warned, a deadly energy rolling from him.

"Mateo," I gasped, getting up onto my knees on the couch and taking hold of his arm as I tried to pull the knife away from Hellfire. I'd only agreed to get him the weapon from the kitchen because I'd thought it might make him happy, but it only seemed to have made him more stabby – and not even in a fun way! I guessed that was the risk I'd run with my gift but enough was enough. "Niall needs his eyes where they are. I know they'd look pretty on a necklace, but we can't just go around making necklaces out of people's eyes because we need some new jewellery." I squeezed Mateo's wrist, drawing his gaze to me and letting him see the pain spilling out of my soul at the idea of him hurting Niall.

Niall didn't seem to care much either way what happened, and as Mateo's arm slowly went slack, he brushed past him and walked upstairs without another word.

My throat burned as I watched him go, wondering if his big bopper bride had upset him or if it was coming home to us that made him sad. I'd been pacing all night (okay for like an hour and eleven minutes) wondering where he was and imagining all the things he might have been doing with her, feeling like a canary in a fish tank while I just waited to see if he was going to return with a worm for me or if he'd given up all of his insects to *Anastasia.* Even in my head, I said her name with a sneer. Maybe he missed her already. Maybe he was upstairs packing a suitcase so he could go and live with her. Maybe he'd leave us here like cats left behind after their meanie bambini owners moved on to a better life without them.

A noise of hurt left me and Mateo moved the knife under my chin, tipping my head up to make me look at him. My breath caught and flutters rushed over my body like tiny wingtips from the contact of that weapon.

I knew Mateo would never hurt me, but I liked the idea that he could. He could cut off pieces of me until I was nothing but blood and bone. He was powerful like that, a god that could create and destroy as easily as he could blink.

"Why do you pine for a man who is nothing but a butcher? He doesn't feel for you, mi sol. He feels nothing. I may be darkness wrapped inside a man's body, but I am capable of protecting you, of making your skin heat and your pulse race with pleasure. That is what I can offer you, what is it that he can offer that is worth this pain in your heart?"

One hard slice of that blade could end me for good, and that was why I gave him the truth. Because I wasn't afraid of death, I was afraid of becoming someone I wasn't. And who I was, was a girl who'd stumbled into a clan of men who were as different as she was. So this was where I wanted us to stay.

"I don't feel odd when I'm with Niall," I said. "He's me in reverse, his cracks are in the same places as mine. You ground me, Mateo, but Niall makes me fly. And I need to fly sometimes as much as I need my feet down here with you too. When you've been as lonely as I have for as long as I have, feeling like no one in the whole wide world wants anything to do with you, and that no one could ever understand what it's like to live in your head, I think it's impossible to let go of feeling accepted once you find that acceptance. I feel like I'm finally home, but I'm terrified, Dead Man, because nothing lasts in this world. It all vanishes, poof. Bit by bit or all at once. One day, it'll be gone. All of the good, the bad, and I've known so much of the bad, now the good is here, I want to enjoy it while it stays. I want you and Niall and Brutus and AJ. I want to stay here for as long as life lets me, and I know that means it'll hurt more in the end when the goodbyes come to claim me, but they're inevitable. Everyone in this world is tied to their own train tracks and a train is coming, they just don't know when. So let me be here, now, with you and him and everyone, because the darkness is going to consume us all eventually. At least let me open my eyes and bask in the sun while it's still shining."

Mateo let out a heavy sigh, lowering the knife so it grazed along the length of my throat before he dropped it to his side.

"Go to him then." He stepped aside. "I'll be here when he disappoints you, chica loca. Because what you think lives in him is an illusion draped in a lie."

I tiptoed up to kiss Mateo's cheek, quietly denying his words before heading to the stairs and jogging up them. I was wearing my comfys, a pair of baggy white sweatpants with stars on the ass along with a tank top that had a skeleton on it with its middle finger up.

I crept up the stairs and crossed the little walkway which looked back down into the lounge before making it to Niall's room, pushing the door open quietly, the darkness thick inside.

I peered into the gloom as a low groan sounded within the space and I spotted him on the bed, his pants unbuckled and his huge cock gripped in his hand as he pumped it hard. My lips parted and my pussy throbbed as I stood there, watching his big hand work the length of his spectacular dick. His thumb grazed over the top of it again and again and I just caught a glimpse of silver there as he rubbed it.

I'd been thinking about the way his dick had been decorated a whole lot since he'd shown it to me, wondering what that little silver ball would feel like if it brushed against my fingertips, my tongue and a whole lot of more interesting places besides, and it looked like he was enjoying the feeling of it a hell of a lot himself.

My breaths came heavier, the urge to go in there and take his cock from his hand rising in me like a monster with her own desires. I swear I could feel every stroke of his hand inside my pussy and I ached as a low noise rumbled through Niall's chest, biting down on my bottom lip to hold back my own moan and keep myself hidden in the shadows.

He grabbed something from beside him as his hips thrust forward and his hand movements got more frantic, and I realised it was a pair of my panties. I watched in awe as he wrapped them around the head of his cock and groaned as he came into them, mopping up his cum with the little thong before laying there panting on the bed.

He shoved to his feet suddenly and I darted to the side of the door, pressing my back to it a second before he stepped past it and headed into his en suite, somehow not noticing me where I lurked. I'd managed to evade being caught and I had to put it down to the sneaking training he'd given me before. I'd had to try and stick a post-it to his back without him noticing me do it and it had taken me weeks and weeks before I'd finally managed it.

I stepped into his room, switching the light on and trying to slow my wild heartbeat as I stared at the spot on the bed where I'd watched him pleasure himself. My mouth was dry and my throat tight, the idea of his cock inside me going round and round in my mind like it was on a carousel, carnival music starting up in the back of my brain.

I could taste cotton candy on my tongue as I spun round and round on a little horse in my head, but then the ride came to a jolting halt and the angry ride man told me to get off. Because I wasn't who Niall wanted. He'd proven that when he'd used my underwear to clean himself up, like a rag that had no meaning to him at all. Maybe I was just a rag holder to him, and my clothes were fair game for scrubbing himself. I clutched the clothes on my body in alarm at that, not wanting them to be used as scrubby rags. I'd fight for them until I was bloody and bruised and-

Niall stepped back into the room and I whipped around, praying he couldn't see the truth of what I'd just witnessed written all over my face. I should have walked away, I shouldn't have just stood there and stared like a duck hit by a loaf of bread.

He pushed the door shut behind him and I swear a vacuum sucked all the oxygen out of the room, leaving me gasping like a fish dragged onto land and left there to flap its little fins.

"What are you doing here, Spider?" he demanded, his hand snapping out to turn the light back off.

The darkness was immediate and drowning, and it had nothing to do with the bulb going out. It was him, all him. It was terrifying and exhilarating, the danger so potent I could feel it crawling down my spine.

"Why did you call last night?" I asked, the question having been driving me to crazy town and back again all night long. He hadn't really said much at all, and phones were for speaking and saying stuff, so why had he not done those things? Had he misdialled, gotten confused? Or had he meant to say something but then I'd rambled on about my Betty Boops for so long that he'd gotten bored and hung up?

"Because I knew your voice would stop me goin' on a killing spree and fucking up everything," he said, but his face flickered with regret like he wished he hadn't said it. Or maybe like he was sad he hadn't gotten to go killing.

"Why would my voice do that?" I asked as my nose wrinkled in confusion.

"It don't matter," he growled, striding past me and yanking his shirt off as he went. He kept stripping until he was down to his boxers and I was drinking in every tattoo and scar on his muscular body, then he whipped the covers back and got into bed.

My heart did a twisty thing as I backed up to the door, guessing he wanted his sleep time to dream about his bride's milky mangoes.

My back hit the door and I fumbled for the handle, still staring at him through the gloom as hurt struck a match against the inside of my ribs and set my whole chest on fire.

"Do you love her?" I asked, the words coming out of my voice box like a tiny ant had put them on his back and carried them out for me. Because I definitely hadn't meant to say that, but my tongue was on puppet strings and the treacherous ant was in control.

"She's my duty," he growled.

"You can still enjoy fucking your duty," I whispered, the accusation right there for all the room to hear. The lamp was definitely leaning closer to listen to what Niall had to say and the pillows' ears were pricking up as he shifted onto them, rolling in my direction to face me.

He pushed the covers back beside him, patting the empty space there.

"I don't much like talking when the dark days come, love. If you wanna stay, then you'll stay in my bed beside me. Otherwise, go and don't step a foot inside this room again until I find my way back outa this abyss and come for you." His voice was a dominion in itself, ruled by a heartless king who sat upon a throne of death and madness. It should have made me want to run, to flee his kingdom to the safety of another land, but instead I was drawn deeper into this man's power and I found myself walking towards him.

I dropped my sweatpants, kicking them away from me so I was just in my panties and tank top, and he held my eye as I unclipped my bra, shimmied the straps off of my arms and yanked it out from under my top. I tossed it away and climbed into bed, his hands seizing me the moment I got close. And I was his captor in an instant, drawn into the heat of his chest, the beast who housed his body binding me in chains and promising me a bloody end if I tried to escape.

My body went slack so I moulded easily against the hard muscles of his chest, hooking my leg over his and sliding my arms around his neck. He stiffened like he'd expected me to fight, but I was content in the company of monsters, especially those who inhabited this house.

I nuzzled against his stubble and his heart drummed furiously in response, our lips nearly brushing as I coiled up with this huge man and he folded himself around me like his body was turning into a cage.

It was morning but I hadn't slept much last night anyway, and I got the feeling he hadn't slept at all, though I didn't like to focus too much on what might have been keeping him awake. Right now, it was just me and him, and there was peace between our chaos, dragging me away.

Perhaps when I woke again, Niall would have turned to iron, never to let me go, and perhaps I didn't mind that at all.

Three days passed while Niall was lost to the dark, and I stayed with him while he rode the black tide and his demons tried to drown him in a bleak sea. Mateo made me food, though I had to cart it all out to him from the kitchen because his collar went all zappy if he tried to go in there, but even when I tried to push cherry tomatoes between Niall's teeth, he wouldn't eat. Not even the extra juicy ones. Sometimes he stared at me and I swear I could see a whole world in his eyes. There were tiny people in there working on a mountain, rolling huge boulders up its hills only to lose their grasp halfway up and watch them crash all the way back to the bottom. It was an endless loop of unfulfilled need and it pained me that I couldn't crawl in there and help with his boulders.

I'd never looked after anyone before - except a little matchstick man I used to keep in my pocket. He was really just a single matchstick with a leaf wrapped around him, but one day he'd fallen out of my pocket and blown away on the wind, his little leaf coat left behind. That was the day I found out that I was no good at protecting little creatures, and Niall wasn't little, he was a huge beast built of muscle and fury. How could I look after him if I couldn't even save my matchstick man? So I did the only thing I really wanted to do, and tried to make him laugh, desperate to see the smile of my madman drawing his lips into that sinister grin which made my stomach flutter.

Niall sat on the couch with a blanket on his knees which I'd put there as well as a snuggly woolly hat on his head. If he couldn't be happy, at least he could be warm and fuzzy. Brutus lay at his feet, gnawing on a shoe and wagging his stumpy little tail.

Mateo stood to one side of the room, a dark shadow always watching from afar. He had barely come near me at all since he'd touched me in the swimming pool, and sometimes I caught an expression on his face that was so murderous, he looked like a vampire in desperate need of blood. But we were in the boring people world and if there was a place out there where magical beings roamed, then I was yet to find it. I'd sure as hell looked too. I'd once spent a night hooting to an owl in a tree just in case he might be hoarding my letter to Hogwarts. And don't get me started on the time I'd stolen a kid's pot of glitter and thrown it in my face just in case it would whisk me away to Zodiac Academy. I was an Aquarius – obvi – but I wouldn't have just had air magic if I lived in that world, I'd have had the whole bunch of elements, earth, fire, water, everything. I'd have taken over the entire kingdom too, stolen the throne from the Celestial Heirs while shaking my ass in their hot, preppy faces.

I'd have been an evil Pegasus queen, a villain to be feared and revered, and I'd bring Mateo and Niall and Angry Jack with me too, and together we'd be an unstoppable band of villains. Mateo could really be a vampire then and Niall would be a basilisk, feeding on others' pain while I rode Angry Jack across the land whenever he shifted into a white dragon and burned all the people we didn't like, especially the stinky ones. Yeah, that was the life for me. Queen of everything, all powerful ruler of a magical world where not even the stars could stop me-

"Mi sol," Mateo's voice cut through my wild daydream and my head snapped towards him.

I was still standing on the coffee table, my arms poised above my head in a ballerina pose and I realised all the blood had drained from them.

"Oops sorry, I got lost in a fantasy of world domination," I said with a shy smile and Mateo twitched a dark smirk at me.

"Your audience is distracted," he muttered icily and I realised Niall wasn't sitting in front of me anymore. He'd moved to the window with his blanket draped around his shoulders, staring off into the mist which clung to the ground outside.

"Niall, I was just about to do a circus show for you," I huffed, jumping off the table and grabbing his hand.

He looked down at where our skin connected, energy sparking into my limbs as I looked up at him. And he did the starey thing again, gazing directly into my soul and weighing it in his palm. Did he find me wanting?

Was the rust that clung to it off-putting to him, or did he like the roughened touch of it?

I reached up to draw one side of his lips higher, frowning as I jammed my thumb into the corner of his mouth and tried to make it stick in a smile. But the moment I dropped my hand, his face fell and a little whimper rose in my throat.

"I miss your happies," I whispered, tears rising in my eyes. "Are you all hollow inside? Just a big, empty cave?" I asked, resting my hand against his chest to try and find his heart. The thump of it made relief rush through me and I lurched into his body, pressing my ear to it to hear it thunder just for me. "Mr Heart," I spoke to it, cupping my hand around my mouth to keep the conversation private. "Do you know where his happies have gone? Where can I find them?"

Niall's arm slid around me and his chin rested on my head, a heavy sigh leaving him and I shut my eyes, breathing in his rich, masculine scent. One moment, two, three, fifty. I stole a whole bunch in the arms of a man who was promised to someone else, then I realised my tears were soaking into his shirt and I lurched away, wheeling around and wiping them out of existence before he could see.

"Face paint!" I announced, running from the room to where Niall kept a stash of the stuff in the kitchen. I grabbed the colour palette along with a cup of water, some brushes and sponges then darted back to the lounge with a smile on my face.

Mateo caught my arm before I could make it back to Niall and my heart rocked like a boat on stormy waters as I looked up at him. His gaze swirled with deadly intentions and his fingers dug deeper into my arm as I stood there, his throat rising and falling. He let me go just as suddenly, leaving whitened marks on my arm and taking two steps away from me as he scored a hand down his face.

"Are you okay, Dead Man?" I asked and he nodded once stiffly, but there was something going on behind his gaze which I couldn't work out.

I jogged over to Niall, guiding him to a chair and pushing him down into it before straddling his lap and setting up my face paint things on the arm, bouncing a little in excitement.

"*Spider*," he rasped and I looked to him with a big ass smile on my face.

"Shhh." I pressed my finger to his lips as I continued to bounce then started work on painting his face.

I knew exactly what he was going to be, a big smiley clown. And maybe when there was a huge red grin painted onto his lips, it would sink into his skin and coax a real smile out of him.

I bit my lip as I concentrated, finding I was pretty good at this actually. Better than a squirrel with an artistic flare, that was for sure.

When Niall's face was ghost white, I leaned in nose to nose with him as I painted his eyes black and drew a line through the middle of them that ran down each of his cheeks and up onto his brow. His large hands suddenly clasped my back and he pulled me even closer, our breaths becoming one.

I fisted my hand in his hair, yanking hard as I pursed my lips at him. "Stay still."

"Okay, little psycho," he exhaled.

I started work on his big red smile, making beautiful work of it as I painted it on. And when I was done, I leaned back to admire it, bouncing in his lap again in joy, drawing a groan of delight from him.

"Mi sol," Mateo snarled from across the room, but I ignored him, bouncing more as I admired my work and Niall's hands fisted in the back of my top.

"Stop," he gritted out.

"Stop what?" I bounced harder and a curse fell from his lips a moment before I felt his cock grow hard between my thighs. *Holy tits!*

I fell still, realising what I'd done as my lips popped open. I did that.

Me. I was a seductress, a temptress of the night, The Peen Piper.

Niall was staring at me, his clown's grin wide while his lips remained flat, but as a silence echoed back to us off of the walls, he suddenly snapped, a booming laugh ripping from his throat.

"Jesus Christ, Spider." He got up so I fell right onto my ass and he adjusted his pants, letting the blanket fall from his shoulders too. "Fancy you bein' there in my lap when I got hard for my fiancée." He stepped over me, striding towards Mateo and I gaped after him, his words slashing my heart open like he'd butchered it with a knife. "Where's the big fella then?" He slapped Mateo mockingly on the cheek and Mateo bared his teeth like a wild animal.

"You mean Jack?" he asked and Niall nodded. "He's in the basement where you left him."

"Well go get him then, el burro." Niall waved his hands at Mateo like he was an arrogant lord speaking to his house maid and Mateo didn't move a muscle, his arms folding as he glared back at him.

"Do you know how many times and in how many ways I could have killed you in the past three days?" Mateo hissed.

"Not one, because I've had this in my pocket the whole time and you know it," Niall said with a smirk as he slid the collar remote out. "And don't you think I haven't seen you trying to cut that thing offa ya neck, el burro. But lemme tell ya, it can't be broke, and if you even get close to breaking it, I've set it up to keep shocking ya until you stop kicking. So, how's about you head off to the basement like a good little donkey and fetch my new prisoner? I'll even change the settings so you can go in there without getting your brains fried."

Niall took out his phone and quickly did just that, adjusting the perimeter on the collar so that Mateo could go into the kitchen at last, and swept an arm towards the door in invitation for him to move.

Mateo fronted him out for several seconds before he finally turned his back on him and marched away towards the basement.

I pushed myself to my feet, my heart still bleeding from Niall's comment about his fiancée. Had she been the one to bring him back? Had she been circling in his mind while he'd blocked me out and thought of her instead?

I wrung my fingers together, the quiet in the room pressing as Niall kept his back to me, but he finally turned my way, the wild light back in his eyes.

"Don't just stand there pouting, little psycho. Come over here and play a game with me."

I frowned, tiptoeing over to him, drawn by the lure of a game. Would it be tic-tac-toe? Rock, paper, scissors? Backgammon? Tag? Hopscotch? Kiss chase? Capture the flag?

He opened a drawer in a little cabinet beside him, taking out a penny and twisting it between his fingers. "This is my lucky penny."

I gasped, reaching for it, but he snatched it away, holding it up to admire it in the light above my head. "You can have it if it lands on tails, okay?"

I nodded eagerly and he flicked it up in the air, catching it in his palm then slapping it onto the back of his other hand and showing me the penny.

Heads.

Dammit.

"Again," I demanded and he chuckled, flicking it again, the coin wheeling high up towards the ceiling before he caught it and repeated the action.

Heads.

Dammit.

"Again," I growled and he did so.

Heads.

Dammit.

"Again!" I snapped.

But Niall did it five more times and still tails didn't come up, defying all the laws in the universe, even the wonky ones. I stared at him in dismay and he grinned through his makeup, almost wider than the clown smile painted across his cheeks as he rolled the coin over on his palm, showing me that heads were on both sides of the coin.

"That's not fair," I gasped in anger and his smile somehow grew.

"No, it ain't. It's swung in my favour every time, love. I always win, see? Life is like that too. I'm the master of it, not you. You live in my house, you play by my rules, and if you're a good girl, I'll grant you the gift of my never-ending fortune. But if you ever try to bewitch me, Spider…" He tutted, shaking his head and taking hold of my chin as he pinched the skin. His eyes were the darkest of nights and a coldness fell across his face like frost. "I will personally drag ya to the stake and burn ya."

My throat bobbed and I pushed out my lips indignantly as I realised what this was really about. The one thing he cared about above all others, the thing that he hoarded like treasure and guarded with the might of a beast bound to protect it. Coco Pops. The real power in this house. And he knew, the moment I got my hands on them, I'd be in charge.

If he thought he could scare me off, he was underestimating me. I'd been hunting for them every chance I got, and I wasn't going to back down ever. One day soon, I'd be the queen of the Pops, and he'd be giving me that shiny little unfair penny too when I took a seat on my throne.

"Game on, Niall," I said with a grin and his brows pinched in confusion.

"That ain't a challenge."

"Game. On." I brushed past him, heading off to find my Dead Man and AJ, the sound of a commotion carrying from the basement.

I hurried to the open door, jogging down the steps, finding AJ there smashing up the bed I used to sleep in. I gasped as a huge piece of it hit the wall and Jack swiped up a leg of it, using it as a hammer to smash the rest of the bed. Mateo stood close to him with an assessing look on his face, but didn't intervene.

I'd tried to come see AJ a banana bunch of times in the last couple of days, but I kept being Mateo blocked, my Dead Man telling me it wasn't safe. But I trusted Angry Jack with my life. He was my big boulder man, he'd never hurt me.

Mateo caught my arm as I went to step past him towards Jack. "Go back upstairs, chica loca," he commanded, but I wasn't going anywhere.

"He'll listen to me," I said firmly. "Let me go."

Mateo's mouth twitched like he wanted to force me to obey him and return upstairs and my clit tingled from the beastly look on his face.

Niall appeared out of nowhere, barrelling between us and forcing Mateo's hand off of me as he ran at Jack, whacking him over the head with a saucepan. Jack whipped around with a bellow of rage, his face twisted with some horrors playing out in his head and I knew they were fuelling his angries. I'd seen him like this when we were in Eden Heights a load of times, seeming quiet for days then snap, crackle, pop, he went on a rage spree, destroying everything around him like he wanted to break the whole world.

He was gone, gone, gone to a pit of fury that lived within him and his eyes were almost red with it, his monster fully awake. He swung a fist at Niall which forced the breath from his lungs and Niall coughed a laugh, swinging the saucepan again, the dong ringing off of Jack's head.

"Come on then, big fella. Let's dance." Niall ducked another deadly punch from Jack and I ran forward as Niall hit him over the head again. One too many of those head bangs were gonna make Jack's brain go splat. And I didn't want that. Not at all.

Niall took another punch that sent him sprawling onto the ground, and he leapt back up with another chuckle, his clown's makeup giving him the look of a true demon.

Niall swung the saucepan and I leapt forward to grab it, locking my hands around his arm and digging my teeth into his wrist.

"Stay outa this, Spider," Niall growled, trying to push me aside, but I grabbed onto the saucepan and yanked with all my strength. My hands slipped off of it and I went flying back onto my ass at Jack's feet. I got back up before the fight could break out again, turning to Jack and leaping onto him, scrambling up his body like a monkey and wrapping myself around him, looking back at Niall and baring my teeth.

"Spider," Niall warned. "Get down and lemme knock the rage outa this fella."

Jack's arm slid around me, locking tight as I clutched his neck for support and shook my head at Niall in refusal.

"He's mine. I won him fair and square. And you're not allowed to bash him over the head," I growled.

Niall spun the saucepan in his hand, considering my words. "But I like bashing fellas over the head."

"Not this one." I rubbed the back of Jack's head where Niall had struck him, finding a bump growing there.

Niall turned to Mateo with a grin, pointing his saucepan at him. "How about that one?"

"No," I hissed, tugging on Jack's shirt and he seemed to know what I meant, walking me over to stand beside Mateo, his angries slipping away on the wind somewhere.

"You can bash some potatoes over the head if you have to – but only the ugly ones," I said firmly and Niall scowled.

"This is my house, woman," he barked. "What did I just tell ya about tryna bewitch me?"

"Alexa, play C'est La Vie by B*witched," I called and the song blasted out from the Alexa device in Niall's torture room.

Niall narrowed his eyes at me as I gave him my middle finger then tugged on Jack's shirt and prodded Mateo into action. Jack carried me upstairs with Mateo walking with us, glancing back at me in Jack's arms with a sneer drawing his lips down.

Niall was hot on our heels as we stepped out of the basement and he shoved past Mateo, spitting swear words as he went.

"Fine, you wanna play happy families?" Niall called back to us.

"Yep," I said keenly.

"Then that's exactly what we'll do, Spider," Niall said lightly, striding into the kitchen. "We'll be the happiest family in the fuckin' state."

Oh good, he's finally coming around to the idea.

Jack carried me through to the lounge, sitting down on the couch and hugging me to his chest. Mateo took up his favourite position in the big grey armchair to the side of the room, watching us closely as I caressed the ouchies on the back of Jack's head.

"Rook," Jack growled, that deep voice of his setting off an earthquake in my bones. I smiled at him, booping him on the nose.

"I know why you get the angries," I said and his muscles bunched. "It's because something in your past makes you ragey. I get ragey sometimes too."

He gazed at me, saying nothing and I took that as a confirmation.

"Everyone in this house is full of noxious secrets. Sometimes the poison slips out and makes us go a little cuckoo. But that's okay, AJ. We're different. And that's so much better than being normal."

He held me tighter and we stayed like that as a clattering sound came from the kitchen, pots banging and curses coming from Niall. Eventually the smell of tomatoes and cheese carried to me and I sniffed the air like a kitten on the scent of catnip as Niall walked into the room, his shirt splashed with red sauce and four bowls of pasta on a tray in his hands.

"Now, here we are. Dinner time for the happy family," he said and I grinned. "Ain't that what ya wanted, Spider?"

I nodded keenly, climbing out of Jack's lap and moving to grab a bowl from the tray. Niall shoved one into my hands before I could grab my own, placing the tray down on the table then claiming his own bowl too.

"Eat if ya wanna eat," he snarled at the guys and I moved to perch on the arm of the chair Niall was in.

I chomped through my pasta, eating bite after bite after bite. Niall ate just as savagely, consuming it all like we were in a race. And maybe we were. So I ate faster, inhaling every piece of pasta more than chewing it and half choking on a piece before I managed to get it down my throat.

Jack and Mateo grabbed a bowl each for themselves and Jack ate almost as fast as the two of us, making my heart squish with worry. Had he not eaten these whole three days? I'd thought Mateo had been feeding him but the way he was ravenously eating made me fear I'd been wrong about that. Mateo couldn't go in the kitchen after all, so how had I thought he'd been doing it? *Stupid brain. Now look what you've done! You almost let Jack's stomach get so small that it slid right out of his butt. How could you be so careless? It's like the matchstick man all over again.*

I finished the last of my pasta, tossing the bowl down on the table. "I win!" I announced a second before Niall threw his bowl down beside it.

"I had more than you, so I win," Niall said smugly.

"Na-ar. That's not how it works," I insisted.

"Is too."

"Is not!"

"Is too."

"Is not," I snarled and he shrugged like it absolutely was. "Right then." Niall stood up and walked straight out of the room again into the kitchen, returning a beat later with a gun in his grip and a package in the other hand. He threw the package into Jack's lap and levelled the gun at his head.

"Niall, that's no way to treat family," I hissed, but Niall ignored me, gesturing to the package with the gun.

"Open that up, big fella," he said, but Jack didn't move. "Do. You.

Comprende?" he asked slowly like Jack was stupid, but Jack was no such thing. He was as sharp as a whistle.

Jack slowly took the package into his grip, tearing into it and revealing a new shock collar in some plastic wrapping.

"Oooh, can I have that one?" I asked keenly, but Niall shook his head.

"That's for Jack. Put it on now, come on, I don't have all day," Niall demanded and I pouted as Jack took it out and slid it around his throat, tightening it in place. Niall walked over to it, taking a padlock from his pocket and fixing it in place with his free hand, locking the collar on as tight as tight could be.

"There now," Niall said, caressing the sharp line of Jack's cheek bone with his gun while Jack gazed up at him without a flicker of fear in his stormy eyes. "If we're gonna play house, then you'll be needing a bedroom. You can sleep in the room next to Mateo's down there." He pointed to the corridor that led to a couple of bedrooms at the back of the house then took his phone from his pocket and started tapping something on it. "Both of your perimeters now allow you in here, to those rooms, the bathroom next to 'em and for a bit of a gander outside if the notion takes you. If you try to go anywhere else, that collar will fry ya. I've set 'em both to the max, so don't go testing me, lad, unless you have a death wish, then be my guest and head on into the kitchen." Niall gestured for Jack to walk that way, but my big man just remained in place, his gaze slipping to me and I swear there was a twinkle in his eyes that said he didn't mind this situation so much.

"Do you understand, big fella?" Niall knocked the gun against Jack's temple and I pouted, not liking how close those bullets were to tickling his brain. Bullets didn't play nice. They'd make a right mess of Jack's head if they popped out and shouted boo, but I liked his head just how it was.

"Yes," Jack said, nodding firmly.

"Good. In return for being a good boy, I'll feed ya on occasion and even let ya stretch those big stallion legs in the garden if I'm feelin' real generous. But if you piss me off, I'll drag ya down to my torture chamber, play Operation with ya and see how many organs I can pull outa yer body before you die."

Shivers took root in me at Hellfire's dark words, and though I definitely didn't want Jack to be the victim in that scenario, I wouldn't have minded him playing that game with one of my enemies.

Jack rose from his seat suddenly, forcing Niall to look up at him despite how big my Hellfire was. He was like Godzilla among skyscrapers, and I was the tiny person on the ground, horny for all of the giants around me.

Jack brushed past Niall, walking straight towards me until I was sitting in his shadow, licking my lips as my new monster reached for me. He scooped me up in his arms and carried me away from Mateo and Niall while they leapt to attention at his back.

"Where the fuck do ya think you're going?" Niall growled.

"Put her down, gigante," Mateo hissed.

"Room?" Jack demanded, glancing back at Niall as he reached the end of the corridor.

"That one," Niall said, pointing. "But ya can't take Spider in there alone."

Jack ignored Niall, shoving through the door and leaving it open so Niall and Mateo spilled in behind us, looking frantic.

"Alone," Jack echoed, but he was looking at me and there was a demand in that word.

I scrambled higher up his body, looking over his shoulder at Niall. "We wanna be alone for a bit, kay?"

"No," both Niall and Mateo said at once.

I looked between them, rolling my eyes. "We need time to speak in our secret language. You can't be here, or it'll spoil the magic." I waved my hands to usher them away and Niall tightened his grip on the gun in his hand.

"Maybe this was a bad idea," he muttered. "Change of plan. You come out to the woods with me, big fella. You can dig a nice hole, about…hm, six foot eight, I'd say, then we'll have a merry song and dance together. A real nice time, you and me, how about that?" Niall grinned and though his little fun diggy hole game did sound like a laugh, I really wanted Jack to myself for a bit.

"No, Niall. Go do something with Mateo," I insisted. "You can have a pillow fight!"

Mateo folded his arms, his jaw grinding. "Mi sol, it is not safe to leave you alone with this strange man."

"Strange?" I scoffed. "If Jack's strange, then I must be an oddball riding a cuckoo." I chuckled, but no one else laughed. Well, Niall did a bit, but he was looking at a bug that had fallen on its back by the window, so I was pretty sure he was enjoying its whirly legs, not my riotous sense of humour.

"Five minutes," I insisted. "And I'll crack the door so you know I'm as safe as a spoon who's best friends with a fork."

"Fine," Niall said at last. "But if I give ya five minutes, then you have to spend the rest of the night training with me, while these two losers stay in their rooms."

"Done!" I cried and Niall turned around, shoving Mateo out of the room and leaving the door ajar.

Jack placed me down on his bed and I scurried up it, whipping the comforter back and gesturing for Jack to get under it with me. He frowned, but did as I asked and I slid it over the two of us, concealing us from the outside world like two crows in a tent plotting a murder.

It was dark in here, but a little light filtered through so I could make out Jack's huge form. He was so big that I had to keep tugging the comforter down either side of us so no cracks were there to let our secrets out.

"So," I whispered, my knees butting against his as I shifted closer and my heart pitter-pattered at the proximity of him. "Tell me all the secrets."

"Rook," Jack growled, reaching out to cup my jaw, his thumb rolling along it then moving up to the corner of my lips. Tension formed between his eyes, a need there that desperately wanted to come out and say hi. I gave it a little wave to see if it might be lured closer, but the creases on his forehead only deepened.

"Tell me what you want, Jack," I breathed, a creak beyond the room telling me Niall was earwigging on us. But he couldn't crack mine and Jack's secret code, our words were spoken in the silence, our thoughts shared between gazes. We didn't need to use our tongues…although as my gaze dipped to Jack's mouth, I didn't think using our tongues would be the worst idea in the world. But not for words, there were far more tempting things than that which we could use them for. Mateo had taught me that.

"You," Jack answered easily and my life flashed before my eyes. Okay, not my whole life. But the me and Jack part where we were stuck together in the boring asylum, wearing boring clothes and watching the clock tick, tick, tick us towards madness. It had felt like being slowly, agonisingly lowered into a black abyss, deeper and deeper, knowing nothing awaited us below, and clinging to the view of the sky above. Jack had been a little glimpse of blue between the clouds. He'd always been there, standing at my back while I beat Cannibal Carol at chess by triple vaulting her bishop and round housing her pawn in the ass, or sitting at my side while I flicked a checker into Small Willy Norman's eye.

Now he was back, I realised how much I'd missed the constant presence of him. Missed our looks that held a million words, missed watching him workout until the nurses came and injected him with a sedative. They didn't like when we tried to be strong, they wanted us weak, unable to fight back. But Jack had never surrendered to that in the way I had never surrendered. Our souls were built from diamonds, and everyone knew you couldn't break those.

"Did you miss me, Angry?" I whispered, a fuzzy little creature rolling through my stomach at the thought.

"Yes," he agreed.

"I missed you too," I said. "We always said we'd be free one day, didn't we? Do you like it here? Niall's fun, isn't he? He plays the kind of violent games people like us crave. He can be cruel too, but I think I like that about him. How he doesn't ever wear masks. He lives his emotions, pretty or ugly, he embraces what he is, and that's something I've always struggled with. I've worn all the masks, AJ. I tried to fit in once upon a time, I tried to make my crazies go away, but the longer you ignore them, the more they build and build and make new friends. They started building villages then towns, then one day, bam, there's a whole city of crazy in your head and it doesn't matter how high you built the wall to ignore it, that city needs food and water and eventually you have to give it everything it needs to survive or else, *poof*, the city falls and you fall with it. Do you know what I mean?"

"Yes," he sighed, taking my hand in his and it was so big that mine was lost within it, never to be found.

"You'll like Mateo. He's got angries too. But his are dark and deep, and I'm not sure I've met them all yet. I think he's trying to hide them, but they'll get out. They always do, don't they? We have to be ready for that, AJ. I think we can handle each other's demons though. I think we were all meant to end up in this house actually, now that I think about it. Me and you and Niall and Mateo and Brutus. Look at us all, we're the sum of all the bad things that have ever happened to us. Brutus would be put down out there in the real world, some mean man in a hat would take him away and stick a needle in his neck, send him right away into death just because he bites the people who touch him. But what if every person who's ever touched him has made him bleed and hurt and cry? That's why I bite, Jack. Because if you don't bite, you die. You disappear into a nothing person made of nothing, and that's so much worse than the world hating you. It's not fair really, is it? We're hated because we didn't disappear quietly into the night when the world cut up our hearts with knives and made us bleed on the inside. We're the bad guys. But what if the real bad guys are the ones who claim to be good? The ones who tell the world what's right and wrong, the ones who try to crush differences out of society so everyone will just go along with what suits them? That's why we have to keep killing them, AJ. We have to wipe out every last one of them until all the bad lawmen are gone and we can make our own rules."

"Like?" he asked and I beamed, loving how deeply he listened to me, how he wanted to hear more of what so many people had called my crazy ramblings before. But I had a point, didn't I? It may have been carved a little wonky, but there was something to it I really, really believed in. Because if I'd been shown one percent of the acceptance that Jack and Niall and Mateo had shown me since I'd met them, maybe I'd have found somewhere to fit in out in that big, wide world. But maybe that was my salvation right there, because I had found that here. Even though I feared it wouldn't last, it was still here right now, right in this second, and I was gonna cling to it with every ounce of strength in my bones.

I leaned in conspiratorially. "If the world was mine to rule, I'd make sure everyone was given a big fancy boat that they could go up and down rivers on. I'd paint mine pink and blue and green and yellow and I'd have ribbons hanging from all the railings so when the wind blew, they went whoooosh." I mimed the ribbons with my free hand. "I'd have wind chimes too, so they dinged and linged all the time and when we docked, there'd be a man with a bell there who announced that Captain Brooklyn had arrived. Then my second rule would be that all the cats and dogs and all the birds and piggies and fluffies and cuties of the world, would all get to go live on big happy farms where they could run and play and be free and no one could ever, ever hurt them. And anyone who did I'd get to kill with a giant catapult and a shotgun. They'd get launched into the sky and – bang! I'd blast them to smithereens." I started laughing at the image and Jack's mouth twitched ever so slightly at the corner.

"Then?" he pushed.

"Then…" I tapped my lips as Jack's intense stare burned into me and I felt like my skin was peeling back to reveal everything that lay beneath. A blush was blazing along my cheeks and I glanced at him under my lashes, feeling all floofy in my chest. I cleared my throat, biting my lower lip. "Then I'd make it a rule that no one could ever be touched unless they agreed to be touched. We could all wear stickers, or pins, or… – hats! And on the hats they'd have the names of the people who were allowed to touch us without asking. But if we ever decided we didn't want them to touch us anymore, we could scrub their name right off just like that. And if anyone broke that rule, I'd get to blast whoever did the unwanted touching out of a cannon and they'd fly into a tank full of sharks who'd play snappies with them until they were all dead and gone." I bounced a little on the bed and Jack leaned closer to me, his eyes roaming all over my face like he was committing my expression to memory.

"Names?"

"The names I'd pick?" I guessed and he nodded and I prodded him in the knee.

"Yours. Niall's. Mateo's. And Brutus's. Oh, and all my favourite weapons. And – oh no -what about all the fluffy creatures? How will I fit all their names on my hat? Maybe animals can just default touch me. Unless it's a peeping squirrel. He can't touch me. Unless…well I suppose he can touch me a little just not while I'm pooping."

"Mine?" he asked, like he'd latched onto the first part of what I'd said and his mind couldn't let go of it.

"Yeah, AJ." I took his hand, tracing my fingers all over the lines and callouses marking his palm. "I like you touching me. I can always sense the bad touches, but yours feel safe. You wouldn't hurt me, would you?"

"No," he swore, the gruffness to his tone making my flesh spark all over.

I leaned closer to him, my eyes on his mouth, his eyes on my mouth and everything felt so warm and good that I just wanted to stay here in our little bed tent forever. I swear I could almost hear his powerful heart pounding, or maybe it was the furious drumming of my own in my ears because suddenly I wanted a kiss so bad it made me feel like my soul was tethered to his and we were being wound together by the hands of fate.

"When I was small, my dad hung these curtains in my room which were deepest orange. But they let the light through, see? So every morning when the sun rose, it would blaze through those curtains and it'd feel so warm and safe in that room, like I was surrounded by a circle of fire that no one could ever get into. You make me feel like those curtains made me feel Angry Jack."

"Rook," he croaked, a demand, a plea. But then the comforter was ripped off of us and a massive palm slammed down on my forehead, shoving me flat onto the bed.

"That's yer five minutes up." Niall grinned down at me then threw me over his shoulder, carrying me away from Jack and yanking the door shut behind us so I lost sight of him staring after me.

Mateo was in the hall, the shadows seeming to hug him as Niall carried me past him and jerked his chin towards his room. "Off ya go. She's mine for the rest of the night. You can all keep yer greedy eyes offa her."

I waved at Mateo and he scowled after us before Niall rounded a corner then carried me through the lounge into the kitchen, planting my ass down on the counter.

"Yer gonna try and stab me," he decided, whipping the drawer open by my legs and taking out a small pointy knife who looked like a bitchy little Natalie.

"Here." Niall placed her in my grip.

"Easy." I jabbed it at him, but he caught my wrist before Natalie could cut him.

"Not yet," he said, releasing my wrist and I pouted as he took something from the counter behind me, showing me a black scarf. He smirked at me then wrapped it around my eyes, tying it tight in place so I lost all my looksies.

"Now you can try and stab me," Niall chuckled as he moved away and I lunged blindly, swinging the knife through the air with a 'yah!" leaving my lips as I sprang off the counter.

I hit the kichen island and a stool went flying, making me curse as bruises blossomed up my legs.

"Come on, Spider. Try harder." Niall called from somewhere to my left and I launched myself towards him, wheeling the blade around and stab, stab, stabbing at the air. I struck something hard and a whoop left me before the microwave beeped indignantly and I cursed.

"Sorry, Michael," I muttered. "I'm looking for Niall."

"Over here." He called from right behind me and I wheeled around, slashing and growling as I tried to get him, but my hand sailed through air time and again. My fist whacked into the fridge and I yelped, almost dropping the knife. Niall caught my arm suddenly, kissing my knuckles where I'd bruised them and I gasped before he let go, laughing as he headed away from me again.

I followed the sound, bumping into what felt like every item in the kitchen, bish, bash, bam. My knees were taking the brunt of it, but as I stubbed my little toe on the way out into the lounge, I squealed in anger and hopped forward in a furious bid to find my mark.

"Niall!" I snapped, slashing the knife through the air.

"Come on, Spider. This is fuckin' pathetic," he taunted to my left and I spun that way fast, the knife driving forward and with a crunch, it slammed into something wooden.

"Nice dent ya made in the front door there, but it ain't gonna kill me," Niall said. "What a disappointment. I thought you were a good killer, I musta been wrong."

"Fuck you!" I cried, leaping in the direction of his voice and my head collided with a cabinet, sending me tumbling backwards onto my ass.

"Ow, ow, ow," I whimpered, rubbing my head and I decided playing victim might be a good angle. I let out a little sob, my lower lip pushing out as I listened to the creak of floorboards as Niall moved somewhere close to my right.

"Alright, lass, no need to cry. Where's it hurtin'?" He dropped down beside me, cupping my chin and with a grin snapping out across my face, I slammed the blade towards him. It sunk in deep. Deeper than deep. It went into the softness of his flesh right to the hilt and I gasped in utter, delayed horror at what I'd fucking done. At how stupid this game had been.

I ripped off my blindfold with his name tearing from my throat in horror, but I didn't find him bleeding out, I found him smirking at me with a bunch of bags of flour strapped to his body on leather belts. He must have made them for this game and slipped them on after he put on my blindfold and he looked fucking ridiculous.

"You wore protection," I gasped as I yanked the knife out from the bag on his side and flour poured from it onto my legs.

He shrugged one shoulder as triumph spilled through my chest. Niall O'Brien, infamous hitman, best killer in the whole damn state, was wearing protection so little me didn't kill him.

"Am I really that good?" I breathed in disbelief.

"No," he scoffed, shoving to his feet. "I just planned on havin' you stab me a lot in the next game. There weren't no chance of ya getting' close to me during this game."

"But I did," I pointed out grumpily.

"I let ya," he laughed, getting to his feet and he yanked me up after him as I hung my head, realising I wasn't as good of a killer as I'd thought.

He knocked his knuckles under my chin then slid my blindfold back over my eyes. "Chin up, love. There's only room for one perfect killer in this state anyways. You can be second best if ya work hard. But probably not.

202

You're more like sixteenth at the moment and I don't see much improvement."

I ground my teeth together and lunged at him, slashing hard and feeling another flour bag tear open.

"Cheat. I didn't say go." Niall leapt away from me as I took chase, hunting him down and crashing into the sofa, going ass over tit and tumbling right onto the floor. Niall was hiding there and I'd landed right on top of him, my face squashed against something hard beneath his clothes and for a second, I thought it was his arm before he ripped me away from it by my hair and I realised that huge thing had been his cock.

"Watch it, ya little hellion," he wheezed and I tried to drive my knife into another flour bag, but he knocked me away, getting up and making a run for it.

I leapt up, immediately slamming into the coffee table and crashing over it, grasping my calf as I cursed my way through the pain.

"Silly little Spider," Niall called to me. "Did you really think you could get the best of me?"

My feet bumped into Brutus and strong hands wrapped around my waist from behind, yanking me away from him just before the sound of sharp teeth snapped together near my ankles.

Niall released me and I swung around to get him, but he suddenly wasn't there again. I slashed and swiped and stabbed, but Niall started moving like a dragonfly, whizzing and zooming around me and my knife only grazed him and his flour bags time and again.

I was panting and bruised, doubling over from exertion as sweat beaded on the back of my neck.

"D'ya give up?" Niall mocked from somewhere close, but he always seemed so close and yet so far.

"Never," I growled, standing up straight and drawing in a ragged breath.

"You look like a rabbit who's outrun a fox, little psycho. Yer done."

"I'm not done!" I protested. "I've got plenty of huffs and puffs left in me. I'll get you this time."

I stabbed at the air, but Niall's hand closed around my wrist and he yanked off my blindfold in the next movement, making me wince against the light in the room. He slowly curled one hand around the back of my neck, his flour bags pressing to my side as he held me there, his fingers finding a pressure point in my wrist that made me drop the knife.

"Do you wanna see what the best killer in the U S of A can do when he's blind, love?" he asked in a growl that sent a tremor down to the tips of my toes.

I nodded eagerly and he unbuckled the belts around his body which were holding the flour bags, dropping them onto the couch before pulling off his flour-covered shirt and tossing it away.

My mouth suddenly felt like someone had stuffed a hairdryer between my lips and turned it on full blast. My eyes ate up every inch of his rippling muscles and the ink covering them. The clown on his chest grinned at me and I fluttered my lashes unable to help flirting with it just a little. Niall grabbed the belts again and disappeared into the kitchen with them, leaving me with the lasting impression of the ink covering his back.

When he returned, he had new bags strapped to the belts and he smirked at me as he approached, jerking his chin in a command. "Arms up like yer a solider of war."

I did as he asked and he started strapping the belts all around me, cinching them tight so the flour bags covered all of my fleshy bits. They were kinda heavy though and it was a little awkward to move about, putting me at a definite disadvantage for this game. I was sure he hadn't had this many on him and he had a huge amount of upper body strength for the ones he had been carrying around, but I wasn't gonna start complaining and making out I couldn't handle the pressure. I was an elite killer in the making, and this was all part of my training.

Niall pushed the blindfold into my grip as he finished tightening the belts. "Cover my eyes then. Nice and tight, don't let me cheat. A man with a soul as dark as mine can never be trusted."

My throated bobbed and I climbed up onto the chair behind me with a little trouble, wrapping the blindfold around his head and knotting it tight. Then I held my middle finger up to his face. "How many fingers am I holding up?"

"Yer swearing at me, I know that much, but I can't see ya, I just know you too well."

I laughed. "Alright. I trust you."

"You shouldn't trust anyone, Spider," Niall said seriously. "Especially not an O'Brien. And especially not the one who has a reputation for being psychotic."

"Well you're the only O'Brien I've ever met and you're my favourite. I can't help who I trust, it just sort of happened. But now it has, I can't take it back, so don't break that trust, kay?"

"Spider," he sighed and I let my eyes drift down to the ink on his neck then further still to his pecs and the tightness of his abs. Fuck a duck in a bucket, he really was a sight for small eyes. And with him blindfolded, I could let myself feast on this sight until the crows came home.

"Hand me the knife then," Niall encouraged and I dropped down off of the couch, picking it up and slipping it between his fingers, my hand remaining on his for several seconds longer than it should have. But sometimes I craved his touchies so bad, it was hard to stop myself from stealing them.

He released a slow breath and I could tell he was excited by this game, his broad chest beginning to heave and I realised my fingertips were tip-toeing up his arm, off on adventure of their own like Frodo and Sam towards the pits of Mordor. I reached out with my other hand, snatching them back and crushing those naughty fingers in my palm, trying to stop them kicking, but they kept twitching for more contact with Niall and the glorious artwork of his skin.

"Three," Niall warned. "Two…"

I darted away, as quiet as a mouse in a hammock as I crept up onto the coffee table and fell entirely still.

"One." Niall lunged at me like there wasn't a thing wrong with his sight, slashing a flour bag open at my hip while I squealed and dove onto the nearest chair. Niall was still coming and I gasped, climbing over the back of it, but he caught my ankle and a quick succession of stabs sent flour pouring all down my back. I kicked out with my free leg, knocking him away as he grunted and I scrambled over the back of the chair, moving as silently as possible towards the front door.

Niall didn't slow, running at me like he was a bat hunting with echolocation, and I ducked down low only to serve myself a knee to the head as his strike hit the door.

"Ha," he barked a laugh as I scurried between his legs, but he caught me by one of the belts and three more stabs sent flour exploding over me.

I undid the buckle as he tried to keep me in place and the belt came free of my body, giving me a chance to crawl through his legs and make a break for it. I dove behind the couch and crawled around the other side of it, pressing myself in close and tucking my head low as I made myself as small as possible.

There were only a few bags of flour left intact on my body and I realised how hot Niall's killer instincts were getting me as I bit my lip and refused to move a single muscle.

Niall was quiet too and I listened for his movements as hard as I could, but the room sounded empty now. But surely he wouldn't have left mid-game? A minute ticked past, then another and impatience got the better of me as I peered up over the arm of the sofa in search of him.

But my foot slipped out at the same time, making a slight scuffing noise and Niall came at me like a warthog with an arrow in its ass. I shrieked and leapt up, but he was already on me, knocking me down onto the couch, his hand grasping the flour bag over my heart and sticking it with his knife. He twisted it too before yanking it out and a spray of white powder rained over my face, giving me a moment to imagine what it would be like to die for him as I pictured the flour as red, red blood.

A moan left me as his hands roamed my body, seeking out the final flour bags and stabbing them as he panted with the thrill of a kill he hadn't really claimed, but he knew he could have in so many terribly cruel and wonderful ways if he'd wanted to.

I pushed the blindfold up onto his head so he could see the destruction he'd delivered, and his pupils dilated as he took in the powder coating every inch of me.

"I'm dead," I whispered in reverence of this murderous deity. "All dead because of you."

He jerked back at those words, his brow pinching and terror crossing his eyes. "No," he grunted, pushing to his feet and carving a hand over his hair, sending more powder flurrying down around him like a mini snowstorm. "Fuck no...Ava."

He turned his back on me and the name of his dead wife made my stomach knot and pain fill me.

"I like when you play killer with me," I said quickly. "I'm not fragile. I know you won't break me."

He didn't turn back around so I jumped up and hurried in front of him, gazing up at him with all the honesty I had to offer blazing in my eyes. "If you wanted me dead, I'd be dead and buried and chopped into pieces by now. But you don't, and your hand won't slip with me, you're the best at what you do, and I need you to keep teaching me. I need you to treat me roughly, to bend me to my limits. Don't look at me like I'll shatter, because I already did, Hellfire, it's too late for that."

His brow pinched and he wouldn't meet my eye so I punched him in the gut, making him splutter a cough and his hand shot out to fist in my shirt, dragging me close enough to devour all of my air and then some.

"You know what they say about people who play with fire, little psycho. Eventually they get burned. This ain't a game. It's the life I lead. I live and breathe death. I'm a reaper and I harvest souls. Killing is far too easy a thing for me, and there will always be a chance I'll accidentally pierce your flesh and steal away the beats of your heart, d'ya understand that? I don't intend it. In fact, I wanna swear I'll never fuckin' hurt ya, but what if I do? What then?"

"You won't," I said, knowing it down to my roots and beyond.

"But what if I do?" he pushed and I shook my head at him, cupping his cheek.

"You. Will. Not. Hurt. Me. Niall. O'Brien," I said, not blinking a single blink as I told him straight what I believed.

"And what if the world hurts ya and I'm not there to stop it?" he asked beneath his breath. "Or I'm not big enough of a monster to save ya from yer enemies?"

I frowned, trying to think of an enemy that this ferocious creature couldn't take on. I heard koalas could be pretty aggressive. Maybe a pack of those could take him down, especially if they were friends with a few muscly kangaroos. *We'd better stay away from Australia.*

"Train me up good and I'll be strong enough to take on anything," I suggested. "I mean, I guess there are some things I'd struggle with alone. Like if there were twelve men with baseball bats and a couple of tommy guns. Or if there was a T-rex with a taste for human blood, I don't know if I could take him on, Niall. I'd probably try and shove a bomb up his butt, but where would I get the bomb? Do you have a bomb? Do T-rex's even have buttholes?"

"Well now that's a fair question," he said, his mind immediately latching onto that as he took his phone out of his pocket. "Let's find out, shall we?"

He slung his arm around me, drawing me down onto the couch and I snuggled closer to him as he read out what the internet man had to say on the matter. It turned out T-rexes did have buttholes. Big buttholes. And that was just the cherry on my cupcake of a perfect evening.

MATEO

CHAPTER TWELVE

The sound of Brooklyn singing drew me from my fitful sleep and I sighed as I rolled over, my body still not used to the softness of a real bed - much to my disgust. I'd been sleeping fitfully ever since returning to the main part of the house, ending up on the floor more often than I cared to admit just so that I could gain a few hours of sleep without tossing and turning my way through until morning.

I didn't know what I was doing here anymore. I was in some kind of strange situation now where I wasn't a prisoner in the way I had been, where I had much more freedom and hadn't been taken for any more questioning, and yet I was still collared like a dog and controlled whenever the mood took my twisted captor.

Niall made comments about finding my treasure often enough, but he didn't make any attempt to get me talking anymore which made no sense, especially as he claimed to want an escape from his family now more than ever.

Brooklyn's voice travelled closer to my door and I stilled, laying on my back in the centre of my bed with one arm behind my head and the covers tossed aside.

"Ding gone!" Brooklyn called before throwing the door open regardless, dropping her shoulder against the doorframe as it swung wide and cocking her head to one side as she looked in at me.

She was wearing a pleated mini skirt in a blue tartan pattern with a pair of knee-high black socks and a strappy black cami. Just the sight of her was enough to make blood start running towards my dick as I took her in.

"It's early and no one wants to play with me," she huffed, blowing a lock of dark hair out of her eyes before letting it flutter back down to cover them once more.

"And what is it that you want to play?" I asked, pushing myself to sit up as she took a step into the room, knowing I couldn't allow that. If she closed that door behind her then we would be all too alone in here and after a fitful night of reliving the darkness of my past, I didn't trust myself with her.

That was the one thing about this taste of freedom which I resented. With this greater range of movement available to me and so many more opportunities for me to get this sweet creature to myself, I was at much greater risk of seeing the worst in me break free and do something I couldn't come back from.

When Niall had left me alone with her while he'd been trapped in his own darkness, it had been all that I could do to make sure that I didn't touch her at all, keeping my distance and encouraging her to sleep in the rooms which my collar kept me out of just so that I could be certain I wouldn't lose control with her.

But the longer I fought the desire I felt for her, the more potent it seemed to grow. The desire in me becoming akin to a need just in the same way as I needed oxygen, water and food to sustain me, I was beginning to rely on a dose of her far more often than I should have to.

But all of this restraint, all of this watching and waiting was building to a breaking point and I knew that I wouldn't be able to sleep well again until I managed to give the demon in me at least a little of what it needed.

And that need was all for her.

"Hide and seek?" she suggested. "It's raining out, so we could hide in puddles, or behind the raindrops, or down the storm drain, or-"

"Perhaps we should just play in the house, chica loca?" I suggested, the sound of the storm outside battering against my window beyond the curtains.

"Boo," she complained and I closed the distance between us in three long strides, taking her jaw in my grip and making her look at me.

"No petulance," I warned, which only served to make her bottom lip push out and I leaned in, taking it between my teeth and tugging just hard enough to serve her a small taste of pain for her disobedience before releasing it just as fast.

Her eyes widened and she sucked her lip into her mouth, tasting the small hurt and blinking at me in surprise.

"I made a game out of hunting people once," I told her, lowering my voice and shifting closer to her once more, the space between us electrifying as it got smaller. "No one ever survived me finding them before you."

"What do I get if I win?" she asked, tipping her head back to look up at me as I crowded her in, dominating her space.

"You won't win," I assured her.

"So what do I get if I lose?"

I let my gaze travel down the length of her body, licking my lips as I considered that. I'd been holding back with her so much that it felt like its own kind of torture and I was more than ready to alleviate some of that need in my flesh.

"Is Niall awake?" I asked her, making her blink in surprise at the shift in the conversation but she nodded all the same.

"He's doing more research on the judge," she said with a huff. "He says this one is a planner. It's super boring. Oh, and he was watching the news too and going on about his nephew being a right sneaky little motherfucker because of some vaccine thingy."

"A vaccine?" I asked, picking out the relevant part of that story as she shrugged, making it clear she had no interest in that which meant I needed answers on it elsewhere.

"He says I have to have my lessons later because he's doing the boring man things and sometimes, he has to be the boring man even though it makes him want to blow his brains out."

I nodded thoughtfully. In the last few weeks, he had been focused on training Brooklyn as often as he could, wrestling with her and showing her how to fight with various weapons, he'd even tried to get me to join in and though I'd refused to pit myself against her, I had gotten into a few brawls with him which had helped me work through some of the rage inside me. Not that it came close to paying him back for the months of torture I'd endured at his mercy, but at least I could glean some sort of satisfaction from feeling my knuckles crack against his smirking face.

Brooklyn had been having lessons of her own too, phone calls with some prostitute who was teaching her all kinds of tricks to manipulate men and I had to admit that she was getting better and better at implementing those moves, wrapping the three men in this house around her little finger on an ever-tightening leash. Although maybe that wasn't a trick at all. Maybe it was just her.

"Go hide then, mi sol," I said, giving her a little push to get her moving.

"Yes, boss," she teased, turning and running from me and my lips lifted in amusement as I watched her go. If she wanted to play sub with me then I was more than willing to fill the role of dominating her.

I started counting loudly, walking down the corridor in my black sweatpants and giving her plenty of time to find a good hiding place as I moved towards the door to the office where Niall did the majority of his planning. For a man who had gotten so angry at me over trying to plan our attack on the Eden Heights facility, he could be utterly meticulous when he wanted to be. The difference in his approach on the two jobs would have been unbelievable if I hadn't seen first-hand the chaotic way his mind worked. Sometimes I imagined his brain to be like a switchboard with a monkey running amuck, throwing the switches on and off at random and activating different traits and abilities with no motive beyond just wanting to see what would happen.

I knocked the door open, finding Niall at the desk, several pieces of paper which looked like blueprints strewn across it before him and what looked like the CCTV feed from the judge's house playing on his laptop. The TV was on too, the newscaster beaming as scenes of laboratories played behind her and she gushed about the world being saved at last.

"They have a vaccine for the Hades Virus?" I asked when Niall failed to look my way, though I could tell by the way his arm was positioned that he held a weapon pointed at me beneath the desk.

"That they do," he agreed, looking up at me and offering a predatory grin. "And our friend the judge just started sending invites out to his closest and wealthiest friends for a party he's going to host to celebrate them all getting their shots."

"It would be unwise to strike at him while he is in a house full of people," I commented, keeping my face blank. I wanted the blood of the man who had harmed my chica loca to stain my hands with a feral kind of desire which got the demon in me purring and thinking up all kinds of brutal acts, but I didn't want Niall to fuck up her attempt on his life with his wild inclinations.

"Yeah, yeah. Leave the planning to the expert, el burro. Don't you have a game to be playing?" Niall asked as my gaze lingered on the blueprints before him. "Run along, children, Daddy is working."

He shooed me towards the door and I bit back the retort I wanted to give him, focusing on what I would be taking as a prize for winning this game instead. Because Niall had a point. Daddy was home – which meant he was nice and close by in case I lost control of the dark in me and needed to be pulled back out of it again.

"Ready or not, here I come!" I called, heading away from him and striding into the front room where the rain washed against the floor length windows and nothing but silence awaited me.

I moved to stand in the centre of the space, turning slowly as I looked all around me, hunting for any subtle changes in the room which would give her away.

It only took me a moment to spot the small bulge in the curtain and I stalked towards it with my heart pounding, thinking about the prize I planned on claiming from her body as I went.

"Found you," I purred, reaching out to tug the curtain aside, but the moment my fist gripped the fabric, Brooklyn leapt out from behind it, swinging a rolling pin at my head which I barely managed to duck.

She came at me again with a feral snarl escaping her lips, her reflexes so much faster than they used to be after all the training she'd been putting in and the rolling pin crashed against my forearm, making her laugh loudly.

"Can't catch me, I'm the gingerbread clam!" she yelled, twisting away from me and making a move to run.

I swept a leg around in front of her as she took off, taking her out and sending her crashing to the carpet where she rolled fluidly, putting more distance between us and swiping the rolling pin my way as I tried to close in on her before she leapt to her feet once more.

I barked a laugh at the game, her hair tumbling into her eyes as she danced from foot to foot, clearly meaning to run again.

I took a purposeful step towards her and she backed up but I took another and another, forcing her to swing her weapon at me and raising an arm to accept the hit.

The solid thump of the wood striking my forearm sent pain rattling up through my bones but as I surged forward, I managed to grab a fistful of her hair and jerked her to one side, pulling her off balance.

She started to fall and I twisted toward her, catching her hip and flipping her around so that her back was to me and the rolling pin in her hand became less effective against me.

I released my hold on her hair, grabbing her with both hands and shoving her face down over the dining table.

"I win," I growled in her ear as I pressed my chest to her back, keeping her there beneath me and running a hand down her arm until I was pinning the hand with the rolling pin to the table and effectively disarming her too.

"Sometimes I lay in bed and dream about the way your cock felt inside my mouth," she panted beneath me and I stilled as that mental image filled my mind, drawing back just a little and stupidly giving her an opening.

Brooklyn threw her head back with a wild laugh, cracking my fucking nose and making me release her as I placed a hand over my face and cursed, checking for a break.

She rolled over on the table, swinging the rolling pin at me again and I dropped my hand, smiling though the blood which had run down over my lips before swiping it away on the back of my hand.

"Is this you playing hard to get, mi sol?" I asked, stepping into her and taking a strike to the shoulder which would no doubt leave a bruise, though I refused to so much as flinch that time.

"I am hard to get," she replied. "Impossible. No one will ever get me ever again."

"Is that so?"

She swung the rolling pin again, making a move to back away across the table, but I twisted so that she just caught my arm with it once more, catching her knee in my grasp and squeezing the sensitive flesh there.

"Open your legs, chica loca, you can finish trying to kill me after I'm done tasting you," I commanded, making her stop mid swing as her lips popped open and she glanced towards the door.

"You want to do that tongue thing to me again?" she asked, her pupils dilating and I nodded, taking hold of her other knee and shifting her legs apart for her.

"I want so much more than just that, mi sol," I told her, my hands moving up her thighs so that I could push that little skirt up and reveal her panties to me. My gaze fell on her little pink thong and I looked up into her eyes again. "Do you like it when I make you come for me, Brooklyn?" I asked in a low voice, watching the way my words made her breaths get shallow and her chest rise and fall in the most beautifully tempting way.

"Yes, Dead Man," she agreed, reaching out with her free hand to run a finger down the centre of the crucifix which was burned into my flesh. I shivered at the softness of her touch, fighting against the urge to smack her hand aside in favour of sampling this delicious torture.

"You tempt the demon in me like no other ever has," I warned her as all of the things I wished to do to her body ran through my mind, the need to possess her consuming me as I fought to keep myself in check. "And that is a very dangerous thing indeed."

"So why haven't you been touching me then?" she asked, a note of vulnerability in her tone which made me look up into those electric eyes of hers and see the pain I'd been causing with my distance.

"Because my touch is the touch of the Devil," I warned her. "And when the demon in me demands a feed, I end up powerless to stop it. I want you, mi sol. I want to own and devour every last piece of you. I want to feel how tight and wet your pussy is when I fuck you so hard you can't breathe right. I want to wrap my hands around your throat and take control of your breaths while I make you come for me in more ways than you can imagine. I want to do so many, many things to you, but I want to keep you too."

"You think you would hurt me?" she asked, her eyes sparking like the idea of that wasn't such a bad thing and I growled.

"The demon inside me wants nothing but pain and misery. There is no exorcising it. There is no burning it out. I have been to the gates of hell and

218

back at the hands of God, and the women sent to do His work in the mission to rid myself of it, but it won't ever leave me."

"Good," Brooklyn said, leaning in so close that her lips brushed against mine and I paused there, finding myself wanting something which I couldn't remember ever wanting as I inhaled her breath and she inhaled mine in return. "Because I like your demon, Dead Man. And I think he just wants to come out and play a little more often. If you let him, I bet he wouldn't be so bad."

I stilled at that, wondering if she had any idea of what she was suggesting or why I fought so hard to stifle that piece of me.

"That demon brings only bad," I warned her, my lips brushing hers in the mockery of a touch as I spoke and she leaned in more, making sure I felt the words she whispered against my mouth in reply.

"I like the bad."

My heart leapt at that admission, my eyes on hers and the truth there before me clear as day while her fingers continued to trace the burn on my chest in the tight space between our bodies.

I pressed forward without thought, taking something from her which I had never taken from anyone, had never wanted from anyone or needed in any way.

I kissed her.

Brooklyn sucked in a sharp breath as my mouth moved against hers, parting her lips in surprise and giving access for my tongue to press between them, my heart hammering as she moaned softly, the rolling pin clattering to the floor as she dropped it and her eyes fell closed.

I closed mine too, giving myself over to the sweetness of her lips against mine, the energy which burned between us as our mouths met in this most simple of acts and yet nothing about it was simple at all.

My lips began to move against hers, teasing them, tasting them, her tongue dancing across mine and making my pulse rocket as I gave in to this act which I had never indulged in before.

Kissing her felt important. Real. Like taking a vow to the heavens and all the powers that may be at play within this world and the next before promising to make her mine.

The kiss deepened as I leaned into her, our tongues caressing, soft gasps and moans escaping her and my name spilling from her lips in a plea for so much more.

I twisted my fingers into the sides of her panties and tugged, encouraging her to lift her ass as I lingered in the taste of her mouth and let the demon in me pledge its allegiance to her and her alone.

I still wasn't sure I trusted it or even myself with her, but as her body pressed to mine and I pushed her down beneath me, laying her out on the table like my own personal feast, I knew that I could give her what she needed.

I dragged her panties over her knees, letting them fall to her ankles where she obediently kicked them off.

I indulged in her kiss a little longer, losing myself in the feeling of her mouth against mine, growling against her lips and devouring her as she met my passion with her own, her thighs widening and hips rolling with need as she writhed beneath me.

I shifted my hand between her thighs, groaning as I found her soaked for me, a whimper of need leaving her as I brushed my fingers against her clit and made her writhe more.

"Please," she panted against my mouth and the request was so sweet that I almost laughed. Nothing about me was sweet. But I could give her what she ached for all the same.

I tore my mouth away from hers, kissing the corner of it before working down the side of her throat, pinning her to the table beneath me as her spine arched and she ground her body against me.

I took hold of her hands as she scored them down my chest, pressing them more firmly to the scars there and groaning in the back of my throat at the feeling of her touching me so freely.

I was tempted to pull her hands from me, pin them to the table or even tie them in place but for every moment that I gave in to what she wanted and allowed her to touch me, I felt like some of the pain of my past was breaking loose of my flesh, peeling away and being cast aside in favour of this pleasure.

I tugged the strap of her cami aside, freeing her breast and taking her pert nipple between my teeth, tugging hard and making her moan loudly before slapping a hand down over her mouth to quiet the noise.

"Not yet, chica loca," I warned, looking over my shoulder towards the door, making sure that Niall hadn't heard her. "He'll ruin our fun if he hears you too soon."

She nodded obediently, pushing my hand from her lips and forcing me back so that she could sit up before me.

"Are you good at being quiet, Dead Man?" she asked, reaching out to touch my scar again and causing a shiver to dance across the entirety of my flesh.

"The best," I promised her and she smiled wickedly.

"Good. Because I wasn't lying before I hit you with the rolling pin."

I frowned at her in question but she leaned in and placed another kiss to my lips before I could speak again, stealing my breath with the boldness of her actions and making it more than clear that she knew exactly what she wanted and wasn't afraid to take it.

She mirrored what I had done to her, shifting her mouth to my jaw and running it down my neck, causing a riot to break out in my chest as she continued to move lower, drawing closer to the burn which marked me out for the hell bound creature I was.

I caught her hair in my fist and made her look up at me, halting her progress as she made it to my clavicle, my chest tightening at the thought of her continuing.

"No one has touched me there without intending to harm me, mi sol," I warned her, unsure if I was telling her to stop or not.

"Tell me what you did to the women who hurt you, Dead Man," she whispered. "Tell me all about it while I give you new memories to steal away the bad."

I frowned at her but as she tugged against my hold on her, I relented, releasing her hair and shifting my hands to her sides instead.

"There were shutters on the windows of the convent where they lived," I said slowly, remembering the darkness of that night and letting my eyes fall closed as Brooklyn moved her mouth to my neck once more. "They used to close them when I was in there. Hide the light from my eyes and keep me in the dark while they taught me their lessons and worked to force the demon from within me."

She made a soft sound of sympathy before moving her mouth lower, a kiss landing against the top of the crucifix which was burned into the centre of my chest and I stiffened at the contact, my fingers biting into her sides. The touch of her lips was sinfully soft, a caress against the reddened, damaged skin which I could feel despite the nerve damage in the area, like the ghost of a kiss and yet so much more than that at once.

She paused there for a moment, giving me the chance to stop her, but when I didn't, she continued, moving her mouth lower and kissing my scar again, a long breath sliding from my lips as she paid it such attention. Her touch was reverent, worshipping, loving, something I had known nothing of throughout my long and torturous life.

I didn't know what I was supposed to do with such affection, but I found myself aching for it, needing it, a dam inside me which had been filled with so much rage and resentment for her gender for so long cracking along one side and slowly allowing this new feeling in.

"I bolted all the shutters closed while they were sleeping," I told her as she moved lower, her fingers skimming the sides of the cross while her mouth continued to move down the central line, unfurling the tension in my muscles and making a quiver start up in the centre of me which felt so fucking real that I was powerless to stop it.

"I crept inside the convent and poured gasoline along every wall," I told her, my voice rough and the memory a mix of triumph and failure all at once because by doing what I'd done, I'd both gotten my revenge and had proven their fears about me true.

"You locked them in and burned them?" she breathed, turning her eyes up to meet mine as I looked down at her, her lips hovering just above the base of the scar right above my navel.

"I meant to let myself burn with them," I told her, remembering the scent of the freshly struck match as I stood in the centre of the church and breathed it in. "I still don't know why I walked away instead."

That was the truth. Every piece of it. I had meant to die in that place with the founders of my nightmares, sick of waking in cold sweats and losing control of myself, sick of lusting after and hating women in equally powerful measures. But somehow, I'd found myself walking away after I'd set the place ablaze, locking the doors and standing outside as I listened to them scream for me.

I hadn't felt anything as I claimed my freedom from those who had caused me so much harm. Nothing at all. And in that moment, I had realised that I couldn't stay there. Couldn't keep on living with nothing to live for, even if I had no idea where I would go or what I would do elsewhere. I'd slipped through the night and stolen from the man who everyone I knew feared far more than the Devil and had taken his riches with me when I ran.

"I know why you walked away, Dead Man," Brooklyn said seriously, slipping from the table and dropping to her knees before me as her fingers hooked in the waistband of my sweatpants and my body filled with more lust than I trusted myself to control. "Because you were meant for me. And you hadn't even met me yet."

I frowned at the simplistic answer to a question which had haunted me endlessly, my lips parting on a refusal which wouldn't come. How could I have been meant for her when I had never even known she existed? Then again, how could I have lived so long when I'd been born with the Devil in me, working for my destruction? My life had never made so much sense to me as it did when I was in the company of this wild, insane girl, so why should I deny that claim when she made it so freely?

Brooklyn made a move to tug my pants down, but I caught her hand despite the throbbing in my cock and the desire which seemed set to destroy me if I didn't give in to it.

"I can't control myself, mi sol," I warned her. "And I don't want your blood on my hands if the demon in me wins."

"Oh," she breathed, her eyes going wide before she knocked my hand aside and dragged my pants the rest of the way down, taking my cock in her hand and making me hiss out a curse as I made a move to catch her and drag her off of me. "I quite like the idea of me all bloody for you, Mateo," she added.

I shook my head, catching her hand and pulling her up again, the heat in my veins making it clear that I would give in to her demands all too easily if she pushed me much further, but I couldn't take that risk. Not with her. Not if she really was intended to be my salvation.

I lifted her up and placed her ass on the edge of the table, pushing her legs wide and dropping to my knees instead.

"When you come for me, I want to hear you calling out my name, mi sol. Let that bastardo in the other room know exactly who makes you feel the way only I can."

She nodded obediently and my mind instantly filled with all the other orders I would love to give her if only I could trust myself to carry out my part in them. But I knew what I was and what I did to pretty little things like her and I refused to be the end of this light of mine.

I took her legs and pulled them over my shoulders, dragging her to the edge of the table and licking the sweet centre of her with one firm stroke.

Brooklyn cried out, trying to snap her legs shut against the suddenness of my touch and only managing to clamp her thighs tight around my head.

"Oh, fuck biscuits," she gasped, her fingers knotting in my hair and I smiled against the sweetness of her pussy before continuing to devour it like a starved man.

Brooklyn ground herself against me as I fucked her with my mouth, and I licked and sucked at her while she moaned and panted so loudly that I knew we had to hurry.

I brought my hand up to help finish her, pushing three fingers deep inside her and loving how tight she felt as I stretched her, rolling my fingers along her g-spot and making her scream as I sucked on her clit.

Her heels drove into my spine and I licked her faster, pumped my fingers harder and she came so fucking beautifully that I almost followed her into her release from nothing other than how turned on I was by seeing her fall apart for me so easily.

She called my name like I'd instructed and I growled into her core as I lapped at her clit, extending her pleasure even as the sound of heavy footfalls approached from behind me and I knew our time was up.

"What the fuck have I told you about laying your damn donkey mouth on my Spider?!" Niall roared, his hand fisting in the back of my shirt as he tore me off of her and threw me to the ground.

I laughed loudly at his fucking insanity because if he seriously thought he could command me away from her, then he really must have been cracked in the head.

"Estas celoso, bastardo?" I taunted right before his booted foot slammed into my side.

"Stop it, Hellfire!" Brooklyn yelled, leaping from the table and landing on his back.

He started spinning around while she clung on tight, whooping and laughing and calling him a bucking bronco.

"Let's go wrestle," she called excitedly and he barked a laugh as if he hadn't just been thinking about dismembering me right there on the front room floor.

I shoved to my feet as he agreed and he turned away from me dismissively, while Brooklyn yelled at him to giddy up and slapped his ass like he was her horse.

I spotted Jack standing there, come to see what the fuss was all about with Brutus at his heels, baring his teeth like he might just attack the guy from behind.

"Come on, Mateo!" Brooklyn called over her shoulder. "Oh hey, AJ!"

They disappeared into the kitchen and I cursed Niall, taking a step to follow just as a wave of electricity slammed through the collar and into my body, knocking me to the floor once more as I twitched and spasmed beneath it, the pain rendering my entire body useless.

"Oh dear, Spider, I think you wore Mateo out," Niall's voice came to me in the distance. "I guess we'll just have to oil up and roll about on the floor without him."

I cursed between my teeth as I fought to regain control of my body and the sound of the door slamming behind them reached me while I was left behind to face my new reality as I lay there on the fucking floor with Jack watching me curiously.

Though as I thought of the way Brooklyn had kissed me and banished some of the dark from my soul, I had to admit, it wasn't all bad anymore.

BROOKLYN

CHAPTER THIRTEEN

I was in my jim-jam-jarmies AKA my snuggliest pyjamas which had two owls perching on my boobs with the words You Are Hootiful arching over them. It was movie night, and it was my turn to pick because last week Jack had chosen Up – although Mateo had been convinced he was just telling Niall to get up seeing as he'd sat himself right on the bag of popcorn I'd been eating. I knew better though. Angry Jack's eyes had shimmered like little rhinestones when he'd seen that house take off into the sky beneath a sea of colourful balloons.

Niall had laughed raucously every time a balloon popped, cheering as he waited for the house to fall out of the sky and smash to pieces, killing everyone inside. He'd been super disappointed about the happy ending, and had shocked Jack and Mateo intermittently for thirty minutes before sending them to bed and playing his stupid coin flip game with me again, making me pick tails even though the damn penny had no tails. He'd been as smug as a bug in a jug though every time it landed on heads and he won, so I'd tolerated his little bullshit game then slipped some drawing pins into his pillow when he took me to bed as revenge. He'd woken up with one stuck right in his temple and we'd both screamed until I'd made Angry Jack pull it out.

"Let's watch…Jaws four," I decided. "I haven't seen any of the other Jaws, but I think it'll be a magical experience to watch them backwards."

"Maybe another night, Spider. I thought we could all have a lovely evening out tonight," Niall said, rising to his feet with a glint in his gaze.

"But I'm in jim-jam-jarmies," I said, looking down at the owls on my tits with a pout.

Then again, I hadn't been out in forever. Especially not out-out. I went out in the yard a lot, and in the pool for my swimsies, but never off the property. There had been whispers though, mostly from Niall, whispers of people forgetting about the hunt for me in the months since my escape and the world getting back to normal now that the vaccination for the Hades Virus was being given out left, right and up the butt. He'd even gone and gotten Jack one after I cried about leaving him vulnerable to the death germs for a whole day and a night.

"Well, you can get back into yer jim-jam-what-the-fucks when we get home," Niall said and that was all it took to have me sold on the idea.

"We can really go out?" I leapt to my feet. "Really, really?"

"Really. You've been a lot less disappointing in yer training lately," he said, his eyes still glimmering and my chest swelled with the half compliment. "So let's go and get ready for some killin', Spider. You can put yer new skills to the test." Niall grabbed my arm and guided me towards the stairs while the others finished eating the pizza my wild Irishman had ordered in for us. I'd eaten mine so fast I was pretty sure I could still feel an unchewed olive floating around in my throat. *Oh no, what if a mouse sniffs that olive out and tries to crawl down my throat while I'm sleeping later? Then what if the mouse gets stuck too and a hawk swoops down to grab it and claws my whole face up?*

"You two play nice while we're upstairs." Niall winked at Mateo and Jack before dragging me up to the landing, but he didn't need to be so pullsy, I was more than happy to get ready for a night of killing. That was my favourite thing in the universe, and I was so, so bored of being cooped up in this house all the time. I needed to stretch my wings, fly like a pelican on the hunt for mean fishes and scoop them all up in my big pelican mouth.

I squealed as I ran away from Niall, shoving into his room and throwing the closet door open where a bunch of my clothes were. I rifled through them, picking out a spangly blue leotard, some fishnet tights that had little diamantes woven into them, some skull crushing white heels which had graffiti painted up the sides of them and a little pink fluffy jacket to keep the chill at bay. I put it all on then tied my hair up in a tight bun and pulled a lilac wig on then snagged a tiara out and put it on, admiring myself in the mirror. Was the tiara a little much? Nah, a tiara was never too much.

Niall stepped out of the en suite, his body completely naked as he rubbed a towel over his cock, casually drying it while a furnace was switched on in my cheeks, the heat turned up high enough to melt the ice caps.

His eyes roamed over me and he slicked his tongue over his lips for a second before muscling his way into the closet and dropping the towel. My gaze was drawn to his ass like it was a magnet, its pull a force stronger than any other I'd experienced on this earth. He had tattoos all over it and my gaze snagged on a string of broken hearts curving around the underside of his left cheek, then hooked on a centaur on his other one.

He pulled on a pair of black swim shorts then dressed in jeans and a long-sleeved black shirt, grabbing a couple of balaclavas and turning to me.

"Go downstairs, Spider. Tell the others we'll be leaving in five minutes," he said, breaking a laugh to himself like he knew something I didn't, but I was too excited about our field trip to question it.

I spun away and ran downstairs, doing a twirl for Jack and Mateo as I entered the room.

"What do you think?"

"Me pones tan duro, quiero matar a todos los demás hombres en este mundo, así que soy el único que queda en la tierra para complacerte." Mateo purred in his sultry language. I knew exactly what that meant. That I looked like a popsicle he wanted to give a lick and I wouldn't have minded that at all.

"Good," Jack said, but in a way that had my whole body humming. The two of them were staring at me like they wanted to devour me, and I didn't think I'd mind that at all. They could cut me up and eat me piece by piece while I watched the whole show as they licked their lips between bites.

Jack moved to get up, then slumped back in his seat, running a palm down his face as confusion crossed his features. Mateo glanced at him then stepped toward me, stumbling a little and catching hold of the back of a chair to steady himself.

"Are you okay?" I asked in surprise.

Jack tried to rise again, his face fixed in determination, but instead he fell forward onto the floor, knocking the coffee table flying.

"Angry," I gasped, moving toward him but Niall's arm suddenly came down on my shoulders and he locked me tight to his side.

Mateo's upper lip peeled back as he lurched towards us, stumbling again and his knees hit the floor as he went down.

"Dead Man." I tried to go to him, alarm rattling my heart, but Niall held me tight.

"Oh dear, you look a little sleepy there, el burro," Niall said sympathetically as Jack tried to crawl his way towards us, knocking into Brutus as he went and making the dog snarl ferociously.

Mateo tried to make it to me too, but instead melted onto the floor with a groan, his fingers flexing and his shoulders bunching.

"Aw, would ya look at that," Niall said lightly. "They're having a nice little nap, ain't that sweet, Spider?" He pulled me forward, stepping over Mateo and dragging me past him as Jack made it further, battling on while Brutus snapped at his heels. Niall kicked him over, sending him sprawling into Mateo, his crotch lining up perfectly with Mateo's face.

"Hijo de puta," Mateo spat, but his voice was muffled by Jack's jeans as Jack tried to get up and only managed to squash his crotch harder against Mateo's face.

"What's wrong with them?" I asked in a panic.

"They're sleepy, lass," Niall said lightly. "It might have somethin' to do with the paralytics I gave 'em in their dinner, but it might not."

"*Niall*," I scolded as he dragged me out the door and I glanced back as Brutus got up, padding over to the guys on the floor with his teeth bared and a growl in his throat. Well, at least he'd be here to look after them.

Niall snapped the door shut, locking it tight and I realised he had a bag tucked under his arm as he led me to his BMW.

He opened the passenger door for me like a real gent and I gave him a curtsy, too enthralled with the idea of going on the hunt to worry too much about the other guys. Sure, I'd miss them. But I'd fill them in on the whole story when I got back, and maybe Niall would let them come play killer next time.

Niall took off down the drive at speed and I snapped my belt into place, getting myself cosy in my heated seat and enjoying the sensation of feeling like I'd peed myself without being wet. Niall played some Eminem while he drove us away into the night and we both sang the words at the top of our lungs – although he kept laughing at me, saying I got the words wrong even when they were definitely right.

We eventually pulled up on a country road where there were no streetlamps and Niall killed the engine, turning to me as he pushed a cigarette between his lips. I instinctively grabbed the lighter from the cup holder, igniting it and holding it up for him. He inhaled deep, the cherry burning bright between us in the dark and making my pulse skip and dance.

He exhaled the smoke from one side of his mouth and it coiled around me like a snake, inviting me closer.

"Can I try?" I asked and he chuckled around the cigarette before plucking it from his lips and sliding it between mine.

"I told ya I don't wanna be responsible for killin' ya, lass. Certainly not like this. If I killed you, it would be a damn poetic thing. Blood spilling, every star in the sky crying out to save ya, but you'd be mine and no force in this world could take you from me in yer final moments. Your life and your death would be mine; I'd take one and hand you the other in the most brutally beautiful way I know how."

Fear and lust blazed inside me and I almost forgot the cigarette perched between my lips as I stared at this man who promised me oblivion so easily. It was tempting to ask to die at his hands. If I hadn't wanted to live so much, I'd have given him that privilege a long time ago.

"Now take a drag, but don't get addicted," he commanded and I did so, drawing the smoke into my lungs as deeply as I could. I coughed hard and the cigarette exploded from my lips, sparks flying everywhere as smoke poured from my mouth and Niall laughed so loudly, I could hear it on the inside of my head.

"Well, that settles that easy enough." He swiped up the cigarette, pushing it back into his mouth and toking on it as I struggled to regain my composure.

"I think I like it," I said through a wheeze, though I was pretty sure what I really liked was the taste of him that had lingered on it. If I was gonna be an addict, it wasn't going to be for some smoky stick. It was going to be for the hot killer man sucking on that smoky stick.

"Alright, now, take off those sparkly clothes and put this on." He unzipped the bag at my feet and took out a black bikini, pushing it into my hands.

I gaped at him in horror. "But there's no sparkles. Or spangles. Or even any jangles!"

"That's the point. Now don't pout, I have somethin' special for ya to wear once we're inside."

I tried to peek in the bag to see it, but he caught me by the throat, shoving me back into my seat. "Don't spoil the surprise," he growled and my heart whizzed around my chest like a wayward snitch trying to evade Harry Potter.

I started stripping and Niall shifted around in his seat, opening his window so the smoke filtered out of it and looking away from me as I said goodbye to each of my pretty items until I was butt naked, pouting at the plain black bikini.

I pulled it on with a sigh, securing it in place before pulling off my wig and tossing it into the footwell, my real hair tumbling down around my shoulders.

"Are ya done huffing and pouting yet?" Niall asked as he turned around and his gaze fell to my little tits which probably looked like grapes in comparison to the melons he was used to on his fiancée.

"What in the fuck is that?" he pointed at the sequins I'd pulled off of my leotard and sprinkled over my cleavage.

"It's pizazz, Niall. God you're so boring," I huffed as he leaned in and brushed them off, taking his time to make sure he got every bit. His large palm was rough against my flesh and my mouth dried up like a desert in a drought as he worked to get rid of every sequin, even when I was pretty sure there weren't any left.

"Right. Well then." Niall cleared his throat, sitting back in his seat and flicking his cigarette butt out the window.

He started pulling his clothes off until he was down to his swim trunks and I took in the ink on his muscular body with heat burning between my thighs. The Devil on his forearm was watching me knowingly, like it could see every dark desire I had for this man that his inky self lived upon.

I shook my head at it in a warning, daring it to tell on me then Niall leaned across me, his arm brushing my leg and the heat of his body sending a dagger of pleasure right to my clit.

He took a black backpack out of the bag then stepped out of the car barefoot as he slung it over his shoulder. "Come on then."

I climbed out over his seat, following him as he shut the door and locked the car, tossing the keys into the bag then leading the way along the dark road where the fog swirled thickly.

The heavy thump of music carried from somewhere up ahead and I glanced up at Niall, waiting for him to tell me the plan, but he said nothing as he turned down another quiet lane and came to a halt beside a wooden fence. He whistled softly as he took a hammer from his bag and used the spiky end to prise a couple of boards off of the fence, making a cheeky hole just for us.

He led the way through the gap and I followed him, my feet sinking into some damp grass as the mist hung about us.

"Perfect night for sneaking," Niall commented as he guided the way through the dark towards a haze of lights in the distance. As we got closer, I realised we were approaching a house and my heart beat harder as I recognised it as the judge's home.

Music blared from inside, a party clearly underway and I frowned as I looked to Niall. "Didn't Mateo say we should come here when there's not a load of people about?"

"Yes he did, Spider," Niall said, looking to me seriously. "And that was a very dull idea indeed, and I don't take stock of those. This here is a challenge, and I like that. Besides, who doesn't love a little murder at a party?"

I grinned at that and Niall caught my hand, towing me off to one side of the house, circling around it until the pool came into view.

Steam plumed up from it and Niall chuckled as he pointed out the open barrier between the indoor and outdoor pool. But there wasn't a sole in the water. It was a way inside without a single thing to stop us.

"See how lucky I am?" Niall muttered. "A damn Leprechaun lives in my soul, I tell ya."

He dragged me up to the pool, moving around like he knew where every blind spot was on this property. And he probably did. He was a professional hitman after all.

He reached into his bag and took out a slim pen knife, stepping behind me, drawing my hair back over my shoulders and winding it up around the knife before sliding it into place, leaving shivers kissing my neck from his touch.

Niall used a little ladder to climb down into the water and I guessed his backpack was waterproof because he didn't seem bothered by it getting wet.

I climbed down next, my teeth sinking into my lip with the anticipation of swimming. I hadn't quite got the hang of the flips and flaps yet, so the deepsy ends of the pool made me a little nervous.

"I got ya, lass." Niall's arms wound around me as I stepped off the ladder and he treaded water to keep us afloat. "Nice and quiet now."

I nodded, kicking my legs to help propel us as we moved through the water, hugging the wall as Niall glanced at a camera pointing out towards the grounds. We were in another blind spot, approaching our prey like reapers come to collect a soul, and I couldn't wait to send it to hell.

We made it into the indoor pool and Niall released me as my toes touched the floor, wading forward towards the ladder that led out into the conservatory, the glass windows climbing up around us.

The scent of chlorine and money filled the air and I followed Niall out onto the white marble floor with little veins of gold running through it, wondering what it would be like to live in a house like this where you could afford fancy things. If I had money, I'd buy a castle and announce myself as a lady. I'd hook speakers up in the grounds that made it sound like a monster prowled through the woods at night, and I'd make all the children of the local town fear that I was a witch who wanted to eat them. I'd even pay a few of them off to tell their friends they'd seen me feasting on the bones of a baby. It would be so much freaking fun.

Niall led the way forward, padding through to a sauna where the heat wafted around us, drying us off as he laid his bag down and unpacked it. He took out a dark pink dress which glittered with rhinestones, the thing full length and like a beautiful ball gown.

He handed it to me and I gaped at him as I looked at the incredible thing, unable to think of a single better outfit to kill in than this.

"Thank you," I breathed as he took out a suit for himself, shrugging at me like it was nothing.

He turned his back on me as he changed and I stripped out of my wet bikini, letting myself air dry for a minute before pulling on the dress, having to go underwear free but not caring as the silken inside of the dress hugged my flesh.

I tried to do up the back, scrambling for the zip, my arms going backways and underways, but I just couldn't do it.

Niall turned to me in his smart black trousers, the black shirt still hanging open to reveal his inked chest. He moved towards me, pushing his fingers into his hair and making me still as he circled me like a vulture and took hold of the zip, drawing it slowly up my spine until the whole bodice hugged my figure.

"Perfect," he said close to my ear, making my breath hitch before he stepped away again, doing up the buttons of his shirt and rolling his sleeves back to reveal his muscular forearms. What was it about forearms that was so sexy? Especially when they were flexing and looking all powerful like that.

He tossed me some high heels and I slid them on, smiling to myself because I'd had a whole lesson on walking in these babies via facetime with Mel and I could seduce a badger from his den with a pair of these bad boys on now, so a man for the killing would be easy peasy. I watched as Niall put on his own shoes and slid a knife into his pocket, picking up the bag and shoving our wet swimwear into it. He tucked it out of sight under a bench and stood upright as I gave him a questioning look.

"Isn't that…evidence?" I asked, going through the top three killer tips he'd given me.

Don't be seen.

Make 'em scream.

Don't leave any evidence behind.

"Yup," he said. "We'll be back for it on our way out."

He offered me his arm with a conspiratorial smile and I took it before he led me out of the sauna and deeper into the house.

The music thrummed through my body, the set of some tacky DJ drumming through the house. The more I saw of the place, the more I disliked it. There was stuff for the sake of stuff. If I was going to buy things, they'd mean something to me. But this stuff was all for show, like the owner cared more about what other people thought of it than he did. And that seemed like such a sad, sad way to live your life.

We finally found the centre of the party, the purple, blue and pink lights swinging about an enormous lounge, all the furniture arranged to the sides of it in nooks and crannies while a dance floor sat beneath a skylight shaped like the sun. The DJ was deep in his feels, his eyes shut, his hand on his headphones as he vibed out to the droning song while a bunch of people danced and swayed to the beat.

I hunted the room for the man we were here for as a waiter sailed by and Niall snatched two glasses of champagne from the tray, handing one to me. I swigged the fizzy bubbles then downed all of it, liking that a lot.

Niall drank his own in one gulp and I pushed my glass into a potted plant along with his, not wanting to hold it anymore. I worked to cover it up with a few leaves, losing my grip on Niall's arm as I became preoccupied with the job, but a seductive, accented voice cut through the air and caught my attention.

"Niall! What in the world are you doing here?"

I swung around, finding a very blonde, very beautiful, very tight-waisted, very lippy woman there. And what was worse, so much fucking worse, was that I knew who she was in an instant, because her tits were pushed up and on display like two perfect cantaloups balanced there on her chest, barely concealed by a tight black dress with a slit between her cleavage that ran all the way down to her navel. Those tits were world class, and they were smirking, belittling every other tit in the room, especially mine. Because they knew, they fucking *knew* what they held over me. Niall. They had my Niall.

"Anastasia," Niall said in surprise, shooting a glance at me before his eyes went firmly back to his fiancée as she reached out and took hold of his arm. The very same arm he'd offered to me not five minutes ago. And he didn't even do anything to take it back. "Fancy seeing you here."

Anastasia's painted red nails dug deeper into Niall's arm. "You must come say hello to my friends. They're dying to meet you."

"Hello," I blurted loudly, needing to be acknowledged, because with her there, it suddenly felt like I didn't exist at all.

Anastasia's eyes flicked to me and I realised my hands were still on the plant leaves I'd folded together to hide our glasses. I let them go, immediately exposing the champagne flutes and Anastasia looked to me with her nose wrinkling. Like I was a rat that had just scurried out of the bushes and dared to look her in the eye, this princess who was worth eighty-five of me and then some.

"Yes? Are you lost?" Anastasia asked curtly. Damn her accent was sexy. It was almost as hot as Mateo's. Gah, fuck her. Fuck her right in the tits.

"No," I said the same moment Niall said, "Yes."

I looked to him in confusion as he waved me away like I was an errant fart blown in from across the room.

"Off ya go, lass. I'll come find ya when I need you." He turned his back on me and it felt like a punch in the face.

I stood there in horror as Anastasia gave me a cruel smile, drawing Niall away from me and giving me a look that told me to stay away.

My heart whined like a kicked puppy and I just stood there with my arms hanging at my sides like two useless lumps of meat. But then my gaze locked on the judge across the room and a vicious smile lifted my lips as I decided to defy Niall. I'd tear out my heart, stomp on it and leave it here on the floor while I went on my own killing spree. This was my kill anyway, not Niall's. And while he was off canoodling with his fiancée, I was going to do what I'd come here for. Because I didn't need him anyway. I was the Bully Butcher. The Pink Pussy. The Peen Piper. And I could do this murder all on my own.

NIALL

CHAPTER FOURTEEN

"Who was that?" Anastasia asked, her narrowed gaze moving towards Brooklyn over her shoulder and I wrapped an arm around her back, tugging her close and forcing her body into the curve of mine to stop her from looking.

I couldn't have that.

I didn't want this woman seeing my little psycho and getting any kinds of ideas about her.

This was the world I'd been working to protect her from, keep her out of and now like a rotting trout in a tornado, my two worlds had gone and collided with one another and it was impossible to ignore, this fishy scent assaulting us all.

My heart was racing as I drew Anastasia further from my girl, not even certain what I was planning to do with her aside from keep Brooklyn as far from the mess of mob politics as I could. This was exactly the kind of shit that had cost Ava her life and I couldn't let it happen again. I wouldn't.

"Just a hooker looking to earn her wages for the night, but she was barking up the wrong tree with me," I replied casually, knowing that there were always call girls at these kinds of parties and that Anastasia would dismiss her easily enough once she thought she was nothing more than pussy for sale.

"I have to say, I'm surprised you showed up. When I suggested you come to this party with me you didn't seem all that interested," she said, her all too suspicious gaze running over my features, though she didn't seem inclined to remove herself from my hold.

I held my tongue on that suggestion, cursing myself for not paying any attention to her when I'd been forced to spend another evening in her company last week at my pa's house. She'd been talking a whole hell of a lot and suggesting all kinds of shit but I had tuned out a good eighty percent of it if not more, indulging in thoughts my little Spider and getting shitfaced on expensive whiskey instead. Though how I had managed to miss this trinket of information boggled my mind because even in my least attentive state, I was sure I would have noticed if she mentioned the host of this party by name considering he was on my kill list. So I had to assume she hadn't.

The cloying floral scent of her perfume was rising up under my nose and reminding me of the flowers which had been heaped on Ava's coffin, but I said nothing of that, focusing on moving her away from Brooklyn and protecting her at all costs.

"How did you even figure out where the party was?" Anastasia pushed. "I didn't give you any details about it."

"You'll find I'm a man who always gets where he wants to be when he wants to be there, glove," I said with a shrug, finding myself heading for the bar and liking the idea of a stiff drink a whole hell of a lot. This was a bitch of a surprise if I did say so myself. But of course, the likes of Anastasia would keep one of the top judges in the state in her pocket, she was probably besties with all kinds of lawmen who could bend rules for her and her conniving little family. And she had been going on about law school and her connections to powerful people as part of her 'marry me and pop your penis in my hoo-ha' pitches the last few times I'd been forced to endure her company.

"I was worried that you might still have been angry with me after our little game the other week," she said, looking up at me and biting her lip in a calculated move designed to get me hard for her. But my cock was about as hard as a cookie in the bottom of a cup of tea when I was in her presence, so there wasn't much chance of that unless she was hoping to slip me another Viagra.

"And there was me thinking that you might have been the one who was angry at me when you saw the mess I made of your bathroom," I replied with a grin because I had jerked off a total of sixteen times during the night I'd spent with a perpetual hard-on while locked in her bathroom, and I had made precisely zero effort to clean up any of the mess I'd made of her shiny tiles, considering she was responsible for drugging me into the act.

Even after that, when the sun had risen and my cock had finally seemed vanquished, I'd ended up rock-solid again the moment I got home and laid my eyes on Brooklyn. I'd had to relieve myself of my desire for her all over again, giving in to it far too deeply as I'd let the fantasies I was having of her grow and grow, using her panties to help get me off and still desiring her just as much when I'd finished as I had when I'd begun.

Though after a night spent lost in fantasies of that beautiful, insane girl, I'd fallen into the dark again. And that was because I knew it was too damn late for me already. She was under my skin and locked in my mind, and there was no removing her.

I'd fought off every physical urge I'd had surrounding her, but I hadn't managed to keep her out of my heart, and now I was in just as much danger from the pain of losing her as I would have been if I just gave in to the temptation of her flesh. But I was still fighting to resist her, working to banish these feelings because I was terrified of them. Terrified of becoming her end and causing what I'd caused in Ava's death simply by being who I was and having the enemies who I was always going to have.

"I'll admit I would have preferred for you to use that energy on me,"

Anastasia purred, tiptoeing up to speak in my ear and causing a shudder to pass down my spine.

I sighed, releasing her as we reached the bar and knowing that I had been the one to cause this problem by giving her an inch of interest there. This woman was thirsty. And power hungry. And all the kinds of empty that made for the most dangerous species. My night of jerking off to thoughts of Brooklyn in this woman's bathroom had led to countless nights spent much the same way, no Viagra necessary and even the feeling of Anastasia's hand on my arm made me want to rip it the fuck off and tell her it already belonged to another. Not that I could do that, obviously. But I did want her to get the fucking message and stop with the pawing.

"Drink?" I offered, not wanting to get into a back and forth with her over the way I would never be sticking my dick into her, and wondering if there was anything that I could do to somehow sabotage this wedding without destroying the union my pa had created with the Russians over it.

"Surprise me," she said, her voice all seductive.

I looked to the fella who was mixing cocktails, catching his eye and drawing him close.

"The lady will have a beer and milk," I said to him, leaning over the bar to be sure he could hear me while Anastasia squealed and waved some more squealers over behind me.

"A beer and...?" the bartender frowned, thinking he'd misheard but she asked for a surprise and no one had made any demands for it to be of the good kind.

"Half a glass of beer and half a glass of milk. Full fat if you've got it, she's lookin' a little bony so no doubt she'll appreciate the calories."

He opened his mouth to protest but I let all humour fall from my face and cut him a look that made my request into a demand.

"And for you?" he asked hastily.

I licked my lips then shook my head. I was already on edge here and this whole plan had clearly gone to shit now my fiancée had shown up. I needed to shake off Anastasia then gather up my little psycho and get the fuck out of here. We'd take out the judge another night. There were too many variables here now and I knew when to cut the cord.

"Nothing for me," I confirmed.

The bartender hurried to pour half a bottle of beer into a tall glass before topping it up with milk and passing it over.

I turned back to Anastasia as she returned to my side after a round of hugging and air kissing with the four equally plastic looking girls she'd gathered and the accompanying gaggle of douchebags who looked effectively inflated with vanity muscles and overly styled hairdos, letting me know they were nothing but a bunch of flashy cunts with little to offer beyond the width of their wallets.

"Here he is," Anastasia cooed, her nails biting into my bicep as she took hold of my arm and squeezed, a little warning there that I was to be on my best behaviour - which in all honesty only made my chaos more inclined to come out to play. "My fiancé." She proceeded to rattle off a whole lot of names which sounded more like car brands or adjectives, and I didn't even bother to look at the correct owner of each one, just giving them a bullshit smile while my eyes scanned the rest of the room and I sought out my Spider.

She couldn't have gotten far and though I didn't want her anywhere near this fiancée of mine or any of the Russians who were sprinkled around the room like a series of ugly statues. I didn't want any of them getting close to my little psycho, and I didn't want her running off half-cocked either.

"Here's your drink, glove. I got your favourite," I said sweetly, holding the glass up to her mouth and damn near forcing her to take a swig unless she wanted to risk a scene.

Anastasia's eyes flashed with disgust and I was pretty sure she gagged a little as I tipped the glass higher, forcing her to drink more.

"That's it," I purred, wrapping an arm around her waist and dropping my mouth to her ear, speaking just for her. "Show me how much you enjoy swallowing, glove."

Girl was a pro, I had to give her that and she deep throated that fucker like she'd been born to do it, opening her throat and just sinking the whole fucking thing.

I grinned at her as I tossed the glass down on the bar behind her, releasing her just as fast as I'd grabbed her and not bothering to point out the beery, milky moustache she was now sporting as she worked to school her features and hide the look on her face which said she wanted to vomit.

"Thank you, baby," she purred, patting my chest and making me stiffen at the contact. She really was looking to lose that hand at this point.

My gaze caught on a flash of pink fabric and I looked beyond a girl who was honest to shit called Pancake – or maybe it was Patty - to the dancefloor where Brooklyn was currently moving to the music like it was running through her soul.

This wasn't the moves she'd pulled on me in our dance battle all those weeks ago. No. That right there was sex given motion, her hips grinding to the beat, her hands trailing up her body and into her hair, her sultry expression set ever so firmly on a motherfucker who was not me.

Fucking Mel. What the hell had I been thinking letting that woman teach Brooklyn how to seduce a man? This wasn't happening. No fucking way.

I gritted my jaw, watching as the judge, Cedric Rawlings, stalked closer to her, drawn like a moth to a flame as she continued to dance for him, turning her gaze away like she was suddenly shy. He was a preppy looking douchebag, clearly full of himself and all of his fancy things with a hungry look in his eyes. He was good-looking, more good-looking than his photos had let on in fact. And I didn't much like that at all.

I took a step towards the dance floor, but Anastasia yanked me back, a laugh so fake it made my ears want to bleed spilling from her overly painted lips as she leaned up to speak into my ear.

"If you try to make a fool of me in public, I will make you pay for it in ways you cannot imagine," she hissed before backing up and giggling like whatever she'd said had been a sweet nothing set to seduce me.

I gave her a false grin, wondering how the hell I was going to shake her off because as much as I didn't care about her threats or any of that shit, I did care about making a scene here. The pretty motherfucker who was now dancing with my woman across the room from me would be dead within a matter of days and he was the kind of prick who the police would actually make a fuss over. They'd be hunting for his killers with all they had, and I didn't need stories of me and Brooklyn causing a ruckus at his party hanging around the murder investigation if I could help it. She was already being hunted more than enough and I was determined to keep her as safe as I could. The heat may have died down over the search for her and Jack due to the fact that the vaccine was now dominating the headlines, but if she made a second splash the cops would hunt for her in droves.

"This one is just so hungry for dick all the time, isn't she?" I joked, looking to the slimy bastards who I'd found myself in conversation with. "I bet you fellas know all about that?"

Enough of them nodded, grinned, or just looked plain sheepish that it was more than obvious that Anastasia had been doing the rounds and a couple of the girls got salty over that. I picked up on the tension there and smiled wider as two of them made a few thinly veiled, snidey comments which Anastasia worked to brush off.

My gaze fell back to Brooklyn as she turned towards me, her back to the judge and her arse rubbing all over his crotch as she ground against him. He let his wandering hands move over her body in a way which was absolutely begging for me to break every fucking finger in them, and an ugly green gremlin crawled through my chest and bayed for blood.

I gave Brooklyn a firm look, jerking my chin in a command for her to get away from him, but she only shook her head, flipping her hair and mouthing "honey trap," at me, winking like she thought she was a fully-fledged hitwoman and didn't even need my help.

I bared my teeth at her, but she ignored me, turning and tiptoeing up to whisper something in the handsy motherfucker's ear before taking his hand and leading him off of the dance floor in what was clearly a 'let's go somewhere else to fuck' move.

"No," I snapped, making the group of arseholes around me all look my way in surprise.

Their little titter over who my fiancée had been fucking settled down to nothing. But that wouldn't do.

I looked between them, hunting for guilty faces and finding one fella who was all burning up in the cheeks while he looked anywhere but at Anastasia, his arm firmly around another girl's waist. That'd do it.

"You fucked her just this week, didn't you, you dirty dog?" I asked him loudly, barking a laugh and clapping him on the shoulder hard enough to make his knees buckle and almost sending him to his arse.

"You told him that?" the fella gasped in horror, looking to my fiancée, whose mouth had fallen all the way open.

"What? No! How did you even find out about-" She turned to me with that accusation, but the girl who had been with the wandering cock in question shrieked and threw her drink in her face before she could get any further with her enquiries.

I stepped aside, only gaining a couple of splashes from the drink before the cat fight broke out in force. I managed to keep moving out of the way while the carnage got well underway, and I left them all to it.

But that was only half my problem, because as I turned my attention back to the rest of the room, I found Brooklyn and her mark very much gone.

My blood was pumping with a jealous, furious rage at the thought of her seducing that prick, letting him touch her, kiss her, and who knew what else before she got around to killing him.

No. Fuck no.

I wasn't going to allow it.

But that meant I had a mansion to scour and next to no time to do it in.

My heart began to race with a panic that was all too familiar, putting me back ten years to that godawful moment when I realised they'd taken Ava and I had no idea where to even begin looking for her, knowing that every second I delayed was only further adding to her peril.

My ears began to ring as I thought of all the ways that this could go wrong, of what a man like that might do to my little psycho if he got the upper hand, of how I'd been the one to fucking bring her here and now it could all be happening again, just like before. But worse. So much fucking worse, because as much as I knew it made me a cunt to even think it, I knew I couldn't survive losing Brooklyn the way I'd managed to survive the loss of Ava.

My guilt over Ava's death had been all consuming, but the life I'd lost with her had been a pretty lie which some part of me had always known would end eventually. But there were no lies with Brooklyn. Only a truth too big to tell and a bond I'd never even dared to wish for before this moment.

I wouldn't let that motherfucker lay his unworthy hands on her flesh. I couldn't. The rage and jealousy inside me from the mere thought of it would be enough to bring this entire building down on the heads of anyone fool enough to get in my way.

So with that fear and anger driving me on, I took off into the house to begin my hunt, determined to find her before it was too fucking late again.

BROOKLYN

CHAPTER FIFTEEN

The judge clung to my arm as he led me to his bedroom upstairs through what felt like miles of corridors, grinning down at me. He didn't recognise me, and maybe that was to do with the drugs he was on, because his pupils were like two huge, dark seas that wanted to drag me down to Davy Jones' locker. Or maybe I was just nothing to him. The life he'd ruined by believing a lie. I'd mattered so little to him that he hadn't even given my face enough attention to remember it, even after it had been plastered all over the news again following my second escape from Eden Heights. I wasn't sure which it was. But he was going to be getting a reminder soon enough.

Rage was coiled tight in my chest like a cobra ready to spring forth, and it was the most venomous creature in existence since Niall had abandoned me. It wasn't like I didn't get it. I was yesterday's breakfast, munched up beyond repair. Even if you wanted to pick at the juicy looking pieces of tomato left behind on the plate, they'd gone cold and mushy. One little lick and you'd know that. Niall had taken that lick, kissed me until I'd nearly burst into flames all those weeks ago. So now he knew that there was nothing to nibble on left in me, but Anastasia…she had nibbly bits everywhere. She was freshly cooked eggs and the crunchiest hash brown perched on a perfectly fried mushroom. I couldn't compete with her mushroom. Who could?

Cedric drew me through a door and I found myself in a huge bedroom with dark blue walls and the biggest bed I'd ever seen at the back of it. My lips parted, the urge to run over there and jump up and down on it filling me to the brim. But I had to act normal for once in my life, play pretend so I didn't fuck up my one chance at sweet, sweet vengeance.

The seduction classes Mel had given me made me the best at this ever. I was a wily temptress and my prey wasn't going to escape me tonight.

Cedric let go of my hand, unhooking the buttons at the top of his shirt as his gaze ran down me. "You're young," he commented like he liked that.

"And you're old," I replied, though he couldn't be more than forty.

He scowled like I'd lit a match beneath his chin and set his face alight. Oopsie. "Old enough to teach me a lesson or two," I added in a purr, remembering the way Mel had taught me to turn everything into a compliment, and his face softened as he smiled widely. "I like that."

I stroked his muscly arm in the way Mel had told me to and Cedric's anger ebbed away fully as he chuckled. Visually, he wasn't awful to look at, but emotionally, he was painful to exist beside. His face was enough to make me bloodthirsty and it took every ounce of control I had not to try and tear his eyebrows off and rip his throat out with my teeth. But I was a professional killer now, an assassin trained by the best hitman in the state. And though that hitman may have been off galivanting with his fiancée who made me want to scream until the ceiling fell down on her head, I wasn't going to miss my chance for revenge because of *her*.

I walked away, heading to the bed as my fingers winced from touching the man who'd sent me to Eden Heights, the man who'd stolen away any chance of redemption I'd ever had. Even the press had believed my story more than he had. They'd termed me the Bully Butcher, even though pretty faced Cedric had denied I was bullied at all. I guessed it had just been a catchy little headliner for the newspapers, something for the public to lap up and spit out. Murder was just another form of entertainment in this world. Everyone leaned in a little closer, gathering the juicy details, then discarding them when they were no longer of interest. Cedric would be the latest gossip now, and I'd make sure there were plenty of details to splash through the news.

I ached for the blade hidden in my hair, to feel it kiss my skin and whisper promises of death against my flesh. I was going to stab and gut and twist and rip. A storm was brewing in here and the weather forecast was red rain.

I kicked my shoes off and jumped up onto the bed, having a little bounce because I couldn't resist then turning to Cedric as he approached me, moistening his lips as he got closer. He looked like a Chapstick kinda guy, spreading balms and oils on his face to try and keep it youthful for as long as he could. It had clearly worked, but the funny thing was, I was about to steal away all the years he'd shaved off his face and then some.

"I like you," he said, squeezing the bulge in his pants. "You got me really worked up out on that dance floor. What's your name?"

My heart drummed as I moved to the end of the bed, looking down at him and remembering him on that stand in court, casting me away like I was nothing but a brat looking for attention. Like what had happened to me in those woods hadn't mattered to anyone. Not him, not the whole wide world. And maybe he'd been right, maybe girls like me were trash in society, the kind no one wanted to deal with, the toxic type which had to be put in special garbage disposals that no one ever wanted to touch. Had he taken pleasure in it? Seeing a girl who'd been assaulted and stamping his big man boot down to make sure his gender remained firmly on top in this world.

"Brooklyn," I told him the truth, wondering if there might be a flash of recognition in his eyes, a glimmer of a memory, a touch of regret perhaps.

But there was nothing.

I'd always been a nothing to him. But I'd be a something now. The only something that mattered in the end. I was his gory, vicious end and all that anyone would remember about him after this night was how he died at the hands of a girl he'd dismissed, who he'd thought would disappear quietly into the dark never to return. But return I had, Cedric Rawlings.

"Let me see you." He took hold of my hips, his hands sliding up my back in search of my zipper.

I didn't want him getting a look at my body, so I grabbed hold of him and yanked him onto the bed with me instead. He grunted as he fell on me, weighing me down on the mattress, his lips pursed in search of mine. But I gave him my cheek, not wanting to upset poor Glenda who quacked frantically in my chest.

His clean-shaven chin dragged over my skin as he moved his way down to my throat and started sucking on it, one of his hands working to open his shirt and the other bunching in the material of my dress. I'd discussed this with Mel, how to switch my emotions off when I was being pawed at, how to turn my mind away and focus on my goal, but it was harder than I'd imagined now that it was really happening, and I remembered something else she'd said about it being okay if I couldn't. That I shouldn't if I didn't want to. But now I was here and I had to, *had to*, so want didn't come into it anymore. This was for the me of the past, the one who'd been cast aside from society and forgotten. She had the right to be remembered, she had the right to be avenged.

I reached for my hair, taking hold of the knife and tugging on it to try and get it free, but it was all jammed up and twisted in there, not doing what I needed at all and making my heart patter with panic as I wondered what would happen if I couldn't get it free. *Dammit on a doughnut, Niall.*

Cedric made it to my cleavage and my body stiffened as he kissed my tits and a grimace pulled at my face. He wasn't exactly bad looking, but my vagina was half way to the north pole by now, its bags packed and my clit riding its back. The urge to start screaming clogged up my throat as I thought of him touching me more than he had already.

No – wait. I didn't want it to go like this.

This wasn't vengeance, this was me on my back in the woods again, my limbs freezing up as unwanted fingers groped me.

"Stop playing hard to get," Cedric said excitedly as I didn't respond to his touch. "Roll over so I can get this dress off." He rutted against me, his cock making itself known and bile rose in my throat. Why wouldn't my body respond? Brain was getting all caught up in the past and I was fighting to resurface from the quicksand those memories were dragging me into.

Slowly, I came out of it, thinking of Niall's training, of Mel's words in my ears and I began to breathe again. I could see this through. It was going to lead to a merciless death, and that was definitely worthwhile. I gritted my teeth as the movement came back to my limbs and I tugged at the knife in my hair again. But it wouldn't come out dammit.

"Come on, sugar tits," he encouraged in what I was pretty sure was supposed to be a sexy voice.

A droning noise filled my ears and my head whipped around in search of a low flying aircraft, but then I realised it was Cedric groaning into my neck. *Ew with fries on the side.*

"Can you feel how hard you've got me?" he asked gruffly.

"No," I said immediately because my radar wasn't focused on his lone soldier. I just hoped it didn't sneak around back and spring up my butt while I was trying to concentrate. Dicks didn't do that, did they? No, they were there in the front to stay.

"What do you mean, no?" He lifted his head, his hips bucking hard against me and a grimace filled my face as I realised his cock swelled even more. "Why are you looking at me like that?"

I tried to fix my expression, but I couldn't do it fast enough and suddenly I feared the wind had changed and it was now stuck that way forever.

"Get your dress off," he commanded, his cheeks turning red. "Get it off right now." He started pulling at it and I reached for the knife in my hair, yanking hard and finally getting it into my grip. But just as I did, Cedric reared up and flipped me over with a burst of strength, grabbing my zipper and yanking it down the length of my back. I froze, my face pressed to the pillow as I was dragged back into the woods that night where the moon had watched the monsters touch me, and I lost all sense of where I was, who I was.

Back then, I'd been weak and stupid with a head full of fluff, but I'd changed. My insides had been painted black and I'd morphed into someone strong and capable. I was a furious creature in my own right now. I wasn't that girl anymore. I was powerful. All fucking powerful in fact, and I was here for blood.

I threw my elbow back with a shriek, hearing his nose shatter under the impact with a surge of victory burning through my limbs.

I rolled over on the bed, swinging the knife, ready to slash his throat open, but a shadow was behind him and a huge, tattooed arm locked around Cedric's throat, hauling him away from me before my strike could land.

My lips popped open in awe as I watched the Devil at work right before me, Cedric's eyes full of fear as I swear he saw his death coming just as certainly as I did.

Niall threw him onto the floor, stamping on his head before Cedric could let out a single scream and in the next heartbeat, my Hellfire went fully feral. He grabbed hold of Cedric by the throat, yanking him to his feet and throwing him into a large armchair before his massive fist cracked across his skull again then punched him in the throat hard enough to stop his screams from getting out. Cedric jerked in agony, trying to cry out for help, but Niall hit him again and again and again. He was half unconscious as Niall beat him bloody, his face and forearms flecked in red as he pounded mercilessly into Cedric's body.

I stared on in shock as Niall bared his teeth and nothing but a cold-hearted killer peered from his eyes. This was the best hitman in the state, if not the whole country and I was seeing him let loose, every strike of his fist a hammer blow dealing death, but each time, Cedric continued to twitch and stay alive. Knowing Niall, that was his intention, delivering as much pain as possible as he snapped bones and had Cedric spasming in agony beneath him.

When he was nearly gone, Niall gripped his hair, yanking his head around to make him look me in the eye.

"You see her?" Niall snarled in his ear, making sure he did.

Cedric gargled something inaudible as he looked at me through swollen, bloodshot eyes.

"She's the Bully Butcher. Brooklyn Meadows. The girl you sent to damnation when what she needed was protection. Your death is for her." Niall moved behind Cedric in the chair, looking at me as his chest heaved and I held the knife higher, clambering off the bed to finish him, but Niall twisted his neck sharply and a loud crack sounded his demise.

My jaw dropped and my heart fell into the pit of my stomach, rattling around in there like a coin tossed down a drain.

"Niall!" I shrieked as he dropped the corpse to the floor with a sneer of hatred. "He was *my* kill."

"He was on top of ya," Niall snarled in a deathly quiet voice.

"I was about to strike," I hissed, raising the knife in my hand.

I threw it at Niall in a fit of rage but he didn't even flinch as it whistled past his ear, the blade just clipping it and making him bleed.

"He was on top of ya," he repeated, his whole body still tensed as he panted from the exertion of the kill.

"What do you care?" I spat. "You've probably been off somewhere with Anastasia on top of you while you sucked on her giant Milk Duds."

The straps of my dress slipped down my shoulders as I stepped toward him in anger, but I didn't give a fuck about my body being exposed before him in light of my fury. Niall had taken something important from me, and even if it had been hot as hell to watch him kill my enemy, he still hadn't had the right to do it.

"Anastasia," he laughed coldly, moving around the chair suddenly and marching towards me. "I wish I wanted that woman, it would be so much fuckin' easier, you know that? But I don't give a fuck about that bitch and her fake tits. The only girl I care about is you. Even when you piss me off, or drive me to insanity or give my weapons incorrect names, because *you* are the only person in the world who's ever made sense to me. The only one who can answer my ramblings with ramblings of her own, the only one who would give a fuck about things that I give a fuck about. Like the fact that sharks have two penises."

"They do?" I gasped, but he barrelled on.

"You're in my head." He tapped his bloody fingers against his skull. "Like a bullet fired from the most beautiful fuckin' gun, and if I carve you out now, it'll end me. You're a savage, barmy, lunatic and I ain't ever known anyone like ya except myself. And I ain't gonna say sorry for killing that fucker or any other who harmed you, because I'm *your* killer now. And that makes me your protector too. That ain't some cute declaration from a fancy man, it's the promise of a heathen. And there's more to it than that, Spider." He strode towards me and I fell into his shadow, consumed by his darkness, finding there was no other place in the world I wanted to be. "It means you're mine in return. All mine, down to that wicked soul of yours which the Devil laid claim to. I'm claiming it back from him here and now, and when we die and he comes running to steal it from me, I'll beat him bloody just like I did that lawman over there. I'll cut his horns from his head and drive them into his chest, then I'll take his throne and announce myself the king of hell. The Devil has nothing on me now, love, because I own his most coveted soul." He took hold of my throat, smiling at me as a line of blood dripped down his cheek. "And I'm gonna keep ya for the rest of time, Brooklyn."

He yanked me into his body and suddenly his mouth was on mine, the taste of my enemy's blood rolling between us before he pushed his tongue between my lips and stole away everything but the taste of *him*. This violent maniac who was announcing me as his and him as mine. My head spun in a vortex made of hopes and dreams, fear and lust. I kissed him back, my anger dissolving in my chest and giving way to the purest, sweetest candy in the universe.

Niall drove me back towards the bed, his hand tightening on my throat and making me moan as he stole away my air, holding my life in his grip and marking a red handprint on my flesh.

We were in a blood frenzy and the hairs were rising all across my body as electricity darted along my skin. I needed more, but I didn't know how to get it as I tugged on his shirt in a demand I had no words for. I ripped it open when the stubborn little buttons wouldn't give and I pushed it over his powerful shoulders as he shrugged out of it, letting the material fall to the floor and leaving me with his heated chest to explore. I pulled him closer as our kiss deepened and the flavour of all the sins this man had committed danced over my tastebuds, making my core clench tightly.

My dress was still hanging off of me and I let it fall, hating the heavy material and the barrier it was forming between us. Niall's lips broke from me as he looked down at my body and a blush blazed along my cheeks as he took in my nudity. It was all I was, exposed for him and asking a question I couldn't form with my tongue.

Niall released my throat and my blush deepened as he stared at me like I was truly what he wanted. But inside, a little voice was telling me I wasn't enough for him, that my tiny tatas and the broken pieces of my sanity weren't ever going to amount to something which could fulfil the ferocious needs of this man.

"I haven't done this in a long time, Brooklyn," Niall said seriously and

I frowned in surprise.

"Anastasia?"

"No," he confirmed, disgust flitting across his features and making a heated drop of relief soak right into my core. "No one since Ava."

I swallowed the rising lump in my throat as I nodded, shocked by that. "Well, I haven't done this in a long time either. Like a *really* long time. Imagine the longest time you can think of. I haven't actually-"

He kissed me, cutting off the words 'had sex before', his tongue slow and commanding mine to move in ways I didn't even know were possible.

He shoved me down onto the bed and my back hit the mattress a second before his body crushed me into the sheets, the scent of blood still thick in the air as he rested his weight between my thighs and the huge length of his cock ground against my soaking entrance through the material of his pants.

I felt like I was in a burning forest, the trees falling down around us, the crack and snap of branches breaking ringing out everywhere. It was the world ending and beginning at once, and I knew with all my soul that I wanted this. Niall had claimed me and I wanted that to extend to every piece of me.

He dragged his mouth down to my throat, biting and sucking and working me towards absolute madness. I writhed beneath him, unsure what to do with myself or how to ease this tension in my body as I dug my nails into his back and moaned. His mouth dragged down over my collarbone, lower and lower until he took one of my nipples into his mouth, tugging it between his teeth and making my back arch, lightning scoring beneath my flesh left and right.

"More," I begged, not knowing what I needed, only that he was the only one who could deliver it to me.

My head was a fog of murder and lust, and if I didn't get an outlet, I'd be cast into a bottomless chasm, never to be found. But Niall was my anchor right now and between us there was something terribly perfect that I was already afraid of losing. All good things turned to ash, but Niall seemed so sturdy and real in my grasp, I wondered if it was me who'd crumble to dust this time.

Niall reached between us, nudging my legs wider as he unbuckled his pants, our movements becoming faster as he shifted back up to kiss me, shoving his trousers off alongside his socks and shoes until there was nothing left but him and me on the bed alongside the expectation which was building like a storm cloud ready to burst.

I gasped against his mouth as he dragged the pierced head of his cock over my slick entrance, a curse falling from his lips as our eyes locked and he hesitated in this moment of almost which had my entire being shaking with the need for that promise between us to be fulfilled.

My hips bucked and I whimpered for him, knowing I wanted this with every fibre of my worthless being and grateful that no one had ever had this from me before now. Niall was my captor, my saviour, my psycho, and I wanted him to take this from me. I wanted to give it to him.

"You said I'm yours, Hellfire. So have me," I growled, a ring of command in my tone that I liked the sound of.

Right there beneath him, I didn't feel like some small, shattered creature, I was reborn in torment and death. He was the prince of darkness I'd craved my entire life and maybe I could be his princess, even if my crown was crooked and my dress made of thorns.

He released a feral growl, fisting his hands against the pillow above my head and drove his hips forward hard. He entered me halfway, his cock so big that I nearly headbutted him as I lurched upwards and cried out like a fucking wild thing as a burn of pain came with his entrance into me, my pussy growing wetter with what I was almost certain was blood. It felt equally good and terrifying, and as he started working the length of his huge dick deeper inside me, I somehow accommodated every inch of him, shredding his back with my nails as I bit my tongue through the pain.

"I'm the biggest you've had," he stated, knowing it, but oh how little he actually knew. *Biggest, thickest, the one and only, take your pick.* But I didn't say that because my tongue was busy being wedged between my teeth as I tried to get used to the pressure between my thighs. I swear to the moon and back, this was like driving the whole of Thor's hammer right up there, and I liked it. I wanted more, every inch and then some.

"Don't stop," I panted, gripping him so tightly that I was almost certain I was making him bleed just as he was me.

"Almost there, love." He grinned demonically and I panted as I clung to him, sure this man was full of more evil than Big Red was. He was a far better fantasy too, a real one made of flesh and bone. He was here, becoming a part of me like no one ever had before him.

He hooked his hand around the back of my knee and spread me wider for him as he sank every last inch of himself inside me, until I was so full that it was on the brink of unbearable. But I had a freaking amazing toleration for pain, and this was the kind I had no problem trying to adjust to.

"Fuck, you're the best thing I've ever felt," Niall groaned, stilling within me as the burn of him stretching me splintered along my insides and made me unable to breathe. But it was the sweetest kind of pain I'd ever known. I wanted even more of it, I wanted his body delivering mine this bite of agony over and over because it was pain gifted from a killer in the purest form I could imagine.

But he didn't move, he just looked at me with a thousand thoughts going on behind his eyes, the intensity of him electrifying the atmosphere and sending a shiver tracking down my spine.

I hadn't done this before, but I had seen some porn and usually the guy got all still and stuff after he finished his thrusts, so was this…the end?

"Is that it? Is it over? Did you have your happy time?" I asked and he growled in answer, taking hold of my hair and pulling to make me look directly at him.

"That's not even close to *it*." He pulled his hips back, drawing his cock almost all the way out of me then slammed deep into me once more, making me cry out, the intense feeling of him stretching me all at once, sending my mind spinning through a whirlpool. But when he did it again, I realised I was getting wetter, high on him as he held me down and started fucking me in a way I'd dreamed of being fucked for years, and the pain of it was fast giving way to pleasure.

I wrapped my legs around him on instinct, my heels driving into his ass as I worked to match his pace with my own hips, getting it all wrong immediately and moving to a completely off beat rhythm.

"Follow my lead, for Christ's sake," Niall hissed and I nodded as he gripped my hip with one hand and started moving me until I caught on to the dip and the rise, taking over from him and making him groan low as I got it right. It was still kinda sore, but I was enjoying the ride more now.

We finally found a natural rhythm between us, and his fingers locked tighter in my hair as he picked up his pace, the piercing in his cock rolling up my inside walls in a way that made me whimper with pleasure beneath him.

I clung to his inked shoulders as his muscular body dominated mine and I licked a line of the blood drying on his cheek, tasting my enemy's death.

Niall turned his head, biting into my lower lip before speaking into my mouth. "I'm the demise of everyone who has every crossed you, love. Aim me at anyone you wish to see die by my hand, and I won't question it. The answer is yes. Always fucking yes."

He slowed his hips, circling them instead and I gasped as his cock ground against a sensitive spot inside me that made my clit buzz with pleasure. There was still some pain but holy hell in a handbasket, there was such good stuff as well. The stuff Mateo had gifted me with his mouth and fingers, Niall knew how to give to me too. As he continued to fuck me like that, I found myself shuddering and moaning, my nails cutting into the back of his neck while he watched me, bracing his forearms either side of my head as he slowed his hips to a torturously delicious pace.

"Look at me, Spider. Look at the man who'd kill an army of men for you," he demanded and another wave of pleasure rolled through my pussy.

I was losing my mind all over again, an insane girl cracked even further by this hellion who possessed my flesh.

He arched over me, his biceps flexing as he took hold of the headboard with one hand and I licked a line along the ink on his chest as he started fucking me deep and fast, his pelvic bone grinding over my clit in this new position and I ground right back on him, my thighs clamped around him and my hips riding his from below.

Sex with him was honeyed torment. And between the ache and pleasure, I found bliss, my head tipping back and my moans picking up as his body cast mine to ruin. There were swirls and whirls in my head, a whole dream world of candy canes and chocolate dipping fountains bursting to life before my eyes. The Grim Reaper was there, floating along a peppermint brick road, tending to flowers which bloomed with petals made of sugar and cherries. Skeletons were hanging from a tree made of marshmallows, their feet kicking in an eternal jig while a squirrel peeped at me from the Coco Pop branches. *No! Get out of here you peeping motherfucker of a-*

"Hellfire!" I cried out, tumbling into a pit of pleasure so deep I was sure I would never climb out of it. He fucked me all the way through it, slow then fast, weaving more and more of my orgasm into existence and kissing me breathless like he wanted to taste my pleasure for himself.

I trembled all over as he let go of the headboard and dragged his thumb over my lips with a low laugh in his throat, savouring me, this moment, everything. I was wholly his, bound and marked forever by this perfect sin.

A smile lifted his lips in that manic way I loved and he stared at me with his eyes darkening to pitch, his cock so hard inside me that it was all I could think about. "Now it's my turn."

NIALL

CHAPTER SIXTEEN

Brooklyn moaned as I thrust my hips again, the perfect feeling of her tight body sheathing mine making my damn head spin as this insanity took me hostage and refused to let go.

I didn't know what I'd been thinking to get me to this point, but I did know that now that I was here, there was no turning back for me. I was a ruthless creature, one born of the worst of men and built on a foundation of sin, but she'd found a way to burst into my life and send everything I knew scattering for the walls, leaving me to scramble for them wildly in her wake.

She was an obsession unlike anything I'd ever known. The only person I'd ever allowed to truly see every part of me, and I wanted to see every part of her too.

This was it now for me. This was us and I was hers no matter what way she wanted me.

Her fingernails bit into my skin, her heated breath making my skin rise with goosebumps and her electric blue eyes drinking in every piece of me.

"I've thought about this so many times," she panted. "Touched myself while I tried to imagine how it would feel."

My lips pulled into a wicked grin at her words and I moved my mouth down to her neck, licking and biting her flesh as I drove my cock in and out, listening to every moan and whimper that escaped her, learning to play her body with my own and loving how damn responsive she was.

"Am I living up to your fantasies?" I asked her, a hand running down her side and seeking out her nipple so that I could tug on it and feel the delicious squeeze of her pussy around my shaft as she arched her spine and moaned loudly.

"I thought you'd be rougher," she gasped, the words practically a challenge, though she didn't seem to be complaining.

I smiled against her skin before turning my head and sinking my teeth into her neck as I drove my hips forward with a punishing thrust which made her cry out in pleasure and carve more flesh from my shoulders with her fingernails.

I lost myself to that feeling as I drove my cock into her like that again, the piercing in my tip rolling through the centre of her, making my dick throb with the need for release while I fought against the urge to give in to it.

I didn't want this to end. I didn't want this lightness in my chest to pass away again. And I sure as hell didn't want to stop feeling her body against mine, the slickness of our skin brushing together, the wetness of her pussy around my cock, the taste of sweat and the blood of my kill mixing between us every time I pressed my mouth to her flesh.

I groaned with pleasure as I thrust harder, gripping the headboard so tightly my knuckles were blanching and the veins in my arm were bulging. I hooked her leg over my arm once more as I reared back and watched her beneath me, her bright blue eyes wild and sparking with electricity which made my entire body buzz with pleasure.

She shifted beneath me, the movement making her leg ride further up my arm and I pushed her ankle over my shoulder before thrusting in even deeper than before.

Brooklyn cried out, gripping my forearms tightly and making me pause for a moment before she gasped out a needy "more" and I gave her a shark's grin as I fulfilled her request, turning my head to bite the soft skin of her leg as I began to fuck her harder, deeper, faster.

Her pussy was so tight that it was making me dizzy, and I kept kissing and biting that soft skin of her ankle while I watched her writhe and moan beneath me, filling her with every solid pump of my hips and growling my own pleasure against her flesh.

I could feel her tightening around me, her cries getting so loud that I was certain she was balancing on the edge of nirvana right along with me as I drove my cock in hard and deep, the feel of her so perfectly alien to me and yet so beautifully essential too.

I'd been burning up inside while I fought this. I'd been a man on the edge of ruin while trying to keep myself away and failing in every way but this. She had me. All of me now. This final piece the only thing I'd come even close to holding back anyway because she'd long since stolen the rest of me, and I knew there was no reclaiming it now.

Brooklyn's spine arched and her pussy spasmed around me, a deep growl rumbling through my chest as my cock swelled within her and I fell forward, releasing her leg and claiming her lips as I crushed her into the mattress beneath me and the two of us fell apart as one.

A roar of pleasure tumbled from my lips as she called my name and I came deep inside her, riding on the back of her orgasm as my entire body trembled with pleasure.

I thrust my dick in as deep as it would go, wanting to feel every inch of her squeezing me tight as I came inside her, the pleasure of my release and the taste of her lips against mine making me groan as the frantic press of our mouths against each other's shifted into this urgent and unyielding kiss.

Her body was wrapped around mine, ankles locked together behind me, her arms looped around my neck and my weight crushing her beneath me as we continued to rock our hips slowly, riding out the final echoes of our release, neither of us wanting it to end too soon.

My tongue caressed hers and her fingers slid down my spine, teasing, caressing, exploring my flesh and dancing across my scars.

"Are you all mine now, Hellfire?" she breathed as we finally came up for air, my nose brushing up the length of hers as I placed a soft kiss to her brow.

"All yours, Spider," I agreed, not even bothering to overthink that vow because right there in her arms, it was the God's honest truth, and we both knew it.

She smiled at that, her fingertips moving to trace the side of my face as she looked up at me with this strange kind of awe in her eyes which made me feel wholly unworthy of her while simultaneously desperate to become the man she thought she saw.

I wasn't sure how long we stole, lying there like that, our bodies still joined and our gazes locked as our fingertips roamed over each other's limbs, faces, hair, memorising the moment because we both knew it had changed everything now.

But eventually the dark began to creep in on me. Little whispers reminding me of all the reasons I'd had not to do this in the first place. I didn't regret it. But I feared what it meant. The target it would place upon her head if anyone ever found out about her.

"I'll keep you safe," I swore to her and something blazed in her eyes at that promise, reminding me that she'd never had a single person in her life who'd given her that or even really tried to.

"I know," she replied but her faith in me only made that fear grow sharper, reminding me that we were currently in a room with a dead man and that she was a wanted woman. We shouldn't have been lingering here, and if this was my attempt to keep her safe then I was already doing a piss poor job of it.

I leaned down to kiss her once more, the sweet, simple touch of our lips making something inside me brighten like a candle flickering to life on the darkest of nights, battling against the storm which raged within me.

I drew back then, forcing myself to break the spell and pulling out of her despite my cock being close to solid again already, my desire for her only seeming to heighten now that I'd gotten a taste.

As I withdrew, Brooklyn hissed, her fingers moving between her thighs as she closed her legs, her wide eyes turning to me.

"I knew it was too big to fit easily," she accused, her lips curving up but her body still tense as if she was in pain.

"Did I hurt you?" I asked, reaching for her, my hand curling around her hip as I frowned down at her. "Was I too rough?"

"I liked the rough," she replied. "I liked all of it. Apart from the sore bit."

My brow lowered as something twisted in my gut and I curled my hand around her wrist, drawing it out from between her legs and blinking at the blood which coloured her fingers. I looked down at my cock as my brain scrambled to catch up to what I was looking at, the traces of blood which were smeared along my shaft.

"Brooklyn," I said in a low growl, my body falling entirely still as a thought pushed its way into my skull, a low buzzing drone of a thought which I couldn't quiet down and which refused to go away. "Why are you bleeding?"

"I know, right?" she said, shifting so that she was sitting up beside me. "I thought horse riding was supposed to break it. And I used to do so much horse riding that I was certain it would have been done already. I mean…it wasn't actually a horse – it was a bike. And by bike, I mean a trashcan on its side with a precariously balanced bicycle saddle which I got in a trade with Janky Lou after he-"

"For the love of fuck, woman, give me a straight answer. Why are you bleeding?" I growled, shifting towards her but stopping short of touching her, my hand opening and closing with the desire to grab her and a sick kind of horror which was entirely aimed at myself if what I was thinking turned out to be true.

"I think it's normal, isn't it?" she asked. "For virgins to bleed the first time?"

A stillness fell around the room and I just stared at her as my heart raced and thrashed and tumbled its way through my chest and panic clawed its way deep inside me in a way I'd never known before.

A virgin?

She was a fucking virgin? *Was* being the operative fucking word.

How the hell could I have done this? What the fuck had I done?

"Jesus," I breathed, pushing to my feet and backing away from her as I shook my head, my fingers clawing through my hair as I tried to think of a way back from this.

I'd known she was too young for me. I'd fucking known it and I'd said it, but I hadn't thought for one moment that her innocence had run as deep as this.

"What the fuck have I done?"

I turned from her, unable to bear the way she was looking at me as I swiped a hand down my face and shook my head in disbelief and self-loathing. Ava's screams finally came crashing back into my skull as every moment of bliss I'd just stolen in that bed turned to a sour taste on my tongue. I'd known I was a damned man long before this girl had ever come into my life. I'd known it and embraced it and accepted every tainted inch of me, but I'd always thought I had some lines. Some few sacred things I'd never done or ruined, but now I had. I'd ruined her. I'd found her in a cage and I'd gone and bought her like a pet to keep me company. I'd brought her to my home and worked to train her in all the worst things I knew without ever once considering the morality of encouraging that behaviour in her. And now this. *This.*

"Don't do that," Brooklyn said behind me, her voice low and full of hurt. "Don't turn away from me like I'm some mistake you made or some burden to you. Everyone I've ever known has always seen me as one of those things or another, Hellfire, but never you. Never before this."

I spun back to face her, unable to take the hurt in her voice and shaking my head in refusal of it, not allowing her to bring those thoughts and fears into this. "You're not the mistake, love," I growled. "*I* am. I'm the biggest fuckin' mistake you ever had the misfortune of meeting."

"You're not," she replied, her eyes brimming with unshed tears, and I snapped because her denial was only further proof of the ruin I'd brought on her, of the thing I'd created here and the reality of what I'd taken.

I stared at her for several long seconds then turned away and upended the nightstand, hurling it against the wall and letting a roar escape me as the self-hatred I was feeling made my mind thrash. Fear filled me over what I could bring down on her head just by feeling what I did for her.

The heavy thump of the music still pouring up to us from downstairs had likely covered the worst of that noise, and I was more than inclined to keep testing my luck on that in the aim of banishing some of the furious energy which was pulsing through my body.

"I know it was a first for me, but it was a first for you too," Brooklyn breathed behind me just as I took a step towards a chair in the corner of the room, having every intention of destroying that too. "And it was beautiful, Hellfire. It was pain and pleasure and all the things in between just like you and me and I wouldn't take it back. You *can't* take it back, it's done now and there's no undoing it, and I wouldn't let you, even if you could."

I looked over my shoulder at her, my brow dropping further as I saw the pain my reaction was causing her and realising that it was far too late for temper tantrums and pointless regrets now anyway. We were past that point. Long past it. And the bloody stain between her thighs which mixed with the evidence of the pleasure I'd taken in her body said that all too clearly.

She didn't seem all that young when I looked at her now, a fire in her eyes and the mark of a warrior blazing through her. But it didn't change the facts.

"Fuck," I muttered, realising that I was only making this worse. Further ruining something which she never should have wanted me to take in the first place. But there was no refusing what I'd done now. No changing it. And if her words were true then that wasn't what she wanted either. So what could I do to fix it? Because if I didn't do something, I was fairly certain I was going to lose my grip on my sanity entirely.

I strode across the room, grabbing my clothes and tugging them back on while her eyes trailed me and those tears continued to threaten to fall. She'd ripped the buttons from my shirt so it remained hanging open but that didn't matter, nothing mattered now besides fixing this.

I headed into the bathroom which joined onto this room, finding a washcloth and soaking it in warm water before hunting the cupboards for a couple of pain pills.

Brooklyn was still sitting on the bed when I returned and I moved to stand over her, grasping her chin and encouraging her to part her lips so that I could give her the pills.

"Will they make me sleepy?" she asked, her eyes brightening with fear. "I don't like the ones that make my head foggy."

"They're just pain pills, love," I promised. "I don't want you hurting for me over this."

She stared up at me for several long moments then opened her mouth to accept the pills, the trust in that simple action enough to make my racing heart skip a beat as she fought aside her fear of doctors and medication in favour of believing in me.

I wasn't worthy of that. Not even close to worthy. But I was damn well going to do what I could to fix this fucking mess I'd made.

The moment she swallowed them, I released her, encouraging her up onto her knees and gently cleaning her blood and my cum from between her thighs with the washcloth, my skin prickling at the small wince which fluttered across her features as I tended to her, but she didn't try to stop me.

"You're angry," she said, not a question but an observation.

"Fucking furious," I agreed and I wasn't sure if she could tell how hard I was working to contain my rage right now but she didn't push me further on it, allowing me to finish cleaning her in silence before I drew her upright and off of the bed.

Her eyes met mine as I lifted her dress from the floor and helped her back into it, my fingers drawing goosebumps up her spine as I closed the zipper for her and a harsh breath escaping me as my damn cock got all kinds of ideas over that.

I released her quickly, turning to the bed and stripping it, bundling the sheets and the washcloth together and scrunching them in my fist as I glanced around for any further evidence. I wasn't on any databases anyway and my pa had had me burn my fingerprints off when I was fourteen, so I never had to worry much on that front. Brooklyn on the other hand would already be a prime suspect in this crime and she needed a whole lot more training when it came to keeping crime scenes clean.

I retrieved the knife she'd tossed at me from the corner of the room, then lifted my phone and took a few snap shots of Cedric Rawlings' body in case she wanted to have a little trip down memory road later over the sight of it.

I held the phone to my ear as I made a call.

"What?" Ronan asked irritably as he answered me and I pursed my lips at needing a favour from a member of my fucking family, but desperate times and all that shit.

"I need the jet," I said in a low voice, making it clear with my tone that this wasn't a discussion.

"When?"

"Now, dipshit," I snarled. "I'll be at the runway in less than an hour and it had better be fuelled and ready to fly when I arrive."

"Or what?" he taunted.

"Or I'll come to your house, cut off your legs and let ya watch while I roast them on that fancy new barbeque ya keep boasting about – you're not MasterChef, arsehole, no one gives a fuck about your new grill."

Ronan was silent for several seconds before he replied. "It'll be ready. What do you want it for anyway? You need it for a job?"

"Mind your own business," I snapped, hanging up on him and turning to find Brooklyn tugging drawers open to the side of the room.

"I can't find it," she complained.

"Find what?" I asked, wanting to give her whatever the fuck it was even if it was my own fucked up way of trying to offer some kind of reparation for what I'd just so blindly taken from her.

"His little hammer thingy. I thought it would be super handy for Death Club meetings."

"We ain't a club," I muttered, a sneer pulling up my lip as I thought of those two fuckers who were currently enjoying the effects of the paralytic I'd slipped them in my house.

"Fine. The Society of Psychos it is," she said like she was agreeing with me, but she absolutely fucking wasn't. I also didn't have time for this or the capacity available to deal with this bullshit without losing my fucking grip on reality entirely and entering into the kind of massacre which made news headlines.

"We need to go," I barked, harsher than I wanted to be with her and really just angry with myself. I had to fix this. Had to fucking fix it and there was only one way that might come close to being able to do so, but even then, I was pretty certain it wouldn't be enough. Ava was screaming inside my skull and the urge to re-watch that fucking video and remind myself of all the reasons I had to keep away was eating at me.

But it was too late for that. Far too fucking late.

"I'll get you a gavel some other time," I added as her face filled with disappointment and I fought against the worst in me as I worked to try and keep my anger from lashing her with its poisonous barbs. "Come on. We need to go."

I held my hand out for her and she bit her bottom lip before crossing the space between us and taking it, my fingers enveloping hers and some of the tension in my chest loosening just a little.

I was pretty certain that I couldn't make this any better, but I was damn well going to do what I could to try.

We headed out of the room, taking the bundled-up evidence with me and leaving the corpse for some sad Sandra to stumble across later. I led the way down through the house, heading towards the kitchen and keeping us out of sight as party goers stumbled about drunk, whooping and cheering, not having the faintest idea that their host was currently growing cold on the floor upstairs.

After I'd grabbed the bag with my tools and our swimwear in it from the sauna, it didn't take me long to find the fuse box and with a simple flip of a switch I cut the power, plunging us into darkness, shutting off the music and making sure the CCTV was unable to see us as we walked straight out of the front door into the night, leading my little psycho back to my car.

I said nothing to her as I drove us towards the private airfield my family made use of for our jet and she remained silent too, the new truth between us cloying and suffocating.

I really was the worst of humanity and it looked like I was going to be dragging her down with me no matter how hard I'd been trying to stop that from happening.

BROOKLYN

CHAPTER SEVENTEEN

The take-off had been thrilling. I'd watched the lights of the runway disappear beneath us as we climbed up, up, up into the sky, my face squashed to the window as I took in the twinkly world below. When we'd risen above the clouds and the huge moon had appeared to light the entire fluffy world beneath the night sky, I'd stared, slack jawed and enthralled by every drop of silver light that kissed the bed of clouds.

There'd been some new clothes waiting for us onboard and even though they were as boring as a bag of beans, I'd changed into the black leggings and snuggly grey sweater, pulling on the socks and curling up in my seat. Niall was beside me in a big cream seat of his own, not seeming remotely interested in the view beyond the window even when I pointed out a cloud that looked like a giant turnip eating a mushroom.

He was wearing a navy tracksuit and his tattooed fingers were flexing against the arms of the chair as he stared at nothing with a deep frown drawn onto his features, like he was working out the most complicated math problem in the world. I'd never been good at math, numbers were tricksy things, always doing cartwheels around my head whenever I tried to wrangle them, giggling at me as I attempted to put a couple of them together and squish them up to make a bigger number. No, that cultured number stuff wasn't for me. My mind didn't put things together, it tore them apart and created fantasy worlds out of the pieces.

For the longest time, that had been all I'd had as company. In my head, I had friends who liked me, and I could be whoever I liked. A villainous princess or a heartless assassin. No one could tell me who to be inside my mind, no one could hurt me there, or reject me, or make me feel odd. That was what the people on the outside did. The real world looked at me and recoiled, but the people I made up in my head couldn't do that. I'd made them up after all.

Niall had been the first outside world person who'd seen who I was and hadn't flinched away. He'd answered my weirdness with a weirdness of his own, and tonight, I'd thought that was it. All those pretty declarations while he'd had me pinned beneath him, all the burning looks and kisses which I could still feel tingling within my lips. It had been beautiful for a minute there, the best feeling I'd ever found in the outside world with its realness and its rejection.

But now he'd gone all quiet, sitting there like a goose who'd lost its beak and nothing I said or did drew any reaction from him. Regrets were settling deep into his features and it left a pang in my heart as I stole glances at him, knowing I was the reason for them.

"I tried to tell you," I said after a stretch of silence, wondering if he might not regret it so much if I could make him see that I'd wanted him to pop my strawberry. "But then it was happening and I was distracted and I liked it so much I didn't think it mattered anyway. But I didn't mean to not tell you, it was more that I didn't get around to it. Like, I was on my way around the mulberry bush, but then I went wandering off to dick city, you see?"

"Brooklyn," Niall sighed, swiping a palm down his face before looking me directly in the eye. "I never would have had sex with you if I'd known."

Ouch. Glenda died. Quacked her last quack and fell down to the ground with a thump and didn't get up again.

I was nodding and my mouth was open, but no words were coming out. Tears were welling in my eyes and before I knew it, they were spilling over like little rivers. I tried to catch them on my fingers to keep them back. I whipped around to face the window again, the moon so bright and watchful as always. And I didn't find it beautiful anymore, I found it taunting, the craters on its face pulling up into a smirk.

"Sure. Yeah. Of course. Okie dokie. Alrighty-roo. Fo sho. Roger that." I saluted him without looking back, dabbing away my tears as I tried to will my eyes to suck them back in.

"Spider," Niall said heavily, his arm looping around me and even though I resisted, he was too strong and he pulled me right out of my seat into his lap.

I looked up at him with a tightness in my throat, not knowing what to do with the big emotions muscling their way into my chest like two rhinos and an elephant. There wasn't room in there for them, and now Glenda was dead, who was going to look after them?

"It ain't you, love," Niall said, stroking my cheek with his thumb. "I tainted the good in ya. You're a dark creature in ways, but you're so innocent in others. And now I'm the ruin of that innocence and I never wanted that. Never," he said fiercely and I tried to force words past the lump of coal jammed in my throat.

"I'm not innocent, Hellfire," I said, giving him an imploring look. "I know I like to play games and dance and do stupid shit, but I'm an adult. A killer. I hold onto the magic in the world because there's so little of it that's truly there. So I create it for myself instead. I run and play and skip and do whatever the fuck I like because I don't have to do what society expects me to do. I'm free of those binds, unlike every other adult on this planet. I didn't conform. I don't school my features, or tuck my head down when someone looks at me weird. I don't correct my behaviour, I don't try to fit in.

Because fitting in is so very fucking boring. It's a cage that everyone walks so willingly into just so they don't stand out. Teenagers put their dolls down, hide their favourite toys and cringe if their friends ever find them. But why do we have to put the dolls down, Hellfire? Why can't I like glitter and fairies and jumping on trampolines just because society decided I'm not allowed to play anymore? It's crab shit."

Niall's eyes softened as understanding poured from him. Because of course he knew. Me and him were the same.

I barrelled on, knowing I was probably babbling but I needed to let it all out.

"It's not about being a grown up, it's about doing whatever we feel like doing, because why the hell not? Why should we put ourselves in a box, dampen our smiles, hold back the skip in our steps when our feet itch to dance? Why shouldn't our emotions pour out of us whenever the wind changes? If I get mad, I wanna be ragingly fucking mad, and if I'm happy I want to be ragingly fucking happy, Hellfire. I don't want to hold it all in and pretend I'm mature, because no one's really mature. They're all just playing the biggest game of pretend in the history of pretending. And everyone just… goes along with it. They let life grind them down into a ghost of the fun person they used to be, the one who followed their dreams and whims and never gave a shit if some boring Betty told them not to. But eventually, bit by bit, they gave into the pressures of society and one day, poof, the real them disappeared. And maybe eventually they'll look up and realise how much time they wasted pretending to be as dull as everybody else. But not us, Niall. Not you and me. We're free. Everyone can judge us and point and stare, but we won't stop playing because we know the truth."

"And what's that, Spider?" he asked, seeming enraptured by me.

"That nothing matters. None of it. If I walk down the street tomorrow wearing a huge crown, a bright pink ball gown, have my face painted up as a lizard and do a rumba for a mile, people will look and judge and maybe even

284

laugh, they might even go home and tell all their boring little friends about it. But I won't remember them, and not a single thought they think about me will ever affect me. See, we figured out the key to life, didn't we? The second you stop giving a crap, it all slots together. Because in a hundred years we'll all be dead and gone anyway and everything everyone thought was important wasn't. It was all just a veil upon a veil of societal bullshit that suppressed generations of people who kept handing it down to each other time after time, blinding them to the truth. We might be cracked in the head, maybe even as crazy as a bag of coots. But when I die, I'll know I burned every last drop of fuel in my soul and felt that fire blazing each day I drew breath on this earth. I'll know I was real and never held myself in check for the sake of suiting someone else's expectations. So please don't pull away from me because you think I'm innocent. I'm not, Niall. I'm just free."

He frowned, brushing his fingers along my arm, opening his mouth to speak but I kept going, unable to stop now that I was on a roll.

"After what happened when I was younger, I thought I'd never, ever want anyone to touch my naked flesh again. But after a while, I started thinking about it, dreaming up scenarios with the only person who I could imagine touching me like that. And he was the Devil."

Niall released a breath of amusement, but his face soon fell flat again.

"Until I met you and Mateo…"

Niall's eyes darkened at the mention of Mateo's name, but I was baring my truth and it included my Dead Man. And maybe a side of AJ, but I hadn't figured that out yet. "You gave me a home, and a space to be myself unconditionally, as crazy loo as I liked. I've never gotten to be me for so long without making everyone around me run away. Freedom is great, but it's sure lonely. But now it's like…like being me is finally acceptable. And not only that, but I think maybe, possibly, you and Mateo and Jack…"

"What, love?" Niall pushed when I faltered, his thumb moving to my chin and skimming along there in a slow line.

"Like me," I whispered, not daring to say it too loud in case the moon listened and she decided to make it not true.

Niall's jaw flexed and his fingers pushed into my hair, drawing me closer so we were eye to eye. "I don't like ya, Brooklyn," he said gruffly and Glenda twitched on the floor, her little duck feet flapping as she came alive long enough just to die all over again. "I fuckin' adore ya."

Glenda rose to her feet like a duck touched by an angel, a glow surrounding her and a choir singing her name as a happy quack burst from her beak.

"You do?" I breathed, not daring to blink away a single millisecond of this moment as I drank in those words, playing them on repeat in my mind, wanting to make sure I had them perfectly remembered for if I ever ended up back on the streets with nothing and no one for company.

"I do," he answered. "I've met a lot of people in my line of work. And they tend to get real chatty when they're gonna die. They start tellin' me all sortsa things about themselves and I've come to realise I don't relate to a single dot of it. I'm a different species to them, we're speakin' different languages, and that's something I've known my whole life, Spider. It's what makes me a powerful tool for my father to wield, and it's why my siblings hate me down to my roots. Because I'm not one of them. I'm not the same as these other humans who go about feeling for things I have no care for. And I thought I was the only one of my kind until I met you." His hand skimmed down to my throat, his fingers grazing my rampant pulse as he lowered his voice to a whisper. "We look like them outside, but on the inside we're black as tar and full of ideas and desires they can never understand. We're the point one percent. The reason people lock their doors at night and set up cameras on their property. We're the unspoken fear that lives in the shadows of society, because there is nothing more terrifying to them than someone like us creeping in their window at night and playing butcher with them until dawn. Because everyone knows, deep down, once someone like us is in their house, it's already too late. By the time the police arrive you'll already be dead, and we'll have taken our dose of pain from their flesh."

I shivered, bloodlust rising in me at his words and a smile curled his lips as he saw that need in me reflected back at him.

"We aim to hurt before we kill, don't we Spider?" he purred and I nodded breathily.

"Especially when they deserve it," I said.

"Especially then," he agreed and my forehead fell to his as we breathed heavily over the idea of the hunt, the splash of hot blood against our bodies, the screams and that final, euphoric end as their hearts stopped beating.

"Killing's in our blood," he said. "But it's more than that. Killers come in brands just like cereals do. You and me are Coco Pops."

"What's Mateo?" I asked excitedly.

"Lucky Charms," he grinned.

"And Jack?"

"I dunno, what's the dumbest cereal? A Weetabix?"

"He's not dumb," I growled.

"Nothing goes on behind those eyes," he said with a head shake.

I leaned back as I pouted at him and his hand dropped to my outer thigh. "Go back to your seat now, lass."

I frowned at his dismissal, unsure what our chat had resolved, or if it hadn't resolved anything. But before I left, I got the urge to do something a little crazy and as I always followed my crazy urges right to crazy town, I didn't hesitate as I leaned in and pecked him on the lips.

A blush immediately rose in my cheeks as I moved back and he watched me with a riotous look as I dropped into my seat. We stared at each other for several seconds before I broke his gaze and turned to the window, painting mindless pictures on the glass with my finger as the best words I'd ever heard circled in my mind on repeat. *I fuckin' adore ya.*

I didn't know where we were going and I'd forgotten to ask anyway, happy to fly off on an adventure into the beyond, although I wished Mateo, Jack and Brutus could be here for the funsies. I did know that I was with a man who adored me, even if he wished he hadn't taken my virginity. But I couldn't have picked a more perfect way to lose it than tonight, and maybe Niall wouldn't regret it forever. He'd said it was me and him now, and though I'd never had many promises kept to me in my life, I was really, really with cherries on top hoping this one would be.

MATEO

CHAPTER EIGHTEEN

Drool clung to the side of my cheek and I groaned as I finally managed to roll myself onto my back, the effects of the paralytic Niall had dosed me with beginning to wear off at last.

Using Jack's crotch as a pillow for the last who knew how many hours while that rabid beast of a dog sniffed at my face and snarled at my throat like it was damn tempted to try and eat me alive had been among the lowest points of my life.

Thanks to Niall, I had plenty of low points to compare it to though, so I was fairly certain it hadn't taken the top spot.

I stared up at the ceiling and began to count the whirls in the paint, my fingers twitching with the desire to wrap themselves around a cocky Irishman's throat at the first possible convenience.

Jack lay somewhere to my left, though his silence made it hard to be certain of that aside from the odd harsh breath which escaped him, letting me know he was as pissed as me.

Minutes crept by and I counted on and on, trying not to let my mind wander to mi sol and what she might be doing at this very moment. I wanted her to have her revenge. I wanted her to end the man who had stolen her life from her and believed the lies of her tormentors for no other reason than their money and status. But I wanted to be there to see it. To make certain she was safe and kept away from the danger that kind of work required.

I could have made sure the job was done cleanly. I could have made it so that no piece of the bastardo was left to find after she was done seeking out her vengeance on him. But instead, I was left to lay here on the floor and count the fucking paint whirls while imagining all the ways I planned to murder the man who had done this to me.

I was trying really hard not to think about the fact that I was helpless lying here, at the mercy of fate or any cruel creature who might stumble across me. Not least that rabid fucking dog who had been brought into the house which I suspected would one day flip and kill all four of us.

This was a feeling I hadn't often endured in my adult life, but which had been all too familiar to me as a boy.

Even while I'd been locked in Niall's cage or strapped to his torture table, I hadn't felt quite so helpless as this, and it was unlocking memories I'd long since tried to bury in the dark.

There was a repetitive dripping coming from the kitchen, the noise cycling every few seconds and reminding me of the way the nun's footsteps had sounded as they paced towards me across the flagstones as a child.

I fought against the memories which were stirred by that noise, but the longer it continued and the more my eyes burned from staring at the ceiling, the harder they were to keep out.

"Have you been praying, Mateo?" the harsh words cracked against my ears as I knelt before the altar long after the Sunday service had ended and all the other children had headed out to play in the sunshine.

My father was away working so I'd known this was coming. When my mother had dressed me in my Sunday finest her eyes has been narrowed to slits, accusation and hatred caught in the depths of them.

"You still have the Devil in you," she'd hissed as she tugged my collar

hard enough to rock me forward, fighting to straighten it and make me as presentable as possible. Not that it ever made the slightest bit of difference in the end.

"No, Mama," I protested but she'd only tsked, tugging me from the house and to the church in the centre of our little mountainside town.

The other boys gave me a wide berth, in part because they'd already heard the rumours of who my father was and who he worked for, but partly because the lies my mother told about me had been gaining truth.

When she'd first started to insist that I had a demon rooted in my soul and begged the sisters who lived in the monastery of the church to help force it out of me, I hadn't done anything that I knew of to make her believe such things. But in the years that had passed, I'd been forced to endure their lessons week after week, and their accusations had gained some truth.

They accused me of welcoming the darkness into my heart and maybe they were right about that.

Because recently I had been. I had taken to creeping along the streets of our town in the dark when I should have been asleep and sneaking up on people when they least expected me. I'd taken a liking to causing pain as a way of paying the world back for allowing me to endure so much of it.

I hunted the other village children through the streets of our hometown and when I found them, I made them fight me. Always the biggest of them. I didn't care if I lost. Though the longer I played that little game of mine, the less often it happened. I just needed the fight. I needed to feel the swing of my fists and taste blood on my tongue.

The other children feared me because when I fell into a fight, I didn't easily stop. I'd beaten more than a few boys unconscious, broken ribs, fingers, left scars. Yet it wasn't ever enough to sate this anger in me.

The nun came to a halt behind me and my muscles locked up as I waited to see what punishment she might have in mind for me today.

The moments dragged on as she used that indecision to torture me further, never just getting on with it, always wasting time on prayer to a god who supposedly told her all the best ways to save me.

But they weren't trying to save me. There was no salvation to be found in what they were attempting to do to me.

Even if they banished the demon in me, the boy I might have been once had long since fled.

I was nothing but the monster they'd painted me as now, both broken and hollow inside, hungry and yet never sated. They'd created a void in me which couldn't be filled. A need I had never understood and which I had no way of satisfying. It hurt. And it didn't. I was numb to it. And yet eternally lost to it all the same.

"I think today we should take a walk down to the crypts, Mateo," the nun murmured, her voice soft as if that somehow lessened the truth of what she was.

Lucifer had been an angel once. Perhaps the women who had given their lives to God in this place had once been pure too. But whatever had corrupted them had done so thoroughly now, and I was left with the truth of what they'd become.

Her hand wound around my upper arm and her fingernails bit into my skin as she tugged me to my feet, drawing me towards the left of the altar where the stone steps which led down into the crypt awaited me.

A tremble raced through my limbs as we approached it, my feet compliant while my soul rebelled.

I wanted to break free of her grip and run from this place of nightmares. But as I stumbled past the pew at the front of the church, my eyes met with my mother's stare, the accusation in her cold gaze chilling me to the core.

"Be gone, demon," she hissed. "And leave my sweet son in peace when you abandon him at last."

My throat bobbed at her words and I forced myself to walk on. I was craving the untold promise in those words, the way I had been for so long

294

that I couldn't remember a time when it hadn't been so.

If this demon could be torn from my soul, then she wouldn't look at me that way any longer. She would get her child back. I would be the boy she always claimed I should have been without this thing lodged inside me.

So I forced my feet to walk on as the nun led me down the steps and into the dark, and I forced myself not to scream while they worked to rid me of my evil too. Because if I could endure just one more day of this torture, then perhaps I could finally be free of it forever.

"Up," Jack's voice broke the spell of the past which had me trapped and I sucked in a sharp breath as I managed to shake off the waking nightmare and found myself on the floor once more.

I blinked away the lingering memories, sucking in a deep breath and curling my hands into fists as I found myself able to move a little more.

I grunted, rolling myself onto my side and finding Jack there, his long, white hair falling into his face while his forehead pressed to the ground and he managed to get his knees beneath him. Though he seemed stuck in that position now that he'd established it.

I cursed in Spanish as I managed to make it onto my belly and began to push myself across the wooden floor by alternating twists of my hips and shoulders, my legs dragging along uselessly behind me.

"I'm going to kill that motherfucker," I hissed, somehow making it into the front room and groaning with the effort of propelling myself across the carpet.

I could hear Jack following me and the sound of my boot being ripped to shreds came from the corner which Brutus currently occupied. The dog looked over at me as I began to shuffle across the floor towards the closest chair, its lips peeling back and giving me the strongest suspicion that it was hungering for a taste of me.

I needed to get up off of the fucking floor where it had such easy access to my throat.

With a grunt of effort, I began to make my way towards the closest chair which was by the window at the rear end of the room, furthest from the fireplace. There was another chair opposite it, a table set between them with a board game laid out on it which Brooklyn had set up and then forgotten about in favour of eating cheese.

I huffed out a deep breath as I reached the chair, looking up at the deep blue wingback from my position on the floor as it mocked me with its height.

I rolled my shoulders, my abs flexing as I fought to gain further control of my body and with a snarl of effort, I managed to lift an arm and grip the edge of the chair so that I could heave myself up.

It took far longer than I would have liked, but eventually, with no help at all from my fucking legs, I managed to heave myself onto the thing and roll over so that my ass was finally planted in the seat.

I sat there panting from the effort of getting myself into a fucking chair and my brows rose as I found Jack sitting in the chair opposite me, looking equally exhausted by the simple act of getting himself off the damn floor.

He was watching me, his grey eyes alight with something far more intelligent than Brooklyn's claims about him would have suggested based on the treatment she believed he'd undergone in that hospital. I eyed the faint scar which skimmed his temple and narrowed my gaze on it as we silently surveyed each other.

The man was a machine. It looked like he'd done little other than work out while he was locked away in that psych facility and those two things didn't make a whole lot of sense to me. Why would a man who had little brain capacity be so driven to exercise like that? I was built, but even I wasn't close to his bulk. Not to mention his impossible height. The man must have been closer to seven foot tall than six. He was intimidating, that was for sure, or at least he would have been to a lesser man. But I was also getting the sense that there was a lot more to him than he was letting on.

The shirt he wore had been misbuttoned when Brooklyn had fastened it over his broad chest this morning and another button had fallen open while he'd been dragging himself across the floor, revealing the top of a tattoo which marked his skin. A tattoo which looked at least a little familiar to me, though with nothing but a bell on the tip of what looked like a jester's hat on show, it was hard for me to be certain.

"So…" I said, letting the word hang there while that vicious dog of Brooklyn's returned to savaging my boot, its eyes narrowing on us like it wasn't wholly decided on whether or not it wanted the boot more than it wanted to attack.

Jack said nothing, his gaze moving over me slowly, studying, penetrating. He had something going on inside that head of his. Something cunning and altogether too calculating to go unnoticed. At least by me. I was a man well used to facing off against men who desired my death or worse things, and I was damn good at reading people who didn't want to be read.

"Chess," Jack said eventually, his eyes moving from me to the table which sat between us, the chess board all laid out and ready to go. I doubted Brooklyn would mind us stealing her game. Besides, I could do little more than lift my arm at this point, so it seemed like as good a thing as any to use to pass the time while the effects of the drugs wore off.

"Si," I agreed, bobbing my chin at the board and indicating he should go first.

Jack lifted his hand with some difficulty, bringing a white knight into play straight off the bat and making my brow lift as I responded by advancing a pawn.

We continued in silence for a few moves, and I fought the urge to keep looking towards the clock which hung above the fireplace, the side of it a little discoloured from the smoke of the fire which Niall had let burn the corner of the room, but the hands still diligently ticking around.

They'd been gone for too long. It set me on edge and yet there was nothing I could do about it either.

Jack focused on his knights, seeming to be fixed on keeping them from my pieces until suddenly he downed one of my bishops and sent the black piece rolling from the edge of the table to the floor. There wasn't so much as a flicker of reaction from him, but that had been no lucky move. No. There was a lot more to this giant of a man than met the eye.

"I was in a gang once," I said slowly though that wasn't quite the truth. The Castillo Cartel were so much more than a gang. "Though they didn't brand me on the outside."

Jack looked up at me, his grey eyes shifting over my face before he replied. "Lost."

"Mmm." I wasn't buying that bullshit. Nothing in his expression told me he was lost on my train of thought. He knew exactly what I was referring to.

I licked my lips, making my own move and setting up a strike for his queen which I was betting he wouldn't see coming.

"That ink on your chest is no vanity piece," I went on. "It's a stamp of ownership. Which means you're a long way from home, amigo."

"Lost," he replied, meaning in a physical sense this time, and I shrugged.

"Not hard to find a map," I pointed out. "If you didn't want to stay lost, that is."

His eyes flickered with something then and the ghost of a smile shifted around his lips, but that was all he gave me to go on. Sneaky bastardo. I was starting to see through him though.

"I've performed a lobotomy or two in the past," I said as he casually took out my knight with a move that came from nowhere and I found myself down two major pieces already. "Not in a medical setting of course. But my previous employer enjoyed making people watch their loved ones live through all kinds of tortures. Especially when he was in need of information. So I looked into the procedure and did my best at replicating it."

Jack said nothing, but his shoulders had tensed at my words. Not much, but enough.

"That scar on your temple doesn't look much like a lobotomy scar to me," I went on. "So why does Brooklyn insist that that's what it is?"

"Rook," he muttered, like even the mention of her was enough to distract him from all else and I could admit, I felt like that about her too. There was something about that wild creature which drew dangerous men in like moths to a flame, but I had to wonder what would happen when the powder keg she was creating around herself finally blew up.

"You going to give me an answer on the lobotomy?" I pushed. "Because I'd put money on that scar being from an entirely different kind of violence. Like…maybe you were skimmed with a bullet?"

Jack lifted his head, looking directly at me through the curtain of white hair which hung down into his eyes from the way he'd been leaning over the chessboard, and I could see that chasm of rage in him there. He had a whole lot of anger bottled up inside him. But then again, so did I. It was why I still hadn't tried to claim Brooklyn the way I ached to. Why I forced myself to hold back every time she was in reach and my fingers throbbed with the desire to grip her tightly and demand she give herself to me in every dark and twisted way that I could think up.

"A little way from here, by the coast where the sun shines all day and the sea whispers sweet promises to those all around her, there's a gang who boast tattoos like the one on your chest," I said.

For a moment I could have sworn I saw something akin to regret in his eyes before he looked away again, his focus returning to the chessboard as he savagely took down my other bishop and moved his knight into a position that put my king at threat.

I muttered a curse, shifting a pawn into his path, knowing I was sacrificing it by doing so.

"Past," Jack grunted but I wasn't convinced that men like us ever got the luxury of leaving the things we ran from in our past. They haunted us like ghosts with fingernails lodged deep within our souls, refusing to let go no matter how much we wanted a chance at a new life. That said, there weren't many men who took the risk of escaping the kinds of lives we'd been given. Organisations like the one I'd been a part of, and the one Jack had clearly sworn into didn't just let people leave. There was one way out and that was bloody and brutal. Even now I knew that eventually I'd find myself paying for the freedom I'd tried to steal while bleeding out at the feet of a Castillo one day, no matter how much time I managed to escape with in the meantime.

"You have a lot of words for a man who never speaks more than one at a time," I said slowly, wondering what I might be able to glean from this man and what I might be able to use.

Jack said nothing, focusing on the game and only proving my point that he was no victim of a lobotomy. His mind was sharp and his moves full of a cutthroat kind of cunning. It had been a while since I'd played this game, but it was one I'd won regularly when I used to play it. I knew the rules and strategies well and yet he danced his pieces across the board, concentrating on his knights and taking down piece after piece of mine while barely taking a moment to consider his next move.

Granted, he could have spent a lot of time playing this game in the facility he'd so recently escaped from but even so, there was something about him which was very much off to me.

"This place," I said slowly. "This house we are in. It was mine before that Irish bastardo came and stole it from me."

Jack looked up with interest as I reached up to the shock collar which was cinched tight around my throat, trying to find some weakness in the lock that secured it for the hundredth time, but there was none. He touched his own collar, his irritation mirroring mine and a clear demand for me to go on in his expression.

"No one knows about it," I continued. "No one at all. This place is like a scrap of gold dust among a pile of soot. And I plan to take it back from him."

"Rook?" he questioned.

"I plan to take her from him too. She's no more his than this house is."

Jack considered that, his hand drifting to the board almost without care as he lifted his knight and casually moved it to lock me in checkmate, making my jaw grit as I realised I'd lost.

I knocked my king on its side in surrender, trying not to be bitter over the loss as Jack supressed a smirk.

"I'm going to kill him," I went on, banishing the memory of Niall dragging me away from my demons when that woman had attacked me during the Eden Heights massacre, because one small act of mercy did not come close to making up for the endless days and nights he'd locked me up and tortured me in my own basement.

Slowly, Jack nodded, his fingers drifting over the collar once more as he clearly found his own motivation to end Niall's life simply enough.

I watched as he reset the board, wondering if I might have earned myself an ally in my war against Niall O'Brien or not. It seemed, at the very least, that he wasn't opposed to me ending our captor's life. And if he could help me to achieve that goal then who was I to look a gift horse in the mouth?

There was nothing to say I couldn't kill said horse once he was done helping me either. Then all I'd have to do was dispose of two bodies, clean my fucking house, and get back to the life I'd stolen for myself here with mi sol at my side and my freedom restored.

It was such a pretty dream. And I was all for making it come true.

BROOKLYN

CHAPTER NINETEEN

We flew right over a glitzy strip of lights, a street so vibrant it made my eyes nearly pop out of my skull and fall into my lap. There was a pyramid with a beam of light cutting right up into the sky, a shiny Ferris wheel and towering hotels, all of them illuminated in white, pink, blue, green. It was a feast for my eyes and they wanted to eat up every piece. I spotted the Eiffel tower and whipped around in my seat, gasping as I looked to Niall.

"We're in Paris?" I cried.

"Las Vegas, love." He smirked and my heart did a dip and a spin then bounced off somewhere into my gut.

I felt lots of things about that all at once. Las Vegas was the most exciting place in the world. It was a city built on a foundation of sin and I had always, always, always wanted to visit. But on the other hand, this was the city my mom had run off to with her fancy new man Esteban. Yuck.

She'd promised we'd see each other regularly, but I hadn't heard a peep from her since. She'd tossed me away like a mouldy potato which had recently been up a convict's butt and I had never forgiven her for it. She was a flyaway hag, a runaway ho, and I didn't care about her one bit. Because she had abandoned me for Esteban. Fucking *Esteban* of all people. The man who'd eaten the last special box of Coco Pops my dad had brought home with us from our trip to England. A snarling creature awoke in my chest, snapping off pieces of my ribs in a fit of rage over that memory.

The plane bumped as it landed suddenly and I gasped in surprise, looking to Niall.

"You're not taking me to my mom and Esteban, are you?" I blurted. "They won't take me back if that's what you're thinking. They don't want me, Hellfire, and I don't want them. Please don't take me to them. They'll put me in a box and ship me off to Peru. And I don't know anyone in Peru. I can't even speak Perusian – I mean, I'll probably pick it up after a while because I'm really gifted with languages, but I hear there's a lot of llamas in Peru and everyone knows llamas are snobs and hate everyone. Even if I can speak their language perfectly, they won't let me into their llama clan, so I'll be all alone again, and I just want to go home. Let me go home with you." I was struggling with my seatbelt, trying to get it off so that I could run and find a space in the back of the plane where I could hide, but Niall got out of his seat, leaning over me and pressing his hands to my shoulders as he held me down in the chair.

"I'm not taking ya back to them, little psycho. Listen to me, I meant what I said to ya. You're mine. Nothing's gonna change that now, understand? Where you go, I go, and vice versa. So if ya ever end up in Peru somehow, I'll be there too, alright? But it ain't gonna be me who sends ya there."

A lump rose in my throat and bobbed there like a ship on a rocky wave.

"You promise?" I whispered, stilling as I stared up at the powerful man above me making such beautiful declarations that they simply didn't seem real. When we'd had sex, it had been such a wonderful dream to buy into it, but now reality was here and she was a blonde bimbo of a bitch, slapping me around the face repeatedly while her friends watched and laughed.

"I promise, Brooklyn," he said roughly.

I swear every time he used my real name some broken piece inside me fixed back into place. But it wasn't rebuilding the old me, it was a new version which I liked the feel of.

I took a slow breath, letting myself believe that dream again, even while reality's laughter tittered in my ear. Niall unclipped my belt and drew me to my feet, tucking a lock of hair behind my ear and leaning into me.

His mouth came down on mine and a nuclear explosion went off in my belly, incinerating every butterfly in sight and leaving mass destruction in its wake. His touch had such an effect on me that when his mouth parted from mine, I felt like I'd just survived the fallout of that blast he'd set off in me, weathered years in an apocalypse where I'd fought zombies and become the queen of a savage land.

His hand dropped to take mine, his fingers threading between my own and he turned, tugging me after him while I raised my chin and walked beside him. We climbed down a little stairway out of the plane and a warm desert wind caressed my cheeks, the dry air so different to the wet stuff I was used to.

A fancy black car was waiting for us and a man in a suit stood there, nodding to Niall before opening the back door and ushering us inside. We dropped into the back of it while the man got in the car and drove off across the airfield, not saying a single word while Niall released my hand and placed it on my knee instead.

"This is the right thing to do," he murmured to himself and I looked to him for an explanation, but he just turned his head and gazed out the window thoughtfully. "Jesus, would ya look at the size of that palm tree over there?" he gasped. "That's got to be the size of two palm trees sitting one on top of the other."

"At least," I agreed.

We were soon driving along the strip I'd seen from the sky and every building blew my mind as I gazed out at them. There must have been a bazillion light bulbs to make this place so shiny and I stared at the people on the sidewalks either side of us, hunting their eyes for that same light. There was such a mixture of misery and joy rolling through their expressions, I couldn't tell if this place was hell or heaven.

There were girls in bikinis with big feathers pluming from their butts while men gawped at them and their wives pulled on their arms to keep them away. Tourists weaved among the crowd in Las Vegas shirts and hats, people dressed up for their nights out on the town, and people who didn't have any shoes or teeth. It was a clash of rich and poor and everything in between, all of them milling along together, so many people even though it was late at night, everyone looked wide awake and ready to find out what Vegas had to offer them. I could feel the energy in the air, the excitement over the world opening up again in the wake of the Hades Virus. I could feel the promise of money against my palm and the sense of it already slipping from my fingers too. Everyone here was rolling the dice, praying their number came up and I wanted to roll one as well and find out if fate was in my favour tonight.

"Can we go there?" I pointed into a casino. "No – there!" I spotted a man dressed as a shirtless Roman soldier. "Actually, there," I changed my mind as another wonder caught my eye. "No, no, I wanna go in there!" I tapped on the window, pointing to every building we passed, each one begging me to come explore it. When the Eiffel Tower whizzed by, I pouted at Niall, folding my arms. "Where are we going? It better be better than – oh my God, look at those fountains!" I scrambled over Niall's lap, squashing my face to the window to see the huge sprays of water shooting towards the sky, the water lit up in an incredible display as Viva Las Vegas by Elvis Presley played through speakers all around it. "Stop the car, driver man," I begged.

"Don't stop," Niall barked and I looked to him with my biggest eyes, a whimper leaving my throat. Niall pushed me back into my seat, shaking his head at me.

"We've got somewhere to be, Spider," he said firmly and my pout deepened as I huffed. "I'll take ya to see the fountains after."

"After what?" I narrowed my eyes at him.

"It's a surprise."

"What kind of surprise? The kind where a ghoul jumps out at me from behind a bush or the kind where a seagull swoops down and steals my ice cream cone?"

"A less spooky surprise," he clarified.

"Will I like it?" I asked hopefully and he frowned.

"I'm not sure," he said, flexing his fingers against his knee. "Ya might, or ya might not. Either way, it's happening."

"Oh," I breathed, chewing on my lip as I tried to figure out what it could be. A kitten in a boot? A whole bunch of evil guys for me to slice up? A new hat with spangles on it?

It drove me crazy as we headed off of the main strip while Niall took out his phone and started tapping on buttons, frowning in concentration as he filled out what looked like some kind of form. Maybe it was a waiver form for the skydive we were about to do. Yeah, I'd bet it was that. I'd always wanted to jump out of a plane with a parachute on my back, my life in the hands of a wiggly little cord that I needed to try and get hold of and pull in time before I went splat.

We eventually pulled up outside the most boring building I'd ever seen in all my life. And I'd just seen some of the most exciting buildings in the world, so it seemed extra dull.

"What is this?" I huffed as Niall got out of the car and pulled me after him.

He dragged me inside and towed me into a line inside what seemed to be some official government building. It was bor to the ing. And I couldn't see a single fun thing in sight. There were a few couples ahead of us in the queue and one woman was wearing a flouncy white dress and a tiara.

I rounded on Niall, shoving him in the chest. "What is this? You've taken me through the heart of funsville only to divert me to boring town. Why would you do this to me, Hellfire, *why?*"

"We need to register for the fun before we can do the fun," Niall explained and I relaxed, relieved at that.

"Ohhh, that makes sense," I said. "Do they need to measure us before we get on the helicopter? Is that how they fit us for the parachute?"

I looked around for the stairway that must have led up to the roof. I spotted a door where a man in a uniform was standing and I gave him a wink. It was definitely that way. He must have been the pilot, ready to take us for our sky dive.

It wasn't long before we reached the front of the line, mostly because Niall took my hand and towed me to the front of it, arching a brow at the couple who had been due to go next and smiling like a demon when the guy bowed his head and let us go in front of them. That was darn nice of him. We were ushered over to a woman behind a window who looked like a prune and an orange had given birth to her.

"I filled out the form online." Niall pushed his phone under the slot to the woman and she checked it before tapping something on her computer. I got bored as Niall started talking to her about some stuff and I looked around and stared at the drunk couple who were making out at the booth next to ours while the attendant tried to get their attention.

Niall took my hand and I realised there was a form waiting for me as he a slid a pen between my fingers. "Sign here, love."

I did so, making my signature into a big, fancy thing with frills and two big hearts instead of the Os. I drew a little man being stabbed in the chest too, but when I tried to add some blood, Niall pulled it away from me and slid it back under the slot to the woman.

She did a stampy thing and signed it herself then handed it back to Niall and he snatched it, dragging me away out of the building and back into the car.

"Wait – what about the sky dive?" I begged, looking back at the building forlornly.

"We can do one later, Spider," Niall said, folding up the piece of paper and sliding it into his pocket.

He leaned forward, murmuring something to the driver and we took off down the road while I tapped my feet impatiently.

"Where's the surprise, Hellfire?" I demanded. "Where is it?!"

Niall didn't answer, his jaw flexing and making me grow impatient as I threw myself back in my seat with a growl.

"This is the most boring trip I've ever, ever been on," I said, but Niall didn't rise to my baiting.

We returned to the glittery part of the city again, sailing all the way along and I sat up straighter in my seat, hope bouncing through my chest as I spotted an enormous freaking castle ahead of us.

"Just drop us off here, fella," Niall growled.

"We're in the middle of the street, sir," he said in surprise.

"I wanna take her in that way." Niall pointed to an escalator that led up to a walkway which went right over our heads. "Now pull the fuck over."

The man didn't object again, getting over to the side of the wide road.

Niall got out of the car, towing me after him and I grinned widely as he broke into a run. We reached the escalator on the sidewalk, climbing it at speed and knocking people out of our way as we made it to the top where a bridge with glass windows led us towards the castle. But as we ran across it, my gaze turned to a huge hotel across the road with the Statue of Liberty standing at the front of it and an honest to shit red roller coaster winding around the high skyscrapers that made up the hotel.

"Holy tits, batman," I breathed, but Niall didn't let me stay staring at it, he dragged me off of the bridge onto another walkway and I stared up at the castle we were heading towards, the red and blue coned roofs on top of the towers sharpening to points above us.

The ground started moving beneath my feet and I squealed as I realised we were on a flat travelator that headed straight down into the belly of the castle.

"Niall," I squeaked, looking to him with the widest smile on my face. "This place is amazing."

He frowned, running his thumb over the corner of my mouth like he wanted to absorb my joy through his skin and I was pretty sure it worked because his own lips lifted at the corner.

"You're gonna need a dress that's fit for a castle then, eh love?"

I nodded excitedly at that idea as we made it into an enormous lobby where huge crests hung on the walls, suits of armour and the name Excalibur blazing on flags around the place.

Niall led the way on, glancing at some signs I didn't care to look at as we hurried along, passing through an endless casino while I watched people crying out excitedly, or banging their fists on tables in frustration. Winners, losers, I wanted to snatch a stack of chips and find out which one I'd be. But Niall didn't slow, turning me this way and that until we made it to a parade of stores. He led me inside one full of fancy dress clothes that could have passed for the real deal, and I bounded away from him towards a dark green maiden dress fit for a warrior queen. It had full skirts and a bodice which laced up at the back, lace detailing and was all the best kinds of beautiful.

I immediately started pulling my clothes off while the attendant gaped at us and Niall grabbed a fancy knight's outfit beside it, pulling off his own clothes and tugging it over the chainmail and tight pants, making me bite my lip as I lost myself in my very own round table fantasy where I was his Gwendolyn and he stole me from the evil King Arnold. It was a bit snug on his huge frame, but he made it work and after he fastened up the back of my dress, I lurched away to pick up a plastic sword, swinging it left and right.

Niall grabbed a little backpack with the emblem of the hotel on it, shoving our clothes and stuff inside it before heading to the checkout to pay and slinging it over his shoulder.

He slid his arm around my waist when he returned to me, guiding me out of the store and further along into the hotel.

"I'll be back in a second, love, wait here." Niall left me by a suit of armour and I peeked into its visor, trying to see any ghosts that might be lurking in there as my devil man headed away.

He was probably going to have a wee, or a poop. Yeah, maybe a poop. Maybe I should poop too before we skydived. I didn't want to poop on the way down. What if it escaped my panties and started falling along beside me and then when the parachute went up, it hit the top of it and splattered all over me? No, that wouldn't be good. But I didn't need a poop...

Niall squeezed my hand as he returned and I noticed a paper bag in his other hand, frowning at it as he tried to make me move, but I didn't.

"What's in there? A pastry? I could eat a pastry. Is it a pan au raisin? I love a pan au raisin, but sometimes you can mistake a cinnamon swirl for a pain au raisin and it's super disappointing. I don't want a cinnamon swirl, Niall, I really, really want it to be a pain au-"

Niall pressed his fingers to my lips to shut me up.

"Here." He took the surprise out of the bag and dropped down to one knee in the same moment, offering me up a knife. A beautiful fucking knife too. It was the shiniest silver with a spider wrapped around the hilt and a beautiful web engraved into the blade.

"This is a symbol of that promise I made ya, love. Always and forever. Here's the proof of that, and if I ever break it, I want you to drive this knife into my worthless heart in payment, you understand?" His dark green eyes blazed at me, like he needed me to swear that to him, like he'd rather die if he ever failed to keep his word to me. And it left me completely speechless.

I nodded mutely, taking the incredible knife into my hand and turning it left and right as I admired it.

"Here." Niall got back to his feet, opening the backpack in offering and I dropped it inside before leaning in and stealing a kiss from his lips. He had such nice lips, like two lines of blueberries all cuddling together.

He caught the front of my dress in his fist and tugged me closer, deepening the kiss with this hungry kind of need which mirrored my own so perfectly that it stole us away from everyone and everything else and just left us suspended in a bubble of *us*.

Niall broke away first and I nearly stumbled as I tried to figure out how to stand on solid ground without him anchoring me to it again before he started pulling me along once more.

We finally reached the place he was taking me and I stared up at the red sign above the entrance in shock.

The Chapel at Excalibur.

Niall didn't look at me as he drew me through the door and started talking to a man in a suit who seemed to be expecting us.

The scent of I dos and heartfelt vows filled my nose and I breathed it all in as I took in the beautiful room with empty chairs either side of the aisle and a medieval chandelier hanging over the altar.

There were only a certain number of events that happened in chapels, and I tried to narrow down which one was the most likely for me to be attending.

A funeral?

A christening?

A Christmas carol service?

No…those ones didn't line up. They didn't make sense.

My brain was all whirly as I latched onto the one event that it had to be. And as there was a man with a collar and a book at the end of the aisle, I was pretty sure I was either about to see Niall marry that strange man he was talking to, or the only other person in the room.

Me.

NIALL

CHAPTER TWENTY

I blew out a sharp breath, turning to look at Brooklyn where she hesitated in the door to the chapel, her eyes wide with wonder and a dawning understanding as she took in the medieval themed room before letting her gaze settle on me.

I jerked my head at her in what was meant to be a command, but which felt like something of a plea as my heart thundered in my chest and my mouth grew dry.

This was it. The moment where she would either make this choice or turn and run from me.

I wouldn't let her leave. Not really. But if she didn't want this then I would have to figure out another way to give her everything she deserved and more in this world that had done her so fucking dirty up until this point.

Her hands bunched in the huge skirt she was wearing, her posture tightening and her head turning to look behind her, making everything in my body tense as I expected to see her bolting from me. But instead, she just looked back to me, her hand lifting and pointing at herself in question like she expected there to be someone stood behind her who I was addressing.

"There's only you, love," I said in a rough voice, making it clear to her that I wasn't just talking about her standing there, but that I meant it in all things.

Brooklyn hesitated a moment longer, scrunching her skirt tighter in her fists and raising her chin before stepping into the room. She took her sweet time walking up to me, sliding one foot towards the other and humming a bridal march until someone took pity on her and played the real thing through speakers hidden in the corners of the room – which was especially appreciated as I was fairly sure it was The Imperial March from Star Wars she was actually humming.

I watched her as she drew closer to me, this wedding so unlike the one I'd taken part in before in so many ways. For one, we weren't being watched by countless people who I hated. Nor was there a family of innocent, oblivious folk taking up the pews to the left, believing in the lies I'd fed them about what I did for a living and who I really was. The girl who walked towards me wasn't drinking in the sight of a perfectly presented lie.

No.

Brooklyn was looking right at me, darkness, bloodstains and all. And she was still drawing closer with every damn step, her eyes lighting up in a way that made my frantic heart pound. I pushed the dark outa my mind, forcing it to recede and make way for something so much better.

She stopped beside me at last, her teeth sinking into her bottom lip as she looked up at me, this tiny little package of mayhem dressed up like a Tudor princess, looking like she couldn't hurt a fly when she had in fact laid siege to the heart of a heathen and claimed it for her own empire singlehandedly.

"Niall," she whispered, cutting a look to the officiant like she thought he couldn't hear us even though he was barely a few feet away. "Is this because you put your cock inside me?"

The officiant cleared his throat, backing up a step and muttering something about giving us a moment and frowned as I looked down at my little psycho, shaking my head.

"No, love," I replied, stepping closer to her so that I was dominating all of her space and forcing her to focus on me as I prepared to cut myself open for her and let her see me bleed. "What we did tonight, what you gave me, only made this fate more obvious than it should have been from the fucking start."

"What fate?"

"You and me, beautiful," I said roughly. "Two of a kind and all sorts of fucked up." I reached for her cheek, cupping it in my roughened palm and tipping her head up so that she was fixed in my stare and her lips hovered perilously close to mine. "All this time, I've been trying to keep you away from me, working to force some distance between us because I feared the fate you would receive if anyone ever found out about you. I have more enemies than I could even count within other organisations like my pa's, from within my own family, from the friends and loved ones of those I've killed and no doubt many more I haven't even given any thought to. People like the Nelsons who took Ava from me."

"Your one true love," she breathed, her eyes welling with tears for a woman she'd never even met, and my grip tightened on her cheek as I shook my head, hating myself for what I was about to admit, but needing her to hear it more than I needed to keep lying to myself or anybody else.

"No, Spider," I breathed. "Ava was…a beautiful daydream. She was sweet and naive, and she liked the things my dirty money could offer her while turning her gaze from the dirty acts which earned it. I was in love with the idea of her, and with the idea of the man she pretended I was. And she was no doubt in love with that man too. We had something which meant a great deal to me, but it was a lie. That's a lot of the reason for the guilt I feel over causing her death. She turned her eyes away from the truth of who I was and by the time she was forced to face up to the reality of me, it had already come to claim her innocence and destroy it as brutally as possible."

"You said you took my innocence," Brooklyn said with a frown and I nodded, running my thumb across the seam of her sweet lips as I drank her in.

"The very last piece of it, I'll wager," I agreed.

"So what are we doing here? Because I don't want a pity wedding based on nothing but the destruction of my hymen, Hellfire."

"You're supposed to give your virginity to someone who matters, Spider," I said to her firmly, gripping her cheek harder as she tried to look away from me and making her listen.

"You do matter," she breathed, her eyes pricking with tears again and I pressed on, not wanting to be the cause of more pain for her.

"So do you," I growled. "And this is me proving it. You matter more than my fear of what my love might cost you. You matter more than my insecurities about not being enough for you or being a burden on your heart. You matter more than the family who I have been forced to stay loyal to for my entire hellish life and you matter a whole lot more than some fucking Russian woman who I've been told I have to marry."

"I don't underst-"

"When we return home, my obligations won't go away. My pa won't give a fuck about you even if I tell him I love you and I want to burn the fucking world down for you."

"You love me?" she breathed, her eyes going wide like saucers and I leaned in to kiss her, making sure she had no fucking doubt about the truth of that fact as our mouths collided and that molten heat which burned between us exploded through my veins, making me want to dive right into it and never stop burning for her.

I forced myself to pull back, touching my forehead to hers as we both closed our eyes and let ourselves feel this thing we'd been denying for too long.

"I'm yours, Brooklyn," I reminded her. "And no man of yours is going to make you into his mistress while he marries some fake, Russian bitch who his pa chose for him."

"You choose me?" she whispered in a voice so small I barely even heard it, and the disbelief in those simple words cut into me heart and soul because I knew that it was my fault that she doubted that. I shoulda owned this thing between us from the moment I realised what it was and now I'd gone and forced a wedge right through her trust in me which I was going to have to claw back out again with every action I took around her until she didn't doubt me anymore.

"It ain't my choice to make, love," I reminded her, pulling back and making myself release her, needing her to really look at me and see what I was offering before she just blindly accepted it. "If I make you an O'Brien, my pa won't have a choice but to accept it," I told her, so she understood the practicalities of this. "He will be forced to call off the deal with the Russians and accept you as one of his own. That means the O'Brien umbrella of protection will fall over you too. He won't allow anyone to harm a hair on your head no matter how pissed he is over me going behind his back."

"What will he do to you for defying him?" she asked and I forced myself not to wince as I thought of the many cruel and unusual punishments I'd no doubt receive for my insubordination.

"Nothing I wouldn't gladly endure in payment for you, little psycho," I promised her. "Besides, el burro might even cough up the location to his treasure at some point and then we can just fuck all the way off like I'd planned and be done with my family and everything involving them."

"So why don't we just do that anyway?" she asked. "If you only want to make sure you don't have to marry Anastasia and her flouncy tits then-"

"That isn't the reason I want to marry ya," I snarled, making her suck in a sharp breath as she stared up at me, waiting for me to go on so I did. She deserved that much from me after all I'd taken from her. "I want to marry ya because I see everything I am and everything I could ever want to be in you, Spider. You wake me up when the darkness presses in on me and you don't shy away from the bloodiest, most brutal pieces of my being. Yer a mirror to my cracked and splintered soul but you're also something so much purer than I could ever hope to be. You're wild and free and endlessly beautiful because you don't give a single fuck about what anyone in this boring world has to say about what is right and normal and you just do you. You shine so bright that I haven't been able to look away from you for a single second since I first laid eyes on ya. I don't want to look away. And if I can offer you any piece of happiness in this world which is too often filled with bad then I want to do that. I want you smiling and dancing in the rain and barefoot in bloody puddles. I want you crying and raging and all the things in between which make your heart pump faster and your electric eyes spark. I want you gasping my name as I hold you tight in my arms and offer you every broken piece of me to do with as you will, Spider. I just want you. So the question is, do you want me too?"

Brooklyn's lips parted as she stared at me, my words and declarations hanging in the air all around us, waiting to come crashing down on our heads and make the whole world quake with our union if only she agreed to it.

She sank her teeth into her bottom lip again and I was trapped in that moment, unsure what insanity had led me here and never wanting to stop experiencing it either way.

"I do," she said loudly, the words ringing out loud and true and making her mine in all the ways that counted for now and for fucking ever.

Brooklyn ran at me and I lifted her into my arms as I caught her, kissing her hard as she wound her legs around my waist and groaning as she rolled her hips against mine.

"You heard the woman," I barked as she moved her mouth along my jaw and I gripped her arse to hold her in place, looking over her shoulder to the officiant and the witnesses he'd brought to oversee this thing.

"Oh, that was the vows?" he asked in confusion while Brooklyn began to tug at the collar of my la dee da outfit, moving her mouth down my neck and making my cock so fucking hard that I almost groaned out load.

"Yes, it was the fucking vows, what did you think we'd come here for, a fucking natter?" I barked. "She said 'I do', I said 'I do', so-"

"Actually, you didn't say-" he began and I growled angrily.

"I do," I barked. "Now give me the papers so that we can go make this thing official."

The fella looked inclined to protest for a moment but as he caught a good look at the murderous intentions in my eyes he skedaddled fast enough and made quick work of signing the papers, getting the startled looking witnesses to sign too and hurrying over so that Brooklyn and I could add our scribbles to the mix.

I forced him to turn around so that I could use his back to lean on while Brooklyn managed to fully unbutton my shirt, shoving the chainmail aside and started kissing her way down my chest, seemingly oblivious to everything else that was going on as she worked to get me naked right in the middle of the fucking chapel.

I fisted her hair, my chest heaving as I forced her back and barked a command at her to sign. Her eyes went all round as she nodded obediently, scribbling her name on the marriage licence and signing herself over to a life of sin at my side.

I swiped a thumb over the corner of my lips to stop the smirk which tried to lift them as I watched her write her name out then snatched the papers from the officiant and told him to wait to file it officially until tomorrow. We were wanted criminals after all. It wouldn't do for the cops to be alerted to our presence in the city until we were long gone and back home where we belonged.

I turned and strode out of the chapel while Brooklyn turned her attention to kissing her way down my neck again, her hands exploring my chest and abs, fingertips carving the lines of scars from wounds which probably shoulda killed me, but I knew now why I'd survived them. It wasn't so that I could go on suffering endlessly in the wake of what I'd destroyed. It was so that I could be here waiting for her when she came seeking a hellion to help her claim the vengeance she'd been owed and to make sure that life gave her only the good from here on out.

"We should get back to the jet, love," I panted, my cock aching with need as she ground herself against me, not giving a fuck about the people who were all milling about the place and looking our way.

"I need you, Hellfire. We have to make it official. The congregation," she insisted.

"Consummation?" I guessed. "I'm pretty sure we covered that earlier on."

Brooklyn reared back and slapped me so hard that my head wheeled to one side and I tasted blood.

"Is this a real wedding or not, Niall?" she demanded as I glared at her, her eyes full of fury which I was feeling myself after that smack.

"Yes," I snarled.

"Then take me in there and make me yours." She pointed at a door which held a staff only sign on it, her eyes flaring with her demand, and I gave in. I was only fucking human after all.

I crossed the space between us and the door, shoving it open and finding a cleaning closet stacked high with paper towels and bleach and all kinds of handy things before I kicked the door closed behind us again and pushed her up against it.

I kissed her hard, my tongue driving between her lips, making her moan for me and she locked her ankles tight around my waist and rolled her hips again.

"I was gonna do it proper next time," I said as I forced myself to pull back. "A big bed and rose petals and whale music, fancy candles and all that shit. I was gonna be gentle and-"

"I don't want gentle, Hellfire," Brooklyn snapped. "I want you."

I met her gaze for several long seconds, the protests dying on my tongue as I found myself nodding, a breath of laughter falling from me and the last of those flouncy thoughts slipping away like daisies on a breeze.

"Well alright then," I agreed, lifting my hand to the top of the fancy bodice she was wearing and yanking on it hard enough to make something rip and let her tits burst free of the top of it.

I groaned as I dropped my mouth to her nipple, sucking it hard and making her whimper as she rocked her hips against me again.

I dropped her to her feet and got to my knees before her as I started tugging on her skirt, forcing the endless layers of it up between us and hunting for the softness of her flesh beneath. She wasn't wearing any panties and as I finally discovered that, I lost all sense of myself, pushing her thighs apart and burying my face between them as I tasted her arousal and lapped at her core.

Brooklyn moaned loudly, her fist thumping against the door she leaned on while I devoured the sweetness of her and worked to get her ready to take me again. She had to be tender from the first time and no matter how much I wanted to give in and claim her as roughly as she expected, I still needed to make sure that she was taken care of too. I wanted her coming for me in all the ways I'd fantasised about while fighting against the reality of us and I planned on making every single one of those daydreams come true now that I'd finally given in to the inevitability of us.

Brooklyn's hips bucked as she rode my tongue and I fucked her with my mouth while gripping her arse to hold her in place, loving the taste of her and the wetness which coated my lips, proving her desire for me was just as powerful as mine for her.

I drove my tongue into her opening, circling it slowly before licking my way up and over her clit and sucking on it just hard enough to make her explode for me.

Brooklyn came so loudly that I was certain anyone on the other side of that door would know exactly what we were doing in here, but I couldn't summon a single fuck to give on that matter as I got to my feet and freed my cock from my pants.

I lifted the chainmail over my head and dropped it, wanting less obstructions between us and groaning as I crushed her against the door and I got to experience the blissful feeling of her tits pressing to my bare skin.

I lifted her into my arms once more, kissing her hard so that she could taste herself on me and making her moan loudly as my cock pressed between her thighs, moving through the slickness of her arousal as I lined myself up to take her.

I pinned her against the door with my body, drawing back so that I could look into those bright blue eyes as she dug her heels into my arse and whimpered for me, her perfect tits pressing to my chest as the space dividing us disappeared.

I dropped a hand to my pocket, taking the ring I'd gotten her from the same place I'd bought her knife. I slid it onto her finger so that she could see the large, black diamond which now sat there before laying her hand against my chest and taking hold of her arse again.

I drove myself into her slowly, groaning at how perfectly tight she felt wrapped around my shaft and listening to the way she moaned in pleasure at the feeling of me filling her.

When I was fully sheathed inside her, she fisted her hands in my hair and drew my mouth down so that it was in line with hers, speaking in the space between us as she looked deep into my eyes and took complete control of me.

"Show me what it's like to be married to a man built of sin and corruption, Niall. I want to know what it is to be yours."

"Anything you say, wife. I'm yours to command," I promised her, leaning in to take that kiss and gripping her arse tighter as I began to fuck her against the door, sealing this bond between us and making her mine in a way that no being on this foul earth could take from us no matter how hard they tried.

Brooklyn cried out for more with every thrust of my hips and I fucked her with a passion I hadn't even realised I was capable of, losing myself in the blissful feeling of her body owning mine and driving my cock into her with the recklessness of the fire which lived between us.

The door rattled on its hinges and my muscles bunched and flexed with the effort of satisfying her while she tugged on my hair so hard it was at risk of tearing from the roots.

She bit down on my neck as she came for me and a roar of passion escaped my lips as the feeling of her body tightening around mine sent me over the edge too, my cock thrusting deep while I came so fucking hard that I saw stars.

I dragged her closer as I held her there, my arms tightening around her in a possessive, protective way which challenged any and all entities within this world to just try and take her from me. Because I wouldn't let them have her. No matter what it took, I'd keep her safe. I swore that as I held her in my arms, the words dancing against the skin of her neck where my lips were pressed flush to her skin and the weight of them settling into the world never to be denied.

I was her creature now and she was mine and no matter what came at us following on from this, I would protect her from it with all I had or burn the fucking world to the ground if I failed.

BROOKLYN

CHAPTER TWENTY ONE

Niall had the driver man take us back to the strip and I watched all the colours whizz by in a flurry. Las Vegas was determined to shine as brightly as the sun, burning away the night and rivalling every celestial being in the sky.

Holy tits, I was a married woman, an old ball and chain, a spouse. Ick, I hated all of those terms. I didn't wanna be a *spouse*. That didn't suit me and Niall at all. No, I was like his…screwball. And he was mine in return.

"We'd best get home now, lass," Niall said, bringing my hand to his mouth and kissing the back of it. "We've risked a lot in coming here."

My heart dropped into the ocean of my stomach and swam away into the dark. "But…"

I gazed wistfully out at the playground of sin beyond the window, my soul aching for a taste of it. There was so much music and sparkles and secrets beckoning me through extravagant doorways, begging me to come explore. I placed my fingers to the window as a whimper built in my throat.

"Oh, Jesus, come on now, don't be upset, Spider. I'll bring ya back here another time, when yer less wanted by the police," Niall promised, but it did nothing to quiet the starving creature in me. She wanted to come out and roam the streets, see the sights, delight in the wicked deeds a city like this could offer.

I turned to look at him, my lower lip quivering and my brows knitting together. "Please. Just for a millisecond. A ladybird of a millisecond," I begged and Niall cocked his head at me, a frown creasing his brow.

"Don't look at me like that, you know how easily I can be persuaded by a bad idea. I'm tryin' to protect ya," he said earnestly.

"But what about Glenda?" I breathed, resting a hand over my heart where my little duck resided.

"What about her?" he asked.

"She'll die if she doesn't get excited once in a while. She needs me to get out there and make her quack."

"Alright, fuck it. Let's go make her quack. Pull over, lad," he barked at the driver and the man veered over to the side of the road.

"No more than ten ladybirds, alright?" Niall said and I nodded, squealing as I lunged at him and kissed him hard on the lips. I sank into that kiss as he pushed his tongue between my lips and I considered swinging my leg over his lap and claiming my screwball right here, all over again. But my ladybirds were already scurrying away and I didn't want to miss out on this big bright city.

I yanked myself away from him and he grinned darkly at me as he threw the door open, stepping out and offering me his hand like I was a countess stepping out of a carriage. I slid my palm into his and he pulled me onto the sidewalk beside the huge pool of water where the fountains had been bursting and spraying before, but now it was all quiet and calm.

I spun away from Niall, looking up at the beautiful glittery buildings, spinning around and around on my heels as I took it all in.

"Where to first then, little psycho?" Niall asked and I stopped spinning, everything still whirring around me in a blur except him. Not him. The wild man who grounded me, who was one of the few solid things in a sea full of light and noise.

"I don't know, um, that – no – that!" I pointed from building to building, my heart thrashing as I tried to decide. "No, that one. That one."

Someone bumped into me as I spun around again and nearly knocked me onto my ass.

Niall was at my side in a flash, his hand pressing to my lower back and a growl rolling up his throat as I stared after the dickmunch who'd knocked into me. He was making his way towards the crowd that was gathering before the fountain and my lips parted with a gasp as he turned his head halfway in my direction, recognition crashing into me.

"Holy tits, that's Esteban," I said, my nails digging into Niall's arm as my psycho's gaze zeroed in on the man my mom had married and left me for.

"Well, he's about to be a dead Esteban," Niall growled, but I squeezed his arm to keep him from advancing on my stepfather.

"No, wait," I said, panicked as my head wheeled left and right. "What if my mom's here? What if…" I drew in ragged breaths, turning to Niall and he cupped my cheek as he saw me descending into a flim-flam. "I don't think I want her to see you. She doesn't deserve to see you." I covered his face with my hands, but Niall knocked them away, clutching me against him as the crowd swelled around us.

"Tell me what you want, Brooklyn," he spoke in my ear, and I knew he was offering me anything. Truly anything. "Tell me what you need."

I looked over my shoulder at Esteban and my nose wrinkled as he drew a woman with black hair under his arm who had a giggle about her that stirred up memories from the distant past. There she was, the woman who'd birthed me and eventually abandoned me. And I was surprised how little I felt towards her after all these years.

"That's her," I exhaled.

"Are you alright?" Niall asked in a low tone.

"Yeah, I actually feel…nothing towards her," I said, then my eyes narrowed on the man beside her.

Esteban swept a hand through his black hair, chortling loudly as Bad Romance by Lady Gaga started playing through the speakers around the fountain. He was a skinny guy and super tall, he kinda reminded me of a lamppost with a face. I might have been done with my mother in all the allys – physic-ally, emotion-ally, ment-ally – but me and Esteban had some unfinished business.

The fountain show was starting, but I couldn't even get my happies back in place because now they were being eaten alive by my angries like Pacman chomping down ghosts.

All I could think of was how Esteban had eaten my final box of Pops which my dad had bought for me, how he'd smirked like it was all just some big joke. He'd never liked me. He'd called me odd, told my mom I was 'too much like my dad'. Well at least I wasn't 'too much like a boring lamppost man.'

"Spider," Niall's deep, accented voice drew me back from the past and my eyes snapped up to his as the killer in me perked up her head.

"You said I could point you at anyone, right? And you wouldn't question it," I whispered and Niall nodded, his throat bobbing and a black cloud descending over his gaze.

"I did," he said roughly.

"Even if it's stupid and reckless and, well-"

"Yes, Spider," Niall said. "Even if it's all those things and more. If you need someone to die tonight, then die they will."

My breaths came raggedly as the thrill of a murder swam through my blood and I gripped Niall's chainmail in my fists just as the first huge sprays of water shot into the air from the fountain with a sound like a cannon going off.

I didn't look at it though, I looked at my Niall, clinging to him as I saw the entire thing reflected in his gaze instead. I remembered that murdering was for the ones who deserved it, and it was too beautiful a thing to gift to Esteban. No…he deserved something that fitted his Pops crime instead.

"He can live," I decided. "But I wanna punish him."

"Alright, a punishment it is." He grinned slowly, the smile spreading like a line of fire up his cheeks and I knew he'd gone to the darkest place that lived within him. He whirled me around, tugging me back against his chest and taking hold of my chin as he made me look at the jets of water spraying fifty feet into the air. I felt his heart drumming at my back and a quake ran deep into my body as he leaned down to speak in my ear.

"Enjoy the show, love. We'll have to bide our time on this one while I work out a plan."

"What about our ten ladybirds?" I asked.

"It'll take as long as it takes. You've chosen a mark and I've made my vow to ya as clear as anything. Now follow my lead and I promise to deliver ya his punishment before the night is out."

The power I held in a single pointed finger made me realise the magnitude of what I'd taken on in marrying Niall O'Brien. He was a hound of death and I was his master. I only needed to give the command and he'd bring me a soul and lay it at my feet. He would just as easily have agreed to kill Esteban as he had to punish him, and the idea made my stomach flutter.

I watched the huge sprays of water, the lights in the pool igniting the tall streams as they shot towards the sky. I swayed to the music and Niall rested his hands on my hips, swaying with me and creating a cage with his elbows so no one got to close to us.

The fountain show ended with an enormous bang as a huge jet of water was propelled upwards and I gasped as I watched it reach its peak then come crashing back down into the pool just as the song ended.

I clapped excitedly, bouncing up and down and Niall nudged me along in the direction Esteban took with my mom. I'd cut the cord which had once tied me to her a long time ago, snipped it right in two and never thought of her since, just like she'd never thought of me when she'd flounced away with Esteban. So we were done as far as I was concerned.

Niall prowled along at my side as Esteban turned towards an impressive hotel called the Bellagio and I hopped and skipped after him as excitement thundered in my chest.

"I want him shamed," I hissed. "Embarrassed and cringing while the whole world looks."

"I can do that," Niall purred.

We walked through the entranceway and I gazed around at the beautiful place in wonder as we followed Esteban through expansive corridors before arriving in a vast casino and sitting at a blackjack table with my mother.

Niall steered me past them to a kiosk, taking out his wallet and slapping down a wedge of cash under the cashier's nose. "Change them up for some pretty chips, please lass. I like the hundreds and the fifties."

"Yes, sir," she said, taking the money and replacing it with some shiny betting chips which had the hotel name on them.

Niall nodded to her in thanks, scooping them all into his pockets and I snagged one to hold onto, admiring it in the light as he slid his arm around my shoulders and led me back towards Esteban and my mom, circling far enough away from them that they didn't catch sight of me.

"Outa interest, what did the fella do to ya?" Niall purred to me.

"He ate the last box of Pops my dad bought me even though he knew what they meant to me," I answered, looking up at him with a fierceness in my soul. "And he was always a dickmunch."

"Hm," Niall grunted, anger crossing his features. "A Pops thief, eh? And a cunt to boot. Well then, we'll teach him what happens to my wife's enemies."

"I hope my dad is watching." I looked down at the floor, giving him a little wave. "Love you, Daddy."

"What's he in hell for?" Niall asked, following my gaze to the floor.

"Um…hookers, booze, cursing, breaking our neighbour's nose with the blunt end of a pitchfork and hating everyone in the world except me." I looked up at Niall and he knocked his knuckles against my cheek, a frown drawing his brow low before he looked down at the floor again. "Right then, this one's for you, old man. I'll be meetin' ya one day when I get down there, and we'll be the best of pals. I'll take care of yer flesh and blood, don't you worry about that. And I gotta tip my hat to ya for making the most perfect creature in this world." He snatched a cap from a man's head, flipping it onto his own and tipping it to my dad.

"Hey," the man snapped, wheeling towards him and Niall pressed his shoulders back and stared him in the eye. The man immediately backed down as he took in the cut of my husband, waving his hand in apology and hurrying away without another word.

Niall twisted the cap around so it was on backwards and I glanced down at his knight's costume, the way his chest was filling it out and the ink which was crawling up his neck. He looked like so many contradictions bundled into one and I freaking loved it.

"I need ya to stay outa this one, Spider, or he'll have the cops on ya before I can stop him," Niall said and I sighed, knowing he was right. "I'm gonna go play blackjack on his table. Sit over there." He pointed to a roulette table across the casino. "I swear I'll give ya a show to remember."

"Okay." I tiptoed up, kissing his cheek and he turned his head to steal a dirtier kiss from my lips, the public display lighting me up from head to foot. He pushed a wedge of chips into my hand as he stepped back. "Have fun, little psycho. Win us some cash, or lose it all in a blaze of glory. So long as ya enjoy the ride, it don't much matter either way."

He walked away, dropping down at Esteban's table and planting a huge stack of chips in front of him, nodding to the dealer who immediately cut him in to the game.

I turned and skipped off to the roulette table Niall had directed me to, taking a seat next to a big man with a fancy metal tie thing hanging around the neck of his red shirt. He had a huge moustache and bushy eyebrows too, looking like a cowboy who'd blown off his horse and ended up here.

"Good evening, young lady," he said in a thick accent which was probably from some southy place. "Are ya bettin' tonight?"

"Yup! Everything on red," I said, throwing all my chips down onto red and the man gaped at me while the dealer glanced my way, seeming completely unphased.

"Holy moly," the guy breathed as he took in the sizeable amount of chips I'd put down.

The dealer waited for everyone else to place their bets then dropped the little ball into the roulette, the tiny sphere bouncing around it then spinning and whizzing and weeeeee. My head moved as I followed it with my eyes, round and round and round it went like a teeny weenie ball of destiny, holding all of our fates in its itty-bitty hands. In that moment, it was the ruler of all our worlds, giggling as it decided on our fate, bouncing from number to number as the roulette wheel slowed. Red, black, red, black, red, black. I was dizzy and thrilled and grinning from ear to ear as the little rock star of a ball held us all in suspense, wiggling its shiny butt at us as it went.

Then it stopped. Right on red.

I screamed, full on whooped my heart out, as the dealer doubled my chips and pushed them back at me. The cowboy man slapped me on the shoulder and I hugged all my chippys before shoving them all onto black this time.

"Gracious, darlin', take it easy there," the cowboy warned, but I didn't need advice from a cow man when I was having the time of my life.

I shot a look over at Niall who now had his arm over Esteban's shoulders, talking animatedly about something as he ordered drinks from a waitress. Esteban seemed to be enjoying the company, and my mom was laughing wildly at something he said.

You don't get to keep my Niall, you can laugh and laugh for now, but he isn't gonna be your bestie. He's playing monster with you.

The cowboy man toyed with a final chip in his hand, contemplating all the spots on the table where he could put it while dabbing at his brow. There were lots of numbers and confuddling thingys, but the easiest ones to choose from were red or black, odd or even. I didn't know why he was taking so long to decide.

"Last bets," the dealer called and the cow man kissed his chip and placed it on red.

The dealer man sent the ball into the roulette wheel and it went spinning around it again like it was on a rollercoaster, its little *tehehehe* laugh giggling around my brain. It slowed, falling into the ring of numbers and colours at the centre of the wheel then stopped.

Black!

I squealed, throwing my arms around my cowboy friend as I bounced up and down and a whole army of chips were pushed my way as I doubled them again.

The cowboy's lone chip was taken away from him by the dealer's chip-stealing stick and he stared dejectedly at the table, looking like his whole life had been riding on that chip.

"Well, darlin'. It's been a pleasure playing with you. I hope the luck stays with ya." He nodded to me, turning away as I gathered up all my chips in a huge hug and nuzzled into them, sure they were nuzzling me back.

"Oh, um, Mr Man?" I called after him as he walked away and he glanced back at me, worries straining his eyes. "You can keep playing, if you like." I scooped up a few chips in my hand and offered them to him, making his big brows pull together in confusion.

"Why in the world would you do that?" he asked.

"Because you look sad and sad people make me sad, especially sad people who wear little dangly metal string thingys around their necks." I shrugged, tossing the chips to him and he caught them as I turned back to the table and shoved all of my chips onto even this time. That meant all I had to do was get an even number and I'd be in double chippy heaven again.

The cow man moved back to my side, placing one of the chips I'd given him down beside my huge stack then he took his neck thingy off and handed it to me.

"It's called a bolo tie, darlin', and it's all yours."

I picked it up with a gasp, not even paying attention as the dealer threw the ball into the wheel. My new tie thingy had a silver bull clasping the two strings together and it had a twinkle in its eye that made my heart nearly burst. I'd never ever been given a gift from a stranger before. Most strangers kept away from me, but maybe it was different in Vegas, maybe they liked odd here. Maybe if I'd grown up in this place, I'd have been celebrated instead of outcasted.

"Yes," he barked suddenly, slapping his hand down on the table and I realised we'd won.

My chip stack was replaced with chips that were worth more so it didn't get too big, but I still had a nice fancy pile of them as I drew them in for another hug.

"Hello Chippy one and Chippy two and oooh, you're Chippy Mcpippy." I kissed that one then another, then shoved them all onto red again.

"Ma'am, if you don't mind me sayin' so, you are the luckiest damn creature I have ever had the fortune to meet, but that luck will run out. Are you sure about this?" Cow man placed two chips next to mine and I beamed at him.

"It's just a game," I said with a shrug. "It doesn't mean anything."

"It's a lot of money, darlin'," he warned and I shrugged again. "It's more than a game."

"It's all a game, cow man. We're all just little creatures who made up a bunch of rules, built tiny houses then listened to the big men when they told everyone to play along, go home, go to work, grind to make more numbers and put them in an imaginary world called the internet. But I don't listen to the rules, I don't live by the system designed to keep me in a box, and I certainly don't listen to big men with their laws and their fandangles. It's free outside the box, cow man, all you have to do is step out of it."

My chips were doubled again and people around the table cheered. I'd drawn quite the crowd, a bunch of hungry money zombies sniffing out new blood. It was sad really, the want in their eyes, the jealous gremlins peering out of them as they watched me claim my stack of plastic while my cow friend claimed his too.

My gaze moved to the only thing that mattered to me in this whole room, this whole city in fact. And I found him watching me back, a feral look on his face as I smiled at him and Glenda did a backflip in my chest. That was what was real. Me and him and a house far, far away where two beautiful, twisted souls and my cuddly pooch were waiting for me to come home.

Niall winked at me, his hand snaking up the back of Esteban's neck and suddenly he slammed his face down onto the table, then flipped him off his seat right up onto it. Esteban cried out as my mother screamed and the dealer lurched backwards in alarm. Niall was upon him in the next second, climbing onto the table, pressing his knee into Esteban's back and yanking his pants down to unveil his ass. He started shoving Esteban's chips between his ass cheeks as two security men came running from across the room. But Niall wasn't done, he started playing Esteban's ass cheeks like a bongo while my mother continued to scream, Esteban flailed beneath him and a bunch of people started recording him on their phones, though the hat that Niall had stolen was somehow perfectly positioned to hide his own face from their nosy cameras like it was in on the joke too.

A wild laugh tore from my lungs and I clutched my sides as I fell completely apart, watching my madman of a husband slapping his huge, inked hands down on Esteban's ass and playing a pretty neat tune with surprising skill.

"Wendy!" Esteban shrieked at my mom, but she just stared on, like her mind couldn't quite catch up to what she was seeing.

Niall slapped Esteban's ass up so good it was turning bright red, and my head bobbed in time with the tune he was playing. I was pretty sure it was Can't Stop by Red Hot Chilli Peppers, so I started singing the backing singer bit under my breath and filled in the guitar part in my head.

The security men made it to the table, but Niall jumped up fast, leaping off of it and kicking Esteban in the head as he flew over him and landed heavily on the floor.

"Wendy!" Esteban cried louder and my mom finally snapped out of her stupor, lurching forward and scooping piles of chips out of her husband's ass crack.

I shoved all of my chips at my cow man friend, snatching the tie thingy he'd gifted me and waving him goodbye. He stared at me in shock as I wheeled away and ran to meet Niall as he came barrelling towards me through the crowd.

I was so small I couldn't see above all the people who were swarming forward to try and get a look at the commotion. I pushed and shoved to get through them, hunting for my Hellfire as my heart jerked and kicked in my chest.

"Niall!" I called to him and a man in front of me was knocked down like a toothpick snapping in half as he appeared, snatching my hand into his grasp as he grinned big at me.

"Time to go, Spider." Niall dragged me along and I ran with him as fast as we could go, racing left and right through the tables before we finally found a door and made it outside before anyone could stop us.

Our driver man was already there and he yanked the back door open and ushered us inside.

I fell into Niall's lap as the door shut behind us and the driver man leapt into the car, taking off down the road just as the security people spilled out of the casino and looked left and right for us in confusion.

The two of us laughed so hard, I swear one of my lungs was gonna leap out of my throat, but instead Niall's mouth came down on mine and he crushed me against him.

Our laughter turned to panting and suddenly he was yanking my dress up and I was shoving down his pants as we clawed at each other ferally.

"If you look back here even one time, I'll cut your eyes out, throw them in a wishing well and wish for all your nightmares to come true," Niall warned the driver, who nodded stiffly before putting up a partition between us.

It was the perfect end to a perfect night, and I couldn't wait to tell Mateo and Jack all about it.

JACK

CHAPTER TWENTY TWO

My muscles recovered slowly, sensation returning to them piece by piece as I sat in the chair across from Mateo and listened to him talk. We'd slept too, both of us having little choice other than to fall asleep in our chairs and hope that the other wouldn't wake first with the use of our limbs and murderous thoughts.

But to my surprise, when I'd woken it hadn't been to the feeling of his hands around my throat or some weapon driving into my flesh. It had simply been to his keen eyes observing me, assessing me, taking in everything about me in a way that none of the people I'd spent time with during my incarceration ever had.

Like I was a worthy adversary.

It was so much more interesting than the simple fear I usually commanded due to my size and unpredictable nature, and I couldn't help but rise to the challenge in his gaze.

No one had paid me this much attention in a long time. No one aside from her. And when she looked at me, it wasn't like this, like one predator assessing another, searching for weaknesses, strengths, ways to use or manipulate the other.

"We have a common enemy," Mateo said as I yawned, pushing my long hair away from my face and adjusting my position in the chair. My stomach was growling with a demand for food, but I was used to being punished with starvation under Madam Lucille's watch back in Eden Heights, so I ignored it.

"Niall," I grunted, knowing what he meant and already prepared for this conversation. It hadn't been hard to predict. Over countless chess games, Mateo had continued to make observations about me, my behaviour, my appearance, and not least, our current situation. I knew he was trying to secure an alliance with me against the man who had collared us like dogs.

"Together we can end him," he hissed. "You and me. If we work together, one of us can distract him while the other strikes. All I need is thirty seconds where he doesn't manage to activate my collar and I can have him bleeding out beneath me."

"Then?" I asked, waiting to hear the rest of his plan and wondering if he would admit that that would leave the two of us with nothing to cement our union anymore.

"Then I can give you money. More than enough for you to start up a new life wherever the fuck you want to go. That's why Niall hasn't killed me in all the time he's held me – he knows I have it and he wants it. Wants to buy his own freedom from the cage his family have erected around him. I couldn't really give a fuck about his motivations. Point is, you scratch my back, I'll scratch yours. You'll have everything you need to start up a fresh life well away from the gang whose mark you bear on your flesh."

He bobbed his chin at the ink poking out from beneath my shirt and I grunted. He'd figured out that small hint of my past quick enough, though it wasn't much of a stretch for anyone to put two and two together when gang ink was involved.

My mind drifted to the life I'd once pledged myself to. The one which had offered me an outlet every time I snapped the way I did all too often.

But the rage in me had only gotten more unpredictable as time went on. Often unleashing when my boss had no use for it, and I wasn't a beast made to fit chains or attack on command. I was volatile, unpredictable, a loose cannon as he'd once called me. And what good was a soldier who lost his shit at the slightest provocation and paid little to no attention to his orders once the rage took me?

That entire enterprise had been headed for disaster since the moment I'd sworn in and gotten my ink. Problem was, there was no backing out of that kind of organisation once you were in. No way out for anyone aside from death. Or perhaps insanity.

My lips twisted in amusement at my work on that front and Mateo's eyes narrowed as he caught the movement.

"Rook," I said simply, pointing out the flaw to his plan because she was clearly fond of the Irishman who kept us captive, and I wasn't willing to hurt her in the attempt to end him. Nor was I inclined to leave her behind with this motherfucker and just head off on my way the moment we freed ourselves from his grasp.

Mateo shifted in his seat. "My chica loca will be well provided for with me," he said slowly, some darkness filtering though his expression, like he wasn't entirely convinced of his own words and I didn't like that one bit.

I tapped my finger on the arm of my chair, uncertain about whether or not I wanted to indulge him in his plans.

The drugs had done the job of calming me at least, so my mind was clear enough for me to form my own plans, and I wasn't sure they had a whole lot to do with the man sitting opposite me.

That said, I would be happy enough to relieve him of the money he claimed to have and take him up on the offer of a free life. I just doubted I'd leave him alive to have much say in what I did with it.

The sound of a car pulling up the drive made both of us look around and my slow pulse began to pound a little harder as I felt the need for the fight surging within me.

"Now or never, gigante," Mateo urged as he pushed to his feet and I nodded, standing too, my legs still a little wobbly though strong enough to support me at last.

"Now," I agreed, walking towards the door with him and positioning myself on the opposite side of it to him as we awaited our prey.

Brutus raised his head from the blankets on the far side of the room, the enormous grey dog baring his teeth at us like it could sense what we planned to do and didn't much like it. I eyed the beast warily, not liking the way it was looking at us and half expecting it to pounce at any moment.

The sound of Brooklyn singing came from outside and I exchanged a look with Mateo, wickedness coating his skin as he rolled his shoulders back and the scent of death curled around us on the air.

It had been a long time since I'd been so free to unleash this part of me at will and I cracked my knuckles as I forced myself to hold still, battling against my nature which was far more inclined towards an outward show of aggression than lying in wait for my prey.

The front door unlocked and I snapped, that switch flicking inside my skull which left no room for anything other than violence as I threw myself through the door and ran full pelt down the short hallway.

Niall kicked the door open before I got there, stepping over the threshold with Brooklyn held in his arms, her head thrown back and arm looped around his neck while she pointed one ballerina shoe at the ceiling and he laughed wildly.

He lifted his head and met my gaze as I charged him with a bellow, tossing Brooklyn aside so that she landed on her feet like a cat before running forward to meet me with a wild laugh tearing from his lips.

Brooklyn whooped, doing a pirouette in her pink ballet skirt which I spotted in the corner of my eye a moment before the two of us collided.

The impact of our huge bodies crashing into each other made my damn bones rattle and the force of his fist sent pain radiating through my side before I managed to throw him back against the wall.

His spine slammed into the brickwork, but he threw his head towards me, his forehead cracking against the bridge of my nose and making blood spill down onto my lips as they pulled back in a ferocious snarl.

Mateo cursed me as he made it into the fight, his weight slamming into us from the side and knocking us through the door into the front room where we all went sprawling to the floor.

The taste of my own blood on my lips made that thin hold I was trying to maintain on my rage snap, and a roar escaped me as I threw my weight forward, swinging fists and knees and elbows as we fell into a brawl. I forgot to even try and keep my entire aim focused on the man who kept us captive, striking any and every piece of flesh I could find.

I was lost to the violence in me as so often happened and there was nothing left beyond the rampant beat of my heart, the smack of flesh against flesh as I swung my fists and worked to destroy everything within range of me.

Mateo yelled something which I couldn't hear over the pumping of my own pulse against my eardrums, and suddenly Brutus dove into the fray, sharp teeth sinking into my arm and splitting the skin as he savaged me.

I tried to shake the enormous dog off me as a fist cracked against my jaw, but before I could do more than jab an elbow into its side, an explosion of electricity crashed through my body from the shock collar.

I slammed down against the floorboards on my back as I jerked and spasmed my way through the feeling of it, agony tearing through my skin and forcing my mind to snap back into alignment once more.

Brutus yelped as the current transferred into him too, releasing my arm and backing away towards the dark goddess who came to stand over me, her ballerina shoe nudging my chest as she tilted her head to one side to observe me.

Niall coughed out a laugh as he stood, straightening his I love Vegas shirt and dropping an arm around Brooklyn's shoulders. He grinned at her as she spun the remote for our collars in her hand, making it clear that she had been the one to intervene in our violence.

"Bad boys," she chastised, biting down on her bottom lip as she looked from me to Mateo who was cursing as he managed to get onto his hands and knees, the shock from the collars finally dissipating.

"Ah now, don't be harsh with them, love. They're just excited to have us home, aren't they?" Niall said, licking his bottom lip to taste the blood from the nasty looking split he now had marking it.

"Did you hear the news already?" she asked excitedly, looking between Mateo and I while he moved to sit on his ass.

I just stayed laying on my back, panting through the afterglow of the fight and wishing it could have gone on longer.

"What news?" Mateo asked, carving a hand through his dark hair and scowling at Niall, though he made no new attempt to attack him again.

The corner of Niall's lips lifted in a cruel smile and he looked to Brooklyn, plucking the remote from her fingers.

"Show 'em, love," he encouraged and Brooklyn squealed as she held her hand out for the two of us to see the ring which now adorned her left hand.

"What is this?" Mateo demanded, his scowl fixing on Niall.

"Niall fucked the virginity clean out of me then took me to Vegas to make an honest woman of me, once he realised what he'd done," Brooklyn cooed and some deep, dark thing twisted in my chest as I looked between the ring on her hand and the heathen at her back.

"What?" Mateo demanded angrily and I shoved myself to my feet as the anger in me began to rise once more.

"You're not making it sound all that romantic, love," Niall corrected her. "It was more like I got myself an order from a higher purpose to claim you for my own once and for all and was powerless to resist it."

"You married this piece of shit?" Mateo barked, staring between Brooklyn and Niall like he was having trouble understanding them.

But I'd heard enough and I snarled as I lunged at Niall again, his death in my mind and this warring kind of rage pulsing through my veins. Brooklyn wasn't his. She was *mine*.

Electricity crashed through my body before I could lay a hand on him this time and I slammed to the floor at Brooklyn's feet, my chin colliding with the floorboards and my teeth damn near severing the tip of my tongue.

"Is it the good tingles?" Brooklyn whispered, squatting down beside me and pushing her fingers into my hair so that she could feel the effects of the collar in her flesh too. A sultry moan escaped her as the electricity transferred into her where she touched me, and I couldn't help but stare up at her as her pupils dilated with lust.

Mateo punched Niall square in the mouth and the Irish bastard laughed loudly as he allowed the strike to fall, stumbling backwards before he hit the button to activate Mateo's collar too, flooring him right beside me.

"You haven't even heard all the things we got up to in Vegas," Brooklyn said with a pout. "You know nothing about my princess dress or the way we got it all messy when we were having sexy times in the back of the car and had to go get new fancy clothes from the ballerina shop."

"I think it was just a standard shop," Niall interrupted. "Didn't you steal that outfit from some girl on her way to a show?"

"Oh yeah," Brooklyn replied wistfully. "Right before I got the stabby."

She rubbed her arm and I frowned at the red mark there.

"What's that?" Mateo demands, his finger digging into the carpet as he tried to claw his way upright again but I just lay there, panting and staring up at Brooklyn as I listened to her story.

"A contraband," Brooklyn said.

"Contraceptive," Niall corrected. "I made mention of the possibility of babies and Brooklyn thought that was a terrible idea for us and I have to say I agree. So we went to grab a morning after pill from a pharmacy, and she got excited when the fella mentioned the option of her getting an implant. I did offer to buy condoms instead but-"

"But I wanna feel your mega-cock, not some plastic cock bag inside me," Brooklyn snapped angrily and I wetted my lips at the thought of her fucking him, watching the way her eyes lit up as she looked at him and letting my imagination run riot on that idea. It wasn't exactly a bad visual. But it didn't make her his either.

"Yeah, the fella got flustered when she said that to him," Niall agreed with a chuckle. "But he went ahead and gave her the implant with a thinly veiled threat in place to hurry him along."

"I'm going to rip your cock from your body and feed it to that fucking dog," Mateo snarled as he started dragging himself towards Niall, but he was stopped by a jolt of electricity as Niall hit the button for his collar once again.

"We'll leave you two to get over the shock," Niall announced loudly, laughing at his own shit joke and scooping Brooklyn into his arms, carrying her towards the stairs while she giggled girlishly. "But I'm impressed by your rage, fellas. Keep up the good work."

By the time I managed to regain the use of my limbs again, the sound of his bedroom door banging shut reached me and I cursed beneath my breath as I lay panting on the floor.

"Do you need any further motivation to want him dead now, gigante?" Mateo hissed beside me and I shook my head, imaging all the ways I'd like to make that man suffer more than any man should rightly be able to survive.

"Dead," I grunted in confirmation and Mateo met my eye as I rolled my head to the side to look at him.

"Dead," he agreed darkly.

By the time Niall emerged from his room, I'd successfully destroyed the coffee table and shattered all of the plates which had been displayed on the dresser at the far end of the front room. If I had thought that losing my mind over the idea of Brooklyn marrying him had been intense, then it was nothing on the blind rage that had possessed me when she began moaning his name like he was a God-given flesh intended solely for delivering her pleasure.

My chest heaved and fell rapidly while I stood in the splintered remains of the destruction I'd caused and sweat slicked my skin beneath my shirt, but Mateo hadn't said a single word.

He sat in the corner of the room beside the chessboard once more, his eyes fixed on the walkway above the fireplace which Brooklyn and Niall would have to cross before returning downstairs to us.

The sound of a door opening and closing made me whip around as Brooklyn stepped onto the walkway at last. She was wearing a white dress kind of like the one Marilyn Monroe wore way back before the world got too much for her and she escaped it into the wings of death.

"Hey AJ," she called as she moved to stand by the railings, gripping the banister tightly and leaning over it so that her tiptoes barely stayed on the carpet.

I moved to stand beneath her, tipping my head back to watch her as she continued to toy with the idea of falling from the walkway above me and finding the anger in me calming.

It had always been like that in Eden Heights too. My obsession with her was enough to drive the madness from my blood. At least for a little while.

Niall exited the room behind her, strolling down the stairs and making a show of leaping the final five, landing before me and grinning widely. He was only wearing a pair of black jeans which hung low on his waist and allowed me to see the scratches Brooklyn had left all over his body during the time they'd spent upstairs.

But as I looked into his green eyes, I found myself unmoved by his show of possessiveness, turning my eyes back up to look at Brooklyn who still had her attention fixed on me. I didn't care about some showboating Irishman while I had her to focus on instead.

Niall sighed, giving up on me and heading across the room at my back, kicking some broken pieces of the coffee table aside and making them rattle across the floor as he headed towards Mateo.

"You got something to say to me, el burro?" Niall taunted and I swear I could feel Mateo's hatred colouring the air.

"I have nothing at all to say you, hijo de puta," Mateo hissed in a low voice. "You are beneath my attention and not worth the breath I would waste on making conversation with you."

"He says while making conversation with me," Niall replied, barking a laugh.

They started to bicker, but I ignored whatever it was that they were so intent on saying, my eyes on Brooklyn as she pushed her tiptoes off of the carpet and swung forward over the banister above me.

She whooped as she almost fell, managing to swing herself back and place her feet on the ground once more before pushing forward again.

"It's not my fault that she chose me, arsehole," Niall snapped loudly. "You're the one who couldn't do enough to convince her to place her bets on you. I can't help being her favourite."

"Who said you're my favourite?" Brooklyn called, causing a beat of silence to pass before Mateo and Niall started arguing between themselves again, the sound of Mateo shoving his chair back and rising to his feet reaching me.

But I didn't look around at them. My gaze was fixed on Rook.

Brooklyn gave me a wide smile, spreading her arms out either side of her like a pair of wings before kicking off of the carpet once more and flipping herself straight over the banister.

Her white dress billowed up around her and she laughed as she fell, not doubting for a single second that I would catch her.

She landed heavily in my arms, but I was never at any risk of dropping her, my hands banding beneath her legs and around her back as I drew her in close to my chest.

She laughed excitedly as she wrapped her arms around my neck and leaned up to place a kiss on my cheek.

"You're my favourite, AJ," she whispered conspiratorially. "You and me have all kinds of special connections that they just don't understand."

I nodded, drawing her closer to me and leaning down to brush my lips over her temple, breathing her in as she leaned into my embrace. She smelled of honey, papaya and sex and I inhaled all of it, wanting more than I was taking and enjoying the attention she was giving me.

"You wouldn't be so fucking cocky if you didn't have the remote to this collar in your pocket, bastardo," Mateo barked behind us, and Niall laughed loudly.

"Are you looking to get your arse kicked as well as your heart broken today?" he challenged. "Because I don't need no fancy collar to grind you into the dirt, my little donkey."

"Prove it then," Mateo challenged.

"Maybe I will," Niall replied.

Brooklyn tightened her grip on my neck and drew herself up to speak in my ear, her lips brushing against my skin and making it tingle from the contact.

"We should go while they're busy," she whispered. "I want to do a Pop hunt while Hellfire is distracted."

I nodded in agreement, turning towards the door and carrying her out towards the kitchen. I was forced to stop before stepping through onto the tiles, reluctantly releasing her and watching as she began hunting through all of the cupboards one by one, cursing every time she failed to find what she was looking for.

"Damn," she muttered as she made it to the fridge. "I keep expecting him to try and hide them in the kitchen where they belong, because that's so clever. It's like hiding something exactly where you'd expect it to be because no one would ever expect you to do the expected, you see?"

"Yes," I agreed though it seemed unlikely to me that Niall would do anything that simple. His mind was a twisted knot of convoluted thoughts and half formed intentions, with a whole heap of violence thrown into the mix ready to come out and play at the slightest provocation. He wasn't the type to do things in an expected way.

Brooklyn sighed forlornly as she stared into the depths of the fridge and started running her hand down her chest, her fingers massaging her breast while she bit her lip thoughtfully.

"Have you noticed how small my tits are, AJ?" she asked without looking at me.

"No," I grunted because they seemed pretty fucking perfect to me, and I couldn't say I'd ever once looked at them and thought they were too small. More like I'd looked at them and wanted to run my tongue over the hardened peeks of her nipples or watch her play with them while I came all over her naked flesh and she moaned my name. None of those thoughts included any kind of disappointment over their size. She was exactly what I wanted just as she was.

"No," she agreed. "Because they're so small they're beneath notice."

I frowned as she reached into the fridge and grabbed a watermelon out of it, watching her as she tugged the front of her dress wide and pushed the fruit into the fabric, forcing it to stretch out around it. She found a second melon and repeated the process for her other breast, flinging the fridge door shut with a flourish and turning to grin at me as she finished.

"Better?" she demanded.

"No," I growled and she pouted at me.

"Well, I'm trying it out, so get used to it, big man, and try not to stare." She stalked towards me, forcing her way by when I didn't immediately move aside.

I followed her as she headed down the corridor, both of us ignoring the sounds of violence from the front room where Mateo and Niall were clearly in the middle of a fist fight.

If I was lucky, they'd kill each other and leave me and Rook to our own devices in this big, hidden house in the middle of nowhere. Then I'd hunt every inch of this place for the treasure Mateo claimed to have hidden somewhere and we could live off of it happily for the rest of our days in peace.

Brooklyn paused to sniff the air, her eyes narrowing as she whipped around and called out for Brutus.

"Come here, boy, come sniff with me!"

The beastly looking creature raised his head from his position blocking the front door, a low snarl escaping his lips as he looked at her.

"Come on you squeaky cheesey," she purred, patting her thighs and hurrying towards him.

The dog snarled louder and I followed close behind her as she closed in on it. But I wasn't really worried that the thing would attack her. Not because I was deluded into thinking it was a gentle creature or only snarling out of fear, but because I knew my Rook and she had a way with violent beasts which somehow equalled her survival against all odds.

Clearly the creature had no problem with savaging any of us if it felt the desire to do so though, and I had the teeth marks to prove it.

Brooklyn dropped to her knees, winding her arms around the snarling dog's neck and squeezing him tight while he barked aggressively. Brutus snapped at her hand as she stood up but she just giggled, taking a can of tuna from her cardigan pocket and shaking it at him.

"Niall says this is your favourite," she said in a cutesy voice as she shook the can at him. "You wanna earn a treat by helping me sniff out a Pop?"

There was a huge crash and a cry of pain from the front room as it sounded like Niall was thrown into something, but Brooklyn just rolled her eyes as she glanced their way before unlocking the door and letting it swing wide.

Brutus turned and raced out into the huge yard which stretched away down the hill and Brooklyn took off after him, not seeming to care that her feet were bare and the grass was wet.

She opened her arms wide as she ran down the hill, her white dress billowing out around her as she started saying hello to everything she laid her eyes on and let the freedom of the outside world consume her.

I broke into a run behind her, sprinting as fast as I could and closing in on her with every passing second, my gaze locked on her back and my desire for her making me heady.

Brooklyn squealed as I caught her and I spun her in my arms, letting her legs swing out as she laughed and the watermelons almost fell out of her dress.

"My tatas!" she wailed, clutching them and I placed her back on her feet so that she could hold them in place, the two of us exchanging a wild grin as I released her.

"I missed you, Jack," she breathed, her chest rising and falling from her run and the wind tossing her dark hair around her shoulders.

I stepped closer to her, grasping her by the hips and drawing her right into my shadow as I dropped my mouth to her ear and gave her my truth in reply.

"I dreamed of you every night that you were gone," I growled, my voice a rough rasp from lack of use which made goosebumps explode along her skin as she shivered for me. "I lay in my bed and imagined you in my arms, the ghost of your smile haunting me in the dark as I held onto the memory of it and pretended you were mine. I thought of the feeling of your flesh against my own and I fantasised over all the things I would do to your body if I ever had you at my disposal again. I've dreamed of hearing you gasp my name while I pin you beneath me and bury myself deep inside the sweet oblivion of your body more times than you can count. I don't think I have ever wanted anything in the way that I want you."

Brooklyn sucked in a sharp breath, her head turning so that her cheek brushed against mine, her lips shifting until they were almost in line with my mouth as her wide eyes met mine.

"Oh my stars, I just read your mind, AJ," she breathed, her hand moving onto my chest and sliding up the thin fabric of my shirt until it rested over my heart. "I slipped right inside your mind and listened to your deepest, darkest secret."

"And?" I asked, wanting a reply to the first real words I'd spoken in so, so long.

"And I dreamed of you too," she whispered, inching closer to me, making the melons she'd stuffed inside her dress press against my stomach. "Maybe I walked right out of my own head while I was sleeping and slipped into yours, even though you were miles and miles away…"

I reached out and took the side of her face in my large hand, running my thumb over the features I'd pictured all too often and committing every piece of her to memory, just in case. Though I had no intention of letting her leave me ever again.

"You," I said in a low voice, trying to convey all that she was to me, the beacon she'd been while I'd been locked away in the dark, the smiles she'd afforded me when I had begun to believe that there was nothing worth smiling for left in this world. While I was pretending I was a man with a brain injury which had left me barely able to speak, giving my enemies no reason to come for me.

Brutus barked loudly and Brooklyn released me, whirling around with a gasp and looking to the dog who was digging at the ground beside a little outbuilding, his lips pulled back on a snarl which made me think he was likely on the hunt.

"Brutus found a trail!" Brooklyn cried, sprinting away from me across the wet grass and forcing me to follow yet again. But I was content to stay in her shadow. She brought me peace in the maelstrom of my mind and offered me a taste of solace which I didn't deserve to sample.

She ran to the door of the outbuilding, scowling at it like she thought it was in on this plan to deny her of her favourite food and reaching for the latch with hesitant fingers.

The knob rattled as she tried to open it, the wooden door creaking but not budging as it remained locked.

"Fuck biscuits," she cursed, looking around at me. "What now?"

I took hold of her wrist and tugged her back a step then grasped the door handle myself and yanked on it so hard that the whole thing ripped off in my hand with a loud bang.

The wooden door swung open slowly without the latch left to secure it and the low creak it made was followed by an excited squeal from Brooklyn as she tore into the dark space inside.

Brutus raced past me, smacking against the side of my leg with almost enough force to knock me over and I stumbled aside a step before following the snarling creature into the dark outbuilding.

The second I stepped over the threshold, electricity exploded from my collar and I cursed as I fell backwards, thrashing and twitching in the mud outside the door through the agony of the blast as it ebbed away again.

"Ooooh yeah, Niall said you can't go into the sheds," Brooklyn cooed as she came to stand over me, her dark hair tumbling down to caress my cheeks while she smiled at me. "I'll bring the Pops out once I find them, kay?"

I grunted, no words escaping me as the pain of that shock continued to echo through my skull and she grinned before skipping away into the darkness of the building once more, leaving me to roll over and scramble to my feet.

The back of my clothes were drenched from the dew-soaked grass and mud stained my knees as I stood once again, looking back towards the house and scowling in Niall's direction even though he was far too occupied with Mateo to see or care.

I moved to lean against the doorframe, gazing into the outbuilding while Brooklyn began to rummage around the piled-up boxes and move between dusty workbenches. It didn't look like this place was used often and I wasn't certain she'd find what she was looking for, but she hunted with a keen determination which said she believed she would find her prize.

I spotted the light switch just inside the door and carefully reached in to flick it on for her, making sure my collar didn't cross the threshold to shock me again.

Brooklyn gasped loudly as the lights came on, swooping down and grabbing something from the dusty floor before raising it high into the air with a triumphant cry.

"I knew we were on the trail!" she called, rushing over to me to show me a little brown thing between her fingers. It could have been a Coco Pop. It also could have been a rat dropping.

Brooklyn tossed it into her mouth and moaned loudly in delight before whipping around once more and narrowing her eyes on the room. To the right of the door was a tall cabinet, the path between it and the exit suspiciously free of dust in comparison to the rest of the space.

"There," I said, pointing towards it and Brooklyn twisted around, hurrying towards the cupboard and grabbing the handle just as I noticed a long, thin wire which was drawn tight across the ceiling and connected to the top of the door.

"Rook!" I roared in warning as she yanked the door open and I threw myself inside after her, my body colliding with hers just as the sharp hiss and thwack of the trap being set off filled the air.

Brooklyn screamed bloody murder as a pair of arrows slammed into her chest before I could throw her aside and the final two struck me in the back just as an explosion of electricity ripped through my being and sent me crashing to the ground on top of her.

Brutus began barking wildly somewhere far away from me as the hot wetness of blood spilled across my flesh and the agony from the collar made it hard for my thoughts to stick together, but one kept rattling through my mind over and over on repeat.

She has to be okay. She has to.

BROOKLYN

CHAPTER TWENTY THREE

Pain was zapping through me, zap, zap, ZAP.

I liked those fiery rockets of electricity normally, but they weren't playing so nice this time. They were hurty and I couldn't make it stop because Jack was weighing me down, and the two of us were locked in the furious grip of lightning which was tearing from his collar right through to my soul.

The hot splash of blood dripped onto my cheek and I knew it wasn't mine. It was my big man's, my AJ's, and panic cleaved my chest in two and let all my demons come rushing out as I tried to move. But I was trapped in a dark, dark palace of pain. Fire was coursing through my skull and washing down my spine. My nerves were screaming, every single one of them crying out in a choir of agony.

My heart was beating too hard and poor Glenda couldn't break free, her wings flapping frantically against the inside of that meaty organ which kept me here on this earth, with my Hellfire, Dead Man, AJ.

And I found for the first time ever, I didn't embrace death, I didn't call for the Devil to come take me away, glad to walk into his arms. In fact, I didn't want him to touch me at all anymore. Niall had been right, he'd claimed me from him and there was no going back, but he wasn't the only one who had stocks and shares in my soul now.

A bellow reached my ears and the crushing weight of Jack lifted from my body, making the electricity stop, but my eyes wouldn't open. Wetness seeped through my chest and I suddenly remembered the arrows. The ca-whooshing noise then the quick thud-thud sound of them striking me.

I was in the lap of someone big and strong who smelled like cigarettes and the echo of a hundred kills.

"Spider!" Hellfire cried and fear coloured that word red as he cupped my cheek and spoke to me in a frantic voice. "Yer gonna need to open your eyes now, love. Show me you're still with me, or I'll take us all down to hell after ya."

My eyelids weighed a ton, but I managed to peel them back and Niall's deep green gaze burned me alive.

"Oh, thank fuck," he sighed, leaning down and kissing me hard. I reached up to cling to him, my thoughts torn apart and nothing existing but him in that second as I tried to remember how I'd gotten here.

"Is she alright?" Mateo barked and I looked for him, but as Niall leaned back, he kept hold of my cheek so I couldn't break his gaze.

"She's fine," he said gruffly, then released a long breath of relief, leaning down and kissing my forehead. "Bad Spider. Silly, stupid Spider."

"Did my tatas make it?" I whispered, reaching for my boobs and finding a mess of juice soaking through my shirt and the two arrows sticking right out of the melons within it.

Niall pulled my dress down and yanked the arrows out of the skewered fruit, tossing the melons after them and inspecting my uninjured flesh beneath. "They made it, little psycho."

A growl of pain made me bolt upright in alarm and I spotted Jack outside the shed on his front with Mateo kneeling over him, tugging an arrow out of his shoulder.

"AJ!" I cried in horror, leaping out of Niall's lap and running to him, finding Brutus barking beside him.

The dog jumped up at me and I thought I was about to be snapped up in his snappies, but then he licked my arm and wagged his stumpy tail instead. I scruffed his head, dropping down beside Jack and looking to Mateo in horror.

"Is he going to be okay?" I begged, realising I was shaking and tears were burning the backs of my eyes.

"He'll be fine if he stops jerking about," Mateo said before sitting on Jack's back to hold him down and gripping a second arrow still stuck in the lower part of his shoulder, ripping it out without mercy.

"Motherfucker," Jack spat.

"So he does say more than one syllable, huh?" Mateo snarled in Jack's ear, digging his finger into one of the arrow wounds and making Jack buck like a crocodile being weighed down by a wildebeest. "What else can you say, gigante?"

"Stop it, Dead Man!" I lunged at him, throwing all my weight at Mateo and knocking him onto the grass beside Jack.

Mateo caught my wrists in his grasp before I could do any more to him, his dark eyes roaming endlessly over my body as he hunted for injuries.

"I'm fine, thanks to Jack," I said. "And my melons. They saved me too. Now let me go."

Mateo didn't release me, looking like he wanted to fold me up, put me in his pocket and run as far away as he could from here before anyone could catch him. But as I tugged on my wrists, he slowly released me and I crawled over to Jack as he started to rise, grabbing his head in both of my hands and kissing him on the mouth. Kissing him felt like the rightest thing in the world, like two dots being connected by a line in a dot-to-dot. We were meant to be joined to help make a bigger picture, it was fate.

He stilled, his hands coming up to grasp my face as he sank his tongue between my lips and my tears broke free, sailing down my cheeks like little boats on a windy river.

A furious growl sounded behind us and Jack was ripped away from me by the hair, leaving me in the damp grass as I looked up at Niall in fury and he waved the remote around in a threat to the others. "Get offa my wife."

"He saved my life." I pouted.

"And you almost cost her it with your fucking booby trap, bastardo," Mateo hissed as he got to his feet.

Jack remained silent, not even bothering to try and break Niall's grip on his hair as he started at me with blood dripping from his back onto the grass and a passion in his eyes that made me ache inside.

"Quiet down," Niall snarled, letting go of Jack and starting to pace around us all in a circle. "Yer all so fuckin' chatty, just pipe down and let me figure out how this is gonna go."

He swiped a hand over his face, seeming all antsy pants and I crawled closer to Jack, moving around him to inspect the bloody wounds on his back, my throat welling at the sight of his pain. I'd dealt so many hurts and aches out to people in my life, but I didn't like to see my giant bleeding.

Niall kept looking at me with a panicked horror in his eyes before his gaze shifted to Jack then Mateo. Round and round, even pausing on Brutus who had come to sit beside me, sniffing the blood on Jack like he was tempted to have a little lick. He was drooling a lot, so he probably really wanted to make him feel better, but I kept nudging him away every time he leaned towards Jack's wound, not wanting his licks to give him more ouchies.

"He needs stitches," I said with a frown, tracing my finger around the wounds in a big circle and Jack relaxed into my touch. "I could do it. I just need a needle and thread and – oh they are quite deep, aren't they? – maybe some gum to stick the holes shut first? Some strawberry gum because that's probably less hurty than mint-"

"I've got it," Niall said, snapping his fingers and pointing between us all. "It's makin' some kinda sense now, what my nephew was saying about him and his girl. How he lets his boys fuck her too. It ain't about the fuckin' – that's important, mind, but I can see how it's more than that. My damn crazy arse will end up killin' my Spider one way or the other if I don't have more eyes on her, you see? I already fear I ain't up to the job alone. I couldn't keep Ava safe after all. And that probably ain't the only booby trap in this house, but fuck knows where the others are, because I was likely on a blood high when I fixed 'em elsewhere. Do ya see what I'm saying, Mateo?" Niall gripped his jaw, making him look up at him. "Is that making sense to you like it is to me?"

Mateo frowned then jerked his chin out of Niall's grip. "You want her protected from yourself." Dead Man looked to me, and I smiled shyly under the blazing scrutiny of his dark eyes, my tummy all of a flutter.

"That's right. And Jack went and protected her from me, didn't ya lad?" Niall approached him, petting him on the head. "Look at you. All those muscles. All nearly seven feet of ya. How many men could you take on at once? How much time could you buy her to run? Enough, I'd say." He smirked like he was the cleverest man on the planet then looked to me. "What do you say to that, Spider? You like these men, don't ya?"

"I like them lots," I agreed, biting my lower lip. "I feel like...like we're..." I couldn't get the words out past the lumpy bump in my throat, feeling suddenly self-conscious in case these men didn't feel the same as me, in case Brutus didn't either. I was getting so attached to them all, so deeply, impossibly attached like I hadn't to any people I'd ever met ever before. And if I admitted it out loud, they might go pop like the weasel. They might vanish before my very eyes and I'd be lost and alone again.

"Say it, chica loca," Mateo encouraged, shifting closer to me on the grass.

"Rook," Jack urged and I looked to him too as Brutus let out a yap like he wanted to know as well.

365

I cleared my throat again and again, shifting on my butt and picking a handful of grass, sorting through the blades.

"Come on now, Spider," Niall encouraged. "Don't hold out on us."

I shut my eyes, scrunching them up super tight as I forced the words to wrap around my tongue, praying that when I opened my eyes again, they'd still be there. That they wouldn't be stolen away from me, and I'd realise they were always just a figment of my overactive imagination. Because I was sitting in the wish I'd made for myself all those years ago on my birthday, blowing out a candle on my little red velvet cupcake. I'd wished for adventure. But underneath that wish had been something so much deeper. I'd wished to feel accepted, to feel loved, and with these men, I felt more love than my little heart could take. But I wanted to try and keep hold of it all, to find a way for my heart to stretch and accommodate all those fuzzy warm feels, because if I didn't, they might escape out of my chest and blow away into the trees to be eaten by an owl.

"I feel so happy here. So, so happy," I blurted. "All of you are my favourite, each and every one, and I don't know how that's possible because usually a favourite means one, but to me it means five. I've never ever felt so loved or content or like myself in any other place, and I think if one of you were to die, I'd die too. I'd cut my throat and let myself bleed and bleed until I went with you. Because I need it to be us. All of us. Or none of us."

My words were met with silence and a crow cawed somewhere in the woods, laughing at me. I bowed my head, heat rising in my cheeks as I kept my eyes tightly shut. They were gone, weren't they? Pop and away. I'd made them up, of course I had. Just like I'd made up imaginary friends when I was little. They were too perfect for me, of course they'd been fake. They couldn't be real, because if they were real that meant life was being good to me, and it was never good to me. Life was a rocky railroad and my train was about to fly off the tracks into a canyon.

"Rook," Jack said softly, taking my hand and I gasped, my eyes flying open as I found him still there, still bloody and hurting, but his eyes so full of love that it made me want to cry.

I looked to Mateo next and he cocked his head at me, his expression full of so much darkness, yet so much desire and want and dedication too.

Brutus licked my cheek where a splash of blood was drying against it from Jack's wound. He was here to stay, just like Jack and Mateo and –

"Niall." I looked up at him as he moved forward to shadow the sun. My monster of a husband, the one who'd brought us all together. Had he known what he was doing when he'd stitched our souls into one?

"Brooklyn," he said roughly, pushing his fingers into my hair, petting me like he had Jack, affection rising in his gaze. "I'm going nowhere. And if you want these fuckers too, then they can stay here with their hearts continuing to beat. But they're on probation, mind. If they prove they're worthy of you, and that they'll do anything to please ya and protect ya, then they can stay." He moved forward, slipping a key from his pocket and unlocking the padlock that was keeping Jack's collar in place, letting it tumble from his throat and fall to the ground. Jack didn't move, watching Niall closely like he was trying to understand him better and Mateo knelt up as Niall closed in on him with the keys.

"Don't do anything foolish, el burro," Niall warned as Mateo's upper lip peeled back.

"If any of you die, I'll die," I reminded them and Mateo looked my way in fury. "I'll kill myself, Dead Man. I mean it. I'll get a noose or a knife or I'll throw myself in the lake and I won't use my kickers and flappers to get to the surface. We all live, or I die. And that includes Brutus." I patted Brutus's back and he growled at me, making me giggle at his grumpies.

"Wait a minute," Niall rounded on me, shaking his head. "The dog isn't in on that part."

"Dogs don't live that long, mi sol," Mateo implored. "And that dog doesn't look very young."

"I said what I said," I insisted, folding my arms and pursing my lips at them. "If one of us dies, I'm dying too. I can't live without any of you, Brutus included, and that's that."

"Spider, for heaven's sake. That's insanity," Niall growled.

"That's rich coming from you, bastardo loco," Mateo muttered then turned to me. "Just omit the dog."

"No," I said stubbornly and the three men around me exchanged a concerned look. I swear it was the first time they'd ever looked at each other without hate in their eyes, and it made me all squishy inside.

"Fine, fine," Niall muttered. "We'll discuss it later."

He unlocked Mateo's padlock, freeing him from his collar and Mateo reached up to touch the skin at his throat which was red from his last zappy. His fingers flexed as he gazed up at Niall, like he was working to wrangle the monster in him, but as he looked to me, he sighed and dropped his hands to his sides.

A grin spilled over my face and I leapt to my feet, capturing Jack's hand and tugging him up after me. "Jack is hurt. We need to get him fixed up."

"I'll fix him myself. Come on, get moving." Niall shoved him along and Jack shoved him back, nearly knocking Niall over from the force he used. Niall spat a snarl, lunging at Jack with his fist raised and I dove into the way, giving him a furious pout until he lowered his arm, a growl rumbling through his chest. I took hold of his hand, keeping hold of Jack's too and Mateo watched us closely, his jaw grinding as we made it back to the house.

"Come on then, big lad." Niall steered Jack toward the kitchen as we stepped through the front door. "Sit down and I'll stitch ya up real nice. Got it?" He spoke loudly, like he didn't think Jack could understand him and Jack gave him a cool look before following.

Brutus trotted off to go and find his favourite boot and Mateo grabbed me by the waist, yanking me against him and speaking in a low voice. "We can go now, chica loca. You and me. We'll take a truck and run."

I laughed, booping him on the nose. "But I like it here, Dead Man. Don't you?"

"I liked it before it was invaded," he said coldly, not letting me go as I tried to pull away.

"Is it so bad?" I whispered, my heart tugging at the thought of him hating it here.

He frowned, drawing me closer in his arms as a heavy sigh escaped his chest. His forehead fell to mine and the warmth of his muscular arms folded me into him like we were a little origami swan. "Being with you is a pleasure like nothing I have ever known. Donde sea que estés, quiero estar."

I smiled at his pretty words, understanding them perfectly. "I like my hair this way too." I twisted my finger into it. "But do you really want to leave?"

"Te deseo," he said heavily and I was sure that meant yes please, and a Coca-Cola to go.

I tipped my head down as tears welled in my eyes. I couldn't keep my Dead Man if he didn't want to stay. I didn't want to be the reason he couldn't go skipping through meadows and picking dandelions on a hillside.

"If you need to go, then…that's okay. I understand. Everyone leaves in the end. But if this is our end then can I at least have a kiss to remember you by?"

Mateo's mouth found mine and the roughened stubble on his skin scratched against the softness of my chin, the feeling lighting me up inside. His tongue met mine and I moaned in delight as I tasted him, needing more, always more. I was a selfish, hungry creature who wanted all the love these men could offer me. I wanted to take and take and take, but I wanted to give back too. If only they knew how much.

"I'm not enough, am I? There's too many of you, and just one of little old me," I said against his lips, but he kept kissing me between my words, drawing me closer like he was getting drunk on my flesh.

"Mi sol, you are enough for an army of men."

"Oh my God, that's a lot of men. A lot of peen too. I'd have to work out an extensive rota. Maybe do it alphabetically, but would I do it by first names or last names? Oh no, I don't want all those men, Mateo, I'd have to clone my vagina, and I definitely don't know the science involved for that. I mean, I'm sure there's glue and a photocopier involved somewhere, but I don't know where exactly."

"Just three men then," Niall said as he returned to the room and I glanced over at him, tasting Mateo on my lips as my husband gave me a heated look. "You can handle three, Spider."

"At once, or one at a time?" I squeaked.

"Whatever you like," Niall said, resting his shoulder against the doorway just as Jack appeared at his back, shirtless and looking like a wicked soul given flesh. "Assuming I can cope with that without the urge to kill rising in me."

He gazed from me to Mateo, not seeming fazed, more curious and I let my fingers roam down Mateo's chest as I decided what to do.

My pulse starting racing and I looked between them all before returning my gaze to Mateo's, the energy in the room shifting to something dark and sinful.

Niall moved up behind me, his fingers pushing into my hair before locking around the back of my neck.

"What do you want, little psycho?" he asked as a quake rocked the foundations of my being.

I ran my hand down Mateo's chest again and watched his eyes fix on Niall with hatred sparking in them before moving back to me. And the hate melted away into something so much more potent.

"Anything?" I asked, moving into the arc of Mateo's body as Niall applied pressure to the back of my neck, encouraging me.

"Anything," Niall spoke in my ear. "You will never be denied anything in this house. The universe has taken too much from you, and I plan on giving it back piece by piece and then some. If you want el burro, then have him in any way you see fit."

"That's not for you to decide," Mateo warned.

"She's my wife," Niall hissed. "But you're right there, el burro, the decision is hers. I just want her to know nothing she chooses will change things between me and her. There's no force on this earth that can break what we have. So if my wife wants you, then she can have ya, and I guess I'll figure out if I can handle watching you with her too. But if you don't please her, then I'll be taking that up with ya, man to man."

"I want Mateo," I said firmly.

Niall pushed the back of my neck again, guiding our mouths together, and I kissed my Dead Man, pressing my tongue between his lips.

I felt his resistance to Niall's involvement give way as he grabbed me, dragging me closer like he was letting himself loose and suddenly I was in his arms, my legs wrapping around him as he ripped me away from Niall and strode across the room with me, laying me on the couch.

I felt Niall follow, sensed Jack's eyes on us too, but it didn't feel wrong, it was how it should have been, and that made a strange kind of sense to me.

Mateo kissed me villainously, weighing me down as he nudged my legs apart with his knees. I moaned as his hand slid under my top and into my bra, his thumb carving over my nipple as my skin came alive for him.

Mateo knelt up and I saw a possessed creature gazing back at me, darkness crawling all over his flesh. He unbuckled his belt, whipping it off with one movement and I frowned as he latched it around his throat and cinched it tight, twisting it around so the long end stuck out at the back.

"Hold onto that," he barked at Niall. "And if I go too far, then pull me off of her."

Niall didn't even question that statement as he grabbed onto the end of the belt and yanked on it with a smirk, making Mateo spit a curse.

"I said *if,*" Mateo growled.

"What's too far?" Niall asked and I was pretty curious to that too.

"Sometimes fucking makes me murderous," Mateo said and my toes curled up tightly, those words only turning me on ten times more.

"I want you so bad," I panted and Mateo and Niall's eyes snapped onto me, making me feel like a monarch in the room.

I pulled my dress up and slid my hand between my thighs, pushing into my panties and feeling how wet I was for them.

"Dead Man," I begged, reaching for him and he grabbed my wrist, rearing forward and pinning it above my head before tugging my other hand up to join it. I gasped as he yanked my panties aside and pushed two thick fingers inside me, my back arching and a loud moan falling from my throat.

Niall stood above him, watching every move he made and I met his gaze as my hips started to buck in time with Mateo's hand.

"Rook," Jack growled as he came into view on the other side of the couch and my gaze ran down the firm lines of his pecs to the tightness of his abs as he watched me with undisguised want in his eyes.

The three of them looking at me like that had me so turned on that I was losing my train of thought, my mind going in every direction as Mateo's thumb rolled over my clit. I was falling to ruin already, my breaths coming heavily as my three sinners watched, and with a few more pumps of Mateo fingers, I was a goner, a cry tearing from my throat as pleasure radiated out from my clit. Mateo continued to drive his fingers in and out of me as I came down from the climax, then he tore my panties clean off of me, shifting forward on his knees and tugging his pants down.

His free hand locked around my throat half a second before he drove his huge cock into me, filling me completely and making my pussy stretch for him. I garbled something against his mouth as he reared over me, a groan of pleasure leaving him before he drew his hips back and started fucking me.

372

Really fucking me. He didn't hold back, keeping me still as he took and took from my body, every drive of his hips demanding I keep up with him and I loved his ruthless claiming. I responded to every thrust by raising my hips to meet him and he cursed in his beautiful language while Niall cinched the belt around his throat a little tighter.

Mateo growled at him, but he seemed completely possessed as he held me down and fucked me harder, more furiously than I'd ever been touched and I gasped and begged for more as his fingers closed tighter around my neck.

I realised I couldn't breathe around the time I was about to come again, forgetting about oxygen in favour of the pleasure Mateo was offering me. His eyes darkened to nightshade as he watched me choke for him, a twisted smile lifting his lips as he filled me with every drive of his hips. And it seemed like the best place in the world to be, hovering between ecstasy and death.

He circled his hips, grinding against some perfectly delicious spot inside me and Niall yanked the belt tighter on his throat, making Mateo struggle for air and his fingers loosened on my neck.

I dragged down a breath just as my clit put on a firework show and I moaned and moaned as Mateo continued to pound into me. I was a fisherman lost at sea, whizzing away on a little piece of driftwood as the storm took me and hell did I wanna be swallowed by the ocean.

My climax went on and on as Mateo kept fucking me, fighting against the strain of the belt as Niall pulled it harder and harder, a jester's smile on his face as he toyed with the man fucking his wife. It was different to how it felt with him, but not any less intoxicating. My body felt made for these men and as my gaze slid to Jack, I had a crazy thought or ten about doing this with him too.

Mateo's hand tightened on my throat again and he looked down at me, all savage as he came close to his own release, his eyes burning from the inside out like two doorways to hell.

"That's enough, let go of her," Niall commanded, but Mateo's grip didn't ease. I didn't mind, I liked the kiss of pain and struggle for breath, but at the same time it was probably best I didn't up and die, even if it would have been worth it.

Niall yanked backwards on the belt as Mateo failed to release my throat and stars burst in front of my eyes as he clung on. Jack grabbed hold of Mateo's shoulder and the two of them hauled him off of me, throwing him to the floor while I sucked in air and touched my throat with a manic laugh leaving me.

Mateo lunged at me again and I reached for him, wanting to give him the release he'd given me, but Niall smashed a fist into his face, knocking him back to the floor and pressing a boot to his chest.

"That's enough playtime," Niall warned as I ran my hand between my legs, the aftershocks of pleasure still skipping through my flesh.

Jack leaned down, scooping me into his arms and carrying me out of the room.

"Hey!" Niall barked. "Where do ya think you're going?"

"Wash," Jack replied, kicking the door open to the bathroom he shared with Mateo and walking me to the large shower unit.

He placed me down and peeled off my dress for me. I unbuckled his pants and he let me tug them off along with his boxers, revealing the leviathan that lived between his thighs. He turned me around, pushing me into the shower and switching the water on, grabbing a sponge before lathering it up with soap and immediately rubbing it all over my body.

I turned to face him, my heart thundering from his touch as he worked methodically over my bare skin, his huge cock becoming even huger as it hardened. I tipped it a salute and Jack chuckled, gripping my chin between his fingers and leaning close to speak to me.

"I enjoyed watching you come for him," he whispered, giving me his words through our powerful mind connection. "But I would enjoy it far more

374

if you came for me. I want your pussy throbbing around my fingers and my name on your lips, would you like that Rook?"

I nodded, getting hot all over again as he crowded me in against the wall and I felt his Kraken cock rise up from the depths of the sea to come and sink my ship.

"Do these men make you happy?" he asked roughly.

"So happy," I whispered.

"Do I make you happy?" he asked, and I nodded.

"Then I'll stay here for you, Rook. I'll stay as long as you want me."

"Then you'll have to stay forever," I breathed and he closed the distance between our mouths, sealing that promise with a kiss. A kiss I wanted to keep in my pocket for the rest of time.

"That's enough of that," Niall snapped as he entered the room, pulling off his own clothes and walking straight into the shower, shoving Jack away from me and I got all of a fluster as I looked between them.

"No. Bad, Spider. You don't play with them unless I give ya the go ahead." He pointed at me and I pouted. "Go get dressed, big fella," he commanded Jack, not taking his eyes off of me and Jack left the room, wrapping a towel around his waist and stealing the sight of his muscular ass from me.

"Did you not like watching me with Mateo?" I asked sadly, hoping I was wrong.

"I coped with it just fine, I suppose," he said airily and I looked down to find he was rock hard.

"You look happy," I spoke to his dick. "You liked it, didn't you?" I reached for his cock but, Niall snatched my wrist to stop me, giving me a serious look.

"Did you like it?" he asked.

"Yes," I said huskily and he smirked at me.

"Yeah, I know ya did." He grazed his thumb up my neck as his brow lowered. "Even when he choked ya?"

"I liked that bit the most," I said with a girlish giggle and his smirk grew darker.

"Alright, it's settled then. You're the boss, love. You tell me when you fancy a whirl with them and I'll give ya the green light, so long as I don't wanna steal ya from them myself." He kissed me deep and slow and I whimpered at the feel of his hard cock against my stomach, knowing this wasn't going to end here. "We need to go tell my pa and Anastasia about our happy news."

"Can I be there so I can watch the exact moment her dreams are crushed out of existence?" I asked excitedly and he nodded. "And Jack and Mateo and Brutus too?"

"Not Mateo," he said. "My family's looking for him and the treasure he hides. They can't have him."

"Okay," I agreed and Niall scooped me up, pressing me to the wall as he lined himself up to take me.

He gave me an expression that made me tingle all over. "We'll give him a visit in a few days, once I've had my fill of ya."

NIALL

CHAPTER TWENTY FOUR

The drive to my pa's house was a quiet one, the night pressing in around us as it fell beyond the windows and the dangerous prospect of what I was about to do laying heavily on my shoulders.

I licked my dry lips, glancing in the rearview mirror at Brooklyn and Jack where they sat in the back of my Ford pickup, her head nestled against his chest while he held her close beneath his arm.

Bastard had barely even flinched when I'd patched him up after the crossbow incident and he hadn't mentioned the pain of the wounds on his shoulder in the three days since, even though they had to be hurting like a bitch. He had taken plenty of fuss from Brooklyn though. No problems for him to accept that. He'd almost gotten her to sleep in his room that first night too, though I'd put an end to that sharpish by promising her a night filled with orgasms which she hadn't been able to resist. I'd have to keep an eye on him and el burro though. This wasn't a society where everyone got equal votes or any of that bullshit. It was a dictatorship and I was head dick. I had the wedding ring to prove it.

Brooklyn was humming a tune as she looked out the window, winding her fingers between Jack's and kissing his knuckles while he just watched her. But as I bumped over a pothole in the road, he raised his grey eyes to meet mine, a twinkle of smugness shining in them which got me all kinds of riled up.

"Any chance you can drive, big fella?" I asked him in a low voice, my fingers tight on the steering wheel as I turned a corner and entered the private street where my family all took up residence, aside from me and my nephew Kyan.

"Yes," he replied and I nodded.

"Then you'll be able to drive this in a getaway if it comes to that." I didn't add the part which stated I'd be dead in that scenario, but he nodded his understanding, letting me know he'd keep her safe no matter what. I'd had that chat with him nice and clearly while she was drowning herself in Coco Pops this morning, and I was confident he got it. He had one role to play here: keep her alive.

"Yes," he agreed once more, letting some of the unease in my gut settle.

I began to pass by the houses of my brothers and sister, nieces and nephews, each of them more ostentatious than the last, each trying hard to win a dick measuring contest which they knew I would easily dominate if only I could summon the energy to participate in their bullshit.

"Did you grow up in a fancy house like one of these, Hellfire?" Brooklyn whispered, the awe in her voice making me shift uncomfortably in my seat.

"Not all pretty things are sweet on the inside, love," I murmured, tension growing in my limbs with every second that we closed in on the heart of my family home.

Brutus barked from his position in the back of the truck. I glanced at him in the mirror as he lifted his nose to the breeze and sniffed at it, no doubt scenting bullshit on the air and wanting to sink his jaws into it.

"You remember what I said?" I asked as I turned onto my pa's drive, pausing for the electric gates to open for me and ignoring the men he had positioned there as I drummed my tattooed fingers on the wheel.

"Stay close to you and Jack," Brooklyn sighed, like that was the most boring instruction she'd ever been given, but she'd be fucking sticking to it or there would be hell to pay.

"And Brutus," I growled. "You don't let go of his leash unless you have to run for your life – got it?"

The seriousness of my tone made her lift her eyes to mine as I turned to look back at her and she nodded.

"I promise."

I glanced at Jack as he tugged her to his side more firmly. "Safe," he vowed and there was something in the set of his jaw and the feral look in his eyes which made me believe him on that. He was her creature just as I was, and he wouldn't see any harm come to her.

I clucked my tongue, wanting nothing more than to turn and drive away from here while knowing this had to be done. I'd have preferred to do it alone, but Brooklyn needed to see it with her own eyes. She needed to let those damn insecurities of hers fall away into the irrelevant nonsense that they were. She was the only woman for me, and I'd spell that out plain as day to all those who thought to deny it.

I nodded once, slamming my foot to the floor the moment the gates had fully opened and tearing up the gravel drive without another word, making Brutus bark in alarm in the back and a whoop of excitement spill from Brooklyn's lips.

Mateo had wanted to come too of course, but even he had been forced to admit that revealing himself to a whole host of Irish and Russian gangsters who would like nothing more than to torture a member of his fancy cartel in the quest for information on their organisation and the riches he'd stolen from them was a bad idea. So he was just stewing away back at the house. I'd even left his collar off when we went, making it clear to him that this arrangement of ours was coming upon a grand change. When we returned, he'd either be ready and waiting, looking to sign up to this ride until the bitter end or he'd be gone, and we'd see the truth of him plain enough. He hadn't run yet, so I suspected he'd be staying.

Strangely, I was hoping for that too. Because no matter my own feelings on him or the behemoth currently sitting in the back of my truck, it was clear to me that they were important to Brooklyn, and I didn't want to see her cry over either of them. So if keeping them around equalled her happiness as well as her safety, then so be it. I could work with that. I never had made obvious choices in life, and this seemed like the kind of lunatic idea I liked the flavour of.

I jerked the parking brake hard, swinging the wheel around and skidding the truck to a halt at the base of the steps which led up to the house I hated more than any other in this world.

"Wow," Brooklyn breathed from the backseat. "It looks like two mansions got together for an orgy with another two mansions, and then all of them had quadruplets and then they all bought really big dogs and then they all kinda squished themselves together to become a mega mansion."

I cleared my throat, glancing at the imposing structure which my father occupied alongside a whole host of staff, and I nodded.

"Yeah, and in each and every room of it is a bastard born of sin, built perfectly to raise more bastards within its walls and coat our skin in darkness, ready to unleash upon the world," I muttered.

"You hate it here," she whispered sadly.

"It's no home," I agreed. "Just a shell built for breeding evil little clones."

"But you're not a clone," she pointed out, reaching between the seats and running her hand down my forearm, her fingers brushing against the Devil I had tattooed there. "You broke the mould, Hellfire."

I grinned at that remark and nodded firmly, taking a cigarette from the door pocket and placing it in the corner of my lips before lighting it up.

"Then let's go remind them of that, shall we, love?" I offered, exhaling a cloud of smoke as her eyes lit with violence and my heart began to beat faster in anticipation of this game.

I rolled my shoulders back, checked the Desert Eagle which was sitting snug beneath the smart jacket I wore in its holster, and I drew in a lungful of smoke before opening the car door and getting out.

I moved to open the rear door next, offering a hand to Brooklyn and she took it, letting me draw her out to stand before me in the long blue dress she was wearing which had tiny silver skulls stitched all across it. She'd paired it with some killer heels which brought her a little closer to my height, but I still dwarfed her even in them. I reached out to tuck a lock of ebony hair back behind her ear while I looked her over.

"Last chance to escape this hell without having to look it in the eye," I offered, toking on my cigarette as Jack got out of the car behind her but she just giggled, booping me on the nose and shaking her head.

"I want to see her tits deflate, Hellfire," she said firmly. "I want to watch all the air zip out of them when she realises she can never have you."

I smirked at that, nodding my head in acceptance of what I'd known had to happen anyway, and exchanging a look with Jack that warned him in no uncertain terms to protect her with his life.

I took a last inhale from my smoke then flicked it aside, moving around the truck and taking the leash attached to Brutus's new collar and whistling for him to jump out of the truck as I opened the back of it.

The big bastard snapped at my fingers as I jerked on the blue diamante leash and I laughed as I managed to escape his jaws with all my fingers intact then handed the leash to Brooklyn.

"Hold on tight to him in there," I warned her. "He's a good boy, he'll protect ya. Only let go if you gotta run and he needs to attack."

"I'm the fastest runner ever," Brooklyn swore. "But we won't have to run, Hellfire. They won't dare attack us."

I grunted my disagreement because I really wasn't certain how this was about to go. I planned on making it quick, that was for sure. I'd lay out the facts, let them see my new bride then fuck off sharpish before anyone had the chance to get too murderous with their intentions.

"How fast can you run while carrying a tiny scrap of a girl, big fella?" I asked, lifting my gaze to Jack as he moved up close behind Brooklyn, his chest pressing to her back and making her inch towards me so that she was sandwiched between us. Brooklyn bit her lip like she didn't mind that at all and I took a step forward myself with a grin, making sure she really was trapped between us.

"Fast," Jack said, his tone serious and the look he gave me swearing it.

I wasn't sure what to make of the big fella, but I was becoming more and more convinced of his feelings towards Brooklyn, and for some reason that made me trust him with her safety. He also seemed to respond pretty well to orders, snapping to attention if he was given a nice clear one and making me think he liked it when someone focused his mind for him like that. I happened to enjoy bossing people about, so we would likely get on like a house on fire once we were given a little bit of time to warm up to one another.

I reached out to wrap my fingers around Brooklyn's throat, caressing the racing pulse point there and giving her a light squeeze, which made her moan softly between us, her fingers releasing the leash and allowing Brutus to wander away.

She liked that, falling into the thrall of my power, but I was pretty sure we both knew she was the real one in charge around here now that she'd gone and shattered the last of my resolve and made me fully hers.

"Come on then, love," I said in a low tone. "Time to show my family that I have a new master now."

I released her abruptly and turned to walk up the white steps which led to the front door, feeling the two of them and the dog close at my back as they followed in silence.

The door swung open before I made it there and I nodded at Martha as she looked between me and the uninvited guests I'd brought with me on this little excursion.

"Find yourself something to keep busy with in the kitchen for a while, eh Martha?" I suggested, not bothering to hide the darkness in my eyes as she looked up at me.

She nodded seriously, quickly taking note of the way this meeting was going to go and doing the sensible thing in heeding my word.

I placed a hand on her shoulder as she quivered before me, giving her a squeeze of reassurance.

"I'm not looking to spill any blood if I don't have ta," I assured her. "Just keep outa the way and you'll be dandy."

"Dandy as a cotton candy," Brooklyn agreed as she spun past me and opened her arms wide, tipping her head back to look up at the obnoxious mural my pa had gotten painted on the ceiling above our heads and cooing softly. There were angels and clouds and all kinds of heavenly things which I very much doubted he would ever experience in any form of afterlife. I'd always assumed it was some kind of twisted joke.

"You ready, love?" I asked, reaching out to snag Brooklyn's attention back and she nodded brightly as she obediently moved to stand beneath my arm.

I drew her in close, whistling to Brutus who still lingered outside and ignoring Martha's shocked gasp as the big brute lumbered through the door with a low growl.

Jack stepped inside last, moving to stand on Brooklyn's other side and looking to me like he favoured instruction over the freedom to act of his own accord. That worked well for me. I bobbed my chin toward the long corridor we needed to take.

"Just keep your focus on our little psycho, big fella," I told him. "Stay close to her and get her the fuck out if things go to shit. Got it?'

"Yes," he agreed solemnly, shifting even closer to Brooklyn and haunting her steps as we began down the corridor.

Martha turned and hurried away after closing the front door behind us, heading towards the kitchens as I'd told her and calling out to the other members of staff to join her for a meeting as she went. Clever old gal.

The sound of bullshit conversations and the scent of expensive aftershaves blended in the air as we closed in on the dining room. I rolled my shoulders back as I prepared to head through the gates of hell and tell the Devil who had fathered me that I had chosen my own path without him.

I whistled sharply to draw Brutus closer to us again and either my command or the scent of expensive meat drew him to obey as he prowled nearer just as I opened the dining room door. I caught his leash, handing it to Brooklyn and giving her a firm look to remind her to keep hold of it.

Brutus stalked inside, drawing an alarmed cry from Anastasia's lips just as I crossed the threshold with Brooklyn very much beneath my arm and Jack hounding our steps.

"What's the meaning of this, lad?" Pa called, feigning amusement while his narrowed gaze took in every single thing about me and the pack of wild animals I'd just brought into his home. "You know I don't allow beasts in the house."

"Do I?" I asked with a frown. "Because you let me in often enough, and I think most of the people currently perched around this dining table would call me a beast, yet I visit frequently."

My supposed fiancée was sitting on the far side of the table alongside her father and several other Russian pricks, so she was getting a clear enough view of the little firecracker who was nestled beneath my arm alongside my Desert Eagle. Brooklyn gave a cutesy little wave to her as she looked right back, owning her power and making the corner of my lips lift.

Aside from the Russians, the table was once again filled with my brothers and sister, their spouses and kids and all other various blood relatives of mine who I disliked almost as much as I dismissed them. They were nothing to me. Not really. Never had been. Just a noose around my neck attached to a dead weight which I had always been fighting against while it tried to pull me down. But here and now, I was ready to cut the damn thing free of me for good.

"I thought you had better taste than to bring a whore to the dinner table, little Niall," Roland scoffed and I drew my gun so fast that the first he knew of it was the bang of the shot being fired and the pain of his shoulder shattering as my bullet struck him and threw him backwards from his chair.

His wife screamed somewhat prettily, diving down after him and a couple of my nieces and nephews flinched, but mostly, the cold-hearted bastards sitting around the table just took note of my demand for respect and started paying a whole lot more attention.

"You'd better have a damn good reason for prancing in here and shooting your kin with a bunch of mutts in tow, lad," Pa growled as he made a move to get to his feet, but I shook my head at him, wheeling my weapon his way.

"Uh, uh, Papa bear, no need to get up," I said loudly, releasing my grip on Brooklyn and leaving her to stand with Jack as I stalked closer to him.

Brutus tugged on his leash and despite my commands to Brooklyn, she instantly released her hold on it, shrugging at me innocently as she let him do as he pleased. I sighed as the dog moved to walk at my side like a wolf drawn to its alpha, scenting the hunt as I locked my kill in my sight.

I whistled to my dog as I made it to the empty chair which had been left for me at my pa's right hand and I pulled it out, pointing to the table in command.

Brutus dutifully leapt up onto the priceless mahogany, sending plates and glasses flying in every direction before dropping his scarred grey muzzle to Liam O'Brien's plate and stealing his lump of prime steak straight off of it.

My father shoved his chair back, his upper lip curling in disgust as Brutus chomped away happily, splashing gravy from his chops and splattering it all over the pristine table linen while Anastasia jumped up with a disgusted cry.

"He won't bite any of ya, unless I tell him to," I said to the eyes which were all clinging to me, never once looking away from the man at the head of the table.

"He does get the chompies sometimes," Brooklyn piped up. "So he might."

"Yeah," I agreed. "He might. Most likely he'll be happy enough eating his way through all of these lovely meals though, so just keep your fingers to yourselves and don't make the foolish decision to try and hurt him, or you'll regret it in all kinds of ways."

Brutus turned from my pa's plate as I finished up my warning, moving to claim the meat from Vlad's next, ignoring the way the Russian was looking at him like he fully intended to cut him apart piece by piece.

"Out with it then," Pa barked. "You've clearly come here with something to say so let's have it."

"I just wanted to make an introduction to all of you fine people," I said brightly, keeping my aim fixed on my pa while turning and smiling at the rest of the gathered villains in the room. "Because I think there may have been a little mix up, crossed wires, miscommunication, that kind of thing, and it seemed like it would be prudent to clear it up before it went on a moment longer."

Dougal shifted in his seat further along the table, reaching for the gun he no doubt had tucked in his belt, but Jack punched him in the back of the head so fast that I'd barely even seen him coming. Damn that man could get a wriggle on when he needed to.

My brother crashed face first into his dinner plate, out cold or maybe even dead, but certainly not moving either way. There were a few sharp inhales as the wild eyes in the room shifted between him, the dog and me like they were trying to figure out where the most danger lay.

Silly them for forgetting my Spider. She was the one who owned all of us after all.

"What is the meaning of this, Niall?" Anastasia demanded, tossing her napkin down by her feet as she glared at me from her position by the wall, and I raised a wicked grin her way as I gave her my attention.

"Can I tell her?" Brooklyn asked keenly, taking a running jump and hopping up onto the dining table too, doing a little spin as she landed off balance and kicking a glass of scotch straight into Dermot's lap, either on purpose or accidentally. Either way, it was fucking funny, especially when Brooklyn asked him if he'd pissed himself.

"Rook," Jack growled, reminding her of why we were here, and he had a damn good point. The element of surprise was buying us this little bit of time, but soon enough one of the arseholes here would pull a weapon and we were planning on getting the fuck out of here before the bullets started flying. Well… before any *more* bullets started flying anyway.

Roland was still sniffling and whimpering over the bullet in his shoulder while his wife tried to stop the bleeding with a napkin on the far side of the table, but no one was really interested in his hysterics right now.

"I'm the cat who got the dream," Brooklyn said excitedly as she hopped and pranced her way along the table, vaulting over Brutus who growled possessively over the fifth steak he'd stolen before pausing to do a pirouette right between my pa, Vlad and Anastasia's pushed back chair.

"You have three seconds to explain why there's a crazy woman dancing on my table, Niall," Pa growled in warning at me and I narrowed my eyes on him.

"You won't speak ill of her in front of me again," I growled right back.

"You can't call me crazy," Brooklyn added. "I'm sanely challenged.

Look it up."

"And why are you on the table?" Anastasia demanded.

"Because of this." Brooklyn waved her left hand in a dramatic little flourish, making the fat black diamond on her wedding ring flash in the low light of the room and grinning widely as she looked right into my ex-fiancée's eyes. "I made a hornet man out of him."

"Hornet?" Vlad hissed, exchanging a look with one of his men who was steadily inching his hand off of the table.

I took a knife from my belt and flung it at said hand, impaling it and halting its progress, finding myself mildly impressed as the Russian didn't so much as squeak in pain, only glaring at me over the hilt of the knife and leaving it there while a red stain spread across the white table linen beneath it.

"See that, Connor?" I called, looking for my newly balding brother along the table and finding him in the shameful position furthest from our father right at the end. "You could take a lesson or two from this fella on how not to look like a pussy when taking a beating from your better."

Connor looked inclined to say something, but Brooklyn whirled on him, tugging a pistol from the back of her skirt and levelling it in his direction.

"Don't open your mouth if you like it that shape, bald man," she warned. "I get shooty when people are rude to Hellfire."

I chuckled darkly as I looked up at her, lust burning through me in a powerful wave while I watched her dancing on the table before a room full of enemies and wielding a gun without a flicker of fear in sight. Though in all honesty, she hadn't had nearly enough practice with that weapon and the likelihood of her actually managing to shoot my brother from this distance was slim, so I whistled to get her attention back on track.

Brooklyn pouted at me in disappointment then whirled around to aim her gun at Anastasia instead.

"I'm sorry for your loss," she said seriously, touching her free hand to her heart and showing off that ring again. "But you can't have my Niall."

"Yours?" Anastasia scoffed, her disapproving gaze roaming all over my little psycho and getting my back up in a way that was mighty likely to cause death.

"Yeah," I agreed loudly, making everyone look my way once more. "All hers."

"He took me up the aisle and rammed my ring and all that jazz," Brooklyn said proudly. "And he doesn't even like your flouncy tits."

"What is she saying?" Pa barked, either genuinely unable to figure this out or refusing to believe it until he heard it from my own mouth.

"That beautiful creature up there," I called loudly, pointing to Brooklyn and making certain that everyone in the room was looking at her before I went on. "Chose my unworthy self to be her creature. To serve and protect her from now until my death. So I'm sorry, glove." I flicked half a glance at Anastasia whose eyes seemed about to bug out of her face as she realised what I was saying. "But I did tell ya I wasn't a good match. And now it turns out I'm no match at all. You can't marry a man who's already married."

I turned my attention back to my pa as Anastasia's feral shriek lit the air and found his furious gaze locked on mine as he took in this act of defiance for what it was. The shattering of his control over me.

Brutus leapt from the table as Anastasia attempted to launch herself at my new bride and the Russians all yelled in fear as the enormous dog slammed into her, knocking her to the ground.

"Time to go!" I barked, snapping my fingers at Jack who immediately moved forward with his arms held wide for Brooklyn. She laughed excitedly then did a running jump from the table straight into them.

He turned and ran with her instantly, not needing any further instruction while everyone at the table leapt to their feet, pulling weapons and trying to escape from Brutus who dove headfirst at them, fangs bared and ripping into flesh left and right as he went.

I turned to leave as well, jerking to a halt as strong fingers wrapped around my wrist and I was forced to look back into the eyes of the man who had owned me up until this very moment.

"You know what this choice will cost you?" Liam O'Brien demanded furiously, all the worst of his demons rising up in his eyes in a way that had once terrified me beyond anything in this twisted world of ours. But I had long since become a far worse monster than he was, and it was about time he realised what he'd created in his cruelty.

"I know what it's cost *you*," I replied, nice and low, leaning in so he'd hear every word. "The feral beast you whipped and chained has finally broken free of its shackles. Question is, old man, are you gonna let me run free? Or will you be fool enough to try your luck in collaring me again? Because if you don't back me in this then you'll make an enemy of me. I won't be yours a moment longer. I won't be a part of this organisation you love so well. And worst of all, I'll make you into my prey the next time I decide to go on the hunt."

His face paled at those words and the truth in them, the reality of what he knew I was and how well he understood those threats as he blinked and damn near flinched out of fear of me. He saw my truth then. Understood my line and in that moment, I knew he wasn't fool enough to try and stop me. This was done. He could deal with the Russians and call me back once they were no longer trying to capture me for their own designs too.

I gave him a shove so hard that he was sent flying back into his chair which almost upended, then fired four shots into the ceiling, sending the rest of the people in the room diving for cover.

"I'll be seeing all of you then. Feel free to give a donation to charity in lew of a wedding gift. My wife has particular tastes and won't be impressed by any of the bullshit you would gift her, so give it to some baby animals or some shit and do something good for once in yer miserable lives."

I whistled sharply for Brutus who was somewhat distracted by the arm he was savaging but he looked up at my command, barking aggressively before taking off after me as I stalked towards the door.

I didn't run. Didn't even hurry myself particularly, giving any of them the chance to take a pot shot at my back if they had the balls for it, but none of them did and in the wake of the carnage I'd inflicted upon all of them, I strode from the room.

"You will live to regret this, Niall O'Brien!" Anastasia's words reached me just as the door swung closed at my back. "No one treats me like this! No one!"

I snorted in dismissal before heading back outside to my truck where Brooklyn and Jack were already sitting in the passenger seat while the big fella aimed a shotgun towards the doors in anticipation of anyone following me.

I dropped into the driver's seat and looked at the two of them as Brooklyn arched her spine and whooped in victory, tipping her head right back so that she would have fallen had Jack's hand not been firm around her spine where she straddled him.

I caught her chin in my grip and made her look at me as I stole a moment of true freedom in her eyes then kissed her hard, letting her feel my passion for her in the press of my mouth on hers.

"You done good, Jack," I said as I pulled back, turning her to look at him next. "Maybe good enough to earn yourself a kiss too?"

I gave Brooklyn a questioning look and she bit her lip as she nodded, her hips grinding over Jack's lap and making me all kinds of jealous.

I watched her as she leaned in, my hand still clasping her jaw as she moved forward and parted her lips in anticipation of the kiss she was offering.

For a moment he held himself exactly where he was, his eyes drinking her in before slipping to meet mine, and I smiled as I saw the question in his grey gaze.

"You want me to give you the order?" I guessed and he nodded, though the hunger in his eyes as he looked to her again said he was damn close to taking what he wanted either way. "Then do it, lad. Make her moan for us."

Tension filled the car as we all waited for him to do it, my heart pounding restlessly as a mixture of jealousy and lust built within me as the seconds ticked by, filling with heat and a promise which made all kinds of fucked-up sense.

Jack shifted forward just as the front door banged open at the top of the steps, and I cursed as I was forced to hit the gas, accelerating away before a Russian or a sibling or someone equally annoying could come after us.

I sped down the gravel drive, the wheels kicking up small stones and flinging them in every direction before I steered us out onto the road and whooped with triumph.

"We should celebrate!" Brooklyn cried. "I want to go somewhere fancy. As fancy as a peacock in a bowtie."

"Fancy it is, then," I agreed, heading out of the private estate where my family all resided and driving fast towards the centre of the city where all the best places to eat and drink were.

Jack kept hold of Brooklyn as we drove, his big hands stroking soft lines against her back while she wriggled and moaned in his lap, no doubt turning him on even more than she was me, and I had to slap myself around the face as we parked up just to make myself concentrate.

"This fancy enough?" I asked, jerking my chin at the exclusive bar where a line extended down the sidewalk and everyone looked fucking rich.

"Oooh, yes," Brooklyn cooed, clapping her hands and I nodded, getting out of the truck and rounding it to open the door so that she could follow.

I took her hand, pulling her out of Jack's lap, and he was hot on her heels as he got out too.

Brutus was crashed out in the bed of the truck, gravy still speckled around his chops and his belly full of stolen steak, so he just ignored us as we headed towards the entrance to the bar.

The man on the door knew my face and he said nothing as we strode past the line, leaving us to our own devices as we walked into the dimly lit space where soft music was playing and people dressed in designer clothes sat around poncy little tables.

I took Brooklyn's hand in mine and strode straight to the bar, pulling out a stool which some fucker in a suit was sitting on and flashing him a threatening grin when he whipped around to protest. He soon scampered away and I lifted Brooklyn onto it, placing her down and kissing her again, my heart racing as the reality of what we'd just done set in. I'd finally told my pa to get fucked, and the adrenaline coursing through my limbs was desperate for an outlet to celebrate the fact.

I barked an order at the bartender who hurriedly poured a few glasses of top shelf scotch for us, and Jack snatched the bottle from his hand before he could retreat.

I waved off his protests, making no complaints as Jack drank from the neck of the bottle, leaving me and Brooklyn to knock our glasses against each other's and sink our liquor.

Brooklyn instantly started heaving and spluttering, cursing loudly and drawing attention from all around us as I laughed at her, and she fought to catch her breath from the burn of the scotch on the way down.

"That's it, girl, cough it all up," I said, slapping her back firmly as she clung to my arm and swore at me.

What's Love Got To Do With It by Tina Turner came on over the speakers and Brooklyn perked right up.

"Oh, this is the song from the Sexy Dancing film," she gasped, forgetting the fact that she'd been near death from that drink thirty seconds ago.

"What?" I asked.

"You know with Patrick Gravy and the baby crying in the corner."

"Dirty Dancing?" I asked with a frown.

"No. Sexy Dancing. I always wanted to do that in-the-air thing."

"Dirty," I growled.

"Sexy," she snarled back.

"Dirty."

"Sexy."

"Dirty."

"Sexy."

"Sexy," Jack agreed and I narrowed my gaze on his expressionless face because he fucking knew it was Dirty and he was just being a cunt.

Brooklyn gave me the murder eyes and I threw my hands into the air in exasperation.

"Gah! This isn't even that song," I pointed out. "And you're getting, like, every detail wrong."

"One of us is," she muttered, exchanging a look with Jack which suggested I was the idiot here. "Are you going to do the dance thing with me, Hellfire? I wanna fly up above all these people and make them jealous of my moves. Be my Patrick Gravy and I'll be your baby. *Please.*"

"We're in a bar, not a club," I laughed, my gaze running over her hungrily.

"Err, I think these people came here for a show, Hellfire. Are we putting one on or not?"

I glanced around at the fancy tables filled with even fancier people who were all paying little to no attention to the music that was playing softly over the speakers. None of whom were so much as shimmying in their chairs. This wasn't a place where people came to dance. Then again, I'd never much cared for what was supposed to happen and where.

"Fuck it." I tossed Jack's rejected glass of scotch to the back of my throat and dropped the glass on the table. "I'll be your Patrick Gravy, but I want you to do something much more interesting with those watermelons when we get out of here than just carry them."

"Put them in my dress again and make them bounce about like big bazingas?" she asked with a pout and I ran my thumb over her lips.

"No, Spider. I love your tiny tatas just as they are."

"You love my tiny tatas?" she echoed in disbelief and I nodded in confirmation.

Her smile lit me up inside and I took her hand, twisting her beneath my arm before encouraging her to jog away between the tables in preparation for her big moment. Not that I knew what the fuck I was doing, but she was tiny, and I was pretty certain I could toss her up over my head without any practice. Either that or I'd drop her on her arse and we'd all get a good laugh out of it. Seemed like a win, win to me.

Jack stayed by the bar, slowly drinking from the neck of the scotch bottle and watching us as we got ready for our big moment.

I had no idea at what point Brooklyn planned on launching herself at me seeing as this was the wrong song, but as Tina dove into another rendition of the chorus, Brooklyn broke into a sprint and raced across the room straight for me.

I grinned widely as she came, holding my hands out and catching her waist as she leapt into the air, raising her up and over my head, looking up at her as she straightened out, shrieking in delight.

Several people started clapping as I held her there, turning her in a circle before tossing her up towards the ceiling and catching her again, her legs winding around my chest as I slowly lowered her down the length of my body.

My heart was thundering at the feeling of her against me and a growl rumbled through my chest as she dropped her head back and I swung her in a circle, making her dark hair fan out as her hips met with mine.

Brooklyn gasped as I yanked her upright in my arms once more, our chests colliding and our lips almost touching as I rolled my hips against hers and held her in place so that there was no doubting just how hard I was between us.

"Here?" she panted, grinding against me and giving me a look so full of sex that I almost gave in.

But one glance at the crowd looking at us told me clear enough that I didn't really want to fuck my wife right in front of them.

"Outside," I countered, keeping hold of her and carrying her straight towards the exit beyond the bar.

Brooklyn ground her hips against mine as I pushed through the emergency exit door, but instead of finding my way out into a darkened alley, I found myself at the foot of a set of stairs with a second door chained up tight in front of me. Seemed mighty dangerous for a fire escape, but more importantly, it was mighty inconvenient for me and my plans to bury myself inside my wife.

"Fuck," I cursed, looking around and Brooklyn slapped me as my attention wavered from her.

"I don't like waiting, Niall," she snarled and damn she was a ferocious creature when she was horny.

My gaze fell on the stairs, but before I could figure out how to make them work, I noticed a sign for the roof instead.

"Alright then," I agreed, hoisting her up in my arms and starting to climb the stairs.

She moved her mouth to my throat and began kissing me in a way that made my entire body fill with need and I upped my pace as I pushed on with the climb.

By the time we made it to the top of the eighth floor, I was damn close to having a heart attack and she had my shirt entirely unbuttoned, her mouth leaving bite marks and bruises on my flesh as well as lipstick stains which I didn't ever want to wash off.

I shoved the door to the roof open and stumbled out onto it, finding a low wall at the edge of the building and sinking down on it as I caught my breath, settling her on my lap.

"I thought you were unstoppable, Hellfire?" Brooklyn teased as I hoisted her skirt up over her thighs and moved my mouth down the length of her throat.

"I woulda carried you up a hundred flights of stairs if it would have bought me a minute between your thighs, love," I swore to her, though in all likelihood, I'd have died in the attempt. Not that I would have given up.

"Only a minute?" she teased and I cursed her as I found the edge of her panties and dragged them out of my way.

"Tell me what you want," I demanded as I shifted my hand between us and tugged my cock free of my trousers, letting the piercing roll over her clit and groaning at the wetness I found waiting between her legs for me.

"I want to scream so loud the stars can hear me," she panted, rocking her hips in demand, and I gave in as I guided my dick to her core before taking hold of her round arse and tugging her down onto me.

Brooklyn threw her head back and moaned so loudly that I was pretty certain the stars really did hear, the twinkly little bastards getting a good old show as I gripped her arse tightly and began to fuck her deep and hard.

She fisted my hair as she rode me, meeting every thrust and begging for more between her moans, the two of us like a pair of insatiable teenagers never able to get enough.

Brooklyn pressed her knees against bricks either side of me, the pressure of her body bearing down on mine making me slip and I cursed as I fell backwards, my weight overbalancing us on the low wall and death calling out as the eight floor drop suddenly looked up at us with a promise to be our end. It wasn't the worst way to go, buried deep in my wife with her smile making me burn inside, but still.

I tried to shove her back, panic engulfing my heart as we began to fall but before we could go tumbling to our demise, a huge hand latched around my ankle and another fisted in her hair, dragging us back to safety.

"Jesus," I cursed as I righted myself on the wall again, blinking up at Jack as he hauled Brooklyn out of my lap, leaving me sat before them with my cock out as my heart remembered how to beat again.

"Rook," Jack growled and I nodded.

"Yeah, you saved her," I panted.

"Like a real-life superhero," Brooklyn breathed, reaching up to run her fingers down the side of his face before leaning in and taking that kiss I'd commanded earlier.

Adrenaline still raced through my veins and my cock throbbed in its abandoned state as I watched the two of them, drawing my hand to it and groaning as I began to work myself over, eyeing the way he gripped her arse and his tongue pushed into her mouth.

Part of me wanted to grab hold of him by his long, silver hair and hurl him to his death on the street below for touching her like that. But another part of me was riled up over him saving her yet again, enjoying the punishment of watching them together and accepting the hurt it caused in favour of how damn hot it was to watch. I'd liked watching Mateo fuck her a little too much, but it had still felt good ripping her off of him and denying him his release. I was very back and forth in my emotions like that.

"You ever fucked a superhero, love?" I panted as I pumped my cock and Brooklyn broke her kiss with Jack as she turned to shake her head at me.

"Only the villains," she confirmed which made me all kinds of possessive over her, but I was into this too.

"How about you give it a go then? Put on a show for this villain of yours and see if I can stop myself from killing the two of ya for it."

Brooklyn bit her lip in excitement over that possibility and I smiled as I continued to pleasure myself in front of her, loving the way her eyes kept dropping to take in the movements of my hand as I ran it up and down my shaft.

She looked back to Jack then slowly started stripping, peeling her clothes off piece by piece until she was standing butt naked before him with nothing but her stiletto heels still in place.

"I'm a bad guy too," she whispered as he watched her in silence, the hunger in his expression making it more than clear how much he wanted her. "And I need all the bad kinds of punishment."

I ran my thumb across my bottom lip as I watched them, but Jack's eyes lifted to me once more, asking for another command and making me laugh as I realised that that was exactly what he needed from me. He really was a pack animal, and he was hungering for the command of an alpha.

"Don't keep her waiting, big fella," I warned. "Or I'm gonna grab hold of her and make her scream myself."

Jack gave in as easy as that, stepping forward and yanking his shirt off with one hand before gripping Brooklyn by the back of the neck and kissing her with a rough kind of passion that made me ache to take hold of her too.

She whimpered in his arms, her fingers fumbling at his belt and the tremble in them made it clear to me how much she wanted this. She was a thirsty little thing. And she wanted to taste all of her heathens as often as she could.

Brooklyn gasped as she freed the leviathan from Jack's pants, and I paused in the movements of my hand along my shaft as I stared at the fucking thing.

"Will it fit?" she gasped, looking down at his huge cock, and Jack grinned like a savage.

"If mine fits, his will too," I barked, glancing between my cock and his and reassuring myself that mine was still damn impressive. And it was fancy too, with the tattoos and Prince Albert I had going. His didn't have any fandangles, that was for sure.

My narrowed gaze met Jack's smug one as Brooklyn panted all over him and I cursed as the desire to throw him off the roof reared its head again.

"Make her come before I give in to the desire to cut that thing off and beat you to death with it," I snapped irritably and in the next breath, Jack had pushed Brooklyn to her knees before me, making her grip my thighs to balance herself.

I curled my free hand around her jaw as Jack dropped his pants behind her, moving to his knees and taking hold of her hips as he lined himself up with her wet pussy.

"Fuck," she hissed as he took hold of her hip and I ran my thumb along the seam of her lips before pushing it inside.

"Bite down on me, love," I said roughly and she nodded obediently just as Jack drove his hips forward and her teeth sank into my flesh hard enough to draw blood and meet with bone.

Brooklyn cried out around the bloody thumb in her mouth and I cursed like a sailor as I took my other hand from my dick and moved it to wind through her hair, caressing her softly.

Jack paused as he looked down at the point where their bodies were joined and Brooklyn whimpered again, easing her teeth from my thumb and releasing it from the cage of her mouth.

"You good, little psycho?" I asked softly and she nodded again, moaning as Jack drew his hips back with agonising slowness.

"I want it all, Hellfire," she panted, her pupils full blown with lust as she gazed up at me. "Every piece of us."

Her eyes fell to my cock which was fucking throbbing between us and I groaned as she lowered her mouth to place a kiss on the head of it.

"Come on then, big fella," I snapped as Jack continued to stare at her and he looked up at me once more before the edges of his mouth lifted into a dark and wicked grin and his grasp on her hips tightened.

Jack slammed himself into her again, making her scream and damn near knocking me offa the roof once more as her grip on my thighs pushed me back.

I released her, grasping the edges of the wall to stop myself from falling and bracing against the force of his thrusts as he upped his pace and made her cry out over and over again.

I still wanted to kill him, but as Brooklyn moaned in ecstasy, I could admit that he was doing a damn good job of making her happy and the sound of her pleasure brought a bead of moisture to the tip of my dick.

Brooklyn dropped her head once more, licking the precum away with a throaty moan before sliding her lips over the tip and sucking on my piercing.

I opened my mouth, meaning to ask what she was doing, but as she took the entire length of my cock into her mouth and moaned even louder, it became all too fucking clear anyway.

The force of Jack's thrusts were damn near knocking me off of the roof, and I gave up on trying to do or say anything other than focusing on the feeling of her mouth wrapped around my cock and enjoying the way his thrusts drove her down onto me even further every time.

Brooklyn's moans got louder and louder, and suddenly she was clamping her lips down around my dick so tight that the vibrations rolling out from her throat had me coming hot and fast between her pretty lips.

She swallowed me down, moaning louder, her nails, making my thighs bleed as Jack fucked her through her orgasm before coming with a roar loud enough to move mountains which made her entire body spasm with pleasure.

We all fell in a sweaty, panting heap on the roof of the bar and I tugged our little psycho into my arms as I trembled in the wake of my release.

"You're officially in, fuck the probation," I grunted to Jack, not bothering to look at him and just staring up at the endless sky above as I held Brooklyn tight in my arms. "Anyone who can protect her and make her come like that makes the cut. I'll work on not killin ya myself every time the urge strikes, but if she wants ya, you're in."

Brooklyn's hand found mine, her fingers tangling with mine and lifting Jack's from her other side so that his were mixed in too and squeezing tight. "I want him."

"Then it's done," I agreed. And just like that, my entire world shifted into something brand spanking new.

BROOKLYN

CHAPTER TWENTY FIVE

I sobbed uncontrollably into my pillow then crawled to the edge of the bed and grabbed the crusty loaf of unsliced bread I had there, leaning up to take a big bite out of it and swallowing it down as it muffled my sobs.

"Spider? What the hell is going on?" Niall called from the doorway of his room and I flipped over, glaring out at him, spotting Jack and Mateo at his back.

"What do you *think* is going on, Hellfire?" I snarled.

"I don't fuckin' know. Yer eating bread and wailing like a banshee," he said, confounded.

"It's my bed bread, Niall," I snapped. "God, you're so stupid sometimes." I hurled the loaf at him and it smacked against his chest before slapping onto the floor.

I looked at it with a whimper, realising I'd just ruined my nice bread, and it had been the only thing making anything better. I sat up, grabbing the bedside lamp and hurling it at all of them with a scream. It smashed against the doorway as the three of them ducked for cover and Brutus barked somewhere beyond them.

"Mi sol," Mateo's gruff voice carried to me as I flipped over and buried my face in the pillow again. My tummy was ouchie and I was on my second foof stick of the morning, but that had nothing to do with anything. "Is it your time of the month?"

I screamed at the accusation, flying out of bed and grabbing the nearest thing to me, my hand closing around a heavy book on Niall's nightstand called Forget-Me-Not Bombshell. And it seemed like the perfect weapon in that moment, because they were not going to forget this. I hurled it with all my might and Mateo cursed as it struck his head.

Jack barged past him, striding towards me with a stern look on his face and I slapped at his hands as he tried to grab me.

"Rook," he growled in warning, but I kept slapping, smacking all his big muscles and his stupid lovely face too.

"The fact that I'm on my period has nothing to do with anything!" I cried.

"Then why are ya upset?" Niall demanded as he and Mateo walked up beside Jack and gazed down at me in concern.

"Because, *Niall*, I was just innocently scrolling your phone on the Tok-Tik app and I found out something terrible. Something I can never, ever recover from." I whimpered again as I remembered it, and tears ran down my cheeks.

"Come on, love, it can't be that bad," Niall reasoned and a snarl peeled back my lips at his dismissal.

"Maybe it is that bad," Mateo said quickly, elbowing Niall hard in the ribs.

"Yeah, *Niall*," I hissed, shoving him in the chest and he shoved me right back. Then we fell into a shoving war where I pushed his chest and he knocked me away, but I kept coming back, shoving and kicking his shins too. He cursed, grabbed hold of me and flipped me off my feet, throwing me onto the bed.

"Now I'm warning ya." He pointed down at me as I did a ninja move to get onto my knees and bared my teeth at him. "You need to be a good, Spider, or you won't get any Pops today. How about that?"

"Explain," Jack cut in, stepping to his side and Niall shot a surprised look at him.

"Bringing out the two syllable words today, eh big fella?" he asked loudly and slowly. "Clever boy." He patted his head and Jack gave him a cool look before turning his attention back to me.

I sniffed, looking at AJ then to Mateo as they all surrounded the bed, penning me in. I wiped my tears away on the back of my hand as I composed myself. "If a female ferret goes into heat and she doesn't mate, she'll die," I choked out and they all shared a look before turning their gazes back to me.

"What's that now, love?" Niall asked, a frown pinching his brow.

"Female ferrets!" I shrieked, leaping off the bed and grabbing hold of the curtains, tearing them down from the window. I balled them up in my fists, shoving the window open and throwing them out. Then I grabbed everything I could around me, hurling it out after the curtains into the rain which was beating steadily down outside. I ripped open Niall's nightstand next, carrying the whole top drawer to the window just as he collided with me from behind, trying to wrestle it from my grasp.

"No," I said through my teeth. "It's mine. Let go!"

"That's *my* stuff, you little hellion," he growled and I looked down at all the things he had in there, from a fancy little knife called Stanley to a shiny broach that had King of the Cuckoos etched into it, a squid pen, a potato, and a small stuffed owl toy.

I released the drawer with one hand, throwing the heel of my palm into his nose and he reared back with swear words falling from his lips. Then I hurled everything out the window, tiny owl and all and Niall lurched forward to try and catch him, his inked hand closing on nothing.

"Owliver!" he yelled as the toy hit the muddy ground.

Mateo wrapped an arm around me, drawing me back against his chest.

"This must be about more than some ferret, chica loca."

"You don't even care," I lamented, biting his wrist until he let me go, then I sprang across the bed, ducked under Jack's huge arm as he tried to grab me and ran out into the hall.

I sprinted downstairs with a sob tearing from my throat as I remembered the fluffy little ferret's face in the video as the handler man at the zoo had explained about their terrible fate. For him to know that fact, there must have been a lady ferret out there who'd been all horny and needy, and no mate had come for her. Or maybe he'd been trapped somewhere, desperate to reach her, but he couldn't get out and he knew, he *knew* in his little ferret soul that his mate would die if he didn't make it to her. And then he'd probably died too from the heartbreak.

I threw the front door open, running out into the rain, only wearing a pair of big black granny panties and a glittery crop shirt which had a partying weasel on it. And weasels were really just less fancy ferrets. *Noooo.*

The rain beat down on me, soaking me through as I ran towards the lake, the mud squelching between my toes as I raced all the way to the bottom of the hill. I fell to my knees before the water and stared up at the grey sky, thinking of all the horny little ferret ladies that had succumbed to such an unjust fate.

"Why?!" I broke down, buckling forward and pressing my hands into the mud as my hair swung forward to cover my face. My tummy was ouchie and all I wanted to do was curl up into a ball and eat chocolate and bed bread, but now my bed bread was ruined and I'd eaten all the chocolate in the house last night. It wasn't *fair.*

"What do you need, Rook?" Jack knelt down at my side and lifted the curtain of hair covering my face so that he could peer in at me. I glanced over my shoulder with a sniff, finding Mateo and Niall arguing back at the house while Brutus barked at them.

I sniffed again, looking out at the lake as the rain made the surface dance with ripples. "I need a hug."

Jack drew me into his arms and he was so big, he easily tucked me in against his chest, rising to his feet as he held me, just like the time Niall had kicked him out of the house. I nuzzled into his neck, his masculine scent floating over my senses and calming the erratic beating of my heart.

"Maybe you should take the ferret shirt off and put something else on, baby," Jack suggested, using our special mind connection to communicate with me and I sniffed again.

"It's a weasel," I said.

"Oh…well, I can only tell the difference between them and stoats," he said and I looked up at him with a frown.

"What do you mean?" I asked.

"A weasel is weaselly recognised, but a stoat is stoatally different," he said, his lips twitching with the joke and my eyes widened before I burst out laughing.

"Oh my God, that's so funny." I clutched my sides as I laughed and laughed and Jack carried me back to the house with a grin on his face.

Niall and Mateo fell quiet as they spotted me laughing and Mateo tugged the bottom of his jeans out of Brutus's mouth as he played snappy snaps with him.

"Are you okay now, mi sol?" Mateo asked hopefully.

"Yes," I said brightly. "Jack told me a joke. Tell them the joke, Jack."

"He can't string a sentence together," Niall scoffed. "He didn't tell ya nothin', Spider."

"He did! There was a weasel and a stoat. And he said that weasels are stoatally cool or something, didn't you? Tell them, AJ!" I said excitedly, bouncing in his arms, but Jack just gave me a roguish look and I tapped his nose, realising he wanted to keep our secret mind language talk between us.

"Poor fella, he ain't got two words to rub together," Niall said, shaking his head sadly. "Ain't that right, big man? Yer a good boy though, aren't ya?

Do you want a snack?" He took a protein bar from his pocket. "Here ya go, keep those muscles nice and big now to protect my Spider." He tossed Jack the bar and it hit him in the face before dropping into the mud. Jack didn't even flinch.

"How about I try and tell the joke?" I said, tugging on Jack's loose fitting tank top before turning to the others again. "There was a bit about a ferret, I think. Ferrets being ferrety, or...dammit, I can't tell it right. Oh no," I gasped, remembering the ferret fact I'd learned earlier and my throat closed up, my mood plummeting out of the sky like an airplane that had been hit by a missile.

"The lady ferrets and their horny deaths," I whispered as my lower lip wobbled.

"C'mere." Niall reached for me and I let him take me from Jack's arms, scooping me against his chest as he walked inside and Mateo looked down at me over his shoulder.

"Can we round up all the lady ferrets who don't have husbands and find them their mates?" I asked Mateo. "We could make an app."

"I'm not sure that would work, mi sol," he said gravely and Niall shot a glare at him as I let out a wail.

"Shut up, Mateo. Get workin' on that app right this fuckin' second," Niall commanded, but Mateo just kept following us to the lounge where Niall laid me on the couch.

I rested the back of my hand to my forehead, hiccups of woe leaving me as the three of them came closer and started pulling off my wet clothes. I kept sobbing even when Niall stripped off his own t-shirt and tugged it over my head and Mateo tucked a snuggly blanket around me.

"Can we get you something?" Mateo asked as he pushed my hair behind my ears.

"I need chocolate," I sniffed as I curled up like a cat. "And a hot water bottle, and a lump of fresh bread, and some Coco Pops, and a glass of milk, and some nuts to nibble on – not stupid almonds though, they don't even count as a nut – oh, and I want a magazine about gardening to soothe my mind, and I want someone to read it to me in a German accent as that's the most soothing accent of all. And I'd like a doughnut with cherry filling and some sprinkles on it, and I'd like a coconut. Not to eat, just an emotional support coconut. And I want a surprise gift. A really good one. And then I want a big hug from all of you while we watch that Disney movie with that person who's stuck working and working and working, and then they realise they can live out their dreams instead."

"Cinderella?" Mateo guessed and I shook my head with a frown.

"You know the one. Where they get to go out at night doing all the things they really want to do, but they can't tell anyone."

"The Incredibles?" Mateo guessed again.

"Nooo." I threw my head back against the cushion behind me with a huff.

"Oh, you mean American Psycho," Niall realised and I perked up.

"Yes! That one. With the stabby man living his dreams," I said with a grin.

"Alright then." Niall turned to Jack. "Get the telly on, big fella, and get her a hot water bottle, el burro. I'll make a call to organise the rest." He headed away upstairs while Jack moved to set up the movie and Mateo walked off into the kitchen.

I snuggled deeper into my blanket and after a few minutes, dreamland called to me and I slipped away into a lovely snooze.

"Little psycho," Niall's voice carried to me from afar, his fingers prodding into my side. "Wakey, wakey."

I growled, burying my head deeper into my blanket and jerking every time he prodded me.

"I think we should let her sleep," Mateo said.

"Nonsense, she'll wanna see what I got her." Niall prodded me again and I cracked an eye open as he drew the blanket away from my face. He shook a shoebox at me and wiggled his eyebrows. "I got ya yer surprise."

I realised my head was now resting on Jack's lap and I yawned as I pushed myself upright, eyeing the box curiously.

"It better be worth ruining my nap for, Hellfire," I said, narrowing my eyes at him.

"I'd say it is." He brushed his knuckles over my cheek and I lunged for the box in his other hand, but he held it out of my reach, chuckling as he enjoyed teasing me.

"Kiss me and I'll give it to ya," he said, leaning forward and I let him take a kiss from me, his tongue sinking between my lips which I decided to bite when he took too much time.

"Fuck," he jerked back, bringing his fingers to his tongue and blood marked them when he pulled them away. "Ya little psycho," he growled like he'd enjoyed that.

Mateo appeared with a hot water bottle and moved to take the one that was already in my lap, swapping it over.

"Thank you, Dead Man," I breathed and he smirked darkly at me before sitting at my side.

Jack played with my hair as I reached for the box in Niall's grip again, and this time he gave it to me. I ripped into it like an animal and took out the gift from inside, finding a black gavel with a gold band around it alongside a wooden block for hitting.

"I told ya I'd get ya one," Niall said with a wide smile.

"I love it!" I squealed then Niall offered up a bag of goodies to me full of all the things I'd asked for. I took out my emotional support coconut and balanced it on Jack's thigh as I rifled through the things until I found what I needed most. My chocolate. I tore into the wrapper with my teeth and took a huge bite, moaning as the sweet goodness rolled over my tongue.

"Thank you," I sighed, eating a few more bites of it before jumping up from my nest and leaping onto the coffee table with my gavel and block in hand. "Now I want to make some new laws! Firstly, I'm officially outlawing the word moist in this house. It's icky and no one needs to use it ever again on pain of death." I held the block in the opposite hand to my gavel then struck it with a bang that made the new law official.

"Death," Jack laughed and the deep tenor of the sound gave me the shivers.

"Yup. Death!" I cried as Niall dropped down onto my seat and hugged my hot water bottle to his chest. Mateo shifted away from him with a moody expression on his face, but found he couldn't get far as Brutus jumped up to sit beside him with a low snarl.

"My next law is that all Pops in this house are officially under my rule. On pain of death!" I hit the block again.

"Now wait a minute-" Niall started, but I talked over him.

"Another rule is that when I take my morning poop, I want coconut smelling toilet paper for wiping. The good stuff, the thick and yummy stuff so I can sniff it while I poop – on pain of death!" I struck the block again.

"You'd better put another order in then, bastardo. Or don't, then I'll watch Brooklyn murder you over her morning shit." Mateo sniggered at Niall.

"But if I kill Hellfire, I'll have to kill myself remember, Dead Man?" I said sweetly and his snigger stuttered out.

"Whatever, I'll get her the toilet paper, but let's circle back to the Pops." Niall turned to me again. "You don't have the jurisdiction to make laws on my Pops."

"The law is made," I said firmly. "Now, for my final law of the day. I am officially forming our club, the Society of Psychos. I, Brooklyn Niall O'Brien-"

"You only took my last name when ya married me-"

"*I*." I spoke louder over him, repeating myself. "Brooklyn Niall O'Brien, am the first and founding member of the Society of Psychos, the second member is my husband, Niall Meadows."

"No, no, no," Niall huffed. "I didn't take your surname. Ya just took mine."

"If you have a complaint to make, Mr Meadows, can you write it down and put it in the suggestion box." I nudged a box of tissues towards him with my toe.

Niall got to his feet, still hugging the hot water bottle to his stomach. "You are Brooklyn O'Brien, and I'm yer husband, Niall O'Brien."

I toed the suggestion box closer to him. "In the box please, sir." I hit the block with my gavel again and Niall huffed, walking across the room to fetch a writing pad and a pen.

"Now, the third member of the club is Mateo Meadows," I said brightly.

"No," Niall snapped, twisting around as he finished folding up his suggestion. "He ain't got yer name. He's Mateo Ortega. Yer not married to him in any way, yer *mine*."

"Hm, well maybe I should marry the rest of you so that it's fair," I said thoughtfully.

"No," Niall hissed as Mateo and Jack sat up straighter. He was being such a negative Nancy today.

"I'll put a pin in that idea." I plucked an imaginary pin from the air and pinned the thought above my head. "So, the third member is Mateo Oregano-"

"Ortega," Mateo corrected.

"Ortega," I amended, then struck Gavin the gavel on my block. "The fourth member is Angry Jack and the fifth is Brutus." I struck the gavel twice. "So, now that we're a killing club, we need someone to kill."

Niall walked over and slid his suggestion into the tissue box and I wafted him back to his seat.

"Hellfire." I snapped my fingers at him just as he sat down. "Fetch my killing rock."

"I'm not yer little bitch, and we ain't a club," he said, folding his arms stubbornly. "I'm gonna spank ya in a minute."

"We are a club, Hellfire," I growled.

"People usually vote before laws are passed, you've become a dictator and you've barely had that gavel five minutes," Niall said. "I'm gonna take it back from ya and use yer ass as a block."

I bit my lip, liking the sound of that, but we had important official things to do, I couldn't get distracted by some judge / naughty jury member roleplay. At least not right now.

"Fine, we'll have a vote. Who votes that we're a club?" I raised my hand and Mateo and Jack shared a smirk before raising theirs too. "Brutus?" I asked and Mateo took hold of his paw, risking a snappy as he lifted it up.

"Hey," Niall barked. "That's not fair."

"You're outvoted, bastardo," Mateo purred, his eyes glittering with victory as he turned to me. "Can we vote for a member to be your little bitch now, mi sol? I'd like to put Niall forward as a candidate."

"All in favour of Niall being my little bitch say 'pie'," I said and Mateo and Jack echoed it back to me.

"For heaven's sake," Niall spat. "I ain't being yer little bitch."

I struck my block with Gavin. "Motion passed. Please fetch my killing rock, Hellfire."

"No," he snarled, throwing my hot water bottle across the room in anger.

I pouted, looking to Jack imploringly. "AJ, he's not cooperating and you're my new law enforcer." I struck my block and Jack got to his feet, dragging Niall up after him, muscles straining between the two of them as Niall fought him. It made me all hot and flustered as I looked between Officer AJ and my little bitch Niall.

Niall lunged toward me suddenly, snatching Gavin and Blocky from my grip before jumping onto the table, knocking me right off of it with his big meaty shoulder. I stumbled and Jack steadied me as Niall gazed down at us with a demonic look, getting drunk on the power of Gavin, just as I had. *Oh no, what have we done bringing Gavin into our world? He's going to corrupt us. Oh wait, we're a bunch of murderous criminals with no morals. He can't make us any worse. Or can he?*

"I'm the ruler of this kingdom," Niall growled, bashing Gavin down on Blocky so hard I swear I heard him squeak in pain. "I'm yer emperor, yer monarch, yer prince of death. This is my land and I'll spread terror across it, turning every light corner dark. You're my pack of heathens and I make the rules, but I'm a reasonable prince, and I'll bow to my ruthless princess when needed to ensure her needs are met. So the club stays. The Society of Psychos we are, and there's one enemy left in this world written on her rock. It's a cold-blooded armadillo, who we'll find even if we have to turn over every rock in-"

"Um, Niall. There's no armadillo. We had this discussion." I rolled my eyes, jogging across the room to the cabinet where I'd last seen my rock. I took it out and moved to join Niall on the table, reading out the name I'd inscribed on it.

"Señor Castillo," I said in a low and ominous voice and Mateo lurched to his feet.

"Castillo?" he spat.

"A fuckin' cartel man?" Niall asked in surprise, his eyebrows sailing up, up and away toward his hairline.

Jack's shoulders tensed and his eyes darkened in recognition of that name too.

I glanced between them all with my lips parted in an O. "You know him?"

"Which one? There's plenty of Castillo scum in the world. Which one hurt you, mi sol?" Mateo moved towards me, all rage and murder in his expression as I saw the vow in him to kill the man who'd made himself my enemy.

"He was the one who they took me to when they stole me from the bridge," I said, unsure how else to describe him. "He looked at me like I was a cow with a bow in its hair, and he had to judge how pricey I could be. He was the one who sold me first."

"You were in America when they took you?" Mateo confirmed, his eyes dark as pitch and I nodded.

"Yep, the United States of Anarchy is all I've ever known. Apart from that one time when I went on a trip to England with my dad and-"

"If he was running the sale of women in this country, then I know him," Mateo interrupted. "Describe what he looked like, mi sol."

"He was a big man, bigger than the moon. And he had angry little moth eyes. Do you know where to find him?" I asked hopefully as Mateo nodded like he knew exactly who I was talking about, all kinds of murderous desires flitting through his expression.

"I know. I worked for him once."

My heart stopped beating, freezing to an ice cap in my chest which was struck hard by the Titanic, making it tremble and shriek inside.

"You…worked for him?" I whispered, pain scoring through my chest. "But he sold people. He sold women like me to bad, bad men who wanted to do bad, bad things to them. They would have done those things to me, taken me, hurt me, made me shatter inside."

Mateo flinched like those words psychically hurt him. "I was never a part of that. I only killed men on his orders or covered his tracks when he left a trail of blood behind him. I'm a fixer, Brooklyn, or I was. I was used by nearly all the Castillos at one time or another. His cousin runs the entire cartel, I was their creature to use a long time ago."

I nodded as I absorbed those words, wanting to believe them and the honesty in his eyes made me think that I could. Trust was a fair-weather friend who hadn't visited me often in life, but she'd moved into this house with a tartan bag under her arm and an umbrella over her head just like Mary Poppins, and she hadn't left yet. This was the first time she was creeping over to the door, packing a few of her things and waving ta-rah. But I didn't want her to go, because trusting these men had kept me sane, okay not sane, but it had kept me happy. And happiness was such a precious, fragile thing.

"Mi sol, I swear to you. I had no involvement with selling women. But here is my truth, because I am guilty in part. I have never done anything to stop such things from happening, because they have always been normal in my world. I'm no hero, I'm the one who got called when blood had been spilled and there were loose ends to be tied up. I have placed bullets in the skulls of men I don't remember the names of, and it does not keep me up at night. I was heartless before you, this place in my chest hollow and vacant." He held a hand to his heart. "But you have made something grow here, something warm and good, and it aches for you, mi sol. Only you. So if a Castillo has wronged you, I will hunt him down and cut him apart for you. I will make him scream until you ask me to silence him for good. And then I will put him in the ground, so deep that he shall never be discovered."

My fingers trembled as I raised them to his jaw, caressing the stubble there as I bought into his words. Because I could see they were true.

"Okay." I leaned down and kissed him hard before pulling away.

"So where can we find this armadillo?" Niall asked Mateo in a purr. "I'm ready to peel the scales from his back."

"Alright then, has everyone got their outfits on?" Niall called from downstairs just as I adjusted the black leather dress I was wearing. It was super short and had metal buckles all the way up my stomach and over my tits, revealing skin beneath and only just hiding my nips. I wore my hair down and thick black eyeliner with diamantes on the outer edges of my eyes. My nails were painted black and I had little net gloves on and platform black heels, my legs completely bare.

Mateo had told us about the fetish club where Señor Castillo did some of his gross auctions and we'd done all the plans and things over the past week – mostly I'd helped pick out the outfits but as I looked at myself, I was confident I'd had the most important role of all.

We were heading there tonight to kill the monster who'd sold me to a death game and I couldn't wait to get stabby. It was an extra special occasion too because it was the Society of Psychos' first outing and we were going undercover to find our mark.

I headed out of Niall's room and walked downstairs where Niall was leaning against the wall, his foot kicked up against it. He was wearing a seriously hot pinstriped suit that made him look like some kind of oldy worldy gangster and he even had a pocket watch chained to his pocket which he was gazing down at in his palm.

He looked up at me, tucking the watch away and my heart burst into song as he looked me over, desire coursing through his eyes. "Well look at you…"

"Hang the fuck on, bastardo," Mateo snapped as he appeared from the corridor which led to his room. "Why are you wearing a nice fucking suit while I'm in this?" He gestured to the outfit he was wearing, his leather chaps assless and his chest bare with a thick leather harness criss-crossing over it. He had a gimp mask on too and adrenaline buzzed through my veins as I ran over to him and took it all in.

"Oooh." I caressed his bare ass cheeks while he gave me a flat look, and though I couldn't really tell through the mask, he seemed like he was all up on Angry Mountain.

Jack appeared in a spiky leather dog collar and full black latex suit which was so tight to his body it showed off every inch of his massive cock where it was stashed away down there. I stared at it for a long, long time, giving it a little wave as I was filled with the urge to write a poem about it and whisper it to the moon. His silver hair was tied into a top knot and he looked just…wow.

"Niall," AJ growled as our boss man looked over at us in his fancy suit.

"Problem, big fella?" Niall asked lightly.

"You're making a fool of me, bastardo," Mateo snarled.

"This is an elite fetish club and we need to blend in. I'm yer master, and you're all my sex slaves, got it? Good. Let's go." He whistled at us and I barked excitedly like a dog, running over to him and looping my hands around his neck.

"Can I do anything to please you, Master?" I wet my lips and Niall looked down at me hungrily.

"There might be a thing or two you can do when we finish up this job, love," he said in a low voice.

"Anything," I reiterated, batting my lashes and he grunted, lingering there for several seconds before Mateo's hand slammed down on his shoulder.

"Come on then, bastardo," he growled, steering him off ahead of me and I skipped over to Jack's side, taking his hand.

"Oh wait, what about Bruty-tooty?" I asked as I looked for him, spotting Brutus on his back on the couch with his favourite boot still clamped in his jaws as he slept. I wondered how he'd feel about donning a gimp mask too, or maybe I could fashion him a coat out of colourful dildos? That would look badass with all his scars.

"He's gonna guard the house, love," Niall said. "He can come on the next job."

"Okay," I sighed then ran over to Brutus, leaning down to kiss him right on the cheek. He woke the moment my lips touched him, snapping and snarling ferociously but I was already gone, dancing back to AJ's side and threading my fingers between his.

We headed out to Niall's shiny new Jeep and piled inside. I hooked up Niall's phone to the speakers, playing Cannibal by Kesha and singing along as Niall belted out the words too while we drove away into the night.

It felt like it took no time to arrive at the club in Hemlock City and we had to enter it through a door down an alleyway, falling into step behind Niall as he talked the talk to the bouncers and bragged about his little entourage of sex slaves.

"That one loves being fucked in the arse," Niall told one of them, pointing at Mateo. "He insists on wearing those chaps everywhere so I can have easy access whenever I like. He douches twice a day just to be sure he's always ready for me, don't ya lad?" He clapped Mateo on the cheek through his gimp mask and Mateo's whole body stiffened before he nodded tightly.

"If he ain't being fucked in the arse, he's thinking about me fucking him in the arse, aren't you fella?" Niall said loudly. "I always find him shoving things up there and jerking off over the thought of me busting in his back gates."

"Yes, Master," Mateo gritted out and I giggled, liking that visual and glancing at AJ who bit the inside of his cheek to hold back his laugh.

The bouncers ushered us inside and I followed Niall through a narrow corridor with black walls lit by pink neon lighting. We headed into a huge bar where ethereal music was coiling through the air. Some of the crowd were dressed up in sexy stuff like we were and others wore suits or fine dresses while leather clad people draped themselves all over them.

The waitresses were pouring high end champagne and whiskey for everyone who wanted it and I stared in awe at a girl covered in body paint as she casually dropped to her knees before a man with silver hair wearing a latex army uniform and started sucking him off right in front of us.

Niall led us through the crowd as the music pulsed around me and the scent of sugar and bad deeds filled the air.

I was fascinated as I watched people making out and touching each other, but things got even more interesting as we turned into a corridor full of rooms with open doors. I looked into each one, my jaw dropping. There were men being whipped and paddled, a woman tied to a huge cross while several people licked and sucked her flesh at once, there were vibrating toys and chains and things that looked better for torturing than pleasuring. But all I heard were moans and pleas for more as I took it all in, making mental notes of everything I witnessed.

It was all so new, so exciting, and I wanted to try every last thing and find out what I liked the most. There were threesomes, foursomes, fivesomes, and more. There were men and women dressed as cats and dogs and aliens, all being fucked in various positions I'd not dreamed of trying, but now I had the dreams. The big dreams. All the dreams. I wanted to be bent over and twisted up like a pretzel. I wanted three Ds at once and I wanted to be chained up while I took them. I wanted to be dommed down, then do the domming myself. I wanted a whip engraved with my name and spiky boob coverings that made me look like a warrior princess.

I wanted it all, I wanted it now.

"Any sign of him?" Niall asked as he looked back at us.

Oh right, the Castillo man. I'd gotten totally distracted by the sex fest around me, and now I wished I had a little notepad or a rock to write down all the things I wanted to try.

I shrugged and the other two shook their heads.

"We'd better split up and look for the auction room." Niall jerked his head at Mateo. "You're with me, el burro." Mateo begrudgingly moved to his side. "Look after her, big fella." He tipped a salute to Jack, and AJ stepped closer to me as they headed off down another corridor.

"That's it, you dirty man," a woman's powerful voice carried from the room up ahead and I crept toward it curiously, peering inside, my lips falling open at what I found. "Take it like the bitch you are."

She stood behind a man on all fours who was chained to a bed, driving her hips forward as she fucked him right in the ass with a giant blue strap on dick. She was dressed like a queen, a crown on her head and her body gilded in a golden bikini with a cape falling over her shoulders. She looked powerful, beautiful and as the man cried out in pleasure, my lips lifted into a wide smile.

"What's that called?" I breathed in awe.

"Pegging," Jack supplied, drawing me away from the door even as I gazed wistfully back at the queen. "Have you got something on your mind, Rook?" he murmured in my ear. "Because you look flustered by all of this. Have you got dirty little wishes in your head that you want someone to fulfil?" He crushed me back against the nearest wall and I gasped as I looked up at him, heat seeping between my thighs as my clit throbbed.

"I want to try it all, AJ," I said, a moan in my voice and he chuckled, leaning down low to speak directly to me.

"You're so wet for this, aren't you?" he growled. "Do you want me to play with your pretty pussy later? I'll do anything you want, anything you tell me. I like being told what to do."

My breathing hitched and I pawed at his huge arms as he caged me in. "I want you now," I demanded, grinding against him.

"Later. We're going to kill for you first, baby. Then you can have me any way you want me. I'll fuck you until you're raw and you can't take anymore of me, is that what you want?"

A ragged breath left my lungs as I nodded.

"Tell me exactly what you want me to do," he rasped.

"I want you to use your mouth to make me moan, AJ."

He leaned down to tease the corner of my lips, not giving me the kiss I tried to take as his huge cock swelled against me.

"I will. I swear it. And you'll be so wet by the time I have you after that every inch of me will slip easily inside you," he said, then he pulled away and locked me to his side as he led me down the corridor. And I was glad he was holding onto me because my legs were like jelly, and I was sure I'd slump right down to the floor in a puddle if he let go.

"You should let Niall know what a filthy mouth you have, why do you keep your words from him?" I asked huskily and he glanced down at me with a smirk.

"Because I enjoy the game of it," he said and I laughed lightly, nuzzling into my big man as wild thoughts ping ponged through my head about what he'd said to me.

I hoped we found Señor Castillo soon and made him bleed, because I wanted to celebrate our kill with my men and try out some of the things I'd seen in this place as soon as I could. My heart was already racing with the thought of it and a twisted smile lifted my lips as we continued our search for the auction room where we'd likely find our mark.

I'm coming for you, Castillo man. And I have a band of monsters at my heels. Come out, come out, wherever you are.

JACK

CHAPTER TWENTY SIX

The pounding music of the club pulsed all around us, drawing Brooklyn to start moving to the beat, raising her hands in the air and swaying her hips as she danced to it. My attention was split between watching her and assessing the room around us for threats as we continued through the club.

Before my incarceration, I hadn't had good instincts, but the man I'd worked for had trusted me and them, insisting I only needed to focus to push through the noise in my head and take in what was all around me with a more careful eye. But he'd been wrong about my ability to focus like that. Bright lights and loud noises made my jaw grind and my muscles flex. Douchebags bumping into me as they stumbled past us while inebriated made me see red and the anger in me built and built until I was prone to snap.

Brooklyn turned to look up at me as we moved between a row of couples who were fucking on various sex swings, leather straps and strange harnesses holding them in position while they moaned and panted for one another.

I clenched my jaw, the muscles in my neck flexing as the pounding music drove into my skull with a fierce determination. But as I felt myself slipping into the pool of fury which waited within me, her hand landed on my arm.

Brooklyn ran her fingers over my flesh, slowly dragging them up and over the crook of my elbow before tugging on the fabric of the latex suit I was in.

"Tell me what's on your mind, AJ," she said, tiptoeing up and pressing her other hand to my chest. "Speak to me in that way you do."

I bent down to drop my mouth to her ear, feeling her shiver as my skin brushed against hers and moving a hand to her lower back as I drew her against me more firmly.

The scent of her enveloped me, pushing out the rage that was filling me and giving me something far more intoxicating to focus on.

"I'm thinking about tasting you just like you asked me, pretty little anarchist," I said to her, my thumb tracing a slow line over the centre of her back. "I'm all caught up on imagining me getting on my knees for you, pushing that skirt up over your hips and peeling your thighs apart so that I can see you bare and dripping for me."

"I have panties on," she breathed, the hand which pressed to my chest fisting in my clothes as I tutted.

"I don't want any barrier between us," I rumbled in her ear. "I want to find you ready for me when you command me to take you. I want to push those soft thighs apart and lick my way up the insides of them until you're quivering with want beneath me, your arousal running down that silky flesh of yours to meet my tongue. I need to taste the want on you while you claw at my hair, dragging me closer while I lick and tease you, making you want me so bad that you can't take it anymore."

Brooklyn whimpered and I carved my fingers down her spine until I was gripping her ass in my hand and squeezing tight.

"I want to hear you beg me for my tongue. I want your fingernails carving the flesh from my body and making me bleed as you force me to give you what you need. And then, when you decide I've gotten you worked up enough, you're going to tell me what you want from me and I'm going to sink my tongue right into that tight hole of yours and lap the taste of you from your flesh. I'm going to lick and suck and tease you while you grind your hips against my face and I fuck you with my mouth, worshipping you the way you deserve to be served."

"Jack," Brooklyn pleaded, looking up at me and biting down on her bottom lip. "Do that now. Take me here."

I shook my head, dropping my mouth to her throat again and running my tongue up the side of her neck just like I was hungering to do to her pussy. The plea in her voice was almost enough to force me into action, but I needed more bite to it, a true command that forced me to bend to her will. Maybe even one that came from the psychotic man who ruled us.

"You aren't ready for me though, are you?" I growled, finding the edge of her panties through the fabric of her dress and tugging on them sharply.

"When I get on my knees for you, you won't want these here. I want to bury my head between your thighs and feel you lock them tight around my neck until I have you coming all over my face and I can't get the flavour of you off my lips. I want to taste you as you come for me and wring your body out until you can't take any more. And then, as soon as you command me to, I'll give you my cock. I'll drive it in fast and deep and make you ride me even though you're spent. I'll make that tight hole work every inch of me in and out over and over again and have you screaming my name as you come for me again, your pussy wrapped around me and my cum filling you up like you deserve. Would you like that?"

I drew back and Brooklyn nodded, her grip on my arm so firm that I was fairly certain she was using it to stop her knees from buckling.

I cocked my head to one side as I waited, my hand falling from her ass and she nodded quickly, grasping the edges of her panties through her leather dress and pushing them down.

She dropped them to the floor, stepping out of them and staring up at me full of want, she made a move to bend down for them but I caught her arm, shaking my head and leaning in closer.

"Show me you own me, Rook. Show me that I am nothing but your servant, born to please you."

Brooklyn swallowed, her eyes two pools of want which drew me in closer as she took in what I was asking of her. What I needed.

"Pick them up," she said in a firm tone, making my cock jerk at the authority she used and I instantly dropped to my knees for her.

She snapped her fingers as she pointed to the discarded underwear on the floor in a clear demand, making my lips curve at the corners as I obeyed without question.

I picked them up, offering the little scrap of black lace to her and watching as she took them from me before lifting them to my lips. I leaned in instantly, licking the taste of her from the seam and groaning as the wet material made my cock throb with need.

Brooklyn's eyes had gone all wide and wanton as she watched me and I slipped the panties into my pocket before getting to my feet and leaning close once more.

"Start thinking about what you want me to do to you, beautiful. I'm all yours after all," I said in a low voice, eyeing the way her nipples peaked through the fabric of her dress and supremely looking forward to acting out that little fantasy on her body just as soon as she said the word.

I took Brooklyn's hand and drew her along the corridor full of couples enjoying the sex swings, leading her out into the wider space beyond where another bar opened up and there were more people with their clothes still on.

Mateo stalked out of another corridor, the darkness of his aura keeping most people away from him though there was a little trail of submissives skulking along in his shadow hopefully, ball gags, whips and cuffs hanging from their fingers and their heads dipped low as they worked to draw his attention.

He moved to join us, barking an angry command at his little fan club as they followed him, telling them to fuck off and they obediently scurried away, disappearing from sight within a few moments. My muscles clenched at the sound and I wondered if he might enjoy commanding me to do a few things to our girl too, the three of them taking control and making me pleasure her in all the ways she deserved. I didn't mind the sound of that at all.

"You gathered a whole tribe of lonely souls, Dead Man," Brooklyn breathed as he joined us, taking her hand and pressing a kiss to the back of it.

"I don't want any soul but yours, chica loca," he swore, pinning her in his dark gaze and making her blush.

Niall sauntered out of another corridor next, a pink feather boa wrapped around his neck and a big grin on his face that said he'd been up to no good.

He jerked his chin at Brooklyn and she took off, running across the bar then leaping into his arms where he kissed her roughly in front of the entire room and she tugged on the ends of the feather boa to choke him during it.

Mateo and I exchanged a look before striding over to join them, the two of us still feeling out the boundaries of this arrangement we were all coming to, though in all honesty, I couldn't see myself backing out of it. If I stayed with them, I got to have my wild girl close, got to touch and kiss her, make her moan my name and offer up my secrets to her. We were safe in the home Mateo and Niall had reinforced away from the world out of sight. The worst of my tendencies weren't frowned upon with them, they were embraced, and I knew I wouldn't find that anywhere else, so what motivation was there for me to leave?

"There's a private entrance to the auctions through the kitchens," Niall said, setting Brooklyn down on her feet and throwing an arm around her shoulders possessively. "I got a helpful little Sandra to tell me all about it while teasing her with the idea that I might take a piss in her mouth. I woulda done it too, but it didn't feel right knowing how much she'd get off on it. My piss is all yours, Spider."

"I don't want your pee water. You can keep it in your danger dick," Brooklyn replied, wrinkling her nose.

"Even so, she can't have it either," Niall promised seriously, tickling her nose with the end of the feather boa.

"Where are these kitchens?" Mateo asked, looking towards the bar and Niall nodded.

"Through there - if my little piss-drinking friend had her facts right." He pushed between me and Mateo, keeping Brooklyn close to him as they led the way to the bar.

Niall released Brooklyn then vaulted the thing, ignoring the shocked gasp from the man serving drinks as he turned back to offer her a hand.

I moved to lift her up so that she could stand on the bar and she flashed me a big smile before taking Niall's fingers in her grip and dropping down on the other side of it where he spun her beneath his arm in celebration.

Mateo lifted the wooden flap so that the two of us could walk through, muttering something under his breath about showboating Irishmen before descending into a few choice Spanish curses.

Niall ignored him, strolling through the door into the kitchen without even trying to explain himself to the bartender. We followed him into the brightly lit space beyond where bottles of drinks were stored and glasses were being placed into washers or stacked up to be brought back out to the bar, none of the workers so much as looking our way as we strode between them.

Another door led into a wider kitchen intended for food preparations and on the far side of that, a beast of a man stood guarding a door.

"How're you doing there, fella?" Niall asked loudly, striding straight up to the man with his hand outstretched and the fool automatically took it, shaking once.

He didn't manage to get a single word out before Niall used the grip he held on the man's hand to yank him close before shoving a taser into his gut and shocking him hard enough that he crumpled to the floor in a heap.

Brooklyn applauded him and gave a little whoop while I stepped forward to haul the man towards a large walk-in refrigerator. Brooklyn skipped past me to open the door and Mateo followed us inside, taking a ball gag and a length of rope from his pocket, which I assumed he'd acquired out in the fetish rooms. He made quick work of securing the unconscious doorman and we threw the refrigerator door closed on him as we left.

Niall led the way through the door, pressing a finger to his lips as he headed into a dark stairwell and began to descend with Brooklyn close on his heels.

Mateo and I headed down right behind him, tugging the door closed at our backs and leaving nothing but dim lighting from somewhere at the base of the stairs to light our way on.

Cheers and shouts came from below us, the roar of men watching sport or egging each other into some game reaching us.

Brooklyn stiffened suddenly, making me walk right into her and snatch hold of her arm to stop her from tumbling the whole way down the stairs.

"Are you good, Spider?" Niall's voice came from ahead of us.

"I just can't help but think how lucky I am that you found me, Hellfire. I was so lost before you came to take me away. And I would have been lost even worse if someone else had bought me instead of you."

"That was never going to happen, little psycho," Niall promised, walking on down the stairs while she lingered with us. "From the moment I laid eyes on ya, I knew I had to have ya. One way or another, we were destined."

"Rook," I agreed, knowing all too well the power she held to captivate wicked men like us and make them her own.

"You're a lure set to trap sinners, mi sol," Mateo said as he shifted to her side. "We were created by a deviant god with nothing but your pleasure in mind. There was never any other fate for you than us."

Brooklyn looked back at me and even in the darkness I swear her blue eyes sparked with life.

"Us," she said on a sigh which seemed to breathe purity into the air, and I inhaled my fill of it as she tugged her arm free of my grip and followed Niall down into the dark.

We made it to the foot of the stairs and found another corridor which led to a set of double doors, manned by another pair of thugs.

I rolled my shoulders back, preparing to force our way past them, but as we closed in on them, they only nodded their heads in greeting to us.

"Welcome," one of them said. "Do you know the rules?"

"Yep," Niall agreed brightly, tapping on his temple. "Got 'em all filed away up here, ready for business."

The man nodded and pushed the door wide for us, his curious gaze lingering on Brooklyn for a moment before dropping away again as we stepped through.

We strode into a dimly lit room where men in expensive suits were drinking and guffawing together, some of them sitting at small tables, while others lingered close to a platform which I assumed they used to showcase the women they were bidding on.

We made our way deeper into the space, drawing a few interested looks from the people smart enough to sense when a pack of predators entered a room, but mostly going unnoticed as a cloud of overbearing entitlement clogged the air.

"We won't make our move in here," Niall said in a low voice as we all gathered around a tall table and Brooklyn hopped up to take a seat on a stool between us. "We just want to pinpoint our mark and follow him out when he leaves. No need for too many witnesses."

"I'm gonna make him squeal for me like a stuck little piggy – not that

I would stick an innocent little piggy but I'd stick *him* alright, I'd stick him good," Brooklyn purred, the darkness in her rising to the surface and making me edgy.

"I know ways to make a man hurt for weeks before he succumbs to death, each and every moment of his time filled with unimaginable agony," Mateo said in a low voice. "I could teach you, mi sol."

Brooklyn moaned low in the back of her throat and all three of us shifted closer to her on instinct.

"I know how to keep them alive for months on end, don't I, el burro?" Niall shot at him but Mateo just scoffed.

"Keeping a prisoner alive indefinitely is easy. I'm talking about cutting pieces from a person hour after hour, day after day and refusing them the respite of death until the very end. Not locking someone in your basement and forgetting to torture them half the time."

"If you want me to torture you some more then you only have to say the word, arsehole," Niall shot back. "You're yet to tell me where you hid all of that lovely treasure you stole from your boss and I haven't forgotten about it."

They continued to argue in low tones, and I blocked them out, my eyes drifting over the men who were moving about the room, laughing and slapping each other on the back. There were a couple of women here too, but it was by far a male dominated room.

Brooklyn sucked in a breath suddenly and I snapped my head her way, my body so in tune with hers that I was tensing for violence without even understanding the threat yet.

"What?" I asked her, scanning the crowd again and a deep frown formed on her brow.

"That man with the boot polish hair dye," she growled in a low tone.

"He's no Castillo," Mateo muttered, noticing our conversation and looking over at him too.

"No," she agreed. "He's not my armadillo. But he did try to buy me. I remember his face. I marked him for death."

Niall cursed and looked around briefly, muttering something to the others about needing to lay eyes on Castillo before we did anything rash, but his words slipped away like water through a crack on the inside of my skull as I fixated on the look of pain and hatred painted across my Rook's face.

She had felt fear at the hands of that man, and that was the only thing which remained inside my head as I snapped.

I took off running across the room, giving the others no time to do anything other than watch as I collided with the man in question with a bellow of rage, knocking him from his seat and grasping his head between my hands.

I started slamming his head against the floor over and over and over again, blind and deaf to everything around me aside from the need to destroy this life which I held in my hands.

My blood thrashed through my veins and there was a ringing in my ears as I looked around at my Rook, finding her eyes wide and alight, full of a need for death and destruction. I held her gaze as I jerked his head sharply between my palms and snapped his neck with a loud crack, the finality of his death making her eyes gleam.

A door flew open beyond the stage as shouts of alarm went up all around me and I twisted towards the new threat, my gaze locking with the eyes of a man I'd long since thought I'd never see again as he stepped into the room amongst a small crowd of cartel thugs.

My attention locked on the brother of the man I had killed so long ago that it seemed like a different life. One of the men who was the reason for me faking insanity during my incarceration. I'd hoped they would stop sending men to kill me in the belief that I was suffering far more in Eden Heights than I would with any death they could deliver. And I'd been right.

Carlos Alonso's mouth fell open as he stared at me, and I dropped my grip on the corpse I still held, my heart thrashing to a rampant beat while I stared my death in the eye.

"There he is!" Brooklyn cried, pointing at the man who had led the group out of the room, but I could barely spare a glance for Señor Castillo while one of the three brothers who had fought to ensure my death for so long met my gaze.

Niall cursed and my eyes widened marginally as I spotted the guns which the cartel were pulling, a bellow escaping my throat as I broke into a sprint and began to charge right for them, intending to leap up onto that stage and dive down amongst them, taking out as many as I could no matter how many bullets pierced my skin.

A panicked scream drew my attention back to Brooklyn a beat before a heavy weight collided with me and I fell tumbling to the floor just as a chorus of gunshots rang out.

Mateo swung a punch into my jaw as I fought to buck him off of me, his angry glare piercing into me through the holes of his gimp mask.

"Snap out of it, you bastardo loco," he snarled while Niall whooped excitedly and began returning fire beyond us.

The other bidders were all running for cover in a panic, but there were a lot of them drawing weapons of their own too and this place was set to become a bloodbath fast.

I bellowed furiously at Mateo, throwing my weight to one side and rolling us before shoving myself upright again and turning my gaze across the room to seek out Carlos. I couldn't let him live. And Brooklyn needed to dole out her own share of bloodshed tonight too.

I started running again, the sounds and screams in the room fading away in favour of the need for violence which sung through my limbs and guided me onward.

Gunfire blasted my way, a bullet catching me in the arm and twisting me aside a heartbeat before another whizzed through the air where my head had been a moment earlier.

I didn't care. It didn't matter. Only my need for death and carnage consumed me and there was nothing else in this world which I could think on.

I ran for the edge of the stage as more bullets flew my way, but just as I was about to vault up onto it, Brooklyn skidded into my path and threw her arms out wide to stop me.

My heart lurched as I found her between me and those bullets. I leapt on her, knocking her to the floor and pinning her beneath me as I shielded her with my body.

A furious roar escaped me as I twisted my head to try and look back at the cartel thugs once more, but she reared up and sank her teeth into my neck to force my attention onto her.

"We need to run, AJ," she urged, her fingers curling around my biceps and digging in as she clung to me in an attempt to stop me from rising. "Fight off your angries and run with me now."

"Five seconds, Spider, or we're leaving him behind!" Niall yelled as he fired a few more shots over our heads, forcing the cartel back and buying her that time.

I made a move to stand again, the need for murder too great in me to back down now, but as I lifted my weight off of her, Brooklyn cried out, snatching my hand and pushing it between her thighs so that I could feel her bare flesh and the slick heat of her core.

"Remember that promise you made me earlier?" she demanded. "We need to make good on that. Right now."

The bark of authority in her voice made my thoughts snap together and I blinked back a little of the red which was pressing in on my vision. My cock swelled at her words before I'd even fully taken them in and my mind turned in the direction she was urging, despite the furious need for destruction which echoed through my veins.

Mateo was suddenly there again, his hand locking around my arm as he yanked me towards the door at Niall's back and I snapped out of it enough to listen, scooping Brooklyn into my arms and doing the one thing I'd sworn to do better than any other. Protecting her.

I curled her up tight in my grip and broke into a sprint as I took off towards Niall, a triumphant whoop escaping him as he managed to shoot one of the cartel men behind me while making no attempt whatsoever to take cover. He may have been insistent that we didn't make a scene here tonight, but now the fray had broken out, he was fully embracing it.

Mateo was right on my heels as we crashed back through the doors and I took off up the stairs at a furious pace, breathing in the scent of my Rook and focusing on that single, most important task as I fought against the need to snap necks and pound flesh.

Niall yelled out in encouragement for us to run faster as he chased after us and an explosion rocked the stairs beneath our feet as he tossed a grenade back over his shoulder with a howl of laughter.

Mateo pushed past me as we shoved our way back into the kitchen and Brooklyn shifted in my arms, pointing towards a window on the other side of the room and shouting, "Onward horsey!" at the top of her lungs.

I did as she commanded, chasing after Mateo who fired his gun out the window before leaping through it.

Mateo ran ahead down the alley, checking for any more armed assholes while I leapt out behind him with Niall's breath warming the back of my neck as he followed.

"Faster, big lad," he snarled, his gaze snapping to Brooklyn's as she beamed up at him.

He stayed just behind us, checking over his shoulder while we ran and my muscles twitched and bulged with the need to turn back and face this fight head on, no matter how outnumbered we were.

We rounded a corner at the end of the alleyway and Niall unlocked the door to his new black Jeep, yanking the rear door open for me to toss

Brooklyn inside before jumping into the driver's seat himself.

Mateo leapt into the front too and I whirled back around, blood pounding against my eardrums, begging me to return to the fray and let my violent needs play out.

"AJ!" Brooklyn demanded, shuffling across the rear seats as she made space for me. "Come use that rage on me," she said, her teeth sinking into her bottom lip and her thighs parting to give me a view of her bare pussy beneath her little leather skirt.

I didn't even realise I'd made the choice to move before feeling the car speed away from the curb, the door swinging shut behind me as I took hold of Brooklyn's hips and shoved her right back against the far door to give myself space to drop my head between her thighs.

Then I did as I had promised her and worked my way to her ruin while Niall cursed me as he sped through the streets of the city and headed home.

"We'll have trouble drawing him out now," Mateo growled angrily as he tossed his gimp mask aside, clearly upset over the missed opportunity to strike the final name from Brooklyn's list, and I knew that I was to blame for that failure.

Brooklyn moaned loudly as I gripped her thighs and I forced them wider, sinking my tongue as deep inside her as I could manage before circling it and tasting just how sweet she really was.

I had failed her. That was the truth of the matter and now I wanted to serve her to make up for it as best I could.

"That's not the first time I've had to cut and run on a job," Niall replied, the car swerving suddenly and almost unseating me and Brooklyn as she gasped and panted my name.

I lifted my head to glare at Niall and found him watching us in the rearview mirror which he'd adjusted to give himself a better view.

"Watch the road," Mateo snarled, shoving the steering wheel and causing Niall to slap him across the face.

I dipped my head back between Brooklyn's thighs, sucking her clit then lapping at it over and over again while she began to thrust and rock her hips against my face.

The overwhelming rage which had held me hostage had switched entirely to lust for this woman beneath me, and as she fisted my hair and I fucked her with my mouth, I found a pure kind of peace that I'd never truly known before.

She came for me with a cry of pleasure and I lapped up every piece of her lust as I held her at my mercy and made sure she felt every moment of it to its fullest.

"We'll come up with a new plan," Niall said as he swung the car around a corner and I was forced to grip the headrest to stop myself from falling.

Brooklyn squealed as she tumbled out from beneath me and I snatched hold of her arm with my free hand before she could make it all the way into the footwell.

I sat up as the car was righted again, freeing my cock and smirking at Niall in the mirror as he scowled back at me. I tugged Brooklyn into place on my lap while holding Niall's eye and keeping her facing him. My cock ached and Brooklyn whimpered with the need for more as I kept her suspended above me, the head of my dick sliding through the slickness of her entrance without pushing inside so much as an inch.

I waited while Brooklyn panted, and Mateo growled curses about her coming for the man who had just fucked up their job.

Niall held us all in suspense. I wasn't entirely certain why I found such relief in following his commands. Maybe it was my years in incarceration, obeying orders and following rules which had awoken a need in me to take orders from others. Then again, I'd always found relief in my old gang too. In letting my crew leader make choices for me so that I didn't have to do so myself. Perhaps it was because I was an orphan who'd never had a parent to give me a single order in my life, and I'd been so fucked up by the lawless way I'd lived that I sought out the structure within the chaos.

Whatever it was, taking commands from the man who had offered me a real chance at freedom, especially when it came to how I got our girl off was something which just worked for me.

"What are ya waiting for, big fella?" Niall barked when he couldn't take the anticipation anymore. "Make my little psycho come all over that monster dick of yours, and don't be gentle with her. The girl has made it clear enough that she prefers it rough."

"Yes," Brooklyn agreed. "Real rough, AJ."

A rush of relief tumbled through my chest at the command and without waiting another second, I tugged Brooklyn's hips down and thrust mine up, sinking my cock into her so deep and hard that she gasped as the feeling of it stole her breath clean away from her.

I gripped her hair in my fist, tugging her head back and leaning in to speak in her ear, low enough that no one but her could hear me.

"More?" I breathed and she nodded. "Hold on to something nice and tight for me then."

Brooklyn garbled an incoherent response as she leaned forward and gripped the two headrests for the front seats.

I reached around to the front of her dress, tugging on the skin-tight leather until her tits spilled free of it and palming them roughly as I began to slam my hips up at a frantic, brutal pace which matched the heady beating of my heart.

Brooklyn moaned loudly, begging for more as I tugged on her nipples and I dropped my hands to her sides, taking full control of her as I began to fuck her harder and faster, pounding my cock so deep inside her that all she could do was cry out in pleasure between my thrusts.

Mateo cursed then unclipped his belt, twisting between the seats and dropping his mouth to capture her nipple between his lips before moving his hand to her clit and rubbing it in time with my thrusts.

Brooklyn moaned and gasped as I fucked her harder, barely able to catch her breath as she took me like the savage I was, and I enjoyed every second of stretching her with my cock and filling her to her limit.

When she finally came, it was with a cry that was a masterpiece, her pussy squeezing around my shaft and forcing me to follow her into ecstasy as I climaxed with a ferocious roar and buried myself deep within her one final time.

Niall's eyes were locked on us in the mirror and I was surprised we hadn't crashed while he'd been so distracted with our performance, but somehow we were still tearing away down the road without so much as a wobble to the wheel to indicate he wasn't paying enough attention.

"Jesus," Niall muttered, shifting his focus to the road once more. "You're in for it now, little psycho. I'm gonna have to work on outdoing that little performance later on tonight and you'd better believe I won't stop until you've screamed twice as loud for me."

Brooklyn slurred something which sounded like an agreement as she slumped back into my arms, making no attempt to disconnect our bodies and allowing me to just enjoy the feeling of having her close.

I held her like that the rest of the way home, breathing in the scent of her and running my fingers back and forth across her soft skin while I let myself believe in her at last after so much time spent having her solely within my mind. My sweet obsession.

Niall parked up and got out of the car, muttering to himself about never having had this kind of problem when he worked alone.

Before we could follow, Mateo hit the door locks and turned to look at us.

"Carlos Alonso knew you," he said in a low voice. "And yet I don't. Which means your vendetta with him must have been personal."

"Why?" Brooklyn breathed as she moved to sit beside me, straightening out her dress and looking like a fucking dream.

"Because I was the creature sent to hunt men who crossed our organisation, and unless I'm mistaken, Jack was sent away to Eden Heights long before I ever left my mountain. If his death had been ordered by the head of the cartel, then I would have been the one to come cleave it from his body."

"Unlikely," I scoffed and Mateo's brow dipped into a frown.

"Three syllables now, is it?"

I offered him a taunting smile and Brooklyn shifted in her seat. "Do we need some of the secrets in AJ's head?" she asked Mateo seriously. "Because I can read his mind and pluck them straight out for you, if he lets me?"

Her questioning gaze swivelled to me and I nodded in agreement.

"Okay." Brooklyn drew in a deep breath then closed her eyes and took my hand. "Communicate your truth, Angry. I'm ready for you to slip it into me."

"I killed Javier Alonso a long time ago," I said and Mateo's eyes flashed with both triumph at hearing me speak and irritation for having been caught in my ruse for so long. "In another lifetime, I was bound to a gang down on the west coast called The Harlequin Crew." I tugged my shirt open to fully reveal the gang tattoo I had there, the skull crowned with a jester's hat, which I'd once worn so proudly.

"He killed a man called Captain Alonso one time," Brooklyn said, her eyes still closed as she relayed what I'd said to Mateo like she thought he couldn't hear me. "And he was into gangbang bondage."

Mateo opened his mouth like he was going to tell her that he could hear me just fine, but he shook his head instead, directing his response to me.

"The Castillo Cartel have dealings with the Harlequins from time to time," Mateo said with a nod of understanding. "They help run some of the cartel's product into the states. But so far as I understand it, they don't let people resign from their organisation. Blood in, blood out. So why are you still breathing if you pledged your life to Luther Harlequin then reneged on your debt?"

I gave a soft smile at the mention of the cold-hearted leader of my former crew, then shrugged.

"Luther had every right to kill me for what I did. I was his tool, his weapon, a beast so full of rage that I used to live for his commands to unleash it."

"Jack was a sub for a bad man who kept him on a leash," Brooklyn whispered mysteriously before I went on.

"But after a while it grew harder to control my violent urges. I would snap and attack people with the littlest provocation. I got to like the taste of blood too much. Luther put me into cage fights, gave me pep talks, tried to keep me in line as his faithful weapon."

"Jack was kept in a cage and had all kinds of urges which made him use his giant weapon," Brooklyn added for Mateo's sake, and I had to supress a chuckle at her interpretation.

"I struggle to believe *the* Luther Harlequin set you on Javier Alonso and you all lived to tell the tale after his brothers found out," Mateo said, pinning me in his gaze.

"He didn't," I agreed. "I just lost it in a bar one night. Picked on the biggest, meanest motherfucker in there and caved his head in with my bare fists. By the time I came back to myself, I was already in a police cell having been hauled there after someone had called the cops and they'd found me still beating the shit out of an already dead body."

"And the remaining three Alonso brothers never came for revenge while you were in prison?" Mateo scoffed lightly before Brooklyn could do her translation and she huffed.

"I haven't told you the bit about him growing bear hands yet. They were all big and brown and hairy with claws and stuff," she snapped, making us both look to her in confusion, but she just kept her eyes closed and squeezed my fingers. "Go on, AJ, slip inside me again."

My gaze roamed down her body in that tight little leather outfit and I considered doing just that before Mateo snapped his fingers in my face to make me look at him.

"Focus, bastardo," he snapped. "I want to know what secrets you've been hiding."

"Yes, they sent men after me in prison. I killed five or six of them, that violence in me always ready for a fight, but I knew I couldn't keep escaping their attempts on my life indefinitely. Luther had no choice but to cut me out of the gang so I couldn't surround myself with them either. He had to protect the crew. I don't blame him for it. But I had to protect myself. So, when they came to give me a psyche assessment, I decided to let them think I was unable to say more than a single word at a time, much less control my violent impulses. It didn't take a lot to convince them to send me to Eden Heights. The last man who had come for me had managed to smack me around the head with a metal bar, so I even had a head injury to back up my story. Before I knew it, I was packed up and shipped out to Eden Heights where I was left to rot, and the Alonso brothers were convinced by my act, believing that I was in a far greater hell than they could deliver with death and were happy to let me rot there in payment for the life I'd taken."

"Until Carlos saw you tonight," Mateo muttered.

"Oh, AJ, I knew you were a cunning creature," Brooklyn purred. "You used your crazies to save you."

She opened her eyes and leaned in to press a kiss to my lips before scampering out of the car, following Niall into the house.

Silence hung between Mateo and I as he digested that information.

"You're a smart motherfucker," he muttered. "But I saw through your bullshit."

"You're the first who has."

He glanced towards the house. "Is that it now? Are you just talking then?"

"No." I wasn't sure why I planned to keep my silence, but I'd grown used to it and found I liked it more than filling the air with empty words for the most part.

"You aren't letting Niall know?" His smile deepened and I shook my head, making him bark a laugh. "Good. That bastardo doesn't deserve your words."

I smiled in reply, already feeling drained by the conversation and wanting to escape it, shift back into the silence and seek out the company of my Rook once more.

"The Alonso brothers will be on the hunt now," he said. "I guess that makes the two of us enemies of the Castillo Cartel."

"At least until they're dead," I agreed and he nodded slowly.

"At least until they're dead."

BROOKLYN

CHAPTER TWENTY SEVEN

"Hellfire?" I called through the house, but instead of my Niall, Brutus came bounding through the lounge and crashed into me with a fierce bark. "Hey Bruty baby!" I squealed, dropping down to hug him and narrowly avoiding a bitey. He was so excited to see me, he kept barking and snapping his teeth all happy-like. I tickled his ears then pranced back to my feet and he lunged at Jack and Mateo as they reached the threshold.

"Ah! You perro loco," Mateo cursed, too slow to avoid a little snappy as Brutus chewed on his arm. It was so cute how much they loved each other.

"Money I'm home!" I cried out, hoping Niall would hear me somewhere, but I pouted when he gave no reply.

I stomped through the lounge in my killer heels then stomped my way upstairs too, stilling as I found him stepping out of his room. He'd shed his jacket and his white shirt now hung open to reveal the ink on his muscular frame. He swept a hand into his dark blond hair, messing it up as he gazed at me with a *come-hither Mrs O'Brien* look, the darkness of the hallway keeping him in perfect shadow.

"Get in here," he commanded. "You need a reminder of why I'm yer number one."

"I see you're wearing your bossy boots today," I purred and he cocked his head, his lips tilting in a psycho's smile.

He opened his mouth to speak but instead of words, out came a tremendous bang that rattled the walls and my heart along with it.

In the next second Niall was barrelling towards me, and I realised that noise hadn't come from his mouth at all, it had come from outside.

I wheeled around, panicked for AJ and Mateo as another gunshot cut through the air and the bulletproof window in the lounge took the hit for us, keeping us safe inside.

"Niall – get guns!" Mateo barked as I spotted him running into the lounge.

Jack was right behind him, gazing up the stairs at me, rage coiling through his expression while Brutus barked furiously at the window and the shadows lurking beyond it.

Niall grabbed my arm, yanking me back along the landing into his room, shoving his closet door open and taking out a bag full of stabbys and shooties. He placed a pistol in my grip and a riot helmet on my head which I quickly threw off.

"I can't see properly through that," I snapped as Niall cocked a shotgun and slung the bag over his shoulder.

"Would ya ever do as I say?" he growled.

"No," I hissed.

"Yes."

"No."

"Yes."

"No."

A stream of gunfire sounded from downstairs and Jack barked 'Rook!" the same moment Mateo roared, "Hurry the fuck up, bastardo!"

We ran out of the room together while my thoughts flashed and banged like dynamite.

"Who's shooting at us?" I asked in confusion as we made it to the stairs.

"Fuck if I know," Niall growled. "I'll be sure to ask 'em when they're dead though, love."

He launched the bag of weapons over the bannister and Jack caught it with an oomph leaving his lungs as more gunshots slammed into the windows and walls outside.

Mateo was sheltering under the window in case any cheeky bullets broke through somehow. Jack threw him a rifle and he reared up like a fearless warrior, cracking the window open and taking shots out into the night. I dropped down beside Mateo, aiming my gun out through the window too and pulling the trigger time and again, the recoil making my fingers tingle with the powerful vibrations.

"I'm gonna carve up some enemies real good tonight," Niall snarled and I glanced back at him, finding him strapping knives and all kinds of bangers and stabbies to his body. The look he and Jack shared told me they were about to do something crazy. And crazy was my forte.

"Wait for me," I gasped as they ran out of the room and I heard the front door open.

"I can see you behind that tree, ya hairy cunt! Shove this up your arse!" Niall cried then a boom set my teeth locking together.

Mateo lunged forward, shoving my head down as the whole house trembled precariously, but we were safe in here, he didn't need to worry his nelly about me.

"Bastardo loco," Mateo hissed in my ear and a wild laugh rolled out of my throat as the tremor tickled my knees.

"You want more, baby?! I'll give ya more!" Niall cried and another boom split the air apart.

The gunfire had ceased on the house and I had to guess our enemies were on the move, heading to meet Niall as he let his demons loose. *Run, run, as fast as you can, you can't get away from my unhinged man!*

"Come on, Dead Man, I don't wanna miss all the fun." I wriggled out of his arms and ran for the door, keeping my head low as I went.

"Mi sol," he growled in a command for me to stop, the heavy sound of his footfalls following me, but I didn't stop. I skipped and jumped my way along with excitement zinging through my limbs.

Brutus joined me, barking loudly, his eyes bright like he was enjoying the chaos as much as I was.

"Let's get 'em, pup!" I whooped as I ran outside, spotting Niall and Jack racing down the drive and firing shots off into the dark. And now it was my turn to play bang-bang.

I raised my gun and hunted for a target, spotting a man taking cover behind a tree near the lake, his arm poking out the side.

I pulled the trigger, boom, boom, boom, the wind whipping my skirt up around me and making me look like some kind of epic supervillain. But that was when I remembered I had no panties on and realised the look was probably more super porn villain than DC Comics.

Brutus took off towards the guy, not a drop of fear in his soul as he charged him down. I kept shooting, making sure he couldn't take any pot shots at my pooch while he was on his way over there to maul his face, but then a gunshot to my right made me flinch.

Mateo slammed into me, dragging me towards Niall's cars to take cover.

We hit the ground on our knees and scrambled out of sight, the skin of my legs tearing open in little grazes and making me feel so freaking alive.

Dead Man got up, peering over the car and aiming his rifle across the yard, the bang of his gun and the animal snarl on his lips making me heady as I stared up at him. His powerful body was rock solid, every muscle coiled like a loaded weapon itself.

I peeped under the car to see Brutus collide with the tree man, taking him down and savaging him like a hungry beast.

"Go on Bruty!" I cried just as more gunfire rattled our way and Mateo dropped down beside me, his back to the car as he reloaded his rifle.

Niall and Jack were further down the drive, wrestling with a man by a fancy black sedan parked there. Jack was fully in his angries, swinging bone crunching punches, clearly preferring to kill with his hands. Niall was playing killer with the same man, choking him out with one arm while stabbing with his free hand. Blood was colouring my men red and it set off a beacon of light within me, making me smile from ear to ear.

A bang made the window of the car explode above me and I covered my head as Mateo shoved me forward to get me moving. Two sets of footsteps were following us around the vehicle and Mateo dropped onto his back, shimmying beneath the car beside us.

"Take the first, I'll take the second," he whispered, disappearing into the dark with a look that told me to keep moving.

I trusted his ideas, so I crawled around to the back of the car, staying low and raising my gun as the footsteps closed in on us.

"Where's that big fucker gone?" one man growled.

"He can't be far," the other murmured. "Check that way. I'll look over here."

The thumping of boots moved closer while another set moved away.

I held my breath.

I was a cobra waiting, ready to strike and sink my fangs in deep. I'd unleash every ounce of venom on our enemy and show them what happened to people who attacked our family. My heart panged as I accepted that that was what we were now. A bonded unit. Dead Man, Hellfire, AJ, Bruty-tooty and little old me. I'd been alone for so long that I'd been waiting for this all to disappear, for me to return to my life on the streets where no one even cared to learn my name. But here, among these beasts of fury, I was somehow at the heart of their wants and desires, and I realised they weren't going to leave.

I'd die defending them. I'd bleed and rot and turn to dust for them. But not today.

As the man rounded the car, he gazed down at me with a sneer and I pulled the trigger of my gun with a soul full of rage and his death singing a ditty in my ear. But there was a click as the chamber rang empty and I realised I'd been a foolish fool.

He grinned as he aimed his own pistol at me, enjoying the look of acceptance on my face as I realised I had no time to do anything but die. There was an entire eternity living in my final seconds on this bittersweet earth. I'd lived a life where all my nightmares had been realised, and all my dreams had come true. I wanted to kick and scream and throw a tantrum at Death's feet because it wasn't *fair*. I'd had so very little time to enjoy the good, to savour the cherry on top of the sweet ice cream of a life I'd finally been served.

A huge shadow rose up behind the maker of my ruin and with a bang that rocked me to my core, a bullet slammed through the back of his skull and out through the centre of his eyes, blood showering over me before he slumped dead at my feet.

Mateo was left standing there, staring down at me with a wild fury as he offered me his hand, his body glistening with the blood of his previous kill. I grabbed hold of him, letting him draw me to my feet as I tasted the blood on my lips and laughed in delight, my brush with death leaving me giddy.

"Why didn't you tell me you were out of bullets?" he hissed, his eyes flashing with the fear of what could have happened because of my little blip.

"I didn't know," I admitted as he tugged me around the car to take cover again. He snatched my gun and loaded it for me as a deep frown formed on his brow.

I reached over to smooth out those angry little creases, but they wouldn't budge. "Mateo-" I started but he cut me off, his eyes snapping up to meet mine as a world of rage stared back at me.

"Eres mi sol. Eres mi luz en la oscuridad. Nunca me dejes," he snarled and my soul rumbled with the power of his words.

"Does that mean…you're mad? And you'd like a cookie?" I translated.

"No," he hissed through his teeth. "It means, you are my sun, my light. And I command that you don't ever leave me." He placed the loaded gun back in my grip and lunged forward to take a savage kiss from my lips. It lasted all of two seconds before he drew back and gave me that burn-the-world-down stare again.

"The next one's mine," I insisted and he smirked slowly.

"All yours, chica loca," he promised before kicking the corpse on the ground and forcing it to roll over. "This is Tomas Alonso, which means these men are cartel," he hissed.

"Like cows?" I breathed.

"No. Like enemies. Jack's enemies. They must have followed us from the club."

A whoop drew my attention to Jack and Niall and I peered over the car, spotting them running towards the man Brutus had on the ground. As the dog backed up, the man was left at the mercy of the new monsters on the scene and my heart beat rampantly as I waited for his death to come. There were no more gunshots, no more men crying out as Niall bore down on the man whimpering from Brutus's bloody attack and slid a knife slow and deep into his throat.

I pouted, folding my arms as the silence stretched right out into the trees and beyond.

"No fair. I didn't get a kill," I huffed.

Mateo ran his thumb over my chin, wiping a line of blood away and frowning at me. "There'll always be a next time."

"I want a now time," I growled and Mateo looked to Niall and Jack, concern blossoming in his gaze.

"We need to figure out a plan," he said heavily. "Stay here." He strode away from me to join the others and my pout pushed out even further as I stared at their little man club.

I didn't even get a kill and now I was being cut out of an official Society of Psychos meeting? This sucked hairy butthole.

My heart shrank to a tiny pea, a pea which tumbled down into my belly, whirling around in there and sobbing as it went.

My men started arguing, pointing at each other as curses carried up the sky and Brutus barked at them like he was in on the conversation too. I didn't care to listen to what they were yapping about. I was the only one who had a right to be a moody Joel, they'd all gotten a kill. But me? No, I was here in the wake of a massacre, and I had no victims among the dead.

I hurled the gun away from me with a snarl, the thing hitting Niall's new Jeep and leaving a dent in the side of it. Then I twisted on my heel and huffed my way back to the house.

I wanted some Coco Pops, but I didn't even deserve Pops right now because I hadn't shed a single drop of blood tonight. I was supposed to be the Pink Pussy, but I was just the Bald Beaver instead. And there was nothing worse than a bald beaver.

I hung my head, stomping to the front door and not even looking where I was going because I just wanted to go sit in the shower and scream.

A large sweaty palm slapped over my mouth, and I jerked to attention before I was yanked back against an enormous body the size of three bodies stitched together horizontally.

I sensed who it was before I even heard his voice, my instincts screaming with the memory of him as the scent of liquorice twisted around me.

Señor Castillo.

"One wrong move and I'll empty my gun into you, whore," he said in my ear, dragging me backwards. "You'll be my shield until I'm out of here."

I fought against his hold, feeling his snooty Simon of a gun poking into my ribs as he towed me towards Niall's truck while the sound of my men arguing still carried up to the sky. The lights flashed on the car as Señor Castillo opened it with a key he must have stolen from the house, but still my men didn't see.

I weighed up my options, not wanting to be made into swiss cheese by Castillo's gun, but also not wanting to play human shield so he could escape.

He drew me down onto his lap in the driver's seat, yanking me tight to his body as he pressed the button to start up the truck. The moment the engine growled, my men stopped shouting at each other and I twisted my head, trying to see them out the back window as Castillo drove the truck in a fast circle to turn it around.

Niall started shooting and I screamed as the passenger window exploded and a bitch of a shard of glass cut my arm.

Angry Jack knocked Niall aside as he heard my scream and Castillo accelerated down the drive, leaning around me as he kept one hand on the gun pressing into my body while using the other to drive.

"Rook!" AJ bellowed as my three men came running our way and adrenaline spilled into my blood.

Castillo had to veer around the fancy car he must have arrived in with the other men and we bumped over the grass, the gun slipping for a second so it was no longer jammed into my side.

That was my moment. No matter how small, how much of a fragment of a heartbeat it was. I wasn't going to be torn away from my heathens. I wasn't going to end up dead in a ditch somewhere at the hands of this sweaty man. I remembered when Dead Man had tried to kill Niall with a windscreen wiper lever and thanked him for his clever idea. I snapped off the lever behind the wheel then stabbed it backwards with all my might in the direction of Castillo's face.

He roared as it sunk into something fleshy and the gun went off with a bang that I felt everywhere. I was so full of adrenaline, I couldn't be sure if I'd been shot or not. But it didn't matter now.

I twisted around in my seat, stabbing with the broken bit of plastic again and again as Castillo clutched his bloody eye, screaming and trying to push me away.

He dropped the gun as he flailed beneath me, snooty old Simon now down in the footwell and stopping him from accelerating any further as it got stuck under the pedal.

The car rolled down a bank and my head hit the roof as we bumped along, but I never stopped stabbing, driving my makeshift weapon into Castillo over and over as hot blood splashed my face. The huge man was no longer in control, it was me who held the power now, the goddess of his destruction come to make him pay for all the cruelty he'd dealt in his life. My mind was in a murder haze as I continued to stab and stab and stab, and it was only when the door wrenched open beside me that I realised the car had rolled to a halt and Castillo had long since stopped moving.

AJ dragged me out of the car, and I was suddenly surrounded by all three of my psychos, pressing against me, our hearts beating as one rebellious creature who defied the laws of life. We were the outcasts of this land, the rejects of the world, but together we had something real and ours which no one could take from us.

Niall drew me from Jack's arms and we shared a bloody kiss that tasted of our fallen enemies. He smiled at me like a jester as he rested his forehead to mine and I felt our souls winding even deeper together.

"It was Señor Castillo," I breathed. "He's the last on my kill rock. Now he's deader than a daisy in winter."

"He came with the Alonso brothers," Mateo said and I looked from him to AJ as relief filled me over their deaths. "They won't be the last to come here. They will have told someone where they were going."

"Fuckin' cartel ruining my safe house," Niall muttered irritably.

"*Your* safe house?" Mateo hissed.

"Yeah. Mine. All mine, seeing as I stole it from ya," Niall said smugly.

"Well, I wasn't the one driving when they followed us back here," Mateo said bitterly.

"I've never once missed a mark on my tail before now," Niall snarled. "Not until you two fellas decided to distract me by making Brooklyn come all over the back seat when I should have been concentrating."

"Your lack of concentration isn't my problem," Mateo snapped.

"Well fuck you for bringing yer enemies to my door, el burro," Niall said as I jumped down from his arms and he stalked away to the house.

"What now?" I asked, looking from Mateo to Jack who was frowning at the closest corpse and seemed more interested in his thoughts than our conversation.

Mateo stepped towards me, his features setting and clarity washing over him. "First, we must destroy the evidence, hide the dead, and wash their blood from our flesh. When that's done, we will make a plan."

MATEO

CHAPTER TWENTY EIGHT

I gripped Brooklyn's wrist and dragged her up the hill, stepping around the body of Carlos Alonso and cursing as I hauled her through the front door then towards my room.

"Where are we going, Dead Man?" she asked curiously. "Did the killing get you all hot under the cobra?"

"The cartel don't do things by halves, mi sol," I said to her urgently, drawing her into my room and throwing the door closed between us and the outside world before releasing her and doing a quick sweep of the place.

Once I was convinced there was no one in the room, I dropped to my knees and hauled the go bag I had ready out from under the bed. I'd gathered up some weapons and found a few of my fake IDs around the house in places Niall either hadn't checked or just hadn't cared about. I knew he'd had a few made up for her, so I'd find them before we left too.

"What's in the bag? Is it a gift?" she asked excitedly, hurrying over to it as I tossed it down on the bed.

"Just some clothes and weapons, things we need if we're going on the run," I explained.

"Oh, I don't really like to run. I prefer to get my cardio from riding huge men."

I coughed out a laugh as I looked at her, my thoughts instantly going to how incredible her body had felt submitting to mine and a low growl rumbling through my chest at the memory. I hadn't taken a single taste of her since, not until tonight when I hadn't been able to resist helping Jack bring her to ruin. Niall had hauled me off of her when we'd fucked after all. Although I kept going over it in my mind again and again, and though I was certain I wouldn't have truly hurt her, I couldn't help but question myself. Maybe he'd seen that demon in me and had feared for her life. Then again, would he have left me breathing if he'd really thought I was close to killing her? It seemed unlikely. And if I hadn't been close to ending her life, then did I have a valid reason to deny myself the sweetness of her flesh while enduring the sound and sight of the others having her?

The thoughts had been driving me to madness ever since I'd been torn away from her with my cock still hard and wanting, but now wasn't the moment to focus on it.

"There will be plenty of that if you desire it, chica loca," I swore. "But right now, we need to leave."

"Why?"

"Because I can guarantee that the Alonso brothers and Raul Castillo didn't just come here on a whim without informing anyone of their plans. There's a chain of command which leads right up to the head of the viper itself and I have worked too fucking hard and suffered too fucking much to fall prey to him again."

"Are we going on a road trip?" she asked eagerly. "I've always loved the idea of going on the road, killing bad guys every time I came across them and seeing all of America. We could see all the states, like Arizona, Nevada, Texas, Canada, Disneyland. Then, when we get back, we could put photos of all our fun times up around the house and-"

"We won't be able to come back here, mi sol," I interrupted her, needing her to understand this.

"But…I like it here," she said sadly, finally understanding what it was that I was telling her. "I don't want to leave."

I blew out a deep breath and closed in on her, backing her up against the door and breathing in her air without quite touching her at all.

"Tell me the things you need in this life, Brooklyn," I commanded as I captured her in my gaze. "The things you truly need."

"You," she replied instantly, making something in my chest settle. "Niall, AJ, Brutus."

I nodded, though a part of me still detested that, but I was willing to accept her desire for them in light of the smiles they brought to her face and the moans they drew from her lips. "You can bring those things with us."

"I need cheese too," she added. "I've gotten a taste for the fancy kind, and if we're going to be homeless, then I want to bring a supply with me. Janky Lou sold cheese down under the bridge, but it wasn't the same. And he kept it in his socks which was less than desirable."

"We won't be homeless, chica, I swear it to you. We'll find somewhere even better than this place and make it ours."

Tears filled her eyes but she nodded, tilting her chin in offering and I closed the distance to taste her, just like she'd known I would.

I pressed my body to hers as I devoured her mouth, sinking my tongue between those delicious lips and making her bend to my will as the darkness in me writhed with lust and the desire to take her here and now.

My grip on her tightened as my cock swelled and a soft whimper spilled from those sinful lips as she felt it, knowing where my thoughts were headed and making no move to resist me.

I forced myself back with a surge of will, swiping a hand down my face and stalking away from her before heading out of the room and into the bathroom.

Brooklyn followed behind me, her steps silent but her presence so potent I wasn't likely to miss it.

"Why do you always do that, Dead Man?" she asked in a soft whisper which spoke to the echoes of a good man who still lingered on within my chest, raising his head on occasions like this and making guilt stir within me as I realised my actions were hurting her. "You pull away from me and it makes my heart hurt. Don't you want me like that anymore?"

I whirled around to face her, a frown etching deep into my brow as I shook my head in a fierce denial.

"The problem is, I want you like that too much, chica," I swore to her. "And that kind of desire only makes me more dangerous. You saw the way Niall had to force me off of you. You experienced the force of my passion when it is unleashed. I couldn't live in a world without you, mi sol, I couldn't bear to be the reason you were lost to it."

Brooklyn gasped, shaking her head violently and rushing towards me so fast that I had no choice but to capture her as she propelled herself into my arms.

"You wouldn't do that, Dead Man, I know it in my soul."

"You can't possibly know that," I protested, but the look in her vibrant blue eyes was so pure and captivating that I found myself unable to look away from it, from her.

"I do," she swore vehemently. "You don't need Hellfire or anyone else to protect me from you. You would never do anything to harm me."

She pushed up onto her tiptoes and kissed me before I could form any other kind of protest, make any further argument and my lips parted for hers because I was a slave to her wants and only a man. A selfish, starving man who had been in need of her for so long that I hadn't even realised why I was so empty without her.

Brooklyn's hands dropped to the buckle of my belt as she started walking me backwards, encouraging me towards the shower while stripping me of my clothes with a new confidence that her experience with the others had clearly given her.

"I don't want to hurt you," I growled against her lips even as my back hit the tiled wall of the walk-in shower and I knew I was passing the point where I would have the strength to stop this.

"Then don't," she snapped. "It's that simple, Dead Man."

"It's not, mi sol. The demon in me-"

"*You* are the demon, Mateo," Brooklyn growled, jerking my belt open with such force that she made me stumble. "One summoned straight from hell just for me. I don't need you to be soft, I don't need you to be kind, I only need you. All of you. So don't leave me waiting for you any longer. Don't keep holding back."

She shoved my trousers down aggressively and my cock bobbed between us, making its desires known all too well as I bit down on my tongue and pressed my hands to the wall, fighting against the urge to grab hold of her and do what she was asking of me.

Brooklyn bit her lip as she looked at my cock, the shyness and uncertainty that she had shown the first time she looked on it now replaced with nothing but hunger and a need for me which I was useless to deny.

She reached out and yanked on the tap, making water crash down over us and stealing my breath with the freezing temperature of it as it began to wash the blood from our skin.

I kicked my shoes and trousers the rest of the way off, leaving myself fully naked before her as the water began to heat and I fought against the warring emotions inside myself, trying to decide if this was madness or if it could truly be as right as it felt.

Brooklyn reached around her back, trying to unbuckle the leather dress she wore but as I saw her struggling, I snapped, giving in to the need in me and trusting her judgement far more than I trusted myself. So I stepped forward and grabbed her.

I spun her around, pushing her face first against the wall and crushing her there with my body, the solid ridge of my cock slipping between her ass cheeks and making me groan as I started unbuckling the thing she was wearing.

Brooklyn pushed her ass back against me and I rocked my hips, unable to resist the urge to feel my cock sliding between her full cheeks and teasing her opening just a little. I wanted to claim her there, wanted to fill her in every way she could be filled and make sure she knew the fit of my body within hers in every way. But right now, I wanted her eyes on me more.

I finished unbuckling the dress, shoving it down and leaving her bare before me, forcing myself to step back as she remained panting against the wall.

"How do you want me, Dead Man?" she breathed, her voice barely audible over the sound of rushing water, but her desire clear.

"I want..." I trailed off as I reached for her shoulder, my fingers skimming along it and working my way towards her neck in a slow and gentle touch.

Brooklyn moaned softly, goosebumps erupting over her skin despite the hot water and as I ran my fingers down her spine, she shivered for me.

I stilled as I brushed my fingers over the curve of her full ass, taking in a shuddering breath and stepping forward slowly.

I dropped my mouth to her neck, not biting or scraping my jaw across her flesh, simply kissing her softly and looking down to see the rock-hard point of her nipple as it dragged across the tiles with the deep inhale my touch elicited.

"I want to love you, mi sol," I murmured against her jaw, taking hold of her chin in gentle fingers and turning her mouth to meet mine, consuming the whimper which escaped her and allowing my lips to move to a slow and heady pace.

"I love you, Mateo," she murmured as I withdrew and the weight of those words pressed into me in a way I'd never known before.

She pushed back against me and I let her turn, watching as the water spilled over her face, catching in her long eyelashes and washing her clean before me.

I traced my fingers along the side of her face, breathing in her air and losing myself in her steady, bright gaze.

I knew we didn't have time for this. We needed to be washing ourselves clean and running for our lives, but in that moment, there was nothing more important to me than her. I needed her. And not in any way I'd ever needed a woman before now. I just needed to be hers.

I leaned down to kiss her, groaning softly at the exquisite feeling of her mouth moving with mine as I dropped my hand to her core and slipped it between her thighs.

Brooklyn moaned as she parted her legs for me, the wetness awaiting me there making my heart beat faster as I began to massage my fingers through it.

I kissed her deeper, my muscles tensing as I anticipated the rise of my demon, the desire to be rough and force more and more from her. Yet it didn't come. I wanted her unlike I'd ever wanted anything in my life and as she moaned beneath the gentle pressure of my fingers, I didn't feel the slightest need to be rougher.

I found her clit and began to massage it for her, loving how wet she felt for me and using the sounds she made to guide me on. I kept my pace slow, rubbing and teasing her until she was gripping my biceps and begging me to finish her, her hips rocking into the movements of my hand.

When she came for me, I groaned with pleasure, my cock pressing against her wet skin while I kissed her all the way through it and my need for her grew uncontrollable.

I moved my hand from her core, sliding it down her outer thigh and hooking my fingers under her knee.

I lifted that leg from the floor and pushed it wide, bearing her to me as

I ducked down enough to make up for the difference in our heights, until I felt my cock pressing to the centre of her.

I hesitated there, right on the edge of oblivion, my fear of my own power and lack of control holding me back even as my desire built to an unbearable level.

"I need you, Mateo," Brooklyn begged. "I need you."

I could no sooner deny this goddess of mine than I could deny the rising of the sun and before I had the chance to question it any further, I was sinking deep inside her and making her moan for me, my cock driving in all the way to the base. The perfection of her pussy wrapping tight around my shaft had me panting, and I looked into her eyes as I rocked back, before slowly sinking in again, every second of this luxurious torment begging me for more.

Brooklyn wound her arms around my neck and I took hold of her other knee, hoisting her all the way into my arms and pressing her back to the wall as I sank into her again, the water crashing down on us and making it feel as if we were lost within our own private storm.

I groaned her name as I drew out even slower than before than sank back in again, loving the way her muscles tensed and relaxed around me in time with my movements.

I'd never felt anything like it, this slow and torturous pleasure which made my limbs tremble and my entire body shake with need.

"Fuck," I gasped as I drove myself into her again, her pussy gripping me tightly while she whimpered with pleasure. "Te amo más que a cualquier otra cosa en este mundo."

"I could eat a pineapple too," Brooklyn gasped and I couldn't help but laugh, an honest to shit smile on my face as I held her in my arms and fucked her sweetly and slowly, relishing the feeling of us joining together and building to a high unlike anything I had ever even thought to claim before.

My muscles tensed as my climax built within me and I swallowed thickly as I realised that I had managed to seize this piece of solace without even a hint of violence linked to it.

Brooklyn's grip on me tightened as she began to come for me and she reared up to capture my lips once more. I fell into the feeling of her body owning mine and came too, a low groan passing between my mouth and hers as I thrust in deep and filled her with my seed.

Our kiss grew slower, headier and more blissful as I held her in my arms like that, my heart thrashing to a pace that was entirely set by her, my lips murmuring words of adoration and devotion in my native language between strokes of our tongues against one another.

"See, Dead Man?" Brooklyn breathed. "You're all kinds of free now, demon and all. You don't ever need to be caged again."

I smiled at her, unable to help myself and getting lost in the depths of her eyes once more.

"You saved me, chica loca," I said. "Only you could calm that darkness in me and make it anew the way you have."

"We saved each other," she countered. "And now you're all mine."

I nodded my agreement as I set her on her feet, forcing myself to release her and remembering what we had to focus on. I needed to get her away from here before the past caught up to me and I was forced to face the reality of the man I'd once been.

We dried quickly and I dressed in a pair of black sweats and a hoody, encouraging Brooklyn to do the same, though she scuttled away and returned wearing a neon pink swimsuit and a pair of lime green leggings, arguing with me over her desire to wear platform heels before finally agreeing to wear sneakers under the promise that I would try some of the things she'd witnessed in the sex club with her once we were safe again.

"We have company!" Niall bellowed from somewhere deeper in the house and I froze, my heart racing as my mind darted over all the possibilities that included. The most likely of which being that we'd already lingered here too long and the cartel had come to finish us off.

I took hold of Brooklyn's wrist again and tugged her back out of my room, grabbing the bag and bringing it with us while I hurried down the corridor towards Niall who was standing by the front door, surveying the CCTV footage which showed a clear view down the drive.

A lone black Sedan was making its way towards us, a little white flag waving from the driver's window which had been lowered to allow it.

I swallowed a lump in my throat as Jack lumbered closer, not seeming to have noticed the blood trickling down the side of his face from a fresh wound though he had also showered and changed since the fight.

"Anyone you know?" I asked Niall and he shook his head.

"Nah. That ain't the Irish and I'm not the type for friends."

The car parked up a little way from the house and a huge man got out, holding his arms wide and still waving the flag. I frowned, seeing some familiarity in him and yet not quite being able to place him at the same time.

"I know you're in there, Mateo," a woman called out, her voice rich with her Mexican accent and recognition struck me then.

"Mierda," I cursed while the others all looked to me for an answer.

"I just want to talk. We can leave the violence to one side while we exchange a few words, can't we? I am family after all."

I swallowed thickly.

"Who is that, lad?" Niall barked, demanding an answer as he twisted a hatchet in his hand.

"My cousin," I admitted. "Carmen Ortega. She's fucking deadly. We don't want to mess with her."

"I have a grenade launcher I could go get?" Niall suggested but I shook my head.

"She's a lieutenant in the Castillo Cartel. Her death won't be forgiven, and I don't think we want to incur the wrath of the Castillos any more than we already have. I should talk to her."

"What if she shoots you in the face?" Niall asked, not like he was concerned, more like he was just discussing the weather.

"Then I'll be ready to kill myself too," Brooklyn vowed, snatching a gun from Jack's waistband and flicking the safety off before pressing the barrel beneath her chin.

"Stop that," Niall barked, yanking it away from her again before glaring at me like that was my fault. "You trust this woman not to kill ya?"

"Tick-tock, Mateo. I'm a busy woman," Carmen called from outside and I glanced between Brooklyn and the men she'd chosen to surround herself with before nodding.

"She's true to her word. If she says she wants to talk without violence, then I trust her. Besides, she owes me. I helped her when she needed support in climbing through the ranks of the cartel the way she has. I killed men who opposed her. She was one of the only things in my old life which I lamented leaving behind."

"Go," Jack said, agreeing to it and Niall sighed as he nodded, reaching out to unlatch the door for me.

I stepped outside with my mouth drying up, the taste of the past coating my tongue and the fear that all my hard work had come to nothing now. This could easily be it for me. Carmen Ortega may have promised me a conversation without violence, but I had seen her talk men into taking their own lives instead of facing the fate that awaited them at the hands of the Castillo Cartel before.

The sound of footsteps close on my heels made the small hairs along the back of my neck stand on end and suddenly, I wasn't alone anymore. A pack of heathens walked at my back, their loyalty somehow surprising and yet not so all at once. There was so much between us. So many hurts and hates and bitter resentments, but there was something else growing there too. A kinship of sorts which revolved around mi sol and the darkness which lay inside each of us. We were a work of art crafted from the messiest of strokes, coloured with brushes dipped in blood and yet somehow, there was beauty in what we were becoming.

The huge man shifted aside to open the rear door of the car and I finally remembered who he was.

"Pepito?" I asked in surprise, trying to marry the memory I had of the scrawny boy I'd fought and tussled with in the streets of our hometown with this mountain of a man before us.

He'd always been a strange boy, seeking out fights with me despite how thoroughly I beat him and seeming to enjoy the humiliation of being left to bleed on the ground beneath me. Then one day he'd just vanished. I hadn't seen or thought of him since. But here he stood, about a hundred pounds heavier and that dull look in his eyes lighting up as he moved to do the bidding of my cousin.

Pepito glanced up at the sound of his name and bobbed his head in confirmation of it, but said nothing more as he moved to open the car door to allow Carmen to step out. There was a thick puddle of mud awaiting the press of her foot, but before I caught so much as a glimpse of her within the luxurious car, Pepito dropped down to lay on the floor over the puddle, causing Brooklyn to gasp in surprise.

A tanned leg fitted with a designer high heel appeared from within the car, pressing down onto Pepito's spine before Carmen unfolded herself from within its depths and stepped out.

"Holy tits, Batman, she's using him as a stepping stone," Brooklyn hissed from just behind me as if we couldn't all see that clearly enough.

Carmen ignored the comment, stepping lightly down from Pepito's back and moving to stand before me, tilting her head to one side so that she could take me in. Her long, dark brown hair was styled into an immaculate knot at the base of her skull and the black dress she wore was perfectly sculpted to her petite frame, making it clear she carried no weapons, though I wasn't fool enough to let myself believe that meant she wasn't dangerous.

"Wow, she's pretty," Brooklyn said in a hiss that most certainly carried. "Like, eat your heart out Adelaide Delecta because you just lost your crown, pretty."

"Who's Adelaide Delecta?" Niall asked curiously, not bothering to lower his voice.

"The most gorgeous woman beneath the bridge," Brooklyn said bitterly. "She had a crown that a magical toad had given her to prove it and everything."

"Well fuck the bridge," Niall growled, hearing the hurt in her voice. "You're the most gorgeous woman beneath the sun and you don't need no toad crown to prove it."

"Oh," Brooklyn replied, her voice dropping into that sultry, sexy tone which always had the three of us panting over her and I cleared my throat.

Brutus barked loudly, racing past us with a furious snarl and making my heart lurch as I yelled at him to back off, lunging towards him in an attempt to catch him as he threatened to make this entire thing blow up in our faces before it had even begun.

"Down, boy," Carmen snapped, her dark eyes meeting the dog's in a challenging glare, and the big bastard skidded to a halt with a whimper before turning tail and fleeing back into the house.

I cleared my throat as silence fell around us in the wake of the dog's attack, and Brooklyn breathed a *wow* low enough that I could only just make it out.

"It's been a while, Carmen," I said, taking charge of the conversation when it became clear she was going to make me do the bulk of the talking.

"I do believe the boss has a timer tracking precisely how long it has been," she agreed. "Marking each and every second that you make him wait for retribution, so that he can be sure you suffer for them all."

I nodded, a hollow kind of acceptance filling me over the horror which I knew would be my reality when this ran its course.

"There's a bit of a problem with that though," Niall interrupted, not knowing when to keep his damn mouth shut as always. "This here fella belongs to our Spider now. And her life is bonded to his. So we can't let you or your fancy boss be chopping him up or baking him in a pie, or putting him in a vat of acid or any of that shit."

"Stay out of this, bastardo," I snapped at him as Carmen's attention shifted over my shoulder with interest which I didn't want falling on Brooklyn or anyone else here.

"I assume the Alonso brothers are all dead?" Carmen asked casually, not seeming in the least bit upset over that fact. "And that horrendous excuse for a man, Raul Castillo, too?"

"What of it?" I asked, knowing that she could see the bodies as well as I could.

Carmen smiled slowly, a goddess surveying a mortal who amused her. "I assume you know what will happen to you if anyone finds out you are here."

"What's that supposed to mean? You already found me."

"Correct. *I* found you. The Alonsos came here for the man who killed their brother. When they told me about the attack in the club, I assumed it was nothing of interest to me, but then I watched the surveillance footage and I have to admit, I was surprised to see you have found such a fondness for fetish play, primo. Pity you didn't think to hide that scar on your chest, or I may never have realised it was you beneath the mask."

I swallowed thickly, my shoulders pushing back as I cursed myself for wearing that fucking outfit. Not many people had seen that scar. In my youth I'd hidden it diligently, hating what it was and what it proved was trapped inside me. I'd grown out of the self-consciousness as my own conscience had slowly died away, but I still hadn't often revealed the disfigurement to my flesh.

Mi sol had only ever looked at it with interest or perhaps even reverence though and in the time I'd known her, I'd lost any lingering feelings of unease that clung to me while showing it to the world. I hadn't thought to keep it covered. Meaning that now I was the one who had destroyed all we had here.

"If you're the only one who knows he's here, then that sounds like good motivation to put a bullet between your eyes," Niall said loudly, moving to step around me but I knocked him back with my shoulder, wanting him to stay close to Brooklyn.

"I wouldn't recommend that," Carmen replied sweetly. "I may be the keeper of your secret as it stands, but I left a note detailing what I had discovered and where I was heading tonight locked up in my office. No one will read it, assuming I return, but if I don't, then I'm sure someone in my organisation will have to check through my things for clues to my demise."

"Why would you keep that information to yourself?" I demanded and Carmen clucked her tongue.

"You and I are products of the same hell, primo," she said to me. "And there was a time that we once used to dream of escaping it together."

"That was before we embraced our demons," I reminded her, and that smile widened.

"And then our dreams grew. You helped me when I needed it a long time ago. You backed me when no one wanted a woman to step into my father's shoes. You helped put me where I am today."

"So?"

"So, I figure I owe you."

Shock spilled through my core as I stared down at this powerful, brutal woman before me, the reputation of ruthlessness and sin which was wrapped so tightly around her cracking open just a little so that I could see the roughened edges of the girl I'd once played with beneath the baking sun.

"What do you want from me?" I asked and she shrugged.

"Tell me the truth of everything that happened. Right back to the night when you disappeared. Was the monastery burning linked to your disappearance?"

"I locked those devils inside the hell they had created for me within that holy place, and listened to their screams while they burned," I replied with my chin high and no regrets in me over the act. "They were demons far worse than any being which they claimed lived within me."

Carmen nodded like she'd expected that.

"And the money?"

"Hidden," I grunted, unsurprised to find that she was seeking that.

"There are many rumours surrounding your disappearance, primo," Carmen said slowly. "Of course, a lot of people believe you stole that money and ran from us, our boss included. But there have been whispers about the monastery burning, people denying your involvement because it made no sense to them for you to attack a place of God. Of course, you and I know that no god ever lived within the walls of that monastery, but to most, they have no idea about the truth of those women and what they did to you."

"I hadn't realised that you knew," I gritted out, my skin prickling at the thought of her having known what I'd suffered with those women all those years ago.

"Your mother might have thought herself a pious woman, but she was no saint," Carmen sneered. "She used to come begging at my father's table for scraps often enough after your father was killed, using the fact that she was the mother to his nephew to plead for money and favours. She often complained of the demon in you and mentioned the work the nuns were doing to try and rid you of it. She never spoke of the details while in my presence, but between her words and my paying enough attention to you whenever I saw you in that church, I managed to figure it out. I tried to get my father to take you in once, begged him to claim you from her, and them, and all of it."

"You did?" I asked in surprised because I knew well enough that her father had been far crueller than mine.

Her smile deepened, though something in her eyes hardened to steel. "He accused me of being your whore," she replied. "Gave me ten lashes with his belt too. I bled for you, primo, but he refused to take you in all the same. I'm sorry for that."

A frown carved its way across my brow as I realised that even back then when we had been hardly more than children, she had seen the suffering I endured and had understood that the brutality of her own household would have been preferable to it.

"I didn't know," I said uselessly.

"He's long since dead now." She shrugged and we shared a look which spoke of her secret surrounding her father's demise and I held my tongue on any further comment. "And like I said, you helped me when I needed it, so I figured I could offer you my help in return now that I am in a position to do so."

"How?"

"By telling my boss that I found you, locked up and tortured half to death, instead of running free and spending his money. We claim you were taken while trying to fight for him. I'll say I lost the Alonsos and Raul Castillo while fighting to get you back. All we need is someone to blame."

I blinked at her in surprise, wondering why on earth she would offer me this lie, this protection.

"If he ever found out that you lied-"

"It wouldn't be the first lie we have shared," she said dismissively, though we both knew the weight of that risk.

"What is it you'll be wanting from him in exchange for this?" Niall demanded, and Carmen flashed him a knowing look, because of course this favour wouldn't come without a cost.

"I'll claim you as one of my men," she said to me. "The ace up my sleeve whenever I have something to deal with which I can't do myself. You won't even have to leave this place if it's where you prefer to be," she added, seeing the way I tensed at the suggestion. "I am based in the states now, most of the time anyway. All I want is to have you on the end of the phone whenever I need someone with your skill set."

I nodded slowly, understanding what she was asking of me and finding myself agreeing to it easily enough. I'd always enjoyed the hunt anyway. If she called me up from time to time with the name of someone who needed to disappear, then I could help with that easily.

"So, who is it that you plan to blame for taking me?" I asked, because that was the real sticking point in her plan. I could tell her the truth of my captivity with Niall, but I knew how Brooklyn felt about him, and I wasn't fool enough to believe that she wouldn't follow through on her threat to kill herself if something happened to him. He was hers, which meant I wouldn't touch him, but that didn't exactly leave me with another option.

"Oooh, we should blame Anastasia and her tits of doom," Brooklyn suggested enthusiastically.

"That's actually not a bad idea," Niall agreed. "Not Anastasia specifically, but the Russians. Vlad is out for my blood at the moment anyway, and my pa keeps leaving me all these angry voicemails demanding I return to the family to help clear up the mess I've made. I think he still wants to forge a deal with them, but from what I've heard, it's marriage or death for me when it comes to our Russian friends. Seeing as I have no intention to divorce my beautiful new wife, I've offered them up the challenge of delivering me my death. Sure would make my life easier if the cartel swooped in and killed them all for me though."

I scoffed at his casual suggestion that we set the Castillo Cartel on the Russian mafia, but Carmen didn't look so sceptical.

"The Russians have been causing problems for a while now," she said thoughtfully. "They bicker over the price of their cut from our imports and blow smoke out of their asses, while trying to claim their own superiority all the time. I wouldn't object to cutting them down a size or two."

"Really? I had the idea that saves us all?" Brooklyn whispered excitedly and Carmen flashed her a look which wasn't even hostile.

"I take it this is your true captor, primo? The way you stand before her tells me you would die a thousand deaths to keep her safe."

I nodded stiffly, unsure if I should be trying to shield Brooklyn from her attention or not, but of course mi sol didn't give me that option. She bounded forward excitedly, offering out a hand with blood still lodged beneath her fingernails and grinning widely.

"I'm Brooklyn with a B, nice to meet you."

Carmen took her hand and shook it without so much as flinching at the blood, despite her own pristine appearance.

"You'll have to return the money," Carmen added, looking to me. "Assuming you still have it?"

"I do," I replied heavily, knowing that she was right, but in the grand scheme of things, returning that money was a price I would gladly pay fifty times over if it bought me a free life with my chica loca.

"Are you gonna be needing help with the Russians?" Niall asked curiously, accepting this turn of events as if it wasn't in the least bit unusual. Like he had ruthless killers show up at his door every day offering peace and striking deals to take down major crime families.

If Jack had any opinion on any of this then he wasn't voicing it, retreating into silence as he so often seemed to prefer.

"No," Carmen purred. "I think I can manage that myself. Besides, Mateo will have to stay out of sight while I pretend he is recovering from the torture he endured. He will return to the fold a hero for never once spilling our secrets and for helping recover the money. I can handle the rest."

"And you'll even have those scars to help sell your story," Niall said enthusiastically, slapping me on the shoulder and making me snarl at him like a rabid beast. "Bet you'll wanna thank me for them now, eh?"

Carmen glanced at me curiously in response to that remark, but I remained silent on the subject as she released Brooklyn's hand then stepped forward to embrace me. It took me a moment to remember what I was supposed to do, and I slowly wrapped my arms around her in return, the scent of her reminding me of a few happy moments we'd stolen together as children and something within me settling as I crushed her against me.

"I don't know how to thank you for this," I murmured as I held her tightly and she breathed a laugh.

"I love you, primo, but that won't stop me from calling in this favour. One day soon, I'll make my move, and I'll need you by my side."

A shiver tracked down my spine at her words because I had the feeling that I knew exactly what she was planning to do in the long term, and the thought of it was terrifying enough to make me flinch. Even so, she was offering me something I had never thought to claim and I would never be able to repay that debt, which meant I'd be there when she called. There was no doubt about that.

"I'm yours to command," I agreed, feeling the weight of that promise settle over me heavily, though I doubted I would have to do anything at all for a long time yet. I'd worry about it when the time came.

"Then it is done."

Carmen moved back, turning away from all of us and stepping over Pepito again as she climbed into her car once again.

Pepito hurried to close the door behind her, and the four of us watched as they backed away down the drive. No one said another word until their car was disappearing into the distance and heading out of sight.

"Well," Brooklyn sighed wistfully. "I really, really like her."

BROOKLYN

CHAPTER TWENTY NINE

I was doing a worry handstand to get all my worries out and my polka dot yellow dress had flipped over to cover my face, so my underwear was on show. Niall had gone to face his dad at last in the wake of Carmen taking out the Russians and ending our problems so far as they were concerned.

That had been about a week ago and we'd all been waiting for the dust to settle following on from Vlad's decapitation and the murder of most of the top men in his organisation. There had been all kinds of news reports about the massacre of the Russian mobsters, but none of them would detail the injuries claiming they were too brutal to describe. No one seemed to have realise that the cartel was responsible for it either, and I was like nine parts impressed and one part turned on by the badassness of Mateo's secret cousin.

I'd been bugging Mateo to arrange a girls' day for me and Carmen to do some murder bonding ever since I'd found out about it, but so far he'd told me she was too busy dealing with the fallout from the attack, so I had had to put a pin in that idea.

A couple of days after the Russians were hit by hurricane Carmen (though sadly Anastasia had survived with her tits intact), Niall's dad had called him up and informed him that with half the Russians dead and the rest of them scrambling for any kind of power they could still claim, he was able to make a deal that didn't involve marrying his youngest son off. So he'd called him back to the house to make peace.

I didn't like it. I didn't like that big house with its fandangles and the money which dripped from the walls and the taste of bad deeds which hung in the air. I didn't like that fancy old man with his smoking jacket and sneering face and salt and pepper hair. I didn't like my Hellfire being forced to play nice and do as he was told either. My Hellfire wasn't made for following orders after all; he was a creature of chaos, and it just didn't seem right to me.

Worst of all, Niall had said I couldn't go with him when he went to meet with his dad, just in case Liam O'Brien decided to kill him. Then he'd run out the front door, locked it tight and driven away in his Jeep before I could follow.

Mateo and AJ had talked me down from trying to blindly drive after him and guess the route he took. Apparently, my intuition wasn't enough of a roadmap to get me there, which was goose crap, but then Mateo had bent me over his knee and spanked my ass when I'd tried to slip out the upstairs window, so now I was under constant watch while I did emotional acrobatics.

"If you want a real distraction, Rook, come over here and let me give you one," AJ growled from across the lounge.

"Let her stay there, I'm enjoying the view," Mateo said and my legs flipped down as I lost my balance.

I stood upright, pushing my dress down and finding them watching me with darkness in their expressions, but I ignored them, grabbing the photo from the coffee table that Niall had left for me to remember him by if he died. He'd taken it last night before he'd fucked me into oblivion, wearing nothing but my favourite pink tutu. He was completely naked except for the tutu, the thin netting pushed up by his fully erect, huge, pierced, tattooed cock and a manic look on his face that made me miss him even more.

"Hellfire," I sighed, kissing his cock in the picture then I looked to my other beautiful men on the couch.

A hiccup left me and I ran over to them, diving onto their laps and nuzzling into Mateo while Jack rested a hand on my back.

"How shall I do it then?" I croaked. "It'll have to be memorable. Maybe I could tie the curtains together upstairs, knot them around my neck and swan dive out the window?"

"What?" Mateo snapped and I rolled over onto my back so I could look up at him.

"If Niall dies, I die, remember?" I brought two fingers to my temple, miming a gun before making a bang noise and pretending to die in his lap.

"Mi sol," Mateo hissed as Jack's fingers curled tightly around my legs. "We need to discuss that clause in our agreement."

"Are we not enough for you?" AJ asked through our mind connection, a note of hurt in his voice.

"It's not that," I whispered, looking between them. "I can't live without Niall, just as I can't live without either of you. If Niall comes home to us, I think we should all promise that when we're old and grey, we'll jump into a volcano together, so that we don't have to go through the pain of losing each other."

The rumble of an engine sounded in the distance and I gasped, launching myself out of their laps and running to the window. I threw it open, clambering out as I spotted Niall's Jeep accelerating up the drive.

I waved my arms in the air with a squeal leaving my throat as I ran to meet him. The moment he stopped the car, he jumped out of it, catching me as I collided with him, his body thumping back against the vehicle as I kissed him and he lifted me into the air.

He tasted like smoke and power and I devoured every bite of him as we kissed with all the passion of two lovers parted by the stars themselves and stealing a moment in spite of them.

"Did ya miss me, love?" he asked as our mouths separated, leaving me breathless and giddy.

"I almost had to hang myself with the curtains," I said seriously and he frowned hard and deep.

"Don't ya ever go killin' yerself over me. I ain't worth that."

"You're worth it all, Hellfire. My heart, my lungs, my kidneys. All of it can go in the ground so I can come find you in hell."

"I'll be there waitin' for ya," he purred, stealing another lingering kiss.

He carried me towards the house, unlocking the front door and shouldering his way inside.

Brutus barked in greeting and Niall cursed as the dog took a little snappy out of his leg. I was actually kind of jealous because I was the only one of us who didn't have toothy scars on my legs yet.

Niall carried me through to the lounge where Mateo and Jack rose to their feet, their eyes full of questions.

"So? What did your father say?" Mateo asked.

"Did he tell you all about his new bakery?" I asked Niall, trying not to snigger as I set up my joke.

"He ain't no baker," Niall said in confusion as he put me down and I bit the inside of my cheek as I kept a straight face.

"Then why are his buns so hot?" I burst out laughing and they all shared a look as I fell apart.

"Are ya talkin' about my father's arse, you little hellion?" Niall asked and I nodded, unable to speak through my laughter, but I raised my hands to pretend I was squeezing it.

Niall roared a laugh then locked me under his arm, biting my ear and tugging on it. "Quiet now, Spider. I got a thing or two to say."

I buttoned my lips as I looked up at him, waiting patiently to hear his news.

"My pa's not happy about any of this, but he's accepting the lay of the land. I told him straight how it is, and he listened. There ain't nothin' more important to him than family and now we're married, Spider, he can't deny what that means. You're an O'Brien, which means you're a part of that family, whether he likes it or not. I told him you're my honey trap and we're a perfect killin' unit if he wants to hire us. He can use our skills anytime he likes and though he ain't happy by any means, there ain't a lot he can do about it unless he decides to have me killed. But he's either fond of me enough not to have me executed, or he can see value in keeping me alive and useful as a hitman for hire. Either way, it seems I've bought us peace for now."

I leapt out from under his arm, hugging him and squeezing with all my strength.

"So, you're off the hook?" Mateo asked.

"Like a fish who wriggled his way free and returned to the ocean," Niall agreed and my smile nearly split my cheeks apart.

"We have to celebrate with a kill!" I cried, bouncing on my toes and tugging on Niall's shirt.

"You really know how to tempt me with a good time, don't ya lass?" He grinned down at me then caught my hand, making me twirl beneath his arm before towing me over to the couch and hooking his laptop off the table.

AJ patted Niall's shoulder briefly as he sat on his other side and I glanced between them, seeing my giant man's relief over Niall's return as clear as day. It made my heart all squishy and warm inside.

"Let's see if we've got any new hits waiting," Niall said, opening his laptop and logging in to some website selling wind-up penguin toys. It took Niall several passwords to get into it and just when I'd picked out which penguin toy I wanted to buy, the screen changed to an email server, revealing an inbox with one juicy message sitting in it entitled Colin Macabee.

Niall tapped on it and I sensed everyone's bloodlust rising as we all leaned in close to look at the message.

Colin Macabee. Hemlock City, 10th Street. Parking Bay 69.

Niall chuckled. "Sixty-nine," he murmured under his breath and I frowned.

"Why's that funny? Everyone knows seven is the funniest number," I said.

"How so?" Niall demanded.

"Because seven eight nine – get it? Like seven *ate* nine." I laughed loudly and Niall chuckled, capturing my chin in his grip.

"I'll show ya why sixty-nine is funny later, love." He gave me a smirk and released me, turning back to the kill as Mateo shifted on my other side, his hand dropping onto my knee and sending a thrill through my body.

Niall read through the rest of the details for the hit while I watched a fly buzz-buzz its way over to Brutus and circle his head. Brutus kept trying to snap up the fly and I giggled each time he missed, the little fly playing a game with him as it diced with death.

"Alright. This one's easy. We can do it tonight. Colin parks at this place five days a week while he's working as a janitor, and he heads back to get his car every day at midnight. He was convicted for sex with a minor a few years back, but he got released early from his sentence on a technicality."

My upper lip peeled back as venom slid into my gut. "I'm gonna ram my emotional support coconut up his ass, then crack it open with a sledgehammer."

"Then we'll be needing Mary the Second for that," Niall got to his feet, prancing off upstairs to get his new sledgehammer and I kissed Mateo on the cheek before racing after Niall to get changed.

By the time we were leaving, I was wearing what was possibly my most fabulous outfit ever. I had sequin rainbow shorts on with a matching bra that had big hearts over my nipples and tiny little sequin straps everywhere else so my tits were barely covered at all. I'd paired it with my short white fluffy jacket and I'd painted glittery tear lines down my cheeks. My hair was pulled up into two Princess Laia buns which had glittery scrunchies holding them in place. My heels were transparent with fake fish floating around inside the platform part of them which were filled with water. I looked like a unicorn dipped in a rainbow and I was ready to get murdery.

Niall drove us out towards the city in his Jeep and parked us down a dark alley behind the parking lot. I had the knife Niall had bought me in Vegas in my hand, the spider engraved on the hilt winking up at me, ready to get bloody.

We left the car in the shadows of the alley and Brutus trotted at my heels, his blue leash looped around my wrist so I could keep my hands free for killing. It was late, the moon hiding behind the clouds like she was in on the plot, keeping us shrouded in shadow as we moved to the emergency exit.

Angry Jack stepped forward, ramming a crowbar into the gap between the door and the wall, his muscles flexing as he worked to force it open.

I sucked my lower lip as I watched his arms strain and bulge, tempted to climb my big man and lick my way up his neck. But I was a professional on a job, a honey trap ready to lure our hit to me tonight when he came back to his car. I was going to play a young hooker, and I'd subtly drop hints that I was underage while the others circled in the wings ready to step in and cut down the monster we were here for.

Mateo stood beside me as AJ worked, running his thumb gently along the nasty little Veronica of a blade in his grip.

"Make him hurt tonight, Dead Man," I said lustfully. "Make it last and last."

Mateo looked to me with his lips curling up in a deadly smile. "As you wish, mi sol."

A shudder ran through me as I got wet for him, but we were here on an official Society of Psychos outing. I couldn't get distracted by thoughts of being triple dicked right now.

AJ got the door open with a splintering noise and Niall moved forward, severing the alarm wire above the door as it let out its first obnoxious bleep. We had to take this way seeing as the front exits were covered with cameras, and Niall said it'd be easier to just avoid them all together instead of trying to cut the power to them.

"Let's go, potato," Niall said, leading the way into a stairwell while adjusting the large bag of weapons over his shoulder.

He led the way up and I jogged at his side, sharing excited glances with him as we closed in on the level we needed. Niall squeezed my ass as we made it to the door, opening it and gesturing for me to step through like a real gentleman.

I curtsied to him and walked through with Brutus sniffing the air, on the hunt for blood as keenly as I was. The parking lot was nearly empty, a few vehicles sitting around the place including a red Volvo in parking bay sixty-nine.

"You two head to the other exit," Niall commanded AJ and Mateo. "If he senses something's off, I want all bases covered."

"Okay," AJ agreed and Mateo nodded stiffly, looking like he didn't much like taking Niall's orders but he turned back into the stairwell with AJ all the same.

"Well then, Spider. We've got some waiting to do." Niall checked his phone for the time and I saw we had twenty minutes left until midnight.

"Enough time for you to show me why sixty-nine is funny?" I asked hopefully and he gave me a burning look before checking the time again like he was considering it.

"Best not, love," he said. "Come on. The light's out over in that corner. I'll get myself hidden for when he shows up and it's time for you to play yer part."

I nodded, following him to the other side of the lot where it was darker, the clip-clop of my heels the only sound in the expansive place, but soon there'd be screams and cries for help, and no one would answer them.

We moved behind a Land Rover with blacked out windows and sat ourselves on the low wall at the edge of the lot, looking down to where a couple of cars were parked on the street two floors below us.

Brutus lay down by our feet and I swung my legs as I waited for the show to start, anticipation making me sway from side to side. A train line ran along close behind the parking lot a big old freight train rumbled down it, seeming a mile long, the noise rumbling around us.

Niall placed his bag of weapons down by his feet and took my hand, his roughened fingers clutching mine. I looked to him with a dreamy smile pulling at my lips and a haze of love filling me up to the brim.

"I can't believe I lived so long without ya in my life, Spider," he said in a low tone, leaning in close so I could hear him over the noise of the train. "I can't imagine a place or time without ya now."

"There won't be one," I promised, painting my finger over his lips. "Our souls will always know where to find each other."

His lips lifted in a hopeful smile at that thought but as he leaned in to kiss me and steal my breath away just like he always did, a bang ripped through the air. Then Niall was falling, tumbling away over the wall and slamming down onto one of the car roofs below.

I screamed in terror, twisting around as the leash looped over my wrist yanked tight and Brutus lunged forward, forcing me onto the ground instead of allowing me to dive after my Hellfire.

I looked to the window which had lowered on the passenger side of the Land Rover, my gaze narrowing on a bald man as he withdrew the gun which had shot Niall, my mind spinning into chaos in seconds.

The leash came off of my wrist as Brutus leapt up at the window, trying to scramble his way inside and another bang roared in my ears as a blonde woman in high heels and a fitted black dress stepped around the car, a pistol raised and my dog falling down between us with a yelp of pain. Horror juddered through me as his name tore from my lips.

493

Anastasia was full of rage, her eyes wide and fearful as she looked over my head to the wall where Niall had fallen.

She glared at the man in the car as I reached for Brutus, and panic welled within my chest. "What the fuck did you just do, Anatoly? How am I supposed to marry a dead man?"

JACK

CHAPTER THIRTY

A bellow escaped me as the sound of gunfire set my pulse hammering in my chest and I took off sprinting towards the ramp which led further up into the parking lot, not caring about cameras or evidence or anything at all other than the scream I'd heard and the girl whose throat it had torn from.

Mateo shouted a warning behind me and through the haze of furious bloodlust which had me blinded, I spotted movement between some of the parked cars on the bottom floor of the lot.

Shots rang out as the men there took aim at us and I roared a challenge as I sprinted straight for them, not slowing so much as a step as I charged them down and saw their deaths in my future.

Gunshots came from behind me too, Mateo returning fire while I opted for the direct approach and as the men in front of us took cover, I managed to close the distance between us.

I leapt over the hood of the closest car and slammed into a man who was trying to hide on the other side of it before he could whip around and aim his gun at me.

I fisted my hand in his hair and started slamming his head against the side of the car over and over again, using his body to shield me against the guns of his friends which were being aimed my way while I cracked his skull and splattered his blood all over the place.

I felt him go limp in my hold and hurled his body towards the rest of them, using their moment of distraction to launch myself between them, fists flying and rage spilling from me far faster than their blood could spill to the floor.

Mateo leapt around the cars too, firing off quick shots and taking two of them out just as I snapped another neck, the final man aiming a furious cry our way as he took in the bodies of his friends and saw what had become of them.

He fired a shot straight at me, but Mateo had already fired on him, a bullet tearing through his skull and knocking him aside just in time to make his bullet shatter the car window behind me instead of puncturing my flesh.

"Rook!" I roared, turning my head towards the ramp which led up to her and hearing nothing at all in reply aside from new gunshots as more men moved to block my path to her.

But that wouldn't do. I wouldn't be kept from the owner of my soul and she wouldn't be left without me when she so clearly needed my help.

"We'll get to her," Mateo snarled, reloading his gun as we were forced to take cover. "She'll be okay, gigante."

My lips curled back on a feral snarl as I held onto his words and turned my attention towards the men who were shooting at us, keeping us from the woman I loved.

I nodded once then let myself go, unleashing the worst of me and thinking of nothing other than her. I lurched out from behind the car and took off running straight towards those foolish enough to try and place a barrier between us and our woman.

I would rip and tear and destroy my way to her if that was what it took to get there. Nothing would stop me from doing so. Not even death itself. I was coming for my sweet obsession and all she had to do was hold on until I made it.

BROOKLYN

CHAPTER THIRTY ONE

Anastasia had one of her two men holding me in place with my arms behind my back as she threw punches at me, her mafia blood on show as she let the darkness in her come out to play. Brutus had scrambled under the Land Rover, a trail of blood marking the route he'd taken and my heart squeezed in pain for my dog, and for my Niall who'd been stolen away from me in a rain of violence. My spider knife was now in Anastasia's pocket, taken just like she'd taken everything else.

I cursed Anastasia with every strike she landed on me, her next punch splitting my lip open and her perfectly styled hair starting to poke out in places and stick to her sweaty face.

"You flouncy-titted-whore!" I shrieked and her fist slammed into my mouth again, shutting me up and making me taste blood instead.

"You ruined everything, you little tramp," she spat at me. "Niall O'Brien was the expansion of my empire. He was *mine*." She struck me with the palm of her hand, sending my head wheeling sideways and the cracks in my mind grew bigger, deeper. The fractures in my sanity were sinkholes now, sucking everything in around them as the walls caved in and left chasms in the essence of who I was. Without Hellfire, I'd die, I'd known that all along, just as I'd die without the others. But when I followed him to the Devil's door, I'd be dragging three Russian souls down with me.

Anastasia got up close to me, her nails tearing into my chin as she forced me to look at her sneering face.

"You're not even that pretty," she hissed, all snake as she filled up with so much venom it made everything about her cold and bitter. "I'm sick of looking at you. Get her on her knees, Grigory."

The man holding me kicked out the backs of my legs and I hit the ground between him and Anastasia, the shadow of Anatoly drawing closer behind her, his head still bowed since she'd bitch slapped him for killing Niall.

"Give me my gun, Anatoly," Anastasia demanded, holding her hand out for it and he shifted foot to foot, not handing her anything. "Now, Anatoly," she barked.

He cleared his throat. "Um, your revolver, ma'am?" he asked in a Russian accent.

"Yes, my fucking revolver. The one with my family name engraved on its side, the one my grandfather was gifted from his grandfather, for generation after generation. The one I kill all my enemies with," she hissed, whipping around to look at him, her hand still extended in a demand.

Anatoly twiddled his thumbs together before adjusting the big gun hanging from his shoulder. "I forgot to bring it, ma'am. But you can have your pistol back instead?" he suggested sheepishly, the huge man scuffing one foot against the ground as he gave her an apologetic look.

"You idiot, Anatoly," she snapped, backhanding him and he dropped his head in shame.

I breathed heavily, barely able to focus on them as my mind went to a place made of nightmares and terror. A clown was there, laughing and laughing as blood ran down from his eyes and he pointed a knife at me. *"Stupid little Brooklyn. All alone again. Just like the world intended. Ha ha ha!"*

He closed in on me, reaching into my chest and snatching Glenda from within my heart, flapping her little duck wings frantically as he brought the knife to her throat and beheaded her in front of my eyes. The pain of it all weighed down on me so heavily that I couldn't draw in air.

A horrible, eerie tune was playing off key in my ears and a carnival of destruction swirled around me, lights flashing, and colours that clashed and glared blinded me. I was snapping thread by thread, falling deeper into a brand of insanity even I'd never tasted before. It was full of all the bad emotions from shock, to horror, and fear, and worst of all, loneliness. Because suddenly all the lights and music stopped, the clown ceased to laugh and the world went quiet and oh so dark. I was in a chamber of endless silence and though it felt like I was screaming loud enough to rip my throat raw, no sound filled the space. I was so dreadfully alone that even my voice had abandoned me.

Then the dark lifted and I was looking up at my enemy, a blonde woman whose name I'd forgotten. All I knew was that she had stolen something so terribly important to me and now Death was sliding an hourglass onto her head and tipping it upside down, the grains of sand trailing down from top to bottom, marking out how long she had left in this world. The rest was up to me.

I threw my head backward with all my might, the back of my skull slamming into Grigory's balls and making him shriek like a school girl, as he stumbled aside.

I was on my feet in the next heartbeat, sprinting to Niall's bag of weapons beside the wall he'd fallen from and dropping to my knees as I unzipped it.

"Get hold of her!" Anastasia shouted just as my hand closed around a grenade. I pulled the pin without a flicker of fear inside me. I'd take us all out in one bloody hit and hunt down my Hellfire in the afterlife.

I threw the grenade at my enemies and Anatoly screamed, running for cover before a bang rang out. I leaned into it, embracing my end, my arms stretching wide as I waited to feel Death's bony hand slide around mine. But instead of that, pink smoke burst from the grenade, swirling up and blinding us all in seconds.

Smoke bomb. Shitballs.

Well then, that just gives me more time to play psycho.

I grabbed the bag, darting for cover between the front of the Land Rover and the wall, taking an Uzi into my grip, stuffing a knife into my waistband and a couple of grenades into my pocket before hurling the bag over the wall to stop them from using anything within it against me.

I kicked my shoes off and climbed up onto the hood of the vehicle then scrambled higher still, as silent as a cat as I dropped down onto the roof. I flattened myself to the surface, waiting for the smoke to clear, fighting back a cough and holding it in my lungs like a beetle in a bug trap.

"Where the fuck is she? Get hold of her!" Anastasia barked somewhere to my right and I swung my Uzi that way, squeezing the trigger with a savage snarl twisting my lips.

Gunfire sprayed out from my Uzi and Anastasia screamed in alarm before a heavy thud sounded.

"Fuck – Grigory!" Anastasia gasped and the smoke cleared enough for me to spot his huge body on the ground, his chest bloody and his eyes gazing lifelessly up to the roof.

I aimed my gun at Anastasia's voice once more, firing blindly towards her, but the sound of my bullets hitting the far wall came in response. Bullets were far too easy a death for her anyway. I wanted to feel her heart stop when my knife pierced it. I wanted her to know that Niall's wife had beaten her in every way that counted.

"Shoot her, Anatoly," Anastasia commanded and gunfire immediately sprayed the Land Rover.

But Anatoly was aiming low, thinking I might be down there on my feet, while I was really up here in a high-hide like that Mr Malcolm man in

Jurassic Park. *You can't find me, Anatoly-saurus Rex.*

My upper lip peeled back as I returned fire and the smoke cleared further, letting me see exactly where Anatoly and Anastasia were taking cover.

I took the real grenade from my pocket, giving zero shits about the consequences anymore, especially as Brutus let out a whimper of fear below the car and reminded me how much these motherfuckers needed to die. The sound gilded my soul in chaotic vengeance and a snarl ripped from my throat as I pulled the pin and launched the grenade towards the assholes in front of me.

The grenade bounced under the car they were hiding behind and Anastasia went running a second before a boom sent the car flying up to the roof. The floor exploded simultaneously and Anatoly lost limbs in the absolute carnage as he fell away into the huge hole torn into the parking lot. He cried out in fear and agony, but the sound was cut off as the wreckage of the car slammed back down on top of him and I felt a twisted satisfaction over killing the man who'd killed my Niall.

The Land Rover started up beneath me and I realised some scared little mouse was hiding inside it. I twisted my Uzi down onto the surface of the hood right above the driver's seat and pulled the trigger, holding on for dear life as the vehicle swung sharply around, revealing Brutus where he'd been laying beneath it in a pool of blood.

A male voice cried out in terror from inside and the Land Rover jerked to a halt as the guy got out of the car, raising a pistol just as my Uzi rang empty. But a blur of motion behind him collided with his back as he took the first shot and it went whistling past my ear as my dog threw off his aim.

Brutus snarled and tore into the man, bringing him to his knees before going for his throat, my little beasty holding his poor injured leg off the ground as he ripped into flesh and bone, and our enemy died in his jaws.

"Thanks, Bruty!" I called, leaving him to chew up his new plaything as I turned to hunt for Anastasia. She was running for the ramp and I grinned darkly as I locked her in my sights leaping off of the Land Rover and tossing my gun. I knew exactly how I preferred to kill her anyway.

I chased after her, blonde hair whipping left and right behind her as she disappeared around the corner. But I was fuelled by the kind of rage and hatred only grief could put there, and nothing would stop me from catching her and making her pay for what she'd done.

I tore down the ramp, gaining on her with every footfall as she threw panicked glances back at me over her shoulder and I knew she saw her death coming for her.

I let out a manic laugh worthy of Niall O'Brien, letting her fear slide in deeper, toying with her as I closed in on her from behind. This was how he would have wanted to be avenged. With all my sanity stripped away and nothing but madness guiding my movements. I was a true assassin now, one more terrifying than anything I could have imagined I'd become. I was Anastasia's monster, a creature stitched together from her worst fears, and I'd be making good on ensuring every one of them came true.

"Dead – dead – dead!" I yelled and she put on a spurt of speed in desperation.

Gunfire sounded off somewhere below us, but my mind couldn't piece together anything beyond my hunt as I focused on the only thing that existed to me anymore. Anastasia. My final victim, and the bloodiest death I'd ever offered up to anyone.

Her heels were slowing her down, but my feet were bare and free, giving me all the advantage I needed to close the distance between us. Before she could round the next turn in the ramp, I collided with her and she slammed face first into the wall ahead of us before we both fell to the ground with me on top.

I threw a savage punch into her shattered nose and she answered with a furious blow of her own, my rib popping under the impact. But I felt no pain. There was a beast of hell housed within this human flesh now, and the wild, frantic look in her eyes told me she knew what had her in its clutches.

I slammed her head down against the concrete, dazing her and giving me a moment to snatch the spider knife from her pocket.

As her eyes refocused, she saw it, the blade glinting above her and the bloody, beaten girl she'd thought she'd had at her mercy holding it ready to end this. I had all the power now, every ladybird of it clasped in my fist, and I held her in suspense for an eternal second before I drove the knife right into her fucking tits.

She wailed in agony, but it was nothing to the second scream she gave me when I did it again. And again, and again, and again. I popped those bouncy Brendas and made her squeal like a piggy sent to market. I was her butcher, her cruel and unforgiving end. But her meat was rotten and rancid, and I didn't want a single lick of it.

"Say you're sorry and I'll call you an ambulance," I growled and her eyes widened with hope, blood bubbling from her lips.

"I'm s-sorry," she garbled and I leaned down so my mouth was next to her ear, sliding the knife under her ribs until I felt the moment it pierced her wretched heart.

"You're an ambulance," I whispered.

The fight in her gave out and I leaned back to watch the life fade from her eyes and her body fell still beneath me, a bitter kind of quiet descending in the wake of my revenge.

The gunshots had fallen silent in the lower level of the parking lot, and that quiet continued to grow, pressing in on all sides and stealing me away again.

I ached for the company of my psychos, but I knew that we would never be whole again without Niall.

I shuddered, the sweetness of vengeance soured by what it was in aid of. Niall was gone. The crazy, unshackled hellhound I'd found a kindred spirit in forever parted from me now. The first man to see me and not recoil, the first to see value in me that no one else ever had. And now he was lost to this world, and I didn't know how to move forward or even if I could.

But as I turned my own knife back on myself, aiming to chase him into death and seek some kind of solace there, Jack and Mateo appeared, bloody and out of breath. They didn't slow for a single second as they saw how close my own blade was to my throat.

Jack gripped my arms and Mateo snatched the knife from my hand before I let out a horrible sob that echoed everywhere and nowhere. Because my Hellfire was gone. And all I wanted to do was take us all away from this world to go and find him in the afterlife.

NIALL

CHAPTER THIRTY TWO

I groaned as I stared up at the cloudless sky, a mixture of numbness and pain radiating through my body as I cursed myself and worked to breathe through the seconds which dragged by endlessly.

The screaming had given way to gunfire, every torturous second of the fight playing out while I couldn't so much as turn my head thanks to the tranquiliser dart which had struck me in the left pec.

Panic consumed me whole and chewed me raw while I waited in the dark, my body cocooned in the metallic embrace of the car roof I'd landed on thanks to my two floor drop right outa the parking lot window.

I had to assume I hadn't been meant to fall otherwise the dart seemed kinda pointless, but the list of people who would want to take me alive was pretty damn short. What kind of fucking amateur tranquilises someone when they're sitting on a wall over a damn precipice?

My lips parted on the name I'd been trying to yell while the drugs kept me trapped here, but I barely managed to force a whisper of it past them.

"Brooklyn," her name wheezed from my chest, my fingers twitching in hunt of a weapon, or better yet, in hunt of her.

There was a pounding taking place in the back of my skull, pain slowly blossoming across my body as whatever I'd been shot with slowly began to wear off. I was a big lad, bigger than pretty much every fucker I'd ever met aside from that giant Brooklyn had brought home from Eden Heights, and I needed higher doses of drugs for them to affect me in the desired way. I was guessing I wasn't even supposed to be conscious right now. Though I couldn't say I'd figured out if that was because someone was hoping to make my end a slow one or if there was something else taking place in this moment.

I had no space for those thoughts in my skull. Only her. Only my memories of the last time I'd failed to protect the woman I was married to and what my failure had cost her.

If I was reliving that worst sin of mine now, then I knew I wouldn't survive it. Not in any way, shape, or form. I'd escape this world in a reign of violence which drenched me in blood and saw me well and truly destroyed by its end. There would be no continuing on for me without her.

The pounding grew louder, solidifying into something so much more real and I realised it was the sound of approaching footsteps, not some echo of pain locked solely within my own mind.

"Hellfire!" Brooklyn's voice sent shock and light blazing through me, this eternal kind of relief surging up to consume me as I tried to call out to her in reply.

My eyes fell closed, removing my view of the sky as I listened to the sound of her approaching, unsure if it was real or just a whisper reaching me from beyond the realms of death, come to call me to it. Either way, my answer was yes. I'd follow her wherever she went and beyond.

A wail of pain filled the air as she reached me, her hand locking with mine and a cry of horror sounding as she pressed her mouth to my flesh, the feeling somehow so intense despite my inability to move my limbs that it roused the fire in me and stoked it until it was blazing once more.

"I told you, he's dead!" Brooklyn cried, true grief echoing through her voice. "It's the end, for him, for me, for all of us. How should we do it? Just slit our throats or pull the pin on a grenade and hug it between us so that our insides can get all mixed up as a final show of our love?"

I tried to speak, tried to open my eyes, but my body was finally giving into the pull of the drugs now that she was here, now that I knew she was safe and the mixture of the relief I felt and the pain pressing into my body from the injuries I'd gained in my fall were enough to force me into sleep.

A hand slapped my cheek as Brooklyn cried out even louder than before, a sob tearing from her throat which carved into me and filled me with the need to show her that I was still here for her.

I felt her moving closer to me, fingers pushing against my pulse point in hunt for a sign of life and I focused all of my energy on the feeling of her so close to me, knowing her lips were only a breath away from mine and needing to show her that I was still here.

With a growl of effort, I managed to lurch forward just enough to close the distance between us, my mouth finding hers and kissing her hard, my tongue pushing between her lips just as I felt the rough bite of stubble grazing against my chin.

My eyes flew open and met a set of startled brown ones half a beat before Mateo reared back and punched me.

The blow sent my head crashing back down against the roof of the car as he started cursing in his fancy language and a manic laugh fell from my lungs as I realised my mistake.

A wild shriek filled the air and I twisted my head towards it, spotting Jack there where I'd expected to find Brooklyn, a pitiful looking Brutus slung over his shoulders, an eyebrow arched at me which I interpreted as utter relief and joy over my continued survival in this world. But before I could get too lost in his grey stare and the tears which would no doubt be welling at any moment, a pocket-sized psycho leapt on top of me and knocked the air clean outa my lungs.

She pressed something cold and hard into my side and Mateo gasped, lunging for it. His hand closed on a grenade in her grip and he hurriedly plucked a pin from between her teeth, smoothly sliding it back into place within the grenade before the thing could blow us to kingdom come.

"Holy fuck, love," I cursed, my heart hammering. That thing could only have had a fraction of a millisecond left on it before it went boom.

"Oopsie," she breathed, blushing cutely. "I almost made us go bang. But now I don't have to! Because you're alive. We're all together. And I killed her, Hellfire," she gasped. "Stabbed her in her tits until they went pop and ended her for hurting you. It's all over now."

She was bloodstained and windswept, her dark hair a mess, falling out of its little buns and brilliant blue eyes wild in the most electric way. She was looking down at me like she was some mythical mermaid and I was a shipwrecked soul she'd found lying on her beach, his heart hers for the taking and his soul endlessly lost in the ocean of her.

I smiled as I observed her in all her bloody glory, not really caring who it was she'd killed or what it had taken to put us here, because the point was that here she was. With me. And there was nothing in this world or any other that could tear us apart now.

"Come claim my soul, little psycho," I urged, managing to move my hands so that they curled around her waist where she straddled me and there could be no doubting how real she was. "It's all yours anyway."

Brooklyn gave me a blinding smile before leaning down and offering the kiss I'd been needing. All the love and devotion a rotten soul like mine never should have been worthy of filled me up, surrounding me entirely as she kissed me like I was her world just as she was mine.

Bloodshed, carnage, mayhem and us. That was all I never knew I needed, and all I'd ever want now. Just me, her, a feral dog and two bloodthirsty arseholes who loved her beyond the point of sanity too. And that was all I desired in this world of chaos, our own little home in the storm.

NIALL

CHAPTER THIRTY THREE

TWO WEEKS LATER

Patricide.

Such a pretty word for such an unwholesome task. Though I had to say, in this instance, killing my father was no loss to the world. Liam O'Brien was a mean bastard who'd long since earned his ticket to hell. I probably should have sent him there myself a long time ago, but better the devil you know I supposed.

Now though, my dear old pa had outstayed his welcome on this planet. He'd had a good run. Eighty-two was decent innings for someone as atrocious as him. Or was it eighty-five? Hmm, eighty-something, for sure. Anyway, the arsehole had had more than his fair share of time ruining lives and wreaking carnage on this earthly plain, and he'd finally pushed me into action.

To be fair to him, I'd stood by while he'd committed countless horrendous acts, even taken part in more of them than I could count, but I had a hard line and he knew it. Ever since Ava had been taken from me. Taken. Beaten. Raped countless times by countless men. Killed minutes before I could get to her. My sweet Ava who had been too fucking good for this world.

Too fucking good for a heathen like me. Anyway, point was, my pa knew my limits, and he'd overstepped. I half imagined he was expecting me. Though on second thought, he likely believed he was far too clever for that.

Had he truly believed I wouldn't figure this out though? That I wouldn't put two and two together and make myself an omelette of the poisonous variety?

I was a hard man, a cruel one, evil some might say, but I had limits. They may have been few and far between, but it was so. I also had a code. A single honourable thing which had been drummed into me and every member of my rotten family since the day of my birth.

Loyalty.

The O'Brien name was sacred. It went beyond petty squabbles and pointless vendettas, it superseded hatred and bypassed hurts and anguish. It was simple. We didn't kill our own. Not unless they betrayed us in the most unforgivable of ways.

The moment someone married in and took our name, they assumed that protection too. It was the only law we all abided by.

Yet here I was, creeping across his roof in the dead of night, because he'd thought to bypass that single, eternal fact.

I crouched down, a hiss of pain escaping me as my ribs twinged from the movement. On doctors' orders I'd been outa commission for a couple of weeks while my bruises and breaks healed after my fall onto that fucking car, but most of them were recovered now. Only the worst of the broken ribs still flared with pain from time to time, and I was past the point of waiting for them to stop.

This needed to be done. It needed to be over.

I dropped to my knee, gripping the edge of the roof before leaning down and taking hold of the side of the window beneath me. A long time ago, I'd created this weakness in my pa's defences of his property just in case a day like this ever arose and I needed to gain access.

There was always a fucker on the roof. I'd told him that a hundred times at least. But no one ever did take my warnings seriously.

I pulled the pin free of the hinge, leaning even lower and ignoring the perilous drop beneath me as I repeated the action on the second hinge before easing the window away from the wall and creating a gap to allow me access.

I slipped inside like a demon in the night, drawing the window back into place behind me and creeping out of the darkened guest room towards the empty corridor beyond.

It was almost three in the morning, clearly a time when any normal man would be fast asleep, but as I turned towards my pa's bedroom, I paused, glancing back over my shoulder.

I mighta been imagining it, but I could have sworn the scent of smoke lingered in the air, calling me back in the direction of the main staircase and beckoning me forth.

I hesitated, my fingers twitching for the feel of a weapon as indecision held me in place before I turned towards the stairs and hurried down them in the dark.

It had been a long damn time since I'd been a rebellious teenager, sneaking in after dark and trying to hide the blood splatter which coated my clothes like a right little ragamuffin, but I still recalled where each and every creaky spot on the stairs was and dodged them all with ease.

I slipped through the shadows in the dark, making my way down the corridor towards my pa's office, taking note of the light which shone around the cracks at the edges of the door and smiling to myself at my correct guess.

I moved to stand to the left of the door, wetting my lips as my heart began to pound, the weight of this decision pressing down on me and reminding me that this would mean so much more than the death of a single man. I was donning a crown in this moment. One I had never had any desire to bear the weight of.

I reached for the handle slowly, drawing in a deep breath and keeping my back flat to the wall before turning it and letting the thing swing wide.

Three shots were fired through the open door in quick succession, the noise of them dulled by a silencer, though the sound of them slamming into the wooden panelling opposite the door was in no way suppressed.

I snagged a knife from my belt, hurling it through the door without risking a look into the room and smirking to myself as a curse followed the act and the gunshots ceased.

"You knew I was coming then?" I called cheerily, the scent of blood and gunpowder in the air making my pulse pick up.

"I'd hoped for both outcomes, if I'm honest, lad," my father's voice came in reply.

I kicked the door wider to get a look at him, finding him slumped back in his wingback chair with my knife protruding from his left shoulder and his gun fallen onto the desk between us.

"Hands where I can see 'em," I said, jerking my chin in command, though I made no move to draw any further weapons against him.

My father obliged, laying his hands flat on the desk as a grunt of pain confirmed that blade made it all kinds of painful for him to do so.

I moved into the room, picking up the fallen gun and inspecting it with interest before tossing it to a far corner of the room. I dropped down opposite the man who had claimed dominion over my life long before my conception, wondering what he thought of the man he'd created now that his moment had come.

"I always knew it would be you," he said, coughing out a laugh which caused blood to ooze from the knife wound and a grimace to cross his features.

"Can't say I did," I replied, leaning across the desk and taking hold of the blade. I met my father's cold eyes as I took hold of the hilt, smiling wryly as I yanked the thing out.

Liam cursed, thumping a fist down on the desk before slumping back in his chair and looking down at the wound which now bled freely, staining his white shirt with the bright redness of his blood.

"It was only ever a matter of time," Liam muttered, his fingers moving towards a cigarette box and I inclined my head as he gave me a questioning look, allowing him to take one and place it between his lips.

His left hand fumbled as he tried to lift the lighter too, the injury I'd given him clearly making things difficult. I snatched it from his fingers, sparking up the smoke for him like a good son before taking one for myself and joining him in his filthy habit.

I leaned back in my seat, inhaling deeply, the flare of the cherry comforting to me like the hand of a father on my shoulder, supportive, loving, kind – none of the things my real father could count himself as.

"So," I said, wondering if he might indulge me with a few parting words.

Liam looked me up and down, his eyes flaring with pride as he took me in and still some pathetic little piece of me enjoyed that, liked knowing that I was finally meeting with his expectations even though I cared not for his opinion. Even though I hated him with all I had. Even though I was here to see his end.

"She's good for you," he said, surprising me. "That little whip of a thing who you went and married."

"Is that so?" I asked, wondering how he'd have any idea on the truth of that.

"I came while you were in the hospital," he went on, shifting the cigarette to the corner of his lips as he inhaled again and parking it there. "Saw her praying to the Devil to bring you back kicking and swinging from wherever he had you trapped. You were off your face on pain meds and waiting on a bunch of scans, but I could see the way you smiled for her. That's when I knew you'd be coming for me."

"Did you seriously think I wouldn't have figured it out?" I asked.

Liam shrugged like he hadn't much cared one way or another. "The deal with the Russians was good for business. They wouldn't keep up their end without a wedding, and I had no one suitable to offer aside from you. They didn't want a grandson or someone too far removed from power. If you'd just done your duty, you coulda had it all, lad."

"I never was one for duty," I reminded him and he coughed another laugh, this one causing a whole lota blood to spill from the wound, making me pretty certain that I'd gone and hit something important with that strike.

"You were one for action," Liam agreed, almost sounding fond over the fact. "Something which is wildly underappreciated in our line of business. Your siblings don't have that same cutthroat ability to make a snap decision and see it through. You're unapologetically single-minded. You don't allow for regrets-"

"I have plenty of regrets, old man," I growled and he shook his head.

"You have one. A pretty little regret who never should have gotten mixed up with the likes of you in the first place. But you learned from that error. Ava made you stronger, whether you wish you could change her fate or not. It took the softness from ya. Made you give up on pretty fantasies and nonsense ideals about good and bad."

I exhaled a lungful of smoke and plucked the cigarette from my lips, letting it hang from my fingers as I considered that.

"You don't regret Brooklyn, do ya?" he pushed, making my spine straighten as he dared speak her name.

"No," I snarled. "But I get the feeling you do."

Liam coughed out another laugh, this one making him slump forward in his chair as he fought to stay conscious through the blood loss before he managed to push himself upright again.

"Turns out, she was the final thing you needed," he said once he regained the energy for speech. "I've been waiting for one of you to grow the balls to end this the way it needed to end. I always knew you were the only one likely to manage it."

"You wanted one of your own children to kill you?" I asked in surprise, his words a clear reminder as to where I inherited my insanity from.

"That I did. No true O'Brien waits for something to be handed to them. The person with the grit and ambition to take it was always going to be the one worthy of it. Tell me, what will you do with my crown now that you have it?"

"I was planning on forcing the others to run everything with as little input from me as possible, only stepping in when I need to kill someone who's fucking up. I figure I can enjoy the fact that I reign over all of them without actually having to suffer their company all too often. Not to mention all of the money I'll have at my disposal."

Liam snorted, not even seeming to care that I wasn't planning some great takeover within his organisation. I was perfectly happy to keep control over my villainous family from afar and take a fat cut of their hard-earned money without needing to engross myself in their affairs too deeply. They'd be fools to try and cross or steal from me, and they knew it. I would rule over them through fear and threats alone and it would do me well.

"Did you expect this then?" I asked. "Did you know I would figure out who told Anastasia about me doing hits with my new wife and accepted the fact that I would come for you after I killed her?"

"Either that, or her plan would have worked and you would have woken from that dart to find yourself widowed all over again, your marriage into the Russian mob back on track, and my plans still in place. Both outcomes were acceptable to me. You weren't ever supposed to have known it was her who killed your new bride after all, but I couldn't be sure if she would be foolish enough to give herself away or not."

I threw my knife again, the blade sinking deep into that very same spot and causing him to stifle a cry of pain.

A ferocious snarl escaped my lips and I pointed straight in his face, the cigarette smoking between my fingers and causing my line of sight to waver through it.

"You speak another word about Brooklyn's death being acceptable to you and you'll find this end of yours taking a whole lot longer, old man," I barked, violence pooling in every inch of my body and only the finest thread tethering me in place, the desire to make him suffer damn near overwhelming me. "You think you know the monster in me, but I can assure you, you haven't even begun to fathom the depths of my capabilities. You have no idea what I can or will do. And believe me when I tell you, you want to die without finding out."

Liam gazed at me with that pride in his eyes again, but this time all it gave me was a feeling of disgust as I sat back in my chair and took a long drag on my cigarette, working to calm my nerves.

"My only regret is in not being here to watch you flourish in this role, Niall," he said roughly, exhaling more smoke and finding himself almost down to the butt. Neither of us had said it, but we both knew that would be his end. The moment that cigarette was done, he would be too.

"I won't think of you again," I promised him coldly. "When I leave this place, I won't return. If I could, I'd let your empire rot and fall to ruin in your wake. The only reason I will take your place is to stop my siblings from doing so in my absence. It has nothing to do with your wishes or your legacy, know that. I'll leave your corpse in this room and leave all memory of you behind with it. Out there is a wild life waiting for me with a beautiful creature taking ownership of the reins. She is my only destiny now, and I won't be burdened by my past a moment longer."

Liam's face dropped at my words, and I knew he heard the truth in them.

"So be it," he grunted, reaching for his phone.

I allowed him the time it took to hit dial on a group call which included all of my siblings, focusing on the taste of smoke rolling over my tongue instead of paying much attention to their voices as they joined the call.

"I'll cut to the point," Liam said, his eyes on me as he took the end of the cigarette from his lips and ashed it between us in the centre of his desk, not bothering with the ashtray which had been waiting to his left. "You've all been waiting on this decision for long enough after all."

A few sharp breaths came over the speaker as my eager little siblings all girded their loins in anticipation of their own names being spoken, none of them for a moment questioning him on what he meant. I waited, a cruel pleasure filling me at the knowledge of their impending disappointment.

"Niall holds the crown now. The time for change has come."

Several of my siblings all started up with some protest or another, but I just hit mute so that I wouldn't have to listen to a word from any of them, leaving them on the line as I got to my feet and ashed my cigarette too.

Liam met my steady gaze and nodded, ripping the knife free of his shoulder with a grunt of pain before moving it over his heart and thrusting it in with the last of his strength.

I let him have the kill, not caring much one way or another how he ended up in the ground, only that he made it there.

My father's pupils dilated as death came for him on swift and brutal wings, and I watched without emotion as he pitched forward onto his desk and fell dead before me with a finality that set me free at long last.

"Long live your new king," I said loudly for my siblings to hear, the smile in my voice as clear as day. "I look forward to ruling in his stead."

I hung up before turning and striding from the room, not even bothering to close the door behind me as I left the oppression of my father's rule in the past at long last. I headed for the life I had claimed for myself with my Spider and her band of fucked-up souls, sure that from here on out, all I'd ever know was the fullness of a life well lived. And what more could a twisted creature like me desire?

BROOKLYN

CHAPTER THIRTY FOUR

"Keep yer hands over her eyes, don't let her peek now, big fella," Niall called as I stumbled across soft sand on bare feet while Jack moved at my back, his huge palms keeping everything from view.

The repetitive sound of a whoooosh and a wet crash kept carrying to me and I tasted salt on my lips as Jack walked me closer to it.

"Have ya got the camera ready on your phone, el burro?" Niall snapped.

"I've been ready for fifteen minutes," Mateo growled. "Get on with it. Let her see."

"Yes! Let me see," I said keenly, a happy little dragonfly whizzing around my chest and perching on Glenda's head. She had stitches all the way around her neck now since she'd been decapitated, but it was amazing what you could do to heal an imaginary duck these days.

"Okay then," Niall said, his voice closer this time. "Let her see."

Jack lowered his hands and the brightness of the sun blinded me for a second, but as my eyes adjusted to that golden veil of light, I ceased to breathe. The ocean spread out before me endlessly towards the horizon, the water deepest blue all the way out there but near to shore it wasn't even blue. It was a colour that lived only in dreamlands, like cyan dipped in liquid turquoise.

Waves rolled against the shore and as a splashy one hit the sand, it rushed up to greet me, running over my toes and tickling my skin. My laughter turned into a squeal and I ran forward, tearing off my clothes as I went, wanting to feel it everywhere.

"Mi sol!" Mateo shouted as I stripped right down, completely naked as I ran into the sea and dove into its embrace.

"Let her have her fun. I'll pluck out anyone's eyes who looks too closely," Niall promised just as I got a mouthful of seawater and spluttered as it went up my nose too.

It wasn't like lake water, or even a swimming pool, this water was alive, playing with me, dragging me out into a depth where I couldn't touch the sand before tossing me backwards again. I squealed and laughed as it threw me about, rolling beneath the waves before coming up for air and finding myself in a spin cycle all over again. It was getting a little harder to find air between all the playtime, but it didn't make it any less fun.

Hands encircled my waist and I was plucked from the water, drawn up against Jack's bare chest as he strode deeper into the sea in his board shorts. Niall was close behind him and Mateo was even closer, the three of them shirtless and looking like the most edible creatures I'd ever seen.

"Keep her angled that way." Mateo pointed and Jack walked with his back to the few people sunbathing further up the beach.

"Do ya like it, love?" Niall called. "Is the ocean everything you hoped it would be?"

"It's better," I said, clambering higher up Jack's body to look over his shoulder at Niall. "It's so big. I've never seen anything this big."

"Except my cock," Jack mind communicated to me, and I snorted a laugh.

"Yeah, except that, AJ," I giggled in agreement.

We played splashy-kicky-swimmy for a while until more people appeared on the beach and I had to wait in the water while Mateo fetched a bikini for me. By the time we were walking back out of the ocean, my tummy was grumbling for lunch and my fingers were twitching for my spider blade to play with.

We'd spent the last six months travelling the states, roaming randomly from town to town in a huge RV that I loved like a second home. But maybe that was because I'd realised my men were my home, and wherever they were, so was I.

We took the little path through the dunes back to the campsite we'd be staying in tonight. I'd begged and begged Niall to take us to the coast ever since we'd started our road trip, but he'd insisted that I only got to see the ocean for the first time once, and the best place for that was California. So we'd taken our sweet time getting here, and I'd had a blast in all the places we'd seen from Montana to Wyoming, right down to Arizona and Nevada.

We'd spent the last month in Las Vegas, partying, spending money, making money, buying all the stuff and things. It had been so much fun, but eventually the noise had gotten too noisy and the baking sun had gotten too dry for my throat, and I'd woken up one day, packed all my bags and demanded we leave in five minutes or I was going to hurl myself out the window. I'd never seen my men move so fast. And now here we were, and the world was so nice and quiet, the sand was hugging my toes and though we'd only just arrived, this was definitely my favourite place so far.

We walked through the campsite, and I waved to all of our new camper friends who were in their sun hats and brightly coloured shirts, sitting on deck chairs outside their vehicles, a few of them barbequing their lunch and making me sniff the air in hopes of swiping myself a corn on the cob off of a grill.

We reached our RV; the huge black van with blacked out windows and fake plates was our getaway whenever we killed. And hell did we kill. That was what this whole adventure was about after all. We were hunting serial killers and dickmunches who needed putting down. We tracked them like wolves in the night then made a bloody mess of them before Mateo would put his fixer hat on and clean up the pieces. He'd been teaching me to do that too, all his clever little ways to hide evidence and destroy a body. I was a certified professional at this point, and I was surrounded by the best team a psycho could ask for.

Niall unlocked the RV and we followed him inside, the air conditioning washing over me and making me shiver. Brutus was asleep in his bed, but his head perked up as we entered, letting out a bark before his tail wagged and he settled himself back down when he realised there was no stranger danger.

"What's for lunch?" I jogged to the fridge, tugging it open and eyeing all the stuff in there with a pout. It was all boring yesterday food, no magical new food had appeared at all. I wanted today food. Something different and scrummy and fresh. I threw the fridge door closed with a huff just as Mateo came up behind me and reached around me, rubbing his thumb over my clit through my bikini bottoms.

"I know what I'm hungry for."

I moaned softly, riding his thumb and grazing my ass back against the huge bulge in his shorts as he laid his free hand on the fridge to cage me in.

"You need more than a diet of pussy to keep you big and strong, el burro," Niall said, smacking him on the shoulder, and Mateo continued to torment my clit while pressing me harder against the cool fridge. Suddenly I wasn't so hungry anymore, my appetite shifting to a sausage sandwich that had nothing to do with food.

"She's so sweet, she's one of my five a day," Mateo said and Niall and Jack chuckled.

"You'd better eat like a gentleman off of the table then." Niall shoved Mateo sideways and my dead man took me with him, dragging me to the table by the window with a bench on either side of it. The orange curtains were open and as Mateo tossed me down on my back with a hard thump, he reached over my head to close them. The sunlight filtered through them and I smiled at the familiarity of it. Jack had shown up with them one day and changed all the boring white ones for these, and now every time I woke up, the whole place was full of amber light and made me feel like a kid all over again.

But I definitely didn't feel like a kid now as Mateo untied the strings holding my bikini in place and yanked them off of me. I gasped as he knelt down and buried his face between my thighs, gripping the backs of my legs as he lapped at my clit.

Niall took two beers from the fridge, cracking them open and passing one to Jack as he sipped his own, watching me like a hawk.

Jack drained his beer in a long, slow drink, his throat working and drawing all of my attention to the muscles within it as a loud moan left me. Mateo ran his tongue up and down my slit, tormenting me before fucking me with it, making my hips writhe and jerk as he devoured me.

Niall and Jack were hard as stone as they watched me, their shorts tented by their cocks as they enjoyed the show. I whimpered as Mateo's tongue slowed, dragging back and forth across my clit in a way that had my toes curling and my back arching. His stubble grazed my pussy as he worked to destroy me and I loved the roughened bite of it, grinding myself against his face to feel it even more.

"How wet is she, Mateo?" Niall asked as he propped his shoulder against the wall and took another swig of his beer.

Mateo brought his hand up, swirling his fingers in my arousal and chuckling against my flesh, the vibrations making another spike of pleasure dance through my clit. "Come find out for yourself."

Niall drew closer, fisting his hand in Mateo's hair and driving his mouth down firmer on my clit as his eyes locked with mine. "Bring her to the edge, but no further."

Mateo growled angrily at Niall's treatment of him, but I moaned so loud in encouragement that he gave in and started licking me again. His tongue was the best sex toy in the world stitched right there into his mouth, and he brought me so easily to the edge of ruin that I was trembling with the need for release in a matter of seconds. But then he drew back, his tongue moving down before he swallowed away my arousal and Niall continued to fist his hair, though he let Mateo take the lead.

"Please, Hellfire," I begged, pushing a hand into my bikini top and toying with my aching nipple. "I'm so close."

Niall smirked darkly and Jack moved just behind him to get a better view, his long white hair drying around his shoulders and curling a little as it did.

"No, Spider. I'm gonna be the first to make you come. Jack will be the second. And Mateo here can wait 'til last."

Mateo defiantly started sucking my clit, refusing to play Niall's game and I cried out as he brought me to the cliff again, about to hurl me off it and send me into ecstasy. But then Niall yanked him away from me by his hair and shoved him back so he could step forward instead. Mateo didn't accept that so easily though, grabbing Niall and throwing him into the fridge, the RV rattling from the impact. Honestly? I freaking loved it when they fought over me.

"You fuckin' donkey. How many times do I gotta tell ya? I'm in charge. I'm the head dick."

"I never agreed to that," Mateo snarled, lunging at him and the two of them fell into a furious fist fight.

Jack stepped forward, pushing my thighs apart and licking his lips. "Look at you," he said in a low voice inside my head. "Left here ready and waiting like the best fantasy I could ever come up with." He fisted his cock through his shorts then shifted them down to free it, releasing the monster and running his fist up and down his thick shaft.

"Do you want me to please you, my love?" he asked and I nodded eagerly, pulling my bikini top down beneath my tits and playing with them for him as my hips bucked with need. "You better say the word then."

"Do it. Take me. I command it," I rasped.

The RV trembled again as a loud thud sounded and Niall and Mateo cursed as they wrestled, furiously fighting to get the upper hand. Meanwhile, Jack lined the tip of huge cock up with my entrance, swirling it around in my wetness and a low groan leaving him. He shoved himself inside me with a fierce thrust and I cried out, grasping at the table for support as he gripped my thighs and started fucking me like a heathen. The RV had a new reason to be rocking now as he drove in and out of me, his teeth bared and his eyes twisting with darkness as he claimed me just how I liked it.

My lips parted and my moans came out in time with his thrusts, his huge cock so much to accommodate, but he angled himself just right to hit the perfect spot inside me, sweetening every thrust he gave me. I panted heavily, lowering my hand to rub my clit and in moments I was coming, already so worked up by Mateo, but my ruin was for Jack alone as my pussy clenched around him and he growled his approval as he felt every second of my climax.

"You fuckin' arsehole." Niall caught hold of Jack by the throat, dropping his whole weight backwards to try and pull him off me but Jack fought to keep fucking me, his cock swelling inside me. I whimpered for him as Niall managed to drag him away, leaving his swollen leviathan cock wanting.

Niall threw Jack into Mateo as my Dead Man ran to intercept him, buying Niall time to grab hold of me. He lifted me off of the table, throwing me over his shoulder and spanking my ass as I let out a squeak, my limbs too heavy for me to even try and get free. Not that I wanted to.

Niall carried me into his bedroom which was the master one in the RV, shoving the door shut and locking it with a key before tossing me onto the bed.

I writhed on the sheets, reaching for him in my lustful haze and he dropped down to kneel between my thighs, leaning over me and caressing my cheek with his thumb. "All mine."

A weight collided with the door, followed by another one and Niall grinned savagely before he stepped back off the bed and dropped his shorts, kicking them away from him as I took in his inked body and his beautiful cock standing ready and waiting for me.

I scrambled up onto my knees, looking up at him and wetting my mouth before I took the tip of it between my lips and played with his piercing with my tongue. Niall groaned, pushing his fingers into my hair and tucking it behind my ear.

"You look so good down there, little psycho."

I took him to the back of my throat, a damn pro at this by now and Niall released a stream of curses as I dragged my tongue up the length of his cock before swirling it around the tip.

Jack and Mateo were battling to break the door down and Niall tossed an irritated glance back at it, watching me suck and lick every inch of him before pushing me off of him.

"No time, love. I need to get inside ya before they get in here." He caught me by the hips, flipping me over and drawing my ass back against him. "Actually…" He dragged the tip of his cock between my ass cheeks, right over my butt where I really, really wanted to feel him. "Stay right where ya are." Niall moved around the bed and my fingers fisted in the sheets as I remained on my hands and knees, shaking a little with the anticipation of him.

He took a bottle of lube from the nightstand and I grinned in excitement. "Yes, Hellfire. Hurry. I want you now."

Niall smirked as he hurried back to me and the door made a cracking noise as my other men slammed into it again. I wanted them to break in, I wanted them to come play with us, but I equally wanted Niall inside me right fucking now.

Niall soaked his fingers in the lube, easing two of them into my ass before adding a third and I moaned, rocking my hips side to side, loving the feel of it. When he had me ready for him, he lined his cock up with my tight hole and pressed into me one thick inch at a time, making me brace against the mattress as I worked to take the pressure.

"Ah," I gasped as he filled me up and his hands held my hips steady, a deep groan leaving him as my body gripped him.

"So tight," he exhaled before he started moving, our bodies falling into a familiar rhythm now as he fucked me and I let my head fall down to the sheets, my arms reaching out ahead of me as I let him take full control.

His thrusts were deep and slow, but they were gaining pace and I loved the feel of him losing control as his fingers started to dig into my flesh and his demons came to say hi.

A bang announced the door giving out and Niall only increased his pace as I garbled his name and begged for more.

"Good girl," Niall said roughly and I glanced back over my shoulder as Mateo's hand closed over Niall's shoulder, a look in his gaze saying he was going to pull him away again.

"No, please," I begged, my voice throaty with need.

Mateo met my gaze and I realised he had some handcuffs in his hand which he'd clearly been intending to lock Niall up with.

I bit my lip, placing my hands behind my back in an offering instead and Mateo's eyes sparked at what I was suggesting. He stepped forward, gripping my wrists before sliding the handcuffs onto them and locking them tight.

"More," I begged. "I want all of you. I want to please you all. Use my body," I said, my inner sex demon awakening to come and be a total kinky freak.

"You heard the woman," Niall said gruffly, slowing his pace, the strain in his posture telling me he was working to hold off his own release. "All of ya use this perfect body like she wants it to be used." Niall fisted one hand in my hair and the other gripped my cuffs as he dragged me upright, remaining inside me as he gave room for Mateo and Jack to approach. Mateo laid down on the bed in the spot I'd vacated and Niall lowered me onto him, Mateo's hands steadying me before he lined his cock up with my pussy and Niall spread me even wider for him.

I gasped as Mateo eased inside me, the two of them within me making me shudder with pleasure as Dead Man sunk all the way into me, stretching me out until I'd taken all of him.

"Follow my lead," Niall commanded, drawing halfway out of me before starting to fuck me again.

"Fuck you," Mateo snapped, starting to fuck me too and I whimpered as they moved out of rhythm, defying each other.

"Stop," I begged and Niall reached past my head, locking his hand around Mateo's throat. "You fuck her right, or you don't fuck her at all."

"Hijo de puta," Mateo snapped, shoving Niall's hand off of him.

"Hold him down, Jack," Niall commanded and AJ's hand closed around Mateo's throat instantly, the sight of that making me nearly purr in delight.

"Good boy," Niall chuckled, fucking me faster. "Now behave little donkey, or I'll enforce a pussy ban on you for a month."

Mateo growled and thrashed, but as Niall weighed me down to stop him from rising and Jack worked to keep him in place too, Mateo slowly gave in, starting to fuck me in time with Niall until my moans were colouring the air like a glittering rainbow.

"Let him go, big fella. He's being good now," Niall said.

I kissed Mateo as Jack eased his hand off of his throat and my Dead Man gave me a look that said he was descending into his dark place. He gripped my hips, fucking me hard and starting to move me, working with Niall as they held me between them and without my hands, I could do nothing but go along for the ride.

"C'mere, Jack. Our Spider looks like she wants more. Don't you, love?"

"Yes," I whimpered.

Jack moved onto the bed beyond Mateo, his large hand moving to grip my face before he leaned forward and thrust the head of his cock between my lips. I moaned around his tip, tasting his precum before taking him in as far as I could.

Niall spanked my ass as he came with a groan that lit me up inside and Mateo kicked him back, forcing him away from me and dominating my body as he claimed it for his own. He locked his legs around mine and thrust up into me with a fury that had me gasping around Jack's cock.

AJ gripped my chin, drawing my gaze up to his, and one final flick of my tongue had him spilling himself down my throat with a beast's roar.

I barely had time to swallow before Mateo tugged me off of Jack and rolled us over, my hands pinned behind my back, turning numb with pins and needles. Mateo pressed me down and drove himself into me, his nails digging into the flesh of my legs as he lifted my hips so he could fill me to the brim. He was always so careful when he fucked me, working not to snap so that he wouldn't go to his most depraved place. But I didn't want him holding back with me this time. I wanted to feel every bite and raw edge of his power. I knew he feared hurting me, but that was a risk I was willing to take because being at the mercy of this monster was a thrill like nothing I'd ever known.

"I trust you," I said breathlessly. "Don't hold back."

Mateo's dark gaze flashed with a mixture of hesitation and heady desire.

"Don't pull him off," I told the others firmly as their shadows drew closer.

"Can't promise that, love," Niall said as he took the new taser from his nightstand that he'd bought in Vegas.

Mateo's hands closed around my throat and a vicious grin lifted his lips as he started to swell inside me and I lost the ability to breathe. He pounded into me hard enough to hurt, but I loved that pain, I loved seeing him lose control and fall into the chaos of the darkness within him.

My ears popped and blackness started to curtain my vision, a sense of euphoria filling Mateo's eyes as he watched, and I loved that I could give him this. That my death might just be the biggest turn on of his life, even if only for a moment. But he wasn't going to kill me. I knew that, really. He loved me, and he'd never actually hurt me.

"Mi sol," he rasped, a moment of clarity finding him and his fingers loosening like I'd known they would.

But then Niall's taser drove into his side and I cried out as the electricity poured through me too, and suddenly I was coming so hard I was almost blinded by it. But if this was the last thing I ever saw, then take my damn eyes and cast them into hell.

Mateo growled in pain, his fingers falling from my throat and as Niall withdrew the taser, my Dead Man drove deep into me and stilled, coming with a groan that set me on fire inside.

Mateo panted and clawed at the sheets, surrounding me entirely as every muscle in his body tensed and I was one with him for an eternal, perfect moment.

His forehead fell to mine and a beautiful smile spread across his lips as he realised he had unleashed his demon fully and controlled it.

"You freed me, Brooklyn," he panted. "From every shackle that has ever been wrapped around my soul. Gracias, chica loca. Te amo más de lo que amo el sabor de la muerte."

MATEO

CHAPTER THIRTY FIVE

SEVEN YEARS AFTER THAT

"Mierda," I muttered, my hand stroking down the cold spine of the big bastardo of a dog who had spent the best years of his life within our family.

It had been weeks of failing medications and a long road to this point, but his time had finally come. He was a good dog, violent, actively aggressive and all kinds of problematic, but then so were the rest of us.

We'd known his end was coming, and in all fairness, he was at least a good five years older than a dog his size really should have lived. But despite having been prepared, I still felt a weight of sorrow in my chest over him leaving us.

I sighed, stroking him again and eyeing the scar on my fingers which would now serve as a memory to him beyond his passing.

I reached out carefully and shook Niall's arm. The four of us had all slept in the big bed in his room with the dog every night this week, knowing his time was drawing close.

Brooklyn had been in denial of course, claiming he was just in need of extra snugs and kisses, but Niall, Jack and I had seen the truth of it.

Niall jerked awake, a blade he'd gotten from fuck knew where pressing to my throat so fast that I didn't even have time to block it and I cursed at him beneath my breath as he blinked himself awake and took in the state of things.

"Ah, shit," he murmured, withdrawing the knife and reaching out to pet the big dog's body, a look of genuine grief crossing his features which bonded us together for a moment as we accepted that the brute really was gone.

Niall's eyes turned to Brooklyn who was curled up against Jack's chest, his eyes open and fixed on us as he took in what had happened.

"We can't let her see him like this," I murmured in a low voice and Niall nodded.

For years we'd all been trying to convince Brooklyn to release the dog from her vow of suicide in the event of his death, but she hadn't budged an inch. And as much as I loved my insane woman, I was certain that she would truly end herself over this loss. She really was that loco. But there hadn't been much we could do in preparation for it aside from make some loose plans to try and cover up what had happened.

"Love," Jack breathed, placing his hand on the dog's head and surprising me as a tear slipped down his cheek in grief over the animal.

It made something deep inside my chest tug and I swallowed thickly again. We were a band of fucked up souls and I hated these two men at least as much as I cherished them, but Brooklyn had been right about one thing – we were a family of sorts. And Brutus had been a part of that for a long time.

I was going to truly miss him.

Niall reached out to clasp Jack's shoulder and I frowned as the lump thickened in my throat before turning my attention to the dead dog once more.

"He went out of this world surrounded by those he loved," I murmured uncertain of who I was even trying to reassure as I ran a hand over his fur again, feeling the scars of his past beneath the soft grey hair. I was glad we'd killed the man who had hurt him, glad we'd offered him a fresh chance at life among other souls who had seen too much suffering in our pasts. He'd had it all for a good while there. And that was all that any pup could ask for.

"That he did," Niall agreed with a sigh.

We all looked to Brooklyn again where she continued to snore in Jack's arms and the need to hurry pressed in on me.

"You have the distraction ready?" I asked Niall and he nodded, getting out of the bed and crossing the room.

He opened his closet and withdrew a box from the back of it, setting it on the nightstand to reveal a fresh box of Coco Pops, a big bar of chocolate, three brand new vibrators, a sparkly pink butt plug and some of her favourite lube, plus a note which told her we love her and want her to enjoy some alone time.

Niall turned the TV on next, leaving it muted and hooking it up to his phone before playing a video compiled of sex tapes the four of us had made over the last few years since Brooklyn decided she wanted to be able to remember our sex life in HD at all times.

My gaze caught on the screen as I watched Brooklyn take my cock into that tight ass of hers and I licked my lips at the look of pure ecstasy on her face while I fucked her like a man possessed.

I dragged my eyes from the show, needing to get on with our task before she woke and realised what had happened. She could never find out that the dog had died, which meant we had work to do.

The three of us carefully got out of the bed, dressing silently and tucking the blankets around her before I gently lifted Brutus's huge body into my arms.

The bastardo weighed a damn ton and his limp weight was a struggle to carry, but I nestled him against me and managed it, following Niall out onto the landing with Jack close at my back.

We headed straight outside, following the slope of the hill down to the very bottom and stepping into the trees there before I set the dog down on a white sheet which Jack had laid out for him.

The three of us stroked him one final time, saying silent goodbyes and feeling the hurt of his loss for a few minutes before urgency forced us into action again.

"I'll head to the pound," Niall said firmly, taking a set of keys from his pocket.

"Make sure the dog you pick looks just like him," I warned. "If you fuck this up then it could mean death for our woman, and you'd better believe that I will make your agony last on eternally if you cause her end."

"Yeah, yeah, you big donkey," Niall said dismissively, waving me off. "I don't need no telling from the likes of you. The pound is full of mean old dogs just aching for a home like the one we can offer. I'll find a nice new pooch to fulfil her needs. She'll never know the difference."

Jack handed me a shovel as he strode away from us and I muttered a thanks to him as we both started digging, the grief of our loss making us maintain the silence as we did this one last thing for our four-legged friend.

It took us a couple of hours to dig a grave large enough for the beast and we had lowered him into it gently, covering him over again and exchanging stories of the men he'd killed with us and the scars we bore on our flesh from his teeth. It had been a bittersweet kind of goodbye. Brutus had been very old and in the last year he'd been struggling with basic things, his mind clearly fading too, until he did little more than eat and sleep and bite the occasional finger. The simple fact was that it had been his time and though we would miss him dearly, we knew that he had lived well with the four of us in our godless house.

Jack had surprised me by fetching a large sack of flower bulbs as we finished off and I'd helped him plant them over the grave, all kinds of beautiful blooms ready to spring up above Brutus's final resting place as the seasons changed and reminded us of him every time we laid our eyes on them. I couldn't say I'd ever done anything so soft, and yet it seemed right to honour him in that way.

The sound of a car pulling up the drive made me turn and we spotted Niall's truck heading towards the house.

I stripped my shirt off, using it to wipe the sweat from my brow as I said a final farewell to Brutus before turning and striding back up the hill beside Jack.

Niall stepped out of the truck as we made it to him and I fell utterly still as I spotted the odd little creature which was perched over his left arm.

"What the fuck is that?" I demanded, pointing at the dog which couldn't have looked any less like Brutus if it had been a damn cat.

"This is Brutus," Niall replied, waving the dog before my face as if it was obvious and I just gaped at him, wondering if he was having some kind of episode.

The dog was black with white patches and looked to be a Pomeranian, like one of those little handbag dogs fancy bitches carried about. Its top lip seemed to be snaggled over one tooth and its eyes were unfocused, staring either at me or at something behind me which it seemed to be both utterly fixated on and yet entirely uninterested in at once.

"Take it back and find one that looks like Brutus," I snapped, pointing a finger at Niall which the dog instantly lunged for, drawing blood with its sharp little teeth and making me curse as I snatched my hand away again.

"See?" Niall said defiantly. "If he doesn't have Brutus energy, then I don't know who does. All the other dogs in that place were wet fishes without a drop of water in sight. They had no flare, no pizzazz. Brooklyn won't be fooled by some two-bit finger licker."

"Rook," Jack muttered and I glared at him for going all one syllable on us at a time like this, but the bastardo still wouldn't speak properly in front of Niall, even after all this time. I didn't know if he was still enjoying the joke or if he just revelled in the way Niall treated him like a mindless heathen sent to do his bidding too much to change things.

A crash inside the house made my heart leap and before I could do anything to stop him, Niall had thrown the front door open and strode inside.

"Wait!" I hissed urgently, tossing the shovel away from me as I hurried to catch him, but it was too late. He was gone, heading straight to the front room and finding Brooklyn there, her cheeks flushed and the little blue pyjamas she'd worn to bed hanging from her hips in a way that instantly drew my eye.

"Morning, love," Niall said brightly, walking towards her with the weird little dog in his arms. "Look at Brutus! He went and got himself reincarnated!"

"What?" she asked, narrowing her eyes at the dog in his arms and stalking closer to him. "That's Brutus?"

"Yeah," Niall said with a grin. "It was damn strange, one minute he was a big old beast, the next he was going all Phoenix and being reborn in another body, fresh and dandy and ready to tear throats out like he used ta."

Brooklyn narrowed her eyes suspiciously and I held my breath, waiting for her to lose her shit as she realised the truth.

"Phoenixes can't be reborn, Hellfire," she said, clucking her tongue. "Everyone knows that's nonsense, just like their tears can't bring people back to life and their farts can't set things on fire. Those are all just conspiracy theories made up by people who can't bear the truth."

"What is the truth, mi sol?" I asked carefully, stepping a little closer.

"That nothing is ever that easy," she hissed, raising a hand towards the dog while my heart thrashed a million miles a minute.

New Brutus lunged at her as she drew close, his teeth snapping shut on air as she managed to shift her fingers aside with a flash of speed before squealing in delight and snatching him straight out of Niall's arms.

"Oh Bruty, it is you!" she cooed. "And you wanna play snappy snaps, just like always!"

Niall gave me a smug grin and I released a slow breath as Brooklyn began to dance around the room with the dog who was working hard to try and bite her face before she placed him on his feet and ran from the room, calling back to him with promises of treats.

The weird little animal gave the three of us a calculating look and I arched a brow at it before it turned and scampered away on her heels.

"Go on," Niall said proudly, turning to me and grinning like an arsehole. "Say it."

I knew what he wanted me to say, but I wasn't going to admit that he'd been right in picking that strange little mutt, so I just shrugged.

"Never, hijo de puta. Never."

Niall started laughing as I headed away to take a shower and wash the grave dirt from my fingers. I found myself hiding a smile as I went. Not that I'd ever admit it, but I didn't entirely hate that bastardo all the time like I used to.

BROOKLYN

CHAPTER THIRTY SIX

ANNND ANOTHER TEN YEARS AFTER THAT

"Oh my god, he's perfect," I cooed, staring down at the bundle of joy beneath me, unable to believe he was really ours. I hadn't planned this. It hadn't been on the cards at all, but now he was here, and I loved him more than I could put into words.

"Hey there, little fella." Niall reached down to tickle him. "I'm ya Daddy."

"How are *you* the father?" Mateo scoffed. "I made him."

"I was the one who made ya make him," Niall growled, throwing his shoulder into him. "And if anyone's Daddy in our family, it's me."

"Hey, baby," I cooed, lifting him into my arms and nestling him against my chest. "Come to Mommy."

"Well, we can agree on that at least. She's certainly his ma. Look, he's even got the same glint about him," Niall said, gazing at me with pride in his eyes as he slung an arm over Jack's shoulders. "Aw, would ya look at that, they're bonding. Have you decided on a name yet, Spider?"

"I think I'll call him…Gabe," I decided.

"Don't call him Gabe," Mateo said, shaking his head firmly.

"Alright, how about Glimmer?" I suggested.

"That's a girl's name. Besides, he looks far too like his Daddy to be a Glimmer. He's made for killin', slicing into flesh and leaving a trail of death in his wake," Niall huffed while Jack moved closer to me to get a look at the new addition to our family.

"Creed," Jack suggested and I looked up at him with a gasp, loving that name. It fit him perfectly. Our little Creed.

"Yes," I said, tears brimming in my eyes as I hugged Creed tighter. "I love it. Open the window, Jack I want to shout his name to the world." I followed him over to it and he swung it wide, the sea air washing around me and making my hair swirl. I looked across the glittering ocean ahead and smiled from ear to ear.

"His name is Creed!" I yelled, then thrust my hands into the air, holding Creed out the window and waving him at the sea.

"Careful! Ya'll drop him, Spider!" Niall cried, lunging forward and knocking into me. Creed slipped from my grasp and I screamed as he tumbled away towards the ground.

The beautiful dagger slammed into the decking, sinking in deep and making a ringing noise as it wobbled there, carving a sizeable hole in the wood.

"For the love of fuck," Saint's angry man-voice carried from down there. He was one of Tatum's men – my new sister-in-law. Or cousin-in-law. Or niece-in-law. I wasn't really sure which. All I knew was I was married to Niall and she was married to Niall's Kyan, so together we were linked, and that made us family.

"Oh, thank my tits." I clasped my tits in my hands. "Creed's okay."

"Kyan!" Saint bellowed. "They're at it again. I told you not to build a medieval forge in the backyard. Now they've gone and forged a dagger. It's lodged in my cedar decking and one of the kids could have been-" his voice was lost as the door to the guest bedroom flew open and a young boy ran in with wayward dark hair growing down to his shoulders, roaring a battle cry.

"To the death!" Rowan leapt onto the bed and started beating our pillows with a baseball bat.

Brutus started yapping from his fancy little bed shaped like a throne – he'd become quite the princess since he'd been reincarnated. Like an angry, snappy princess who liked eating fingers for breakfast.

Caesar ran in next, Tatum's kids all little warriors in their own right, and this one had an air of cunning about him too that made him a real little demon – in all the right ways of course. Rowan was an absolute savage and, as the oldest two of their four kids, they were always competing for position as top dog. I was pretty sure the two of them were around six and seven years old, but I wasn't very good at judging kid's ages. I'd thought the baby was three days old when I'd met him, but apparently he was nearly two or something.

Caesar leapt onto the bed with a snarl and Rowan swung the baseball bat at him which was adult size and a deadly little Donner of a weapon. Niall caught hold of the bat before it could smash Caesar in the head, plucking it clean out of Rowan's hands – although he held on for a good few seconds, hanging right in the air with his feet kicking before he lost his grip and fell back onto the bed.

"Don't hit him like that," Niall growled, throwing the bat up towards the ceiling so it spun in a circle before he caught it again. "Hit him like this." He raised it above his head and Caesar gasped, running from the room while Niall took chase, their laughter carrying back to us a beat later.

"Uncle Jack, can you do the danger swing again?" Rowan asked, jumping off the bed and tugging on Jack's sleeve insistently.

"Your mama told you you're not allowed to do that again, niño salvaje," Mateo said with a grin as Jack scooped Rowan into his arms.

"But Mom won't even know about it," Rowan said with a look of mischief about him. "Swing me, Uncle Jack!" he begged.

"Danger swing! Danger swing!" the little toddler MJ ran into the room chanting, absolutely covered from head to toe in what looked like blood.

"Uh oh – the little one has killed someone. We'd better help hide the body," I breathed.

Jack took hold of Rowan's ankles and wrists in two hands and started swinging him around the room, so high he almost hit the ceiling as he whooped in joy.

Mateo hurried over to MJ with me, bending down and sniffing him. "Strawberries." He frowned.

"Oh, fuck!" Tatum cried from downstairs.

"Fuck, fuck, fuck," MJ echoed brightly, marching back out of the room, his blond hair stuck to his head from all the red gloop.

"Fuckety fuck a fucking duck," I laughed, prancing after him then scooping him up in my arms and balancing my ass on the shiny banister that curved downstairs.

"Weeeeee!" MJ cried as I kicked off from the stairs and we went whizzing down towards the bottom floor.

Mateo ran full pelt after us as the end of the banister loomed, catching us both in his arms before we could go smash and bang.

My Dead Man kept his hand on my lower back as we headed into the kitchen and I found a massive red cake smashed all over the floor, part of a squid's head still made from the icing at one end, but it looked like the rest had been jumped on. A lot. I kinda wanted to jump on it too, so I set MJ down and hurried forward to dive headfirst into the mess.

Kyan came striding into the room, all muscles and tattoos and cocky grin before he spotted the mess and his face fell. "Oh man," he groaned. "What happened?"

"MJ." Tatum bit her lip as she laughed then hurried forward to pick up the little toddler as I crept closer to the sticky mess, peeling off my socks as I went. "You wild little thing. Did you smash all this cake, you naughty boy?" He nodded as she kissed his cheek, no sign of anger in her eyes as she hugged him tight.

Tatum was the best mom I knew. I mean, I didn't know many moms. In fact, she might be the only mom I knew, and she was also my first proper, for-true best girlfriend. She liked my crazy, she even had a little crazy of her own in her soul, and whenever we were together, we got up to a bunch of chaos that left our men chasing around after us. It was the best. Like one time, we went out drinking, stole a boat from a guy who'd groped my ass, and drove it out to sea. We'd been having so much fun with the beer we'd found onboard that we hadn't noticed when the wind had picked up and a storm had blown in, the hours ticking on by.

Saint had tracked us with some fancy fandangle he made Tatum carry around and they'd all shown up on his big ol' speedboat, looking to spank us and drag us home. I hadn't minded the spanking, or the bit where Niall had made me promise I would keep one of Saint's tracking fandagles on me too while he was buried deep inside me, holding me on the edge of bliss. That was the easiest promise I'd ever made.

"I'd better get him changed," Tatum said. "I guess that's the surprise for Saint's birthday ruined."

"Wait, wasn't Saint the one watching MJ?" Kyan asked suspiciously.

"Oh dear," Saint said lightly as he entered the room. "Whatever has happened?"

I looked to him just as I slid my right foot deep into the smooshy cake and found him offering Kyan a smirk.

"You did this," Kyan hissed, pointing in accusation.

"Perhaps. But you let Mateo forge a blade in our house, and now it is lodged several inches deep in my cedarwood decking," Saint said with a shrug.

He was so…scary. Like a good scary. Like he might just eat you alive in the night scary. He was extra on edge when we came to stay too, probably because things got broken a lot when we were around. But what was the fun in keeping everything whole? Some things looked much better in pieces.

I jumped fully into the cake and giggled as it squished between my toes, flapping my arms like a bird and drawing Saint's attention to me, his right eye twitching a little.

"Please desist," he asked, but I kept jumping and kicking up cake everywhere, splattering it all over the pristine kitchen and beckoning Mateo over to me.

"Come on, Dead Man! Jump with me. Take your socks and shoes off, it feels better that way!" I cried, my laughter carrying up, up and away, and an answering cry came back to me from a room upstairs.

"Great, now Beau is awake," Saint growled, carving a hand over his face while Kyan laughed at me. "Stop her," he commanded Mateo, but my Dead Man just slid off his own socks and came to join me in the cake.

"I'm on it!" another of Tatum's men called from upstairs and I jumped faster and faster up and down, holding Mateo's hands and making him jump too.

Kyan started pulling off his own socks and Saint swung a finger onto him.

"Don't you dare, brother," Saint hissed. "You need to clean up this mess and fix my decking."

"*Or*, I could jump in this cake," Kyan said with a wolf's grin before leaping into the cake beside us and jumping up and down too, causing Saint's jaw to grind.

"Come on Saint!" I yelled. "Come play squishy-jumpy!"

"I will not play squishy-jumpy," he said coolly.

Kyan dropped down, scooping up a big blob of cake in his hand and hurling it at Saint, hitting him squarely in the centre of his crisp white shirt. Saint's upper lip peeled back and I squealed a laugh, dropping down as he came striding towards us all angry-like just as Niall came chasing Cesar down the stairs with the baseball bat still raised over his head.

Cesar darted past us, but Niall's foot slipped on a rogue piece of cake and he went crashing into Saint, sending him flying forward and landing right on the floor, his face slamming into the icing squid head. Saint pushed himself half way up with a snarl on his lips and I thought I was genuinely about to be murdered for good this time, but it was so damn funny seeing all that red icing and the big squid eye now stuck to his forehead that instead of running for my life, I started laughing.

"Oops, sorry fella. Oh hey! Cake!" Niall grabbed some from the floor, shoving it into his mouth while Saint glared at him and I laughed so hard my sides hurt.

Everyone else laughed too until suddenly Saint cracked, an amused grin pulling at his mouth as he shoved to his feet with a pile of cake in his hand which he slapped against Niall's cheek.

Cesar dove into the mess at our feet and Saint finally embraced the chaos as a full-on cake fight broke out.

Jack appeared with little Rowan tucked under his arm and we were soon all making such a mess that it awoke all my demons for a party. This was where I thrived, amidst the mayhem while the people I loved more than anything in the world surrounded me. And the most impossible thing of all was that they loved me back.

I was so happy in this life that it was hard to remember a time when I'd just been a lonely girl on the streets, wishing on rainbows and fishes to bring me the company I craved. I guessed they'd been listening all along, because now they were here at last, my reckless, carefree family.

We were a deck of cards, a club, a heart, a diamond and a spade, all of us made for dealing in death. I had my Joker, my Jack, my King, and my scruffy little pooch of an Ace. Somehow, I'd become the Queen of all that, and together we made a full house, even if it didn't look like anyone else's version, even if it was a jumble of suits and colours. It didn't make us any less real.

We were bound by blood and carnage, and I was no longer afraid to lose them. Because I knew in my heart, deep down where Glenda was nestled, snoozing and content at last, that these tethers that held us as one were made of an unbreakable twine. No creature of evil or purity could sever us now.

We were one entity.

One guild.

A Society of Psychos.

And long may we reign.

NIALL

CHAPTER THIRTY SEVEN

ANOTHER TWO YEARS AFTER THAT

"I can't believe I'm seventy-five," Brooklyn sighed wistfully as she strode into the bedroom all dolled up in a lacy black scrap of nothing and giving me the sex eyes where I sat waiting for her on the bed.

"Forty, love. You're forty today, we went over it, remember?"

"Oh right, yeah," she agreed with a nod. "I always get those two muddled up."

I snorted at her, my gaze shifting to the door at her back as Jack and Mateo slipped into the room, both of them shirtless already and the tension rising as the anticipation built between us.

"Have you decided what you wanna try this year?" I asked curiously. This was Brooklyn's birthday tradition, one I'd started around fifteen years ago when I'd started to find it difficult to get her an exciting gift each year on account of the fact that I bought her everything she wanted at the drop of a hat and never remembered to hold anything back for special occasions.

"Yes," she said, biting her bottom lip and Mateo chuckled darkly, clearly knowing what she had planned and well in the mood for it.

Sometimes the things she wanted to try involved just me, other times she got one or both of them involved too. The only rules were that it had to be filthy, and that I'd say yes to whatever it was. At first, we'd experimented with various positions and toys, but as the years passed it had gotten harder to find anything new which we hadn't already tested. She had been excited about this one for weeks though, so I knew it was going to be good.

"Strip for me, Hellfire," Brooklyn commanded and I grinned, doing as she wanted and taking my clothes off for her, fisting my rock-hard cock as I looked her up and down and groaning a little in anticipation. I'd been off on a job all week on my own, so I hadn't gotten to sink my cock into her in far too long already. The day of wild birthday celebrations should have worn us all out already but now that it was time for this, I found myself wide awake.

"Remember, you can't say no," Mateo purred, that wicked grin on his face making me frown a little.

"When have I ever said no?" I replied with a scoff. "I'd suck your cock if that was what she wanted from me, el burro, and don't forget it."

"Boo, why would I want you to suck his cock for me? Then I wouldn't get to do it," Brooklyn cut in with a pout, and I cocked my head at her as I wondered where this was going.

"Alright then, little psycho, tell me what we're working with tonight," I pushed and her smile grew almost shy as she turned to Jack who was holding a large white box.

"I'm really excited for this," Brooklyn breathed and I nodded, wrapping my tattooed fingers around my shaft and giving it a few strokes to relieve some of the need in my flesh while she made me wait.

Mateo moved across the room and grabbed hold of a chair, picking it up and placing it down near the head of the bed before dropping into it where he would have a perfect view of whatever sinful act me and my wife were about to commit.

I was so distracted by him that I didn't even see Brooklyn open the box and when I looked back to find a big, pink strap-on in her hands, I grinned.

"You want me to fuck your arse and cunt at the same time?" I guessed, leaning forward and holding my hand out for the huge rubber cock but she shook her head.

"No, Hellfire, I want you to get on your hands and knees for me," she replied with a grin, letting Jack take the strap on from her.

"You want me to what now?" I asked, blinking in confusion as I watched Jack roll her panties off and position the strap on carefully, tightening the buckles which secured it to her body.

"It vibrates," Brooklyn whispered excitedly.

"Uh-huh. Go back to the bit where you said you want me on my knees," I said, releasing my hold on my cock and frowning at the two of them while Mateo laughed loudly from his corner.

"It pulses too," Brooklyn added, handing Jack a little remote and moaning as he pressed a button on it.

Brooklyn held her hand out and Mateo obediently filled her palm with lube for her while I started shaking my head and his laughter grew louder.

"I think we need to discuss this further, love," I said slowly.

"Why? Are you going to say no to her on her birthday, bastardo?" Mateo taunted, making me turn and narrow my eyes on him.

"Of course not," I snapped.

Brooklyn wrapped her hand around the rubber dick and started working it over like she was jerking it off, moaning every time it was pressed against her body more firmly and making it more than clear that the thing was designed to work her clit while she used it on someone.

"You're looking intrigued there, Jack. Maybe you wanna give it a whirl?" I said loudly, switching my gaze to him.

"No," he replied simply, his eyes all sparkly with amusement like a cunt.

"What is it you like to say to her oh so often? 'I am your creature', isn't it?" Mateo said, not even bothering to try and hide his smirk. "So be her creature."

"Err…"

Brooklyn stepped towards me, her eyes alight with anticipation. "This is my birthday wish, Hellfire," she said firmly. "Besides, I'm a pro at butt stuff. I know how to make it good for you."

She bit her lip again and damn it all to hell, I was a sucker for that woman of mine.

I swiped a hand down my face then nodded, wondering what in the hell I was thinking as I agreed to this carnage before rolling my shoulders back and straightening my spine.

"Alright then," I said boldly, refusing to let Mateo think he'd seen me rattled at last after all these years. "Give me a slap to get my blood pumping, Jack," I commanded and the arsehole smacked me so hard my head wheeled to the side and I tasted blood as I fell down on the bed.

Brooklyn giggled, hurrying forward and giving my arse a shove to make me roll all the way onto my front and I cursed as I gave in, moving onto my knees before her and bracing my forearms on the mattress.

I refused to look at Mateo who I could feel smirking at me once more, focusing instead on the feeling of Brooklyn climbing onto the bed with me, her fingers roaming over my arse cheeks before one rounded my body and found my cock.

I groaned as she pressed herself against me, my thoughts not lingering on the thick length of rubber which I could feel resting against my thigh while I focused instead on the grip of her hand around my shaft.

She began pumping her fist, her other hand moving down my spine just as Jack squirted the lube over my arse. I grunted at the coldness of the liquid, but Brooklyn began to massage it into my skin, her fingers moving to my hole and pushing in just as she upped her pace on my cock.

I groaned as she began to move them. Fingers I could do. Fingers we'd done before many a time after she figured out how to use them to make me come so hard I damn near blacked out.

"I'm gonna fuck you so good, Hellfire," she purred in my ear and the longer this sweet torment went on, the more I found myself liking the idea, nodding my head in agreement as she shifted her hips and the strap on shifted between my arse cheeks.

Brooklyn moaned in excitement, removing her fingers and pressing the head of the rubber cock to my arse just as I started to question the life choices that had gotten me to this point.

"Hang on a-" I began but my words were drowned out by Brooklyn's moan as Jack turned the vibrate function on and the fucking sex toy got to work on her as well as me.

Brooklyn didn't hold back, her hips driving forward much in the same way as I liked to slam mine down when I was taking her, and my eyes flew open in alarm so that I met Mateo's gleeful gaze right as the fucking thing sank deep inside me, and my damn breath was stolen from my lungs.

"Jesus," I gasped and Brooklyn fucking spanked me, drawing back before driving the thing in again.

My hands fisted the sheets and I tried to look away from Mateo, but I was locked in the trap of his dark eyes, the evil little smile he was giving me making me feel all kinds of ways in combination with the vibrating rod of fire which was currently pounding in and out of my arse.

Brooklyn moaned louder, spanking me again and fuck me, I wasn't sure if I liked it or hated it, or what way I was feeling about it, but every time she pumped my cock in time with her thrusts, I was only left more confused.

I managed to draw in a shaky breath as I started to get used to the feeling, finding pleasure among the discomfort and bite of pain which I mighta been able to get a taste for, if I only got into the rhythm of it.

"You must be feeling so empty, chica," Mateo said loudly while I still worked to breathe between thrusts and couldn't do any more than curse him within the confines of my head. "I bet Jack could help you with that."

"Yes," Brooklyn panted and I started shaking my head as I realised what he was suggesting, but no one seemed to be interested in me or what fresh fuckery was happening down here at the bottom of the heap. "Fuck me, AJ, fuck us both."

"Rook," Jack replied like a cunt because I knew he knew there wasn't a world in which I wanted to feel the power of his thrusts driving that rubber cock into my arse, but as I tried to bark out a command for him to stop, Brooklyn got him to spank me instead. And holy fuck, that bastard had a good swing on him.

I needed to take back control of this situation, I needed to finish my woman and stop this madness before it got any more out of hand.

I started driving my arse back into her thrusts, making sure those vibrations were working hard on her clit and making her moan even louder while I took the rubber cock deep inside me, all the way to my shadowy soul and beyond, where nothing had ever ventured before.

I was an old man these days, I shouldn't have been risking my heart on rubber cock acrobatics like this and yet here I was, letting my wife peg me while I forgot to breathe, and a Mexican bastard who I had never liked grinned at me like the fucking Cheshire Cat.

My attempts to finish her worked beautifully, the sounds of Brooklyn coming filling the room, and somehow while she thrusted herself into me and pumped my cock in a firm demand, I found myself coming too, a strangled cry escaping my lips which sounded nothing like I'd ever heard before.

It was incredibly intense, the pleasure and pain, my arse gripping the fucking strap on like a vice and my cum spilling all over the sheets while I listened to her come for me too. I didn't even know what I felt about it. Was I having some kind of sexual awakening, or was this a new nightmare which would draw me from sleep in the dead of night? It was all very confusing.

I was just glad that it was done and I'd given my girl the birthday dream she'd wanted.

But instead of her drawing back, Brooklyn slumped forward, her body pressing mine down flat onto the sheets where we fought to catch our breath together and that thing remained lodged in my arse, making a little home for itself there like a bird roosting through a cold winter night.

I panted beneath her, sparks dancing behind my eyelids at the intensity of my climax and in that moment of blissful uncertainty, a giant clambered onto the bed.

"Hold on, Bessy," Jack growled, slapping my arse where it poked out from beneath Brooklyn and making me curse. "We aren't even close to done, yet."

"You can talk?" I yelled angrily as all the times Brooklyn had insisted that her and Jack had a secret language came to mind and I realised it had never been a figment of her imagination at all. "You sneaky motherfucker, I'm going to-"

My breath catapulted from my lungs as Jack slammed his cock deep inside Brooklyn's pussy, the force of his thrust driving the rubber strap on to all new depths within me and making my entire body tense beneath the weight of the two of them.

"Oh, fuck yes," Brooklyn cried in ecstasy while I was left struggling to take the weight of him beneath her.

Mateo's deep laughter filled the air and I managed to glare up at him from my position at the bottom of the sex pile, a snarl on my lips and a promise of death in my eyes.

"I forgive you, bastardo," Mateo said with a big fucking smile which I planned on slapping clean offa his face if I survived this. "For stealing my house and torturing me. This moment makes it all okay."

He laughed again and I took a swipe for him, but he just caught my hand and held it tight.

"You can squeeze my fingers if it helps," he chuckled. "And when it's done, I'll admit we really are family and forget our feud at last."

"Deal," I hissed, though I wasn't certain I would survive this at all.

I gritted my teeth and squeezed his hand so fucking tight that I was likely to break bones, holding his gaze while I was pegged by the love of my life as she took the cock of the violent criminal we'd set loose on the world.

And if that wasn't a happily ever after, then I didn't know what the fuck else one might look like.

AUTHOR'S NOTE

So, you have officially spent two books deep in the general insanity of our day to day thoughts. I'm not saying we go about the place killing people, but do we create conversations for wild animals and inanimate objects? Do we give back stories to pieces of furniture or stop halfway through a conversation to comment on some random thought that just popped into our heads?

Maybe.

So to all the people who live with peeping squirrels and little Glendas in their chests, we salute you. And to everyone questioning our sanity based on that statement, go back to assuming I'm joking and that we're totally normal and don't get your knickers in a twist worrying about the day to day workings of our minds. It's alllll good. We're totaaaally sane, and definitely don't feed our inner murdery needs by killing off characters.

Niall, Brooklyn, Mateo, Jack, and Brutus (in all of his carnations) took up a special crazy place in our hearts and have honestly been some of the funnest (totally a word – I'm an author so I should know) characters we have ever written.

There is something so freeing about a character who never grew out of announcing to the whole world when they need a poop and who isn't afraid to run wild in public dressed as a unicorn while singing out of tune and living their best life without a single shit to give about what anyone else thinks.

We're trying to take a leaf from Brooklyn's book and give less shits what other people think of our strange behaviour and focusing on the fun times, so if you take anything from this crazy duet then let it be that – alongside the mental image of Niall at the bottom of the pegging pile while wondering if his hip might give out before they finish, obvs.

As always, we want to thank each and every one of you for reading and enjoying our books in all of their forms from high fantasy to crazy contemporary and everything in between, without all of you we wouldn't be living our dreams and we can never express how blown away we are by your continued love and support.

So here's to finishing another motherfucking series!! Here's to the anticipation for the next time we get to throw you from a cliff! And here's to all of you pooping without a squirrel peeping.

All our love,

Susanne & Caroline xx

ALSO BY
CAROLINE PECKHAM
&
SUSANNE VALENTI

Brutal Boys of Everlake Prep

(Complete Reverse Harem Bully Romance Contemporary Series)

Kings of Quarantine

Kings of Lockdown

Kings of Anarchy

Queen of Quarantine

**

Dead Men Walking

(Reverse Harem Dark Romance Contemporary Series)

The Death Club

Society of Psychos

**

The Harlequin Crew

(Reverse Harem Mafia Romance Contemporary Series)

Sinners Playground

Dead Man's Isle

Carnival Hill

Paradise Lagoon

Harlequinn Crew Novellas

Devil's Pass

**

Dark Empire

(Dark Mafia Contemporary Standalones)

Beautiful Carnage

Beautiful Savage

**

The Ruthless Boys of the Zodiac

(Reverse Harem Paranormal Romance Series - Set in the world of Solaria)

Dark Fae

Savage Fae

Vicious Fae

Broken Fae

Warrior Fae

Zodiac Academy

(M/F Bully Romance Series- Set in the world of Solaria, five years after Dark Fae)

The Awakening

Ruthless Fae

The Reckoning

Shadow Princess

Cursed Fates

Fated Thrones

Heartless Sky

The Awakening - As told by the Boys

Zodiac Academy Novellas

Origins of an Academy Bully

The Big A.S.S. Party

Darkmore Penitentiary

(Reverse Harem Paranormal Romance Series - Set in the world of Solaria,
ten years after Dark Fae)

Caged Wolf

Alpha Wolf

Feral Wolf

**

The Age of Vampires

(Complete M/F Paranormal Romance/Dystopian Series)

Eternal Reign

Eternal Shade

Eternal Curse

Eternal Vow

Eternal Night

Eternal Love

**

Cage of Lies

(M/F Dystopian Series)

Rebel Rising

**

Tainted Earth

(M/F Dystopian Series)

Afflicted

Altered

Adapted

Advanced

**

The Vampire Games

(Complete M/F Paranormal Romance Trilogy)

V Games

V Games: Fresh From The Grave

V Games: Dead Before Dawn

*

The Vampire Games: Season Two

(Complete M/F Paranormal Romance Trilogy)

Wolf Games

Wolf Games: Island of Shade

Wolf Games: Severed Fates

*

The Vampire Games: Season Three

Hunter Trials

*

The Vampire Games Novellas

A Game of Vampires

**

The Rise of Issac

(Complete YA Fantasy Series)

Creeping Shadow

Bleeding Snow

Turning Tide

Weeping Sky

Failing Light

Printed in Great Britain
by Amazon

41590564R00324